Praise for the novels of

STELLA CAMERON

"If you haven't read Stella Cameron,
you haven't read romantic suspense."
—Elizabeth Lowell

"Cameron captures the Bayou Teche ambience."
—*Publishers Weekly* on *A Marked Man*

"Hard-boiled and hard-core."
—*Booklist* on *A Grave Mistake*

"Those looking for spicy...fare will enjoy a
heaping helping on every page."
—*Publishers Weekly* on *Now You See Him*

"Cameron returns to the wonderfully
atmospheric Louisiana setting...for her latest
sexy-gritty, compellingly readable tale."
—*Booklist* on *Kiss Them Goodbye*

"A wonderful, fast-paced, furious page-turner."
—*Philadelphia Enquirer* on *Tell Me Why*

"Steamy, atmospheric and fast-paced."
—*Publishers Weekly* on *Key West*

Also by New York Times *bestselling author*

STELLA
CAMERON

STELLA CAMERON

A COLD DAY IN HELL

MIRA®

ISBN-13: 978-0-7783-2495-9
ISBN-10:   0-7783-2495-8

A COLD DAY IN HELL

www.MIRABooks.com

Printed in U.S.A.

For CameronRex and Chairman Liao.
Always an inspiration!

ACKNOWLEDGMENTS

Love and thanks to Jill Marie Landis,
friend and fabulous writer.

Your encouragement, input and partially
successful attempts to teach me how to "be"
as well as "do" helped me reach my goals for
A COLD DAY IN HELL!

1

Pointe Judah, Louisiana
Late November

They never should have been there.

"Stop walking. Now. Stand still, dammit!" Aaron Mogge-ridge shouted at the retreating back of Sonny DeAngelo.

"Sonny," Aaron yelled. "I'm out of rope with my mom. If she finds out about this, I'm toast. She'll kick me out of the house."

"Yeah, yeah," Sonny said. "I got a lot more worries with my uncle. How would you like to have Angel trying to straighten you out? And Eileen's too soft to quit on you. Shit, come on, will ya?"

Aaron pulled a foot out of the sucky mud and stomped it down on a white cypress stump. "We're lost," he pointed out. At least Sonny had quit walking away. "Do you know which way to the bayou?"

Bayou Nezpique had been behind them when Sonny had insisted on striking out into swampy ground, but who knew where it was now? "You don't have a clue, do you? I told you fooling around in swamps was a bad idea. Why did you really want to get into this stuff? And don't give me that ecosystem crap again."

Sonny turned around and retraced his steps, smacking his sodden sneakers through a thin layer of brown water covered with frothing scum into the bottom sludge. He looked like he was enjoying himself.

"You're like a stupid kid," Aaron said. "Jumpin' in puddles. I'm calling for help. It's getting dark, Sonny. You want to be out here in the dark? It'll get colder and it could rain buckets. Where'd you think all this water came from? It's almost December and we're getting a helluva lot of rain." He reached for his cell phone and started punching in numbers. He was scared. Sonny was a city kid, a New Yorker; he didn't know shit about a Louisiana swamp.

"C'mon," Sonny said. He poked at Aaron's cell, messing up the number. "If we call home like a couple of scared girls, we're done for."

"Look around," Aaron said, raising his arms. "We don't know where we are. It's gonna get dark. This isn't Brooklyn, it's a swamp. Y'know what kind of stuff hangs out in swamps?"

"Pretty much what hangs out in parts of Brooklyn."

Sonny kept his head shaved and oiled but the shadow of his thick black hair always showed. It came to a point in the middle, in front. His eyes pissed Aaron off. They *looked* innocent. Big, brown and soft, and they lied. Sonny DeAngelo was the toughest kid he had ever met. Sonny was seventeen and Aaron would be before long, but most of the time Aaron felt like Sonny was years older.

"Okay," Sonny said, his voice dropping. "I'm an ass, just

like you say. But we're in it now and we gotta get out, so quit panicking and start working with me."

"Shit!"

"Shit, what now?"

"I know this place. I've lived here all my life and I know where I don't go. This is a big *don't go.* But I let you talk me into it. You don't get to tell me to work with *you,* because you don't know jack shit. You work with *me,* ballhead."

Sonny grinned. "Sure thing." He posed like a scarecrow with its head on one side, and his thin black sweater hung from his arms and body. His flat belly showed above the black pants that hung on his hip bones. He pointed one long forefinger. "I do know where we are. I didn't tell you in case you chickened out, but there's a guy I want to get a look at."

What Sonny had just said didn't compute for Aaron. He shook his head.

"I'm not making this up," Sonny said. "We got to that busted dock and I knew we had to come this—"

"What guy?" Aaron asked. "What guy, Sonny? You didn't say anything about looking for a guy."

"He lives around here. The bartender at Buzzard's Wet Bar told me about him."

"Buzz's? You were at Buzz's?"

Sonny shrugged. "I just wanted to see what it was like in there."

"If someone squeals on you, Angel's going to take you apart. It's gonna be *ugly.*" Aaron made a circle, searching for something familiar, anything that would steer them out of there.

"We gotta concentrate," Sonny said. "That broken dock where I stopped? Back there on the bayou? That was the marker for us to head into the trees. His place is around here and we're going to stumble right over it any second now."

"Liar," Aaron said. *"Ecosystems."*

"They said I wouldn't do it," Sonny said. "I'm gonna show them. Wait till I prove it to them tomorrow. There's no such thing as *voodoo*. Or a root doctor."

Aaron moaned. "A root doctor? You're off your head. If one of those guys was around here—and he isn't—I sure as hell wouldn't be stopping by for a visit. I'm calling Matt Boudreaux."

"The police chief?" Sonny's voice squeaked. "For crissakes, let's move. All I want to do is see where this guy lives and get me a memento."

Aaron looked up through the trees. They weren't dense but they were all he could see in any direction. Cypress, their feet in standing water. Moss hanging like grey-green slime. Broken stumps scattered. "A frickin' minefield," he muttered. "If there…whatever you're looking for, how will you prove you saw it?"

"If I take a bit of wood back and say it's from his house, they'll have to believe it. Maybe I'll haul along a dead rat, too."

"You don't know a thing about this place," Aaron said. "Okay, we've got to choose. Back the way we came or straight on."

"Straight on," Sonny said, frowning now. "We'll get out to an old logging road eventually. I just want to see his house and—hey, we can ask him how to get out of here."

"Our bikes," Aaron said. "We've got to find them or we'll never get home. That's it." He gritted his teeth and dialed 911.

"Don't," Sonny whispered. "Please don't do that. You know I'm supposed to behave while I'm here. That's *why* I'm here. Uncle Angel's—"

Aaron held up a palm. "No signal," he said. His skin felt

tight. Just like he'd been expecting, raindrops began tunneling down through the trees.

He heard a sound that didn't fit. One look at Sonny showed he had heard it, too. With a finger to his mouth he got to Aaron, took his arm and backed him into the nearest cover—three tall stumps crowded together.

The sound came again and again, then turned into a steady splashing and stumbling racket.

"If that's your root doctor, there's no use hiding. He already knows where we are." Aaron spoke softly through barely moving lips.

"And if it's somebody else?" Sonny said against his ear. "Give me the voodoo man over some others it could be."

"What d'you mean?"

Sonny's features weren't as clear anymore. The light was just about all sucked out. "Stay here," he said. "I'm going to try running to that tree, the really big one there. If we split up, we're more difficult to catch. That's if there's someone planning to catch us. If it was Angel, he'd be calling our names."

"I wish it was him." Aaron twisted the neck of Sonny's black sweater and hung on. "You're not going. We stay together."

The splashing, the cracking of branches stopped abruptly.

"We can take him," Aaron murmured.

"Not if he's got a gun."

Aaron felt puzzled and said, "Root doctors don't carry guns."

"You know any of 'em well?"

"Never met one."

Only the creaking of winter-pale tree limbs and the slapping of raindrops broke the silence, these and the critters on their way home. Those raindrops whirled, catching what light came from above.

The splashing started again, then stopped—then started.

Sonny put his mouth to Aaron's ear again. "He doesn't know where we are for sure. He may not be looking for us at all. Hang on. I think he'll go away."

Aaron nodded and held his breath. With his body so quiet, his heart slammed at his eardrums. He took another breath. "Nothing now," he murmured. They were in big-time trouble. Getting out of there was all that mattered—as long as they could do it alive.

He pulled way back between two trunks and inched around, looking for any movement. The cracks through the stumps weren't big enough to see through. He worked slowly sideways until the fingers of his left hand touched the smooth edge of a cypress.

Sonny caught at Aaron's right shoulder but he shrugged him away.

A loud click, a crack, a flash of light, and Aaron could have sworn he felt the bullet slice through the air close to his face.

"God." He froze in complete panic for a moment, then rolled back the way he had come. He and Sonny didn't speak. The time for that was over.

They were trapped with a shooter who was just waiting for them to make a tiny move.

"Strangers a-coming!" A man's full, deep voice sang out the words and Aaron squeezed his eyes shut. He felt light-headed.

"Strangers a-coming!" Louder, even richer this time. "What they want? Who break the peace? You be sor-ry!" The laugh that followed started with a gurgle and hurtled up the scale.

"That's not the guy with the gun," Aaron said. "He's behind and to the right. This one's…" He wasn't sure where the guy who had shouted was, but there were two men out there.

Sonny put his fingers in his ears. He didn't look gutsy and fearless anymore.

Aaron gripped his arm. "I think the screamer's way over to our left now. Maybe he's trying to help us." He let out a yell and ran toward the big voice.

Air burned his throat and his eyes. But he shouted and screeched louder and louder.

He saw a searing flash, just like the other one. It definitely didn't come from the same direction as the mouthy guy.

A thud into Aaron's back, way to the left side, spun him around. "I'm shot!"

There was pain. Dull pain. Then numbness, heaviness.

He hit the scummy water, face-first, before the lights went out.

Sonny turned one way, then the other. *Don't let him be dead.*

A racket set up, like nothing he'd ever heard before. The clink of sharp things rattling together, and bells—or at least metal clinking on other metal surfaces.

Coming out of the boggy haze, a figure loomed. Tall, in a fever of movement. Great head shaking, voluminous cloth billowing behind, and a glow that picked out a bumpy, shiny red face with holes where the eyes should be.

The creature paused, humming, shaking his noisemakers softly. At first Sonny thought the freak's head looked big because he had a mass of shaggy hair, then he saw a bulbous, colorful turban built up to outlandish proportions.

And Sonny heard more splashing, this time made by someone fleeing, throttle wide-open, from the red, shiny-faced guy. Suddenly he realized that the creature wore a mask—a bright red mask, with a skeletal face painted in black.

Sonny had to get Aaron.

He had to get the hell out of here, they both did.

This was the voodoo man. And damn if it didn't look like he was staring at Aaron, but hadn't noticed Sonny.

Long arms shot out. Spiking his knees skyward with each step, he made for Aaron. In the glow that went with him, he twisted his hands this way and that. Fingernails inches long, glowed white and clicked together. The tips glinted silver.

Amid unearthly sounds, the man—if that's what it was— reached Aaron, stooped and brought his head close, listening. Even at a distance, Sonny saw him nod and hoped it meant Aaron was alive.

With both arms, the man scooped up Sonny's buddy as if he was a baby. Scooped him up, holding Aaron's left side tight with both hands.

Sonny saw blood drizzle through the fingers. "Oh, my, gawd," he muttered. Aaron was done for. They were probably both done for.

"Chuzah, me," the man cried. "He wants you to follow." And he loped rapidly away. "Come you—the other boy hidin' in the three stumps. That one back there with the gun, he gone, but he could come back." All that rattling came from garlands of bones, little bones, big bones, skulls, strung around the man's neck and waist. The bells were gold, Sonny saw them glitter. He shouldn't have pushed to come here. Look what he'd done to Aaron.

Sonny couldn't make his feet move. He couldn't feel his feet or his legs, but he felt how he was rigid and his blood fluttered in his veins.

"You follow Chuzah. Now! This boy bleedin' to death."

2

Eileen Moggeridge slammed the door of her van and locked it, keeping her right hand on the gun she carried in her jacket pocket.

Tonight she had met with someone she'd thought she would never see again. He had stood in this parking lot, nodding toward Poke Around, her gift shop, with a smile on his face. "I'm happy for you, Eileen. I only ever wanted the best for you—and Aaron." And the smile was sad, his expression guilty, apologetic, humble.

As far as she could remember, he'd never regretted a thing he did and she didn't believe he'd changed.

He wanted something, and it wasn't an opportunity to take back responsibility for the family that was no longer his.

Chuck Moggeridge had left her, and Pointe Judah, several years ago. There had been talk about another woman but Eileen had not known who that was. Didn't want to know, didn't care. Chuck had beaten and humiliated her one time too many and she still hated herself for not getting rid of him a lot sooner. In the end, her so-called husband had barely beaten Eileen to a divorce lawyer.

Now he was back.

He had called from his car in the parking lot, asked her to

talk to him, *"Tell me about Aaron. Just for a couple of minutes. He's my son as well as yours."*

His car had been parked only slots away from hers in the Oakdale Mansion Center lot, but Chuck didn't know what she drove anymore. Or he hadn't, but did now. Eileen had walked to her van and seen him hurry toward her. She got quickly behind the wheel, locked the doors and opened her window a crack.

For too long they had looked at each other.

Strange how two people who had made a life together, made a child together, could become strangers.

He didn't ask to get into the van with her, or for her to go somewhere with him. At least he knew better than that—tonight. Eileen didn't trust him not to push for more, not when his parting words had been, *"I know my responsibilities. You should have let me know he was in rehab. Aaron's had a rough time and he needs his father. It's good to be back so I can make things right."*

Lies. Mostly lies.

How had Chuck found out about Aaron's problems with alcohol? They weren't an issue anymore. Aaron had gone through rehab—quietly, although she didn't fool herself that no one knew—and he was just fine. When he had needed Chuck, the man hadn't been around and now she wanted things to stay the way they were.

She had met Angel DeAngelo—his first name was really Christian—through his nephew Sonny. Sonny and Aaron had become fast friends and Angel had stepped up to give masculine support to Aaron when needed. Eileen liked him—a lot. Sonny wasn't nearly as high on her list. Surly and silent around her, he was an Aaron-rescue. Aaron had a history of championing misfits.

She held the gun so tight her fingers ached.

The thought of being afraid of Chuck was not new. When they'd been together she dreaded the sight of him and never knew what he might plan to do to her. But she hadn't worried about him since he'd made a complete break. His timing for coming back couldn't be worse. She raised her face, grateful for the fine moisture on her skin.

If she didn't get back inside the shop, Angel would arrive before her and ask where she'd been. She wasn't ready to tell him.

Eileen and Angel had moved slowly together, each of them scalded by past experience, but she wanted them to have a chance at something more and she thought he did, too—if he could ever stop thinking of her as his good buddy. Most afternoons, around closing time, he stopped by for coffee but their conversations tended to revolve around Aaron and Sonny.

Damn Chuck for showing up now. He shouldn't scare her, but he did.

The rain had eased off, but the evening remained damp, the air heavy. Eileen hurried away from her van toward the lighted windows of Poke Around. The shop was in what had once been the conservatory of the beautiful old Oakdale Mansion and she had strung white icicle lights around the roof and outlined the windows with twinkling multicolored strands.

Chuck's call came only moments after Eileen's employee, Suky-Jo, had left. They had been stocktaking—not so easy when the shop was crammed with holiday merchandise. All but the low lights were off in the patisserie and the new salon that flanked her place. Old friends ran the salon and Eileen had an investment in that, too.

The business was hers—at last.

Eileen could not get over the excitement she felt whenever she looked at the shop. Her shop. She had come a long way from being Chuck's mostly ignored wife, the woman who belonged at home—who mustn't ask for anything, so got nothing.

Angel's offices were also in the Oakdale Mansion Center. He was the operations manager for her brother's construction firm and worked late. Then he liked to walk over and pick her up. Within the hour he'd be at the shop door. She wanted to see him. In the months since they had started their tentative relationship, her need to be with him grew daily.

They circled each other and knew that's what they were doing. Eileen wondered how much longer Angel would be satisfied with being her close friend. She couldn't face the question tonight.

Her cell phone rang in her purse and when she looked at the readout she saw Angel's number.

"Hi," she said, smiling to herself.

"Where are you?"

Eileen frowned and slowed her pace. "Where I almost always am."

He took his time to respond. "And that is?"

"You're not interrogating a suspect in your former life." He admitted to several years' service as an ATF—alcohol, tobacco and firearms—agent but wouldn't discuss what he'd done before that. "I'm at the shop," she said. Or she soon would be.

"No you're not. What's going on?"

Eileen's scalp prickled. She felt colder than she should on a humid night. He'd never spoken to her sharply like that. He had no right to. A few feet from the sidewalk, she stopped and stared at the shop. Angel stood inside the door, staring out, his face set, hard and cold, the way she'd seen it several times before, but never when he was speaking to her.

He had his own key.

In a way, since Aaron and Sonny met, they had almost become a family—with some notable things missing.

His tone turned her stomach. It also made her angry. "What do you think is going on, Christian?" She winced. Her habit of calling him Christian when she was either really happy or really unhappy with him gave her away every time.

He kept the phone at his ear but didn't say anything. So far he didn't know she was only yards away and staring at him.

Angel was one of those men who took up a lot of space. When he walked into a room, there was a subtle change in the atmosphere. People looked at him, and conversation faded.

Eileen crossed her arms. The open line between them unnerved her. She tapped a hand at her throat. When she and Angel had met, she and Matt Boudreaux, the local police chief, had seemed to be moving toward a serious relationship. But Matt had been taking his sweet time, often treating her as if they'd been married for years—and she shouldn't mind a broken date, and another and another. Eileen's patience had run out. She would always love Matt in a certain way, but Angel's attention had eventually distracted her.

Sometimes she thought Angel didn't trust that it was over between her and Matt. He'd never made a romantic move but he did give the impression that she was his property.

Suddenly, Angel slipped his phone into the breast pocket

of his dark blue shirt and stood with his big arms spread. He gripped the door frame on either side. Those arms and shoulders weren't just big, they were massive. She thought about his arms and the way they moved—too often. Just touching him messed with her mind.

Eileen put her own phone away. She had about thirty seconds to see his face, his usually cool gray eyes, before she approached the door and he saw her.

She paused again. Cool didn't have anything to do with his face now. Emotions, none of which Eileen wanted to explore, passed over his features. She could see a white line around his compressed lips. Below his rolled-up sleeves, the muscles and tendons in his arms stood out. He squeezed the door frame.

That's enough. Where does he think I am? Or maybe that should be, who does he think I'm with? She hated the thought because playing the field wasn't her style.

She arrived in front of him and they stared eye-to-eye through the glass. He wore his dark blond hair short and at the moment it stuck up as if he'd pushed at it. He had thicker, darker eyelashes than a man should have and he lowered them to half-mast so he could fix his gaze on her face.

Before she could find her keys, he swept open the door and stood back.

Eileen walked inside and he locked up behind her.

"You're early," she said.

"So you thought you had more time to get back before I found out you'd left?"

"Hey, buddy." She walked to the back of the store where a soft red velvet couch stood, and threw down her purse. "You're out of line. I'm *not* having a wonderful evening and

I don't need you to make it worse. I had to step out and deal with something. That's all, and I don't have to explain every move I make to you. Can I get you an espresso or a glass of wine—or a beer?"

"No."

She turned toward him and found that in his naturally uncanny manner, he'd closed the space between them soundlessly. Although she was a tall woman, she was forced to look up at him.

"A woman doesn't belong out there alone, in the dark," he told her. When he narrowed his gray eyes they became almost black. "It probably used to be that folks didn't have to lock their doors around here, or worry about crime. Times have changed."

"I walked to my van. Then I walked back from my van when I'd finished my business. Really, I do appreciate your concern." She tried a smile, but his expression didn't change. "As I said, thanks, but I'm a big girl."

"That depends on what you mean by *big girl*."

There would be no discussion about what he thought it meant.

Angel rubbed his face. "I tried to check on Sonny but his cell's off. You know it bothers me when he does that."

She sympathized with his worry about his nephew. Sonny had come to Pointe Judah because he needed a strong hand if he wasn't going to end up in jail. "He and Aaron were out riding bikes," she said. "You know how that goes. They always go farther than they say they will."

"That's fine for Aaron," Angel said. "Sonny's got limits. He's got to be where I can reach him at all times."

She took out her phone again and placed a call.

Angel moved closer, so close she could feel him. "You calling Aaron?"

She nodded. *Pick up the phone, Aaron.*

"So Aaron's gone dark, too?"

"Don't put it like that," Eileen said. "They'll check in just as soon as they're close to home. You've got them scared stiff."

He tapped his chest with spread fingertips. "Me? Crap, I'm a pussycat. I care, is all."

She believed the last bit, but he was no pussycat. "Sonny's likely to stop by my place before he goes home. He likes the food. I'll make sure he gets back in one piece."

The following silence unnerved Eileen. She took a deep breath and put the phone away.

"Eileen," Angel said, his voice softening, a little raspy. "I'm sorry I came on too strong. I was worried."

She avoided looking at him. "Forget it."

"I will when you do. You're mad."

"No. Edgy is all."

He put a hand beneath her hair and held the back of her neck. "You said you weren't worried."

Eileen held quite still. Her scalp tightened and she felt as if a subtle breeze lifted her hair. They might be trying to pretend they had no physical effect on each other, but it was a lie.

If she told Angel about Chuck, how would he react? He'd never understand that she couldn't just brush it off. "I'm not worried," she told Angel. He rubbed her neck and she shivered. When she glanced at him, he was frowning.

"Is there anything you're not telling me?" he said.

She looked at the floor.

"Eileen?"

"Leave it. When I can talk about it, I will."

He took her by the hand and led her into the stockroom. Once there, he turned her to face him and held her shoulders. "Not good enough. What is it?"

She kept her gaze on his chest.

"C'mon," he said quietly. "Don't do this to me." He kissed her cheek, pushed her hair away from her left ear and stroked his thumb across it.

"Stop it," Eileen said, without conviction. He had bad timing, choosing tonight to make moves on her.

"I'd rather not stop." He pulled her against him. "I've already waited too long."

"Christian, don't." He was a big man. If he decided to hold you, you were held.

"Sorry—I think we both need a little warmth sometimes." He stepped back at once, but still held her arms and made it uncomfortable to look at him. It would be more uncomfortable to look away. "You've got a gun in your pocket," he said.

She felt her face heat up. "Yes, I have."

"I didn't know you owned one."

"You're the one who's always saying that even people in quiet places like Pointe Judah should take precautions."

His fingers tightened on her arms. "Do you carry all the time?"

This was the problem when you hung around with a man who had interrogated people for a living. "No."

"You keep a gun in the shop?"

She tried to wrench away but he didn't let her go. "Yes. Are we done now?"

"And tonight you decided you needed to be armed when you went out to do this business in your van you talk about?"

Eileen looked him in the eye. She felt the prickle of tears and blinked several times. "This conversation is over."

"I don't think so."

"Leave it, okay? Just leave it." Chuck had driven away. What if he'd come back and was skulking around outside, hoping she'd leave on her own?

"I'm sorry I'm so snappy," she said.

"Me, too." He looked at her mouth. "Do you want me to leave?"

She shook her head. He was sending her messages he'd kept under wraps before. Or perhaps she subconsciously wanted that to be true.

"You sure you don't want to tell me what's on your mind?" he said.

She wasn't sure, but she'd wait anyway.

"Eileen, would this be a bad time to talk about us, too?"

He'd done a great job of behaving like Aaron's strong, benevolent uncle and her friend. And he'd done the things a woman wished for when she wanted to know a man.

He dropped his hands.

"No it's not a bad time," she told him, lying. She laughed a little. "We are so grown-up about things. I'm proud of us. We should get a prize for being reasonable." And if she concentrated on something else, she wouldn't keep trying to figure out what Chuck might or might not plan to do.

"As soon as we're sure the boys are at your place, why don't we go to the Boardroom for a drink?" Angel said. "And something to eat. The music's good. We might even dance."

"Dance? You told me you can't dance." Going to a club

didn't appeal to her much, but she said, "Yes. Looks like Delia and Sarah Board have a success on their hands with that place." He was asking her out on a date. They'd had meals together before, in places like Ona's, but there had never been any planned dates.

Located in the middle of Pointe Judah, the Boardroom had been open just a few months. It revved up when the town revved down and there was nothing else like it around.

Delia owned a cosmetics firm with offices and labs around the country but liked living in Pointe Judah. Her daughter, Sarah, was a chemist at the local lab and the club had been her idea.

Eileen hitched her bag over her shoulder and turned out the lights in the stockroom. "I've got extra help coming in tomorrow and I need it. It's easy enough to get part-time people but I need someone full-time."

"You're working too hard," Angel said. "Why don't you put the gun in your purse if you're going to keep on carrying the thing? It could fall out of your pocket."

She did as he suggested without comment.

"Give me a couple more minutes," Angel said. "If you don't want to say anything, at least listen."

In the darkness, piles of boxes loomed all around and unpacked merchandise was piled high on tables. Much of the stuff on the tables sparkled, even in the gloom. Eileen glanced at the high windows but all she saw was rain speckles heavy enough to make the glass look pebbled in the glow of the icicle lights at the roofline.

"Eileen?"

"Okay. Sorry I got distracted."

"Something's wrong—something you're not telling me."

When he nailed her like this she felt trapped. "And I told you I'll talk about it when I can."

"What's changed?" he said, ever persistent. "If there's something to be worried about I need to know what it is or I can't help."

"There's nothing to worry about." Yet. And there probably wouldn't be. "Angel, has Sonny done jail time?"

A silence followed and went on so long she wished she'd kept her mouth shut.

"No, he hasn't," Angel said, opening the door again. "What made you think he had?"

"Oh, forget I said anything. He's a lot more mature than Aaron and sometimes I worry there could be things Aaron doesn't need to know yet, that's all."

Angel propped himself in the doorway. Behind him, colored lights blinked on and off on display trees. "How did you make the leap from Sonny being mature to his having done jail time?" Angel asked.

She felt ashamed, and judgmental. "He was sent to you for some reason. You told me he needed extra discipline."

"I said he needed a man's hand, a man's guidance. He doesn't have a father."

Like Aaron didn't have a father. Or hadn't. And Eileen wanted Chuck out of town again. Now.

"Look," Angel said. "I don't want to say this but I've got to. You give me the impression you think Sonny's no good for Aaron. You've pegged Sonny as a bad boy."

"No!" Was she that transparent? "Aaron got in his own trouble. He's not perfect." She hadn't told him how silently belligerent Sonny often was with her.

"But Aaron was just acting out and he did it quietly. You

told me that and I believe you. He got muddled up after his father left. Finn told me all about it. He tried to fill in but Aaron got the idea it was his fault his dad ducked out."

Finn Duhon was Eileen's brother. His wife, Emma, used to own Poke Around but sold it to Eileen when she came into money from the sale of the Duhon family home. Finn had insisted she take all the proceeds because he didn't need them. That money had changed Eileen's life.

"Say something," Angel said.

She thought she saw movement outside the front windows of the shop. Her heart missed a beat, then another, then pounded rapidly. She was getting too jumpy. "Leave it, I said," she told him, hearing her voice rise. "I can't do this now. You're pulling me apart like you're suspicious of everything I say. Let me be."

"Eileen, please—"

"No. I'd better go home on my own. I'm not good company."

"I'm coming with you." He reached for her but she tried to evade him. Angel caught her as she backed into a file cabinet. "Hold it," he said quietly.

She began to shake and she had to stop it. Some things had to be dealt with on her own. "I'm fine," she told him. "I'm just overworked."

"You're not fine," he said. He pulled her against him. For an instant she resisted, but then she softened and leaned into him. "You're making too many excuses and you're trembling. If I'm not scaring you to death, something else is. Now tell me because I won't quit asking until you do."

She wanted to close her eyes, breathe him in, hold on tight. How many times had she dreamed about this moment? Now she couldn't relax and enjoy it.

The phone in his pocket rang and he switched it off.

"That could be Sonny," she said.

"We're going back to your place now. I'll deal with him when I get there. Hold my hand. You're important to me. Let me be here for you." He held her hand and led her into the shop.

Nobody had ever told her such things, and he said them without pushing for anything more intimate.

Hammering on the front door made her jump so hard her teeth ground together.

"It's okay," Angel said, but he shoved her behind him and opened the door. "Hell, will you look at this!"

Sonny just about fell inside. Drenched, covered with mud and, unmistakably, smeared with blood, he staggered and Angel stopped him from tripping.

"What's the matter?" Angel said.

Eileen rushed to him. "Where's Aaron?"

"I gotta get back," Sonny said, dragging in breaths, not looking at Eileen. "You gotta come with me, Angel." He looked into Angel's face, a hard stare as if he was sending a silent message.

"Where's Aaron?" Eileen felt herself losing it. "Sonny—"

"Hush," Angel said, but his face wasn't expressionless now.

"It's all my fault," Sonny said. "I shouldn't have been…I went where I shouldn't have and talked to the wrong people. They kind of dared me. I got Aaron and me into trouble. It's bad." His big, dark eyes stretched wide and she could feel his fear. "Angel, do you think someone—"

"Let's go," Angel said.

"Tell me where Aaron is," Eileen begged.

"Oh, God," Sonny moaned, hanging his head. "He's in the swamp. North of town. I know how to get back. Chuzah made sure. I hope he made sure. He sent me in his, er, car."

"Stop it," Angel said. "Calm down, both of you. Chuzah is?"

Sonny looked as if he could cry. "Um, a doctor."

"Oh, thank God," Eileen said.

"In the swamp?" Angel said. "This doctor just happened by, huh?"

"He lives there."

"Aaron hurt himself?" Eileen said.

"No, someone else…" Sonny swallowed. "He got hurt."

"But there's a doctor there? A general practitioner?"

Angel pushed them both through the door and locked it behind him. "Eileen, we'll have to take your van. My truck's at home."

"I've got to drive Chuzah's vehicle back," Sonny said. "I'm afraid he'd do something awful to me if I didn't get his car back. I know the way. Follow me."

Angel grabbed Sonny's arm and spun him around. "What do you mean, something awful?"

"Oh," Sonny said. "He's a root doctor."

Eileen felt faint. She held Angel's sleeve. "We need a real doctor. I'll get on to Mitch Halpern. And let's call Matt—"

"No," Sonny said. "Chuzah knows about other medical stuff. If we show up with some new guy he doesn't expect, he won't let us find him."

"You said you knew the way," Angel said.

Sonny scrubbed at his oiled scalp. "Do what I'm tellin' you. Please. I know how to get to where there'll be someone waiting to guide us in."

To the right, at the curb, was a dark green vintage Morgan sports car. Again, all Eileen could do was stare.

"This root doctor threatened you," Angel said.

"Well…he was nice about it."

"I'm calling Matt now," Eileen said. "Some voodoo practitioner has kidnapped my son."

"Anything could happen if you call the law," Sonny said, with his familiar hard stare. The streetwise kid from Brooklyn was back. "I know Aaron's okay with Chuzah. He helped us."

"That isn't his Morgan, is it?" Angel said.

"Uh-huh. He's really weird."

"And you left Aaron alone with him?" Eileen said.

Sonny broke away and hurried toward the driver's door on the Morgan. "He saved Aaron's life," he said and climbed in, then slammed and locked the door.

3

"I'm worried about complaints," Emma Duhon said. "The merchants like the pedestrian traffic that comes to the fair, but they don't like competing with the stall owners for business."

She looked around the circle of women gathered at Ona's Out Back—Ona referred to it as a tea shop—to discuss the finer details of the Pointe Judah Christmas fair. The event was only days away and lasted over a weekend. They sat in a motley collection of armchairs pulled up to a big low table intended for magazines. The magazines were stacked on the floor to make way for coffee, wine and empty dishes formerly piled high with fried shrimp.

Emma doodled on a looseleaf notebook. "It's really late to be haggling over this. Why not suggest the shopkeepers have tables at the fair, too?" She'd been in a good mood when she agreed to help with the fair, but wished she'd thought it over for much longer before saying she would. How she got to be in charge, she couldn't remember.

"They'd have to pay rent for their tables, just like all the others," Lobelia Forestier said. She had been president of the Pointe Judah Chamber of Commerce for five years. "They should want to do their share for a good cause."

The truth was that nobody else would take over Lobelia's unpaid job which, apart from guaranteeing prime gossip rights, had no function other than to sit in on other people's meetings.

Delia Board, Sabine Webb and Gracie Loder made up the rest of the committee. Delia was Pointe Judah's most celebrated inhabitant and ran a world-famous cosmetics firm. Sabine, Delia's housekeeper, also moonlighted at the Boardroom, and Gracie worked at Buzzard's Wet Bar during the day and the Boardroom at night.

"How do we insult these shopkeepers without insulting them?" Delia said, running her fingers through her hair and drawing a laugh. She crossed her elegant gray boots at the ankle. "No fair, no extra traffic. End of problem. The fair benefits everyone."

Emma clamped her hands behind her neck and grinned at Delia. "Sometimes I think a really small town is more difficult to run than a major company. You would know, Delia."

"You're right, but we have to suffer for all the village charm we get around here."

Lobelia grunted and Emma shared a private smile with Delia and Sabine.

"You got a lot done tonight," Gracie said. "Sorry I was late but I'd better get on to Sarah's place. There's not much more to do except for deciding about the shopkeepers. And we've got to make sure everyone turns up to finish the decorations. We want this to knock everyone's eyes out. More flash, that's what we need, so folks will come from all over to see it."

"And buy," Lobelia said.

"That, too," Gracie said. She shook out her damp jacket and swung it around her shoulders. "'Night, all."

Lobelia shook her head. She coated her entire face with loose powder, including her eyebrows, and flecks clung to strands of dyed brown hair. "Barhopping the way you do isn't good for your reputation, Gracie," she said. "You go on. We'll finish up without you."

"Barhoppin'?" Sabine said and laughed. The red and green beads in her many braids clicked together. "Gracie works at Buzzard's, then she works at the Boardroom. She's busy makin' her way is all. You never had to rush around trying to keep your head above water. Gracie's either going to work or coming from work, so give her a break." Her deep bronze skin shone, especially where a dusting of gold sparkles curved over her high cheekbones.

Lobelia gathered herself up and pursed her lips.

"I'm already parked at Sarah's. I'll take a shortcut through Ona's kitchen and walk over." On her feet, Gracie made for the kitchen that separated Out Back from Out Front, Ona's licensed diner that faced the street. Rounded in the nicest way, with short black hair and large, smiling brown eyes, Gracie pretended to stagger into the kitchen.

Everyone but Lobelia laughed. "That girl's trouble," she said. "She knows Ona doesn't like people in her kitchen."

Emma was tired. In her seventh month of pregnancy, she ran out of steam much more easily than she was used to. "Can I leave you three to talk about the best way to make everyone happy?" she said. "If we're going to charge the business owners, it shouldn't be as much as the stall people just in for the fair."

"I'll give you a call tomorrow," Delia Board said. Her red hair expertly cut to sweep up, and her makeup flawless, Delia managed perfect posture even in a sagging armchair. "You're doing too much, Emma."

That wasn't true, but Emma enjoyed the concern. She had parked in the lot behind the building and set off, glad she'd remembered to bring an umbrella.

Finn would be waiting for her and fussing that she was late. Whenever she went out these days she was automatically late. She smiled, concentrating on her white leather sneakers as she walked the gradual incline toward her car. Out Front was busy tonight and an overflow of vehicles from the diner filled many of the slots on this side of the lot, too.

The baby did a slow somersault and Emma stood still, a hand on her belly. This was the longed-for child she and Finn had come to doubt they would ever have.

She walked on, warm with happiness.

"Mrs. Duhon?"

At the sound of a man's voice, she paused again and looked around. She couldn't see anyone. No moving shadows. Maybe she'd imagined the voice.

The lights inside Out Back seemed a long way away. The wind plucked at Emma's curly hair, tossed it across her face and back again. She fought with the umbrella. Branches shook on a row of trees between the parked cars.

The wind died.

Emma's skin crawled but she carried on.

"Wait, Mrs. Duhon! I want to talk to you."

"Who are you? What do you want?" Emma made sure she was in the middle of the open space between the rows of cars. She calculated how far she'd have to run back to the restaurant.

"You don't think about Denise anymore, do you, Mrs. Duhon?"

Emma's heart seemed to fill her throat.

"You're too important to waste your time on the past."

Denise. Poor, dear Denise. Dead two years now, murdered at the hands of a sick pervert. Emma and Finn had literally run into one another after a whole lot of years. They had stood talking and catching up on their lives, when Denise's body had tumbled from a nearby garbage container. The killer had been caught, but the horror never quite went away.

"Of course I think about Denise. She was my friend. I loved her."

"Did you? Doesn't stop you from carrying on like she never lived. Do you think that's fair? I don't think it is. Do you remember how Denise died?"

Emma considered running. She was fit, she always had been. Of course she couldn't move the way she did when she wasn't pregnant, but what choice did she have?

"I always said pregnant women were sexy."

Emma didn't know the voice. A shadow separated itself between two trees.

She was a little closer to Out Back than he was and he wasn't likely to draw attention to himself by causing her to fight him…she *would* fight him if she had to.

Since she was a bit nearer to the building, she had a chance of catching him off guard by running. She sidestepped back the way she'd come.

"Aw, you don't want to do that. All I want is to talk. You start trying something fancy and you could do damage to that baby of yours. You wouldn't want that."

Emma opened her mouth but only a rasping sound came out. She needed to scream and yell and draw attention to herself.

"You want your baby, don't you?" he said, his voice difficult to hear now. "They say you didn't think you could have one. What a shame if you killed it now."

She backed away from the place where the shadow hovered, skidded on one heel and dropped her purse. She left it where it fell and turned to run. Clumsy, she was so clumsy.

"No, no, no," he shouted. "You stop that right now or you'll hurt yourself. You're overreacting."

She kept running, the weight of the baby pulling her forward.

"You want to murder your kid? Is that what you want? You want to kill that baby you don't deserve?"

His voice kept up with her.

Emma's knees shook. She felt tears on her face.

He had followed, and he intended to catch her. The notebook flew from her hand and she saw a sheet of yellow paper dip and sail. She managed to hold on to the umbrella. It had a point at one end. She might need that.

"Why are you runnin'? What d'you have to be afraid of? Your conscience? Stop, right now."

No, no, no.

She heard the singing sound of something lashing through the air. A cord or rope coiled around one of her shoes. Emma couldn't run anymore.

The toe of her other sneaker jammed against a crack. Her umbrella slid through her fingers and tangled with her legs. Stumbling toward a parked pickup, she grabbed for the truck's tailgate.

Emma missed; she hit her shoulder and hip on cold metal. Sound hammered, louder and louder, in her ears. She was going down.

Her hands slammed into the gritty ground, then her belly.

Tearing pressure under her diaphragm winded her so hard she couldn't breathe. Then her knees gave out.

She skidded under the back of the pickup.

"You stay where you are, and keep still," the man said. He kicked the sole of her shoe and acid rushed to her throat. "You move before I say and you and that kid are finished—if the kid isn't done in already."

4

"Don't let his taillights get too far ahead of you."

"I'm doing the driving," Eileen said, without raising her voice. "You're safe with me. I won't lose Sonny."

At least he hadn't made the mistake of suggesting he take the wheel. He could only imagine what the response to that would have been. "I trust you, Eileen. You're a good driver." His face felt tight. Everything about this evening was wrong—or had gone wrong.

"Thanks," she said and he could hear the sarcasm in her tone.

There were things Eileen didn't know, like the true story behind Sonny being in Pointe Judah. Angel didn't want her to find out. She had already carefully minced around whether or not Sonny was a good role model for Aaron. She hadn't been so subtle that Angel missed the message, but at least she didn't know how close she was to the truth.

Sonny was a kid with potential—and a lot of past baggage weighing him down. Angel's job was to keep the boy alive until certain people forgot about him—if they ever did.

She stared sideways at Angel. "I think Sonny was telling us Aaron got shot but he didn't like saying it right out." Her voice shook.

"That could be. He didn't sound completely sure."

"Aaron will be okay, won't he?"

She wanted him to say yes, because that's what she needed to hear. "Of course he will," he said. He'd better be, and there had better not be anything that suggested whatever had happened was anything other than an accident.

"Could have been a hunter who made a mistake," Eileen said.

Angel wasn't aware of hunters firing indiscriminately in the swamps. "Could have," he said. "This rain makes it hard to see. Sonny's getting farther away."

"I don't mind anything but the fog," she said, leaning forward. "Look how thick it's getting." She rolled her window down an inch and succeeded only in letting cool, heavy vapor into the van. "Your headlights bounce back at you."

She reached for the gearshift and her fingers closed on the thigh he'd hitched up instead. Eileen whipped her hand away. Angel felt singed. He got a backlash, a hot backlash all the way to the base of his spine. They had touched so little— mostly accidentally.

Tonight he'd planned to be alone with her, for as long as he could keep her with him. And he'd planned to point out the benefits of getting closer, much closer. Eileen had been the perfect, immaculate mother for long enough. Too long, from Angel's point of view. When a woman's accidental hold on his thigh gave him pre-orgasmic spasms, the waiting game had gone too far.

"I should have kept a closer eye on what Aaron's been up to," Eileen said.

Shit. "You're not on your own with this. Not that I think

there's anything to worry about." Unless someone had put out a hit on Sonny.

Angel gritted his teeth.

"This isn't a road, it's an overgrown, abandoned track," Eileen said, and right on cue the van bumped up and over the buckled blacktop.

"You're right, it's not much of a road." He turned in his seat to peer through the fog toward the trees. "The bayou can't be so far away." He had never explored out here.

"Farther than you think," Eileen said. "It's close back toward town but around here there's a lot of swampland before you get to the water."

"What's in there?"

"In the swamp?" She glanced at him. "It's not pretty unless you get-off on mud and standing water and sodden ground in every direction. And critters—the kind you'd rather not meet."

Angel said. "And voodoo stuff, too, huh?"

"I don't know anything about that."

"Are you afraid of that bull?" Angel asked. "Don't waste fear on superstitious crap. Unless you fancy one of those little velvet spell bags filled with—grave dust, is it? That's supposed to keep you safe, isn't it?"

"I doubt it."

"Make you wildly passionate then?" Angel said, deliberately trying to catch her off guard. "Mixed with snake droppings and skunk hair? A pinch of dried fire ants to make you hot, and puree of hundred-proof alcohol to make you helpless? Sounds good to me."

He saw how she bit her lower lip and figured she hardly heard him babbling to fill up any silence. Just as well.

She surprised him when she said, "There are things in

these parts that you don't mess with. Ignorance can get you into big trouble."

Angel bit back a retort. Eileen was the last person he would have expected to believe in the old arts.

The little red taillights on the Morgan glowed, then faded to pink as the fog thinned and thickened.

"Watch out! Will you look at that?" He grabbed the dashboard. "The kid slammed on the brakes with no warning."

Eileen pumped the brakes on the van and came to a stop with inches to spare behind the Morgan

"I'm terrified for Aaron," Eileen said. She found his hand and wound her fingers in his. "Call Matt Boudreaux now. We ought to have the police here. And our own doctor. We could get hold of Mitch Halpern. You know he'd come right out."

"You heard what Sonny said. This Chuzah doesn't want any official company." He rubbed her hand between his. It wasn't her way to reach for comfort.

"If it turns out we have to go to Matt about this, he'll be steamed."

Angel made sure he didn't show how much he liked that idea. "Go with me on this. Matt would do the same if he was in our position." Maybe he would; maybe he wouldn't. Eileen didn't need Matt Boudreaux around—for any reason.

Reluctantly, he let go of her hand and pushed out of the van. Sonny didn't appear but Eileen walked toward the Morgan.

Angel said, "Sonny?"

Sonny didn't answer. Angel reached Eileen and they saw that Sonny wasn't in the sports car. He stood a few yards ahead at the very edge of the road. His back was rigid and he repeatedly looked around the area.

"Look," Eileen said, backing into Angel. "Over there. What is it? Sonny!"

"Quiet," Sonny said clearly. "Keep it down. He doesn't like noises."

"Chuzah?" Angel and Eileen asked in unison.

Angel peered into the darkness at the side of the overgrown road. Two small, pale lights blinked on and off. "Get back in the van and lock the doors," he told Eileen.

"Forget it," she whispered hoarsely. "I'm going after Aaron. He's my son."

He reached for her; the backs of his fingers met the side of her face. "You're burning up," he said. "Are you sick?"

"No! It's humid."

It *was* humid. Rain fell hard enough to stick his shirt to his back. He had water inside his shoes. Eileen's long, dark hair clung to her neck and shoulders and her face shone pale and wet in the near opaque darkness.

"Those lights," Eileen said. "They're not normal. They look like shiny stones. What are they?"

"Probably nothing. Just something picking up reflections." He'd never seen anything like them before. And he didn't like that one bit.

"Angel," she said, tugging at the sleeve of his shirt. "They're moving. They go one way, then the other. I want Aaron."

"Look," he said quietly, "it would be quicker if I went on my own with Sonny. Please, wait in the van."

"Don't say that again. I'm getting a flashlight." She turned around and started back.

Angel didn't try to stop her. Instead, he took a few steps closer to Sonny and said, "Eileen's gone for a flashlight. Quick, tell me what happened."

"No flashlight." Sonny hissed. "Chuzah doesn't do flashlights."

The silver lights drew closer and Angel said, "Get away from there. What are those glowing things?"

"It's Locum," Sonny said. "Chuzah's buddy. He's come to guide us into the swamp."

"Don't play any stupid games," Angel said. "Eileen's already scared out of her mind."

"No, I'm not," Eileen said, arriving at his side again. "I'm worried about my boy. Sonny! What's that thing?"

"Don't use the flashlight or we're done for," Sonny said. "Cool it, will ya? Just follow me."

"It's a ghost," Eileen whispered. "My legs are wobbly."

"There aren't any ghosts." Angel eased the flashlight from her fingers and pushed it into his waistband. He put an arm around Eileen and guided—or half pushed—her forward. With each step she leaned back against him.

"It's a ghost," Eileen repeated. "It's floating. Look! The lights went out but I can see a silvery shape wafting above the ground."

"It's Chuzah's friend Locum," Angel whispered. "Sonny told me." He had a wicked temptation to laugh.

"Locum?" Eileen said. "Do you think Chuzah's a ghost, too?"

A few steps behind Sonny, they left the overgrown road and set off onto ground that soon became soggy beneath damp brush. Trees loomed, their pale trunks hung with strips of peeling bark.

"It's a shape-shifter," Eileen said. "Sonny! You come here at once. Don't you go anywhere near that thing."

"He's not twelve," Angel whispered.

Her face turned to his. "Sometimes they behave as if they are. Do you know what that thing is?"

"Looks like an animal."

"Exactly," she hissed. "Aaron's been taken by a shape-shifter."

"No such thing."

"Oh, yes there are. I've read about them."

Angel kept a tight hold on her. "That's called fiction."

"It is not."

"Will you two keep it down?" Sonny said.

The trees had closed around them. Each time Angel lifted a foot, it broke from a seal of sticky mud. When he set his foot down again, water splashed. The overpowering scent was of mold and dank, wet things. "You should have a coat on," he told Eileen.

"So should you." Her voice got higher and suspiciously squeaky.

"You're crying," he said.

"You ought to be crying, too. We shouldn't be here like this. We should have called the police."

"To report that Aaron's been taken by shape-shifters?"

"Sonny said Chuzah was a root doctor."

"That gray thing up there is an animal and—"

"A wolf! Angel, make Sonny come here."

"Relax. Some joker's playing a number on Sonny. They set him up for this."

Eileen sniffed now. "You do think Aaron's okay?"

"Yes." He didn't damn well know. "Sonny—I see more lights. They're different."

"They're colored," Eileen said. "Like Christmas lights. Oh, they're way up high. This is all horrible. I'm getting out my gun and I don't want any arguments from you."

"You won't get 'em unless you start firing," Angel said.

Sonny came back to them. His eyes resembled blank, black circles and Angel could see him shivering.

"We've got to do what Chuzah said, but I feel like I'm going to be sick," Sonny said. Angel only recalled one other time when the boy admitted to fear. That had been on the night his father—a gutsy guy who went against the family—died.

"That Locum is a shape-shifter, isn't he?" Eileen asked, and jumped. A rattling noise reached her, growing louder.

"What's a shape-shifter?"

"Never mind," Angel said. He listened to the eerie sounds.

"Don't worry about that," Sonny said. "It's just Chuzah sending a signal to Locum—I think."

"That's it," Eileen said, shaking away from Angel. She ran, as best she could, toward the lights strung somewhere high in the trees ahead.

Angel took off after her and said, "She's got a gun," over his shoulder.

Eileen couldn't stop crying. She sniffed, swiped at her face. "I've got to hold myself together," she muttered, and skidded to a halt, her mouth open.

She had broken into a clearing, a clearing just big enough for a large wooden cabin built on stilts about six feet tall. No, the clearing was bigger than it had seemed at first. Around the structure, there was enough space for a shed, on shorter stilts, what looked like a carport, and a row of lockers. Sure enough, the roof on the cabin was strung with unevenly looped, multicolored lights. Four small windows in the front were covered with patterned curtains and a faint glow showed from inside.

A hand on her shoulder all but sent her to her knees. "It's just us," Angel said into her ear. "Put the gun out of sight. Quickly."

She sighed, but put the Glock in her purse. "Where's the wolf?" she said.

He stroked her back. "There's no wolf."

"Don't you try to tell me I was imaging things," she told him. "You saw it, too."

Sonny moaned.

"I'm going up there," Eileen said and went to the bottom of a sturdy-enough flight of stairs. She stopped and covered her face. Through her fingers she saw a big gray animal, a dog with silver eyes, standing halfway up the flight. He had huge teeth and she could see every one of them. "Help." She mouthed the word but didn't hear a sound. "Help!" Still she couldn't hear her own voice.

The shack door flow open. "Aha," a great voice, a very deep, right from the boots voice, called. "You would be Eileen, perhaps?"

She nodded. "Where's my son?"

"Are you, Chuzah?" Angel asked. "Sonny's told us about you. Sounds like we owe you."

The keeper of the major voice appeared in the doorway and spread his arms. A rope of bones and bells clanged and clacked around his neck.

"Welcome, welcome. My humble home is your humble home. If you see what I mean. You come in. We been waitin' for you. They here, Aaron, and they look like they been seeing ghosts. There's that quiet boy, too. You come on up, quiet boy. Chuzah, he don't bite." He threw back his head and laughed, showing two rows of gleaming teeth.

Eileen pursed her lips and started to climb. The dog didn't move.

"Locum," Chuzah said, "you get your sorry ass up these

steps and get in the house. You ain't nothin' but a poser. Fierce? You don't know about fierce. You embarrass me. Excuse him, please."

The dog's mouth took on what looked like a smile and he tootled up and inside, looking back once with his tongue hanging out of his mouth and, Eileen was almost certain, giving her a wink.

"You three takin' your time," Chuzah hollered. "We gettin' tired of waitin'." He whirled one hand above his head in an exaggerated queenly wave. A turban and billowing kaftan, both in a Hawaiian print featuring palm trees and hula dancers in grass skirts, and nothing else set off his black skin. "You like my seasonal decorations? In your honor. I don't get many guests around here." He swept back inside.

"Up we go," Angel said, but before either of them could move, Sonny passed them, taking two steps at a time.

Chuzah's laughter spilled from inside the cabin. Angel and Eileen gave each other a final look and walked through the door, which slammed hard behind them under the master of the house's foot. His long, well-shaped bare foot.

"Here we are," he said, rocking onto his heels. "I am Chuzah, and this is my friend, Locum. My assistant. Like a locum tenens, he takes over my practice when I am forced to leave for a while. And I must be forced, I assure you, because this man don't want to go nowhere but right here."

"Sir," Eileen said. She couldn't handle this politely anymore. *"Where is my son?"*

"All in good time, madam," Chuzah said. "All in good time."

A would-be Shakespeare thespian in a Hawaiian-print getup.

An altar took center stage, at least Angel thought it was an altar. Lit by many candles, giving off a variety of questionable odors, the tall, gilded base stood in the center of the room with a screen about a foot high on top. The screen, gold and enamel, stood open and Angel couldn't begin to figure out the heavy load of items in front. He did note sticks of incense burning. He saw no reason to go closer.

There was nothing rustic about the furnishings—other than the oil lamps. Soft suede furniture in deep red invited you to sit or lie. Green and gold rugs covered the floor.

Root doctoring had to be paying better than Angel would have thought.

"Right this way," Chuzah said and Angel stared at him. "You want to see the other boy, of course. Master Aaron, the curious. What amazement, discovering the depths to which an inquisitive youth will sink in order to investigate what he has no right to know about."

Angel closed his mouth.

Chuzah walked on the balls of his feet to a door at the back of the room. He opened it gently and put his head inside. "We got company, boy. You put on your best face and make me proud, y'hear?"

Eileen didn't dare to look at the other two. The gray dog returned, a wooden bowl in his mouth. This, he pushed at Angel.

"Water," Chuzah said, flicking his fingers. "The dog, he need water."

"Weimaraner," Angel said. "Just remembered what he is. I've only seen a couple before. He's a beautiful guy." He took the bowl and looked around for a source of water.

"He has a large ego," Chuzah said. "Do nothing to inflate

his head. You'll find water in there." He indicated another door.

Eileen lowered her head, marched directly to the second door and passed Chuzah. She made it three steps into the room and stopped. "Aaron Moggeridge. What are you doing? You scared me out of my mind."

"Mom—"

"No, don't say a word. Be absolutely quiet while I take this in."

"Mom—"

"One more word and I won't be responsible for my actions."

"Eileen?" Still holding the dog's empty dish, Angel came into the room and had to fight not to laugh. "There you are, Aaron. Having a rough time, I see."

Propped against multicolored silk pillows on a fluffy divan, Aaron wore a robe not dissimilar from Chuzah's. As usual, his curly black hair was pulled into a tail at his nape. True, his eyes looked huge and very dark in his unusually pale face, but apparently he felt well enough to eat chocolates out of a huge box.

"Shee-it," Sonny muttered. "I tell ya, last time I saw him he was dyin'."

"Dramatist," Chuzah said, examining incredibly long, curved nails with silver tips. "There was an incident. Oh, yes, an incident. I'd lie if I denied that, but the boy is mending nicely. He's fortunate he had his little episode right under my nose." He turned up his hands and shook his head with exasperation. "Oh, Angel. It *is* Angel?"

"Yeah."

"Aaron here told me about your former career. I've got

something I think you might find interesting. Would you excuse me please, Eileen? Such an elegant name, *Eileen*."

Eileen nodded. "Start talking, Aaron." She sat on the edge of the divan and Aaron promptly pushed the box of chocolates under her nose.

5

His kaftan billowing, Chuzah led Angel back into the other room, closed the bedroom door and swung to face him. "Let's be honest with each other, shall we?" He waved Angel into an armchair and sat on a couch himself. "We must use what time we have well. It wouldn't do for your lady or the boys to hear this."

Seated, Angel propped his elbows on the arm of the chair and tapped his fingertips together. "Your lady," was an interesting choice of terms from a stranger.

"You do know what I'm talking about?" Chuzah said, keeping his voice down.

Angel raised his eyebrows. If this clown wanted information, he was going to have to prove he had a right to it.

"Very well." Chuzah shrugged. "You're going to be difficult, not that I blame you."

"I don't know you," Angel said. "From what I see here, I never will."

"You carry a grudge against…" He swung out an arm, taking in the room, and Angel noted what he hadn't noticed before, rows of herbs hung to dry on rods at the tops of the walls. And more bones, skulls and various shrunken lumps of unrecognizable material.

On the altar, one of those lumps sizzled on a tiny spit above a candle flame.

A chest with many small drawers, like a Chinese herbalist's cabinet, covered an entire wall.

He turned toward one of the sash windows. The curtains billowed inward and he saw how an artfully placed skull propped the lower window open. A loop of the colored Christmas lights outside cast cheery spots on the shiny white dome that had once contained a human brain.

Angel took it all in. "I've always believed in creative freedom."

Chuzah's knowing eyes revealed that he was more amused than offended by Angel's careful verbiage.

"You want to tell me your story?" Chuzah said.

"First," Angel said, holding up a finger, "would you like to tell me why you sound as if you have a split identity?"

Chuzah gave another huge grin. "You mean my accent, mon? Me, I like to keep my options open. All o' dem options. Now, are you going to tell me about yourself?"

Angel let a few beats pass. "I think I'll pass. Who are you?"

"More questions about me," Chuzah said, turning his head to give a view of his dramatic profile. "I am a being. A creature of particular talents. I use my skills as I wish, and I trouble no one who recognizes my superiority."

"That explains a lot."

"I do not like company," Chuzah announced. He pointed at Angel. "You should be grateful I was meditating when the boy, Aaron, had his unfortunate…encounter."

"Thank you," Angel said. Antagonizing unknown quantities was a don't in ATF 101. "I'd appreciate knowing what happened."

"I approve of sharing information."

So if Angel didn't toss the man a bone...some sort of supposedly interesting detail, there wouldn't be any useful insight coming his way, either. "I'm making my home in Pointe Judah. Sonny is my nephew and he's living with me. He's been having problems settling down. Know what I mean? Teenage stuff."

Chuzah shrugged. "I prefer high places," he said. "Do you understand?"

"No," Angel said honestly.

"My home is a high place. It's peaceful up here. When I attend to my physical fitness, I use high places. Preferably trees. My skills are extraordinary. Some might say I fly."

"I see." Angel didn't.

"Is the lovely Eileen your wife?"

Angel sucked in a breath. "No."

"So Aaron isn't related to you?"

"No."

"But the lovely lady is your lover."

"So far you're batting zero." Angel sighed. "Unfortunately."

"Is Eileen your friend?"

"Yes."

"But you would like her to be a closer friend. You are wanting sex with her?"

Angel puffed up his cheeks but wouldn't let himself look away from the man. This was a test, he was sure of it, and he didn't want to fail. "Yes, I am."

"She's luscious."

"Hey—"

"A compliment, Angel. You have outstanding taste in

womanly flesh. And she may even have a strong mind—or so her eyes suggest."

"Is there a point here?" Angel said.

Chuzah folded his hands behind his head and looked to the ceiling. "If I am to help, I must understand all these currents I feel passing between the subjects. But—" he leaned forward abruptly, his handsome face stern "—there is a great deal at stake. There are those who wish harm. Not simple harm, but ultimate harm. You would do well to humor me.

"Now I understand what I feel between you and the woman, I can separate it from the other currents. Strong passion can cloud the messages that come to me. You may do well to consummate—"

"I don't need your advice on how to deal with my personal affairs."

"Of course not. But she is deeply disturbed. She desires you as much as you desire her. And you will not be disappointed with her nor she with you. You will ignite great fires together."

Holy hell. "Is that right?"

"Without doubt. But there are other currents. I don't understand all of them yet, but I will. Others I read very well now that you have explained some issues to me.

"I can tell you that the lovely Eileen fears she will lose you if you do not become lovers. But you will have to be the, er, aggressor, because she is tied by her duty to the boy. She will sacrifice her chances for satisfaction unless you prove to her that it is right for the two of you to find mutual heaven." Chuzah rolled his eyes then closed them. "If you could see what I see, you would not waste another moment. Her naked body is your vessel to fill, your ecstasy. Her breasts like white melons tipped dusky dark and only waiting for your lips, your teeth. When your manroot sinks slowly into her for the first time, the she-creature will explode with passion. She will draw you in again and again, scratch your skin, sob out her desire for more and more of you, until—"

"Right," Angel said, finally finding a voice. "It won't be easy, but trust me to—"

"Exactly. And I am fascinated by your strengths. Both those you have learned and those with which you were born."

Angel cleared away any expression, a skill he'd learned when he was in the CIA, a part of his life he preferred to ignore.

"An important man to have around," Chuzah said. "Your visions, are they as strong as ever?"

Angel's heart made a momentary full stop. How did this man know anything about Angel's premonitions or his ability to visualize trouble already in action? He was doing his best to forget these unwelcome gifts and he'd been doing well since he left the CIA. Until very recently, that was. Vague hints of the old plague had started to return.

"Not *as* strong, but nevertheless still with you?" Chuzah said. "Good. They will be useful, more than useful. They may save…I have smelled death."

"Do you always talk in code?" Angel wanted to drop the subject. "Not that you're right about me." He knew he didn't sound convincing but Chuzah had caught him off guard.

"I will be very clear." Chuzah glanced toward the bedroom. "Soon there will be questions from your woman. We must finish. What has happened is not as it appears. The injury to Aaron was minor—no more than a small bruise or two."

"When Sonny came for us he said Aaron was bleeding badly."

Chuzah shrugged. "He saw blood—probably from a cut somewhere. He thought it must be serious, no more."

Angel glanced away. "There's blood on Sonny's clothes."

"What we know, we know," Chuzah said softly. "But it's best that the truth be denied. The injury was intended to be deadly. What I don't know is which boy was supposed to die."

"Damn," Angel said under his breath.

"But you knew there was doubt," Chuzah said. "Or you suspected it." Locum rose from the floor abruptly, loped to Angel and looked up into his face. A faint scent, wood-smoke, hovered around the animal and his silvery-blue eyes didn't blink. Angel felt the hair rise on the back of his neck.

"You cannot deny your intuition," Chuzah said. "See how Locum feels it. Down, boy."

"What is it you want to tell me?" Angel said.

"You believe Sonny is in danger?"

"I wish I didn't."

"I was in the trees when the trouble came," Chuzah said. He stood up, breathing deeply, expanding his big chest. "Meditating. I saw the boys. They meant no harm. Curiosity about the practices is common."

"Boys will be boys?" Angel said, biting his tongue, but wanting to hurry the man to the point.

"Mmm. That one who was quiet. The one you say is your nephew."

"Sonny."

"He is not your nephew. You are not related."

Angel had regained control over his reactions. "You don't know that."

"I do know that. And I know the boy is in trouble. He fears a hunter."

"Where are you getting all this?"

"Each of us has different talents."

"I want to get Eileen and the boys home."

Chuzah came toward him and Angel automatically got to his feet. The other man's eyes were black, large, uptilted. And mysterious. But Angel saw no malice in him.

"Take them home," Chuzah said. "But when you need me, I will be here."

"Thanks. We'll manage."

"I will be here. And remember this. Out there—" He pointed both first fingers toward the outside. "Out there is an evil force made more fearsome because it has no discipline. What you face is a bitter desire for vengeance. I don't know the reason yet, but I will. Do you know the reason?"

Did he? What was he thinking? This joker had practiced his act and what he said could mean whatever he wanted it to mean. What Angel didn't know was what the man wanted from him.

"You're off-base," Angel said. "Thanks for looking after Aaron. But you're deliberately talking in circles. Were there really shots? Or did he scare himself into a collapse. He doesn't look as if he was wounded."

Chuzah smiled. "Perhaps not. You'll see. I may be off-base, as you say. Regardless, don't let your guard down." He stood still and his smile faded. He turned toward the bedroom and back again. "It's important not to make a mistake. It would be disastrous to misread the signs."

"What signs?" Angel said. "If you've got something I need to know, tell me."

The haughty face was all sharp angles. "Until you are ready to trust me, I cannot be certain I read the signs correctly. Trust will take time. I understand. But you don't have much time, my friend.

"I can tell you one fact," Chuzah continued. "Today someone was supposed to die. The attempt failed, but there will be another attempt."

"Someone tried to kill Sonny?" Angel said.

"When the trouble comes again, it will be when you don't expect it. You must guard against what is least likely. One death may not come close to satisfying our killer's appetite."

6

Bucky Smith turned his head, tried to focus. Flashing lights. He fucking hated flashing lights. They never meant anythin' good, or they never had for him.

He hated this town. If he hadn't just about run out of places to be, he'd already be gone.

Cops driving down the side of Ona's.

So what? Nothing to do with him. He just had to take a leak and he'd be out of here.

Nobody gave a shit about him. Never had.

Would you look at that? He was in the damn kitchen. What he wanted was the can, the *can,* dammit.

Where was everyone back here? Yeah, Ona's Out Back. *Tea room,* she called it. Shit. He could smell the booze even if the place was empty. Empty, not a single piece of ass sippin' *tea.*

The cop lights were out back.

Out back of Out Back.

Damn, he ought to be a poet or somethin'. He needed that can and another drink. If anyone was still workin' around here.

The fryer smelled good. All those leftover bits of food bubblin' in the fat. Best part of this nowhere, the food.

Bucky turned back, frowned. He must have passed the can on the way in here.

The side door to the outside slammed open and a guy came in—fast. Bucky turned his head the other way, blinked to look at him. Just a guy in a wet coat.

"You lost?" Bucky said. "Same's me. Shit. You lookin' for the can, too?"

The guy just stared at him, his hair dark and sopped, stuck to his face.

Bucky raised his palms. "Friendly, ain't you? Well, fuck you." He stumbled toward the passageway to Out Front.

He didn't see the hand coming.

Fingers dug into his windpipe and he gagged, took a swing at the face that wouldn't stay still. He clawed at the man's chest.

Deeper the fingertips gouged. Bucky's mouth opened. A shove and he fell backward. His skull hit something hard and he felt his bladder let go.

All he heard was the sizzle of the boiling fat.

7

Finn Duhon drove into the parking lot behind Ona's restaurants. Emma had called him, whispered for him to come, but she wouldn't say why.

A cream-colored Jeep passed him and the driver honked. Finn honked back but didn't recognize the vehicle or the driver. Seeing someone drive by as though everything was normal didn't make him feel any better.

He stopped his car and jumped out. The lights were on in both Out Front and Out Back. It wasn't that late.

He didn't see anyone in the lot and started to run past parked cars. He saw Emma's Lexus and broke into a sprint. His left shoe scrunched on something and he paused to look down.

Car keys. He picked them up and knew immediately that they were Emma's. Finn breathed through his open mouth. Heading for her car again, he punched the number pad on his cell, got through to the police station and demanded to speak with Matt Boudreaux.

He heard Matt's voice and said, "Get to the parking lot behind Ona's. Something's happened to Emma. I think she's been kidnapped," then cut off.

The Lexus was empty, just as he'd known it would be. No wonder she'd whispered; she must have been in someone else's vehicle.

Maybe she was in a trunk. Emma was no dummy. He could hope she'd find a way to put out a taillight to get air— or puncture the spare tire.

How long had she been in trouble before she could call him? Finn stared around.

He heard a siren and saw the reflection of flashing lights against the sky.

What should he do first? This wasn't like jungle warfare— the only kind of warfare he knew about. He didn't have the automatic reactions that would work here.

My God. He didn't know where to start.

People who wanted children badly enough cut babies from their mothers' wombs.

He bent double and took a deep breath. Finn Duhon didn't panic. He'd been a warrior and that was something that changed you forever. He needed the police and they'd be here any moment.

Breaking into a jog, he headed back toward his car.

"Finn!"

He jumped, searched in every direction.

"It's you." And it was Emma's voice. An instant later she broke into sobs.

Blood pounded into Finn's head. He followed the sounds and found her easily. Under a pickup truck, on her poor, swollen belly, the side of her face resting in the dirt. She still clutched her cell. Her very curly, honey-blond hair fell over her face.

"Hold on," he said, on his knees, peering at her. "Don't

move. Matt's coming. I'll call the medical-aid car now. And I'll see if I can get Mitch Halpern to come over."

"Take me home," she said in a small, broken voice. "Help me out of here and take me home."

"Cher, please don't move." He stayed on all fours where he could see her and make sure she didn't attempt to move. And he called emergency again, this time asking for medical response.

Emma dropped her phone and reached out a hand. Finn closed his fingers over hers. "Has the man gone?" she asked quietly. "I didn't hear him go. Be careful, Finn. He could creep up on you."

Sirens grew louder.

"Man?" Finn said. "There was a man? Did you recognize him?"

"No, it was too dark. Look around. Make sure he isn't coming back."

Finn did as he was told but the only movement was a guy coming around from Ona's Out Front to get on his motorbike, which he'd parked near a wall. He kicked off the stand, climbed on and roared away. He didn't even glance toward the parking lot.

"How long have you been down here?"

Emma pushed at her hair. "I don't know. A long time. Finn, I can move my hands and legs just fine but it was hard to calm down. I listened to the baby. There wasn't any pain. That's good, isn't it? I thought blood would come—I expected to feel it rush out."

"You're both going to be fine." He realized he believed it—he had to. "Sounds as if the aid car's right there with the cops."

"I don't want all kinds of people, Finn. I'm fine now you're here. I didn't get out before because I thought he might still be waiting for me."

Finn got on to the dispatcher at the station house and spoke to Officer Carley, whom they all knew well. "We need to find Mitch Halpern," he said. "You know, Dr. Mitch?" Carley kept it short and efficient and assured him she'd get the local doctor over there fast.

Waves of tremors shook Emma. She heard the sound of many approaching feet and voices, breathless, high voices. And Lobelia Forestier's rose above them all.

"Is she dead? Has Emma been murdered? Was she raped? If Matt Boudreaux had done his job properly in the past, this wouldn't be happening now."

"Can it, Lobelia," Sabine Webb said. "You're embarrassin' all of us."

"You doin' okay, Emma?" Ona asked.

"I am," Emma said.

She saw a pair of extremely high, gray ankle boots, gorgeous legs and a deep green swishing skirt. Delia Board was there, of course. Ignoring her knees and her hose, she got down beside Finn.

A police car, lights flashing, rolled in, passed Finn's car and stopped. Chief Matt Boudreaux got out, leaving the door open, and Officer Clemens came at a trot.

"No," Emma said. "Not the police, please. He told me not to tell anyone. He said he'd make sure our baby died, if I did. And me."

"Who told you not to tell anyone?" Lobelia said. "What did he do to you?"

Cold, the sweat on his body abruptly icy, Finn looked into Emma's face and said quietly, "He won't get near you again."

"What happened here?" Matt Boudreaux asked.

"I think some guy was drunk," Emma said, keeping her voice strong. "He threatened me. I'm moving out from the truck now."

"Don't," Finn said. "Please, cher, just stay where you are."

"Take it easy," Matt said. "Tell me what went on. Take it slowly."

"This is what happens when the police chief is too young," Lobelia said. "We need someone with experience in the job. Every woman in this town is in danger of being raped in her bed. We'd better all make sure we lock our doors."

"Can it, Lobelia," Sabine Webb said again.

"I'll have to ask you ladies to move along," Matt said. "The aid car's comin' and you're in the way."

"The idea!" Lobelia said. "Don't you forget who pays your wages, young man. If you don't want to lose that cushy job of yours, you'll watch your tongue."

Finn glanced at Delia who shook her head slightly. "Emma, how are you feeling? What hurts, darling?"

"I'm going to be fine," Emma said. She planted an elbow and pushed herself out from beneath the pickup. She smiled at Delia and whispered, "See if you can get Lobelia out of here. Sabine will help."

"Consider it done," Delia said and stood up. She flapped her arms at Lobelia. "This is too much for you. Much too much. I insist we go back inside and have some coffee. With a little something stronger in it."

"I've got just the thing," Ona said. "It's my own special recipe for shock."

Lobelia tutted.

"I insist," Delia said, and the four women headed back toward Out Back.

"Where the hell's the aid car?" Matt asked, and more flashing lights appeared as if he'd summoned them. "Well…well, we've got a good portion of the police force. But I want medics." Another cop car pulled in, followed by a dark-colored Prius.

"The aid car could have been called to an emergency," Emma said.

Matt opened his mouth and Finn as good as heard that the other man intended to say that this was an emergency. "Good thing everything's under control here," Finn said quickly. "Rusty's arrived. I don't think we want a whole lot written about this in the papers, at least not yet. Whoever did this needs to be caught, not scared off."

Rusty Barnes ran the local newspaper and he was also a close friend of Finn and Emma.

The arms that closed around Emma were the only ones she wanted to feel. She looked up at Finn, into his dark, troubled eyes, and he managed a half-hearted grin. "Sit still," he said. "When I get you home I'm keeping you there. You're too dangerous to be out. What have you got on your feet? You've got to wear sensible shoes."

Emma just listened to him and kept her head on his shoulder.

Rusty arrived. He had a camera slung over one shoulder. Like most very-small-town newspapers, *The Pointe Judah News* didn't run to many employees. In fact, Rusty and two production people were it.

"Emma?" he said, dropping down beside her. "What's happened? You okay? Finn?" Anxiety tightened his voice.

"Can we talk about it when we get back home?" Finn said, looking straight into Rusty's eyes. "I'm going to ask you for a favor. Please don't write about this."

Rusty nodded, showing immediate understanding, then backed off to give them room. "You bet."

"Emma," Matt said. "Do you feel up to telling me what happened to you?"

"Yes." She suddenly wanted to. She wanted that man arrested. "A man waited for me out here—in that line of trees. He said horrible things about my baby getting killed. And me. He talked about…he talked about something that happened before and he was angry because he said I'd forgotten it, only I haven't."

"What was he talking about?"

She sucked in a deep breath. "Denise Steen and how she died such a horrible death. He said everyone's forgotten her and I'm just getting on with my life like she never lived. I didn't expect that to be brought up again."

Finn's arms tightened around her but he didn't interrupt. Denise Steen had been murdered in Pointe Judah two years ago. He and Emma had found the body.

Clemens was taking notes.

"So he threatened you and took off?" Matt said.

"He chased me," Emma said in a small voice. "I was almost to my car but I knew I shouldn't try to get in with him so close. I think he would have driven away with me."

"He chased you," Matt said. "But he didn't catch you."

"I dropped my purse. It's black leather so you'll have to use a flashlight to find it. And the pages from my notebook went everywhere. I couldn't hold on. I just ran and I thought I was going to get back to Ona's, but he used a whip around my ankle and I tripped up."

Finn took her by the arms and looked into her face. "He *what?*"

"He flipped a whip thing around my ankle and yanked it to stop me from running."

Finn rubbed both hands over his face.

"Sampson and his partner are going over the carpark," Clemens said. "There's the aid car coming right now."

The boxy vehicle squealed around to pull up close to Matt's car.

A medic hopped out, followed by a second one. Both men leaned over, hands on knees and one of them said, "Hold still, Mrs. Duhon." A good-looking blond kid, he had a reassuring smile on his face.

"She was under that pickup," Matt said, brushing dirt from her face.

The medic looked at her and his eyes flicked down to her belly. "I don't know how you managed to get where you were, but you wouldn't be able to get there again if you wanted to."

"Don't bet on it," she said, laughing weakly. "I'm a talented klutz."

"Are you in any pain, ma'am?"

"I ache," she said. "But I'm not really in pain." *Except in her mind. She was so scared.*

Officer Sampson's partner hurried up. "We're not seeing any purse, or any notepaper sheets," he said. "Did you hear a vehicle leave, Mrs. Duhon?"

"No. Even if he took my purse, the papers went everywhere. They did, I tell you. Yellow pages—"

"It's all right," Matt said quietly. "We'll have a better look."

"A Jeep left when I was arriving," Finn said. "I didn't recognize who was driving but he honked so he obviously knows me. I'd say the guy didn't even know anything had happened. How long ago did this man leave, Emma?"

"I'm not sure. I left the restaurant around nine-fifteen. I don't think the whole thing took long to happen and then everything went quiet. I just stayed under the truck and waited."

"That's more than an hour now," Matt said, looking at his watch. "Which ankle did he get with the whip?" Matt asked.

Emma stuck out the appropriate foot.

Immediately the blond medic examined the skin. He undid her shoe carefully and slid it off, then the sock. "You did mean it hit your ankle? Not somewhere higher?"

"No, my ankle."

"How long ago was this?" Matt said.

"Forty-five minutes?" Emma said. "I guess. I don't know."

"There aren't any marks," the medic said.

"It was my foot really, not my ankle." With difficulty Emma bent over to study her foot. "I'm all muddled." She looked up. "The marks must have faded."

She saw the medics glance at each other and suddenly felt angry. "I'm not making this up. I couldn't come up with something like that if I tried."

"I'll ask the questions," Matt said. "As soon as Mitch gets here and says it's okay, we'll move you Emma. I want more blankets, please."

At that moment, Dr. Mitch Halpern ran up. "Had to park at the side," he said. "You guys have about filled this place. Hi, Emma. How are you feeling?"

"Great," she said, wanting only to get into Finn's car and leave. She could see that Mitch was, as usual, in a track suit and exuding health.

He unzipped his bag and tugged out a stethoscope. "Kneel behind her so she can lean on you and relax," Mitch said to Finn, hitching the blankets more tightly around her. He listened to her heart and lungs, smiling directly into her eyes as he did so. "Ready to run a marathon," he said.

Mitch moved on to her belly and Emma held her breath.

"Breathe," Mitch said, laughing. "We don't want you to pass out. Junior sounds as good as Mom. Good. I would like you to go over to the clinic so I can take a better look, though, Emma. Best go by aid car."

"There's something wrong," Emma said. "Isn't there?"

Mitch shook his head emphatically. "If I was worried, I'd say so. I believe in caution."

"I'll come with you, cher," Finn said. "There's nothing to worry about. This is my baby, too, and I want to know both of you are perfect."

"Sir! Chief Boudreaux!" Officer Sampson, who had put on a few pounds since his recent marriage, puffed toward the group. "Could I have a word, please?"

"If you've got something to say that's to do with us, we'll hear it if you don't mind," Finn said.

Emma leaned harder against him and reached up to hold one of his hands.

"Sir?" Sampson said to Matt.

"Okay, it can't be that big a deal," Matt said. "Shoot."

Sampson shuffled forward and held out a hand. "This was on a chair in Out Back, sir. And this was on the floor."

Emma couldn't see what they were talking about.

"So?" Matt said.

"Mrs. Forestier says these are Mrs. Duhon's purse and notebook. We can't find any pieces of yellow paper out here."

8

At Aaron's house, Sonny asked, "How long d'you think they'll be gone?" He propped himself beside Aaron on his bed and they watched the back lights on Eileen's van bob up the driveway. She had dropped the two of them off after they got back from Chuzah's. Now she was driving Angel back to his place.

"What is it?" Aaron said. "About twenty minutes each way?"

Sonny slanted a glance at him. "If your mom goes straight there and straight back."

"She wouldn't be running errands at this time of night."

"Nope," Sonny said. "Too bad he chose today to run to work."

Aaron swallowed from a can of Coke. He followed this up with a handful of jelly beans.

Maybe it wasn't easy to talk about your mother, Sonny thought. He tried not to think about his, but that was easy.

"D'you know how to use that gun Angel gave you?" Aaron asked.

Sonny sat up straighter. "He wouldn't have given it to me if I didn't. I grew up around guns. Makes sense to make sure

I can look after us, especially now—unless we want Angel glued to us 24/7."

"Will you teach me?"

They were from different planets. Sonny crossed his arms and took a deep breath. "Angel's the one to do that. We'll ask him."

"Then my mom will find out."

Different solar systems. Sonny drew up his shoulders. "I dunno, then. I guess…"

"Drop it. But, thanks. Maybe I'll talk to Mom about it, just feel her out."

"*She* has a gun."

"Yeah," Aaron said.

Sonny figured it really was time to drop the subject. "Didn't Eileen ever date before?"

It was a long time before Aaron said, "She was married to my dad."

"Like how many years ago?" Sonny said.

"A couple of years." Aaron tipped back his head and poured more jelly beans into his mouth, lifting his hand higher and higher but never dropping a bean. He coughed. "She went out with Matt Boudreaux last year, but they were just friends."

Sonny felt guilty—just a little guilty. He'd known about Matt from something Angel had said. Angel didn't like Matt Boudreaux.

"Off topic," he said. "How close are you and Sally? She's hot." He needed to change the subject again and girls were close to his heart—and other things.

Aaron treated him to a slit-eyed stare. "None of your business."

"Okay, but those eyes aren't all she's got that's big. She's got—"

"Cut it out."

Sonny sighed loudly. "I think I'm getting through to Miranda. It's about time she figured out I'm the best thing likely to happen to her in this hick town."

"Yeah?"

He liked Aaron a lot, but talking to him took a lot of effort. "I'm thinking about a double date."

"Keep on thinkin'," Aaron said. "Those two aren't panting to go out with us."

"Well, I'm panting. I'm in pain…you're, well, we'll work it out."

Aaron looked like his mind had moved on. Time to get back to the Angel-Eileen question. Sonny thought it would be good for Angel to have someone else to fill up a lot of his time. The guy was decent, but he cramped Sonny's style.

Sonny slid down flat and watched the muted television flicker colors on the ceiling. "My mom dated."

"Yeah?" Aaron stopped chewing for a second, then carried on. "How long after your dad was dead?"

"He wasn't."

Aaron choked on his jelly beans. "Sorry."

"S'okay. They're both dead now." Now what had made him spill his guts to Aaron? True, he'd never had a good friend before, but he knew better than to get loose lips. Angel would kill him if he found out. "Aaron?"

"Yeah?"

"In my family we don't talk about personal stuff. I'd get in trouble for that. You understand?"

Aaron landed a floppy punch on Sonny's chest. "What you tell me stops here."

"Same for me," Sonny said.

They both fell silent.

It would be good to be able to talk about stuff, Sonny thought. What was going on was hard. Angel was the best but he had his own crap to deal with.

He'd waited long enough to ask the big question. "Hey, I don't want to pry, but you were majorly bleeding when Chuzah picked you up out of that swamp." He twisted up his face. Swamps would never be big with him.

"Was I?" Aaron turned his head away, looking for another subject to distract Sonny. "I got to get rid of all the kids' books in those shelves. Mom won't let me toss 'em, but I can box 'em up."

Later he'd go back to what happened out there. He wasn't ready to talk about it.

"I'll help you with the books," Sonny said.

"Thanks."

"I just about live over here. Your mom must get sick of it."

Aaron looked back at him. "My mom likes you, even if you are an asshole around her most of the time. She doesn't give up on people."

"She will," Sonny said and felt mad because he sounded like he felt sorry for himself. He wasn't sure why he couldn't loosen up with Eileen—except she was a woman. "Was your mom always on her own, before Angel came along? Except for when she was seeing the cop, I mean."

"She worked at the shop. Same as always. And she had me and some girlfriends. She and Matt still get along."

"No other men?"

"No." Aaron sat up straighter. "You keep pushing about that. She's never been the kind to look for men."

"She's pretty."

"Yeah."

"I can tell Angel thinks so, too. You've seen the way he looks at her?" Sonny was really warming up to the idea of Angel and Eileen being more than just friends because their boys hung out together.

"My mom's quiet," Aaron said. "I don't think…Angel's big and tough."

"He's not tough with her. I think he wants to be real soft and gentle with her."

"What are you sayin'?"

He shouldn't have mentioned this, Sonny thought. He cleared his throat and thought about the way his dad had taught him to say things carefully. "I just think Angel and Eileen would be a nice, er, couple. They don't do much except work and look out for us. They ought to go out for dinner, maybe a drive."

"Where would they drive?"

"Oh," Sonny shrugged. "Around. You know. To some nice places. They could even go to Mississippi. New York's great but it's a long drive."

"Okay," Aaron said. "Quit pussyfooting around. You're talking about them having sex. Go on, say it. You think your uncle's horny and my mom's convenient."

Holy crap. "Watch your mouth. Don't talk about your mother that way. I meant just what I said. They're nice people and they could do worse than be real good friends. You ought to be thinkin' what's gonna happen to Eileen when you move on. Or are you sticking around Pointe Judah for the rest of your life? Maybe going to work selling hedgehog boot-scrapers at Poke Around?"

Aaron sighed. "When I get caught up with school I'm

going to college. Okay, I'm sorry I got pissed at you. I just don't like thinking about my mom having sex, okay?"

"Sure." Sonny smiled to himself and wondered what Aaron would have done if he'd walked in on his mother having sex—with two men—and neither of them was his father.

"Angel's okay."

Sonny's stomach flipped. "He's the best guy I ever knew. Cares more about me than anyone else ever has."

"You think my mom will come right back?"

I've got a big mouth. "Probably."

Aaron scrubbed at his face.

Sonny drew in a long breath. "Chuzah said your clothes were too messed up to clean so he threw them away. That's how you got to come home in a dress."

He expected the elbow he got and laughed.

"Chuzah's okay," Aaron said. "He said we could go back there if we wanted to return the kaftan."

"I don't think I'll want to."

Aaron took a bit to say, "I'm going to. I like Locum. When I was a little kid we had a dog and he went everywhere with me. He was only a mutt, but he was the best."

"What happened to him?" Sonny said.

Aaron frowned and sighed. "I don't know. Ran off, I guess. One day he was there, the next he was gone. It was tough. Wouldn't you like to have a sidekick like Locum?"

"He's okay for a dog. There was blood on my clothes, too. I got it on me when Chuzah carried you back to his place. It was comin' through his fingers."

"Forget it, will ya? It must have been something from the swamp. It just looked like blood is all."

"You were shot," Sonny said bluntly.

Aaron didn't answer him and Sonny sat up. He put on the bedside lamp and glared at the TV. Some black-and-white movie had come on. Loads of men in fedoras and ties hanging undone arguing with some guy behind one of those old-fashioned windows, the ones they used to have inside banks. Looked like a major heist gone wrong.

He touched Aaron's side and saw how he recoiled. "So show it to me," Sonny said.

Aaron got off the bed and shoved his hands in his jeans pockets. He paced back and forth.

"Look," Sonny said. "We're in this together. All of it. Whatever happens, I'll be there for you."

"And I'll be there for you."

"So show me."

Aaron hauled up the left side of his T-shirt and walked close to Sonny. "Satisfied?"

Sonny sat on the edge of the bed and touched a round, brownish bruise on the skin just beneath Aaron's ribs. Aaron turned slowly around to show a matching mark on the other side.

"Entry and exit wounds," Sonny said. "Or that's where they should be. That's too freakin' creepy."

9

Angel lived on an oxbow lake not too far from The Willows, the building project he was currently managing for Finn Duhon.

When Eileen had asked him why he'd chosen to buy an old house by the lake when oxbows disappeared eventually, he had said, "Because almost no one else lives there. Anyway, whoever built that place of mine had imagination. They knew it would stand, lake or no lake, and maybe there would always be someone to love it. I'm going to do a lot of the renovating myself."

He had big hands. Eileen watched them on the wheel while they drove the winding road west and out of town. His hands gave her a funny feeling; she wanted to take and examine them, to find out how the bones and the veins and the muscles felt. "You do think it was okay to leave the boys like that?" she asked.

"They'll be fine. Aaron's a smart kid and Sonny knows a lot about how to look after himself. I pity anyone who tries to get in there after them. Anyway, Sonny would call me if he needed to." He smiled at her. "We can't keep them locked away. Learning to react effectively in bad situations takes practice."

She wasn't sure how she felt about that. "That's good then, I guess. It's quite a way from your house to your office."

Angel worked with Finn in a suite at the old Oakdale Mansion but spent a lot of hands-on time at whichever building site needed his attention.

"I never liked living in towns." He chuckled. "Not even little burghs like Pointe Judah."

"How early do you start out when you come into town?"

"Early." He smiled. "A lot earlier if I run. I don't do that too often."

The road narrowed and Angel took a half-right where tire tracks intersected shaggy grass and the old oaks made a tunnel. Ahead the area was black and rain continued to fall. Eileen didn't relish the drive home once she'd dropped Angel off.

At last the headlights picked out the house, three stories of faded faux antebellum. The place might have been pretty if it were the real thing, but Angel said the land was a find and he intended his new house to sprout out of this old one and look similar—only better.

"Light by the door went out again," Angel said. "I've got to take a look at the wiring."

"Must be nice to be so handy with those things."

He put on the emergency brake. "Anything you need done, just call and I'll do it. You like gardening and plants?"

"Yes," she said, smiling and looking toward sets of double doors to the left of the entrance where Angel was having a conservatory refurbished. "That's going to be so lovely. Your conservatory. If I were you, I'd probably just about live out there."

"Hey." He turned sideways. "Christmas is coming. I was trying to think what to give you. How about a greenhouse? Unless I build it from a kit, it won't be finished in time, but it wouldn't take so long. I'd rather build one from scratch. That way I could help you design exactly what you want."

She felt awkward, flustered. "I wasn't angling for any favors. And a greenhouse is a ridiculously expensive gift, but thank you."

"You've never angled for anything from me, Eileen. I often wish you would."

She looked at her hands and blinked rapidly. He couldn't know that she hadn't had any practice asking for things from a man in her life.

"What is it?" Angel said. "Why do you look…scared, if I say I'd like to do something for you? There would never be any strings attached."

"No! No, I would never think of that," Eileen said. "I'm so unpolished. I never got all the finer points of interacting with people the way other girls did. I think I must have been the most unpopular girl in school. I'm so sorry if I insulted you." She closed her mouth. Why did she babble like that? Well, she didn't, except with Angel. And why was that?

"Eileen," he said, leaning closer. "If you weren't the most popular girl in school, then every guy in the place was dumb. I never saw a woman more beautiful than you."

She grinned and immediately covered her face.

Angel chuckled softly and ruffled her hair. "I'd like to tell you all the ways you're beautiful but you'd kick me out of the van and never speak to me again."

"Why?" She frowned and slid her hands down enough to look at him.

He gave her an evil look. "Don't ask. Ahh, you can ask. I'd describe all your positive points, and they are many, and then you'd slap my face."

She punched his arm. "Get outa here, you soft soap. I've got to drive home."

"Nope," he said.

"Okay, enough joking around. It's getting late."

"I can get my motorcycle in the back of the van. Then I'll drive you home and ride back."

"You will not. That's the craziest thing I've ever heard."

"Don't fib."

"You're incorrigible."

He was very near to her. "I know," he said. "Don't you love it?"

Eileen didn't answer. What she felt wasn't new, just a little rusty. It shortened her breath and she was aware of a very strong man who could make light of almost anything, but a man who was tough and whom she barely knew. What did she know about him really?

"It won't be any use arguing with me, Eileen. Besides, I've got your keys." He pulled them from the ignition and rolled a little to put them into a pocket. "Let's go in and have some coffee before you go home. This night has been hard on you."

"Please give me my keys. I just need to get back."

"No you don't. Didn't you hear Chuzah say he thought Aaron collapsed from shock? So if there was a gunshot, it missed him. That means we aren't dealing with something to worry about—as long as we keep the boys out of the swamp after dark."

Eileen processed what he'd said. "Anybody can miss a shot, can't they?"

He looked straight ahead. Dim light caught in his eyes, and showed how his mouth turned down. "I should have known you were too smart to miss that slip. No, *anyone* can't miss a shot. There are people who never miss."

She swallowed. "What kind of people?"

He half-lowered his eyelids and she saw him bare his teeth. "The kind you're never going to meet, thank God. Now, let's get that coffee."

"No."

"Eileen."

Now he was trying the forceful male on her and she was through with that stuff. "I don't take crap from any man."

He turned his head sharply toward her. Too much time passed for her to feel other than edgy. "Sorry," he said finally. "You're right. I got out of line there. Come on in and I'll explain what I mean. I want you to accept one thing, though. Will you do that?"

"If I can."

"Promise."

"Angel, I don't know. You haven't told me what you want me to accept."

He snorted. "I didn't, did I? Trust that I can look after you and Aaron. Sonny already knows I can. I admit I had a moment earlier when I thought someone had gotten through the net, but I was wrong."

"You're scaring me."

"Do you believe I'll look after you?"

What was he asking her to agree to? He knew nothing about Chuck or the problems he could present. Was Angel telling her he intended to be more than a friend? She was a fool. He was offering to take care of her and Aaron.

"Yes, Angel, I believe you will. It's a good feeling. I never had that before, not that I'm such a slender-stemmed flower I have to be staked up all the time."

"You can stake me up any time, my flower." He laughed and the laugh was full of fun. "Let's go."

She had been inside the house before, a few months earlier

when Aaron had first become fast friends with Sonny. At that time it resembled the set of a horror film with curtains of cobwebs festooned between sagging ceiling beams and rotting carpets on the floor. She remembered walking into a spider and feeling smug because she wasn't afraid of it and had just brushed it aside.

Those months had made a huge difference. Gone were the old rugs and the cobwebs, the damp wallboard and broken windows. They walked to the right, through the large hall, passed a central staircase leading up to a gallery and went into what must have been the grand salon. From what she saw, the place had a long way to go but Angel had spent a lot of time, and money, on his pet project.

"What do you think?" Angel asked. He turned on the recessed lighting in the high ceilings. It shone softly down pale caramel walls. Refinished oak floors glowed. White canvas drops covered areas of the floor where decorating and building materials were stacked.

The only furniture in the room was an oversized circular ottoman, antique; its heavy pink brocade upholstery and fringe shabby and torn in places.

"It's wonderful in here," she said. "You've done so much. Congratulations."

He smiled and looked as she'd never seen him look before, carefree and boyish. "Take a seat on the ottoman, my lady. Or, let me see—you could always sit on the ottoman. I decided to keep it because it seems to fit in."

"Wait till it's reupholstered," she said. "It'll be a knockout."

"You think?" He frowned.

"I know. You've got great taste."

"So have you, Eileen. I like you in red."

She shrugged. "Thanks. It's just an old sweat suit."

He looked her over from head to toe—rapidly. Not rapidly enough for Eileen to miss the sexual appreciation in his narrowed eyes.

"I can't put it off any longer," he said. "I'll have to show you the kitchen."

Rubbing her hands together as if in anticipation, she caught up with him and followed through a long corridor framed with open studs, to the kitchen at the end. The lights were on and she could see a lot of umber color.

"Are you going to have a dining room?" she said.

"Sort of."

"If it's as far away from the kitchen as that salon is, you'll never get a warm dish on the table."

Angel didn't respond. He bent to straighten some loose boards just in front of the kitchen door and stepped inside.

Eileen followed and hid a smile. "You're enjoying this moment." The kitchen was part of a great room with a huge, wooden-topped island delineating the two areas. Already Angel had an iron rack hung with pans immediately above the island, and a table and chairs stood in the as yet un-touched—apart from newly sheet-rocked walls—dining and sitting room areas of the space.

In a corner, where an uncurtained window wrapped around, stood an undecorated Christmas tree.

Angel saw her looking at it and crossed the room to quickly push in a plug. A zillion tiny colored lights blossomed. "Voilà," he said. "I haven't got any ornaments for it, but I wanted Sonny to have a tree."

From the way he looked at the lighted tree, Eileen decided Angel wanted it for himself, too.

"Now coffee," Angel said. He returned to the kitchen and pulled forward a stainless steel coffeemaker on a stone-topped counter. The appliances were all stainless. The stove was gas, an Aga, and all business.

"Would you mind if I just had something cold?" Eileen said. "I'm so thirsty."

"Sure. You want to go back to the other room?"

"I'll sit at the table."

The smell of fresh paint hung around and Eileen wrinkled her nose. She liked it, all clean and new. At the level of the high ceilings in the kitchen there were narrow plaster moldings of vegetables, fruit and loaves of bread in a lighter shade than the umber walls. She felt a twinge of envy. It would take time, but one day she'd be able to think about moving from the tiny house she'd shared with Chuck. At least with him gone, she and Aaron had enough space to spread out.

Chuck was a subject she wanted out of her mind.

Angel came around the island with a large glass of white wine in one hand and red in the other.

She smiled up at him. "I had water in mind."

"Then you should have said so." He put the white in front of her.

"I thought you were going to tell me to take my pick," Eileen said.

"You prefer white."

"Mmm."

She sat at one end of the table. He pulled a chair close and dropped into it so that their legs touched under the table and their elbows touched on top. Eileen felt too aware of him but she wasn't about to make a fool of herself by moving away.

"This is nice," he said and sighed. He drank from his glass and watched as she sipped from hers. She passed the tip of her tongue over her upper lip, caught him following with rapt concentration and felt herself turn the color of the crimson sweat suit.

Eileen looked away. "Now you can tell me what you meant about feeling better because if someone shot at Aaron, they missed."

"I could. Why spoil a nice moment?"

"For most men it takes a whole lot more than a drink at a kitchen table to…make…a nice…moment." *Careless chatter.* "I didn't mean that the way it sounded."

"I was afraid you didn't. Sonny is with me under unusual circumstances. He is here because he's had difficulties, but they weren't anything to do with him getting into trouble."

She frowned and moved the base of her glass back and forth. That wasn't what she'd expected him to say. "Could I taste the red?" she said, buying time.

Angel hesitated, then gave her his glass. She drank and made a face. "Cranberry juice. Ouch, that's bitter after the wine."

"The wine's dry," he said, sounding defensive.

"And you're getting me drunk while you stay sober," she said with mock annoyance.

"I have to drive," he pointed out.

"Oh, boy, you are so holy," she said.

"Wanna bet?"

Eileen whistled out a breath. "I think I'll pass on that. What's the deal with Sonny?"

"I've told you most of it. He got caught up in something— none of his doing—something really dangerous. There was some possibility that bad types saw him where it would have been better for him not to be. If they did, they might well have decided to get rid of him. When he showed up tonight, that was my first thought, and I think it was his. But we were both wrong. Those guys don't miss, and they don't make mistakes like shooting the wrong person. They can't afford to if they don't want to end up on the wrong end of the next gun barrel."

After much too large a swallow of wine, a big enough mouthful to make her cough, Eileen collected herself and said, "You're talking about the Mafia."

He shook his head. "We don't talk like that anymore. The scene has changed."

"Who is *we*, Angel?"

"Just people in the business." He waved an airy hand. "You know I've been in various kinds of enforcement over the years."

"I thought you were out of all that now."

"I am." His expression was so innocent, there was no way she believed much of what he said. "This is just something I had to do for an old friend."

"You're not used to making up bedtime stories for soft women, are you?" she asked. "Or women you think are soft. Who is this old friend?"

"Eileen. I've already told you far more than I have any right to say. I have rules I must live by. They're for good reasons."

"You're still involved. You said you weren't, but you lied to me."

He got the bottle of wine and refilled her glass. Eileen made no attempt to stop him.

"I didn't lie. I'm not on active duty. I quit because I had other things I wanted to do. I came here to talk to Finn because he went through the same thing, changed his lifestyle pretty drastically. And now I'm his manager of operations. That's not a lie."

"But you're doing something that could bring gunmen after you."

He reached for her hand but she put it in her lap. "Don't be like that," he said.

"Who is this friend? You don't have to give me his name, just tell me what kind of person he is. What he's mixed up in that makes him so dangerous to know."

Angel leaned against his chair, tipped it onto its back legs. "He's not dangerous to anyone anymore. He's dead."

She pressed a hand on the wooden tabletop and her mind raced. "I'm sorry. So, why do you—"

"He was Sonny's father."

"Oh, no. Your brother. Oh, Angel—"

"Don't. It's okay. He was doing something the people he worked for didn't like." He looked at the ceiling. "They *really* didn't like it." He let the front legs of his chair slam to the floor and put his face closer to hers. "If you talk about any of this, someone could die. Do you understand?"

She nodded and whispered, "Yes." He looked so desolate. There was a mountain of bad stuff on his back. Loneliness and isolation were the only reasons he was telling her all of this.

"You don't have to worry about me," she told him.

"Good. They shot him, emptied a Beretta submachine gun with a forty-round magazine into him."

Eileen held the wine with both hands and drank. "You know these things happen, but most of the time you can pretend they don't. They thought Sonny saw this, but he didn't? They may have figured that out by now and they're leaving him alone."

"They *could* think that," Angel said. "I hope they do. But he did see his father shot. He saw him die."

"Oh, God." Eileen shuddered. "The good people shouldn't come out last."

Angel didn't answer and she caught his eye. She felt so cold. Knowledge you didn't want could freeze you. "He wasn't a good guy?"

"I think we've said enough," he told her without inflection.

"Poor Sonny. I don't know why he isn't a worse mess. No wonder he acts so surly and bitter."

Again he was silent.

She held his wrist on the table. "Thank you for being honest. It helps to know what's going on…or could be."

"Not necessarily. If you weren't involved, I'd never reveal any of this to you. But you are in a way and you need to be too scared to open your mouth about anything. You don't know anything about Sonny, right?"

"I understand." Like this, he was scary. "I'll do anything I can to help. And you'll never have to wonder if I've said anything to anyone or if I might for some reason. Nothing could get it out of me."

"Good," Angel said, looking at her hand on his arm, "because I can sense things, like when someone is wavering. I'd know if you were thinking about running your mouth off to someone."

"I never would. Angel?" Her heart thumped. "I really wouldn't."

"Good. Because if I got that feeling, I'd have to kill you."

10

No man's eyes should look that cold.

Eileen noticed the lines that flared from the corners of his eyes. Laugh lines? She pictured him squinting into the sun through dark glasses, a gun in his hand.

"That was a joke," he said. "A bad one."

Maybe it was; maybe it wasn't. She stood so quickly, her chair screeched on the wood floor. "Thanks for the wine."

"Eileen." He got up, too, and she was aware of how big he was. Fear and intense excitement mounted her spine.

"I've stayed too long," she told him. "Aaron will wonder where I am."

Angel walked behind her and she held her ground with difficulty. "You never have to be afraid of me," he said.

"I'm not."

"Yes, you are. I can smell it. Men like me have a particular relationship with fear."

And with danger…and violence.

"I know you've had a hard life," she said.

"I chose it." He didn't even pretend to smile now. "Aaron isn't worrying about where you are. Both of them know you're with me."

She colored. "I shouldn't be any longer."

"Why? Because they might think we're doing more than driving to my place and sharing a drink, maybe?"

Eileen laughed nervously. "No, of course not. I'm pretty tired. All the hocus-pocus in the swamp must have worn me out. I'm so grateful Aaron's okay."

He moved again and this time he stood behind her right shoulder where she could almost, but not quite, see him. She could feel him, hear him breathing.

Eileen stood straighter. She wished she wore high heels because they brought her closer to his height and she felt more powerful then. "Let me wash these glasses out for you." She reached for them but Angel's hand on the back of her neck immobilized her.

"Forget the glasses. You're scared and I don't like that. Not when I'm the one you're scared of."

"I'm not."

As long as she stayed with her back to him she would appear nervous. She faced him. His hand slid from her neck, over her shoulder and down her arm. He circled her wrist and stroked the tender inside skin there.

The lightning climbed her back again, matched by the same feeling low in her belly, between her legs. Was she that kind of woman? The kind who got sexually excited by fear? She ran the fingers of her free hand across her brow and they came away damp.

"It's probably not a good idea to call voodoo *hocus-pocus* in these parts."

She raised her chin. "I've lived here all my life. I know to be careful what I say about those things in some circumstances. These aren't those circumstances."

"Did you look at Aaron's body?"

"He wouldn't let me. You know how boys are."

He grinned. "Only until they grow up and the women they're with aren't their mothers."

She had to smile. "I guess you're right. I don't suppose Aaron counts as a boy anymore, either."

"I've made more progress in the house. Let me show you."

She couldn't bring herself to repeat that she ought to get back. "I'd like that."

Still holding her wrist, he took her to the far side of the room where an archway was framed into a wall. Once on the other side, with the unfinished conservatory to their right, he headed directly for the stairs and climbed. Eileen went behind him, every heartbeat feeling bigger and harder.

"What do you think of Chuzah?" she asked. "I don't know whether to accept that he was kind to the boys, or be terrified of him. That dog is strange."

"A shape-shifter?" Angel said, and chuckled. "That was a strange comment you made. He's a great dog. It's the breed. Silver ghosts."

"He looked like a ghost when he moved through the fog," Eileen said.

"Maybe he is. Maybe Chuzah is, too. He surely doesn't fit any profile I've encountered before."

She paused, frowning.

Angel stopped a couple of stairs above her. "Eileen, something's going on. Something happened in that swamp. Sonny said Aaron was bleeding—a lot—and he had blood on his own clothes. But there wasn't any coming from Aaron when we got there."

"Don't. Aaron's fine."

"Chuzah said he threw Aaron's clothes away because they were such a mess. That doesn't sound unreasonable to you?"

Eileen thought exactly that. "The man's unusual."

"That's enough for you?" Angel said.

"I'm trying to make it enough."

He produced his cell phone and pressed a button. Almost at once he said, "You guys okay? Uh-huh. No calls before this one? Good. We're taking things a bit easy. It's good to get away from you two now and again."

Eileen suppressed a smile and shook her head.

"Okay," Angel said. "Stick with the instructions. See you eventually." He put the phone away and gave her all of his attention. "I want to kiss you."

She stood absolutely still, looking up at him in light that hadn't been upgraded. He was in the gloom but the glint in his eyes, the sexual intensity, was clear. So was the downward tilt of his lips and the tight movement of the small muscles in his jaw.

"That's abrupt," she said.

He pulled on her arm so she had to go up another step, and another. "It wasn't abrupt. You've been taking up most of my mind for months. How about you, Eileen? Have I been on your mind?"

Without taking her eyes from his, she nodded.

His expression turned predatory, possessive—and determined.

If she wanted out of this, there wasn't much time. There wasn't *any* time.

Angel spread a hand behind her head and lowered his face over hers. He kissed her and she felt instantly weak, and wet, and wanted to get closer to him.

Eileen wanted to be naked with him.

She started hard enough for Angel to raise his face. A new element had appeared, a feverishness. "What?" he said. "You jumped."

Parting her lips, Eileen stood on tiptoe and delivered her own kiss. She worked their mouths until he groaned and dragged her hard against him. She swayed a little and grabbed for him to steady herself.

Angel put an arm around her waist and walked her up to the gallery, kissing her repeatedly as they went. Without warning, he unzipped her sweat suit jacket and slid a hand inside. She hadn't put on another top underneath. There was no mistaking his satisfaction when he weighed a breast, hooked a thumb inside her bra.

She pulled out his hand and moved away a little. "You believe in moving right along."

"And you aren't ready for that?" Angel said.

"You're going to show me what else you've done to the house, remember?" That anxiety, that conviction that somehow she must be wanting when it came to being with men, returned. Chuck had always said she was boring in bed.

Angel took her from the gallery into a passageway. He reached through an open door and flipped a light switch. The room they entered wasn't large. The walls were paneled with warm cherry; a deep window seat had yet to be finished, but the floor matched the paneling and, almost in the center of the room, stood a piece of furniture that made Eileen frown. "What's that? Are you starting an ottoman collection?"

Walking around it, he put his fists on his hips and looked pleased with himself. "I could be. It's a tête-à-tête."

"So you say. It looks like a big, square ottoman to me, with a fat post in the middle. It's really old, isn't it?"

"It's something else I salvaged from all the stuff that was here. I was told it would have been in a public room of some kind and people liked them, particularly the young and lovelorn, because it was easy to *accidentally* brush shoulders and arms while sitting side by side. Their legs might even have touched. Imagine that. All that pent-up desire in the heat of a Louisiana night and in a room much bigger than this one but packed with dashing young men, and girls with trembling white breasts spilling from their bodices."

Eileen stared at him. She swallowed. "I can imagine it. I wouldn't have expected you to."

"I'm interested in the history of the area. Particularly the social history. I've had enough of war."

"You and Finn fought together, didn't you?"

"We met in a field hospital. We kept in touch."

He wasn't inviting her to probe further.

"I'm seeing a new side of you," she said. "You'll make this a fantastic house."

"I'll try. But I'm only showing you and talking about it to keep you with me." He offered her a hand and she held it. "This is going to be part of the master suite. I'll show you the best bit to date."

Double doors, which he closed behind them, took her into an amazing bathroom. Tiled from floor to ceiling with large, unglazed white stone, a shower large enough for an intimate party sloped down from all sides, and had no doors. Stone benches lined the sides and several showerheads jutted from each wall.

"I've never seen anything like this before," Eileen said.

It was too intimate, too personal—but he knew that and had brought her here deliberately.

Angel turned a knob on the wall and she expected lights to brighten. Instead, a fan of white fabric finished like parchment swung open to reveal a skylight. Tonight she saw raindrops on the glass and heard more falling, but on a clear night it would be filled with stars.

She lost the battle to keep her attention away from a bathtub made of heavy glass. It stood on pewter feet in the center of the room and since vertical strips of mirror were incorporated into each wall there would be no way to bathe without seeing yourself from every angle.

And the tub was huge, curved, almost an oversize Victorian shape.

Eileen would not keep looking at that bath. "You must have brought in a designer," she said. "What an imagination!"

"A guy over in Toussaint," Angel said, "Marc Girard. Finn's cousin Annie recommended him and he's responsible for all the plans. He's my architect, but someone in his firm consults on design."

"I know Annie. She used to live in Pointe Judah."

Small talk.

Another set of double doors, also closed, stood on the other side of the bathroom. Angel caught her looking at them. "That will be the bedroom but it's pretty basic at this point. Okay to sleep in, though. I haven't tried out the bath yet. I'm always in a hurry so I shower—not that the bath would be much fun on my own."

The glow Eileen felt had to be visible. She must be luminous.

"Don't you think there's something sensual about water, Eileen?"

She drew in a breath through parted lips. "Yes. Yes, I suppose so."

He turned on the bathwater and almost at once, steam rose.

"What are you doing?" Eileen said.

"Showing you how it looks with water in it. We could put in some soapy stuff, if you like."

How was she supposed to answer a comment like that? She didn't.

Angel stopped smiling. He pulled his dark T-shirt over his head and Eileen took a step backward. His body shouldn't be covered, ever. Muscle and sinew, every line defined. Not a millimeter of spare flesh. His jeans settled low on his hips and she couldn't look away from his hard belly, the bands of muscle; the start of dark hair she didn't have to see to know how the rest of it would look.

He walked straight at her, unsnapping his waistband as he came. When he reached her, Eileen backed up and kept backing up all the way to the wall where steam had dampened the tile. Her back hit solidly and she raised bent arms, palms out.

"We don't want the bath to overflow," he said.

"Christian?" she said. His real name came naturally. "We aren't thinking."

"I always know I'm supposed to be in trouble when you call me that." He unzipped her jacket and pushed it from her shoulders. "Sure we're thinking. I'm thinking about what I want and what you want." Quickly, he pulled down her pants and panties, went to his knees and freed her feet.

He parted her thighs with inflexible hands, pressed his face low against her belly, and drove his tongue into the folds between her legs. Eileen cried out and pulled at his hair with both hands.

If it hurt him, his shudder said he liked it. Pushing up on her buttocks, he lifted her legs over his shoulders and held her in place while he nipped and probed at her pulsing flesh. She released his hair and threw out her arms, tossed her head from side to side.

A climax ripped through her. Eileen sobbed and heard sounds she knew she made, but hadn't heard before.

Moving so fast that he disoriented her, Angel tossed her over his shoulder and went to turn off the bathwater. Then, with no ceremony and her bra still on, he dumped her into the tub. It was deep and she slid, dousing her hair and face. When she sat up, she swiped the water away and slicked back her hair.

There was nothing she could think of to say to him. She still throbbed, her heart still raced, but she wasn't a fresh girl and she knew what he wanted.

He stood over her, his head on one side, studying her. And he took off his jeans. His penis sprang free of his underwear and when he turned his hips to toss the clothes aside, she gasped at the sway of his flesh.

Eileen burned inside. Her skin tingled.

Then he was in the water, too, pushing up her knees, settling between them. With his palms, he made circles over her nipples and she shivered at the friction from her lace bra.

"Christian," she said. "Hurry. Please."

His face was dark, the veins at his temples distended. The wet bra didn't come off easily enough to please him but he was careful with the fastening.

With his forearms beneath her back, he stretched on his stomach over her and rubbed their bodies together, inciting her with the hair on his skin, with the sensation each time he pushed inside her a little, only to withdraw again.

He blinked, his expression tense, then kissed her. With his hands supporting her head, he coaxed her with the tip of his tongue on the tip of hers. Eileen softened, she wrapped her arms around his neck and they kissed for a long time.

She reached between them to touch him, to guide him, and he swept into her, huge and hard, demanding—perfect. They fought each other in the water, demanded more and more.

Eileen's nerves strained, rushed toward another release, and she saw when Christian's eyes fixed and his teeth clenched.

The skylight exploded overhead, sprayed pellets of glass in a stinging shower.

Then a deafening crack burst like lightning.

Gunfire. Someone had shot out the skylight and now they were firing into the bathroom.

Christian covered Eileen, held her face against his neck. "It's okay," he said and she felt his body tense, as if to spring. "Hold on." He hauled them both from the tub.

Another shot came as they slithered, drenched, across the floor with its bruising scatter of glass pebbles.

Christian all but threw Eileen into the shower and followed, covering her again. "The angle would be hard with us here," he said.

What did he mean? What was happening to them?

The next sound was of someone scrambling from the roof. Instantly, Angel was out of the shower and rushing, naked, for the door. "Don't go after him!" Eileen screamed.

"If he knows what he's doing, I'll never catch him. But I might see his vehicle," he yelled back at her. "And I need to look for anything he's left behind."

Eileen crouched in the shower, shivering.

Shattered beads of safety glass glinted all over the bathroom.

A fractured mirror showed where the first bullet into the room must have ricocheted.

Water ran from a second bullet hole in the bottom of the tub.

11

Eileen hobbled across the floor to rescue her sweat suit and haul it over her wet skin.

Water pouring from the bottom of the tub ran into a drain in the floor, but not fast enough to keep the tiles dry. Angel's discarded jeans were soaked from waist to hem on one side, but Eileen grabbed them and headed out the door. She didn't get away without punishing her feet on the glass fragments.

He'd turned out the lights in the next room.

Fumbling, bumping into a wall, she made it to the gallery. The rest of the house was in darkness. So, he preferred to work in the dark. Or, more likely he was trying to make sure an intruder couldn't pick him out—and pick him off.

She dropped to her hands and knees and crawled forward until her hand, and her head, bumped a bannister. Then she was on her feet again, Angel's wet jeans slung over her shoulder. She felt along the stair railing all the way down to the hall.

Cold air blew through the open front door, bringing rain with it, and leaves. Faint light also slanted across the hall and Eileen remembered the gun in her purse—in the salon.

Every move she made was painfully slow, but she knew

better than to touch the lights. Somewhere outside, Angel…what could he be doing out there? The man who tried to shoot them should be away by now.

Who was it? Why had he tried to kill them?

She swallowed rasping sounds from her throat. At last she held the weapon in her hand and retraced her steps, working toward the vague glow from the open front door.

Inside the door, she stood with her back to the wall and listened. Gusts of wind and the muted clatter of rain on windows were all she heard.

When she had time to think, she'd consider how unreal this night had been.

Eileen slid outside and ran to the left, for the cover of tall, thick bushes. With her arms in front of her face, she forced herself into them and paused, listening again, parting branches to peer back at the front of the house. She was even more wet than when she'd pulled her damp sweat suit on.

Whoever had shot at them would be well away by now but she still whispered, "Angel?" and a little louder, "Angel?"

He didn't answer. She strained to hear any indication that he heard or was in the area. Nothing.

Holding his jeans in front of her, she doubled over and crept along. The ground squelched, pushed mud between her toes and she grimaced.

"Darn it all, Angel," she muttered. "You go rushing off into the night and I'm supposed to stay hiding in a shower?" She got more furious by the second. It hadn't been her idea to go into his house and hang around longer than was good for her.

She wrinkled her nose. So, okay, it might not have been good *for* her, but it *was* good. It might be chilly, but she had a heat all her own. In fact she felt pink all over.

Staying here was out of the question.

Very carefully, her gun against her shoulder, Eileen eased back out of the bushes and away from the driveway. If she approached the house from the side, she could stay out of any reflection on the front windows, just in case someone was watching from the driveway.

A hand, clamped over her mouth, and her feet being hauled from the ground, took months off her life. Her heart seared, fluttered, and didn't seem inclined to settle in her chest.

Twisting violently, she kicked out at the shins behind her, bit down on the fingers over her mouth. Eileen tried to scream but only managed strangled squeaks from her throat. She scissored her legs, used her heels to bombard her assailant's shins. And she twisted her body from side to side.

"Eileen." It was Angel's voice very close to her head. "For God's sake, stop it. I thought you were the enemy." He set her down.

"And you scared me sick." She went limp, put a hand behind her to touch him and quickly withdrew it.

"The shooter's gone," Angel said. "When I heard you, I thought he'd come back."

"I've never been so terrified," she said. "I brought your jeans but I've dropped them." With her back to him, she peered around in the bushes and on the ground.

"Better not look at me," Angel whispered. "You're too tender for what you'd see."

"Smart ass." She located the jeans, deliberately faced him and slapped the pants against his chest. "Put 'em on."

He held them out. She could only barely make out his face. Inside, she clenched and trembled.

"A lady would turn her back," he said.

Eileen crossed her arms, settled her gun in the crook of an elbow and put most of her weight on one leg.

Angel did foot-to-foot hops to get into his jeans, sucking in a breath as the cold wet denim must have raked over his skin. He jumped some more and grasped the waistband. She watched every move and looked down when he started to close the zipper.

"Better be careful how you do that," she said.

Angel adjusted himself, grinning all the time, and finally snapped the waist closed. "When did you learn to be forward?"

"Aren't you going to ask why your jeans are soaked?" Eileen said.

"They were on the floor. The bathtub's got a hole in it."

"And it's leaking water all over the place," Eileen said, her mouth twitching. "Good job there's a drain."

"I'm sorry," Angel said. "I never wanted you frightened like that."

"Yes." She curled a hand over one of his shoulders and dug in her fingers. "The bullets were meant for us." Her stomach flipped.

"Don't think about it. I didn't get a look at him, or his vehicle. He must have parked on the access road—I heard his car."

"Did you call the police?"

"Not yet," Angel said. "I want to look around first. I'm going up on the roof to look for casings."

"It's so dark."

"I'm used to working in the dark. Can you use that gun?"

"Yes, I can. My father—who was the local police chief— taught us."

Angel sighed. "Good."

"We can't keep all this to ourselves any longer, Angel," she said. "I was almost ready to believe the swamp thing was—"

"Really an accident? But now you're not. And neither am I, but I want you to bear with me. Give me a little more time before making me throw something to the cops. They're going to be out of their league anyway."

"You're so quick to put people down just because they aren't big-city types."

"Garbage," he said. "Come here." He took her by the shoulders. Trying to twist away would be pointless. Angel kissed her. He broke the contact slowly, settled his lips at her temple and stroked her wet hair. "We have something to finish."

And right now his timing wasn't good. "What do you think may be going on?" she asked. "Do you think those gang types or whatever they are may be involved after all?"

He pulled her face to his neck. "I'm not sure. Really not sure."

"Where did you learn to work in the dark?" she asked. There was too much mystery about him.

He hesitated, then said, "In South America. In the jungle. I put in some years with the CIA."

In the distance a vehicle engine rumbled faintly, growing closer. Her van remained where she and Angel had left it, its dark paint shiny-slick. Eileen didn't know what to do next. She reached for him. "There's someone coming now."

The engine grew louder. "Who the hell is it?" Angel asked, listening. "He's got to be coming here—there's nothing else around. You didn't call anyone?"

She shook her head no.

They stood side by side and watched headlights burst on the scene. Eileen opened her mouth to breath.

"No one comes here," Angel muttered. "Stay where you are. Don't—and I mean it, Eileen—don't get in my way."

"Someone already was here, remember," Eileen said. "We're supposed to be dead in your glass bathtub. He could be coming back."

"He wouldn't risk it. I'm not in a vulnerable position now."

Eileen shivered a little. She was too uptight to argue.

"Shit," Angel muttered. "What d'you want to bet it *is* our gun-toter being real clever. First the rear attack, then right in the front door with some big excuse. He must have heard us yell and known he'd missed us."

The headlights went out, the engine cut and a figure got out of a nondescript sedan. A man. He walked toward the open front door and Eileen felt blood rush to her feet. Her face prickled.

"I think it's time to surprise our visitor," Angel said, his gun in his hand.

Eileen gripped his elbow tightly. "That's Chuck!"

He turned his face toward her. "Who? Chuck, your *husband?*"

"Ex-husband." She could scarcely get the word out.

"He's back in Pointe Judah? How long have you known?"

She swallowed. "I knew this afternoon. That's why I went out to the parking lot at Oakdale. He was waiting there in his car. He called me to go and talk to him. Chuck was the *appointment* I told you about."

"And you went? Just like that? The man's been a pig to you. Why didn't you tell me?"

"Don't," Eileen said. "I want him to go away again, is all.

Getting mad takes too much energy." And she was confused, confused about his return and about his coming to Angel's. How would he know where she might be tonight? He didn't know anything about her life since he'd left. Or did he? "I hate this," she said through her teeth. "He was never supposed to come back."

"You're sure that's him?" Angel said. Chuck had approached the front door and they could see him with his head inside, listening.

"I'm sure."

"To do what?"

"I don't know." No longer warm, she pressed her fingers to her mouth. The wind picked up again and tossed wet leaves around. "I didn't think he'd ever leave the rigs but he said he's come back to be here for Aaron…and me," she finished in a tiny voice. She wanted to close her eyes, open then again and find that Chuck had never been there.

"Really?" Angel said. "If he works on the rigs, he shouldn't have difficulty climbing around on rooftops."

"He wouldn't do that."

Angel fell silent.

She touched his arm. "I mean he's a selfish man, and he wasn't faithful to me, but I don't think he's physically dangerous." Except when he was alone with a woman who couldn't defend herself.

"You don't think? But you don't know for sure?" Angel wrapped an arm around her. "You're shaking."

She knew Chuck had a twisted imagination and there had been no end to the punishments he'd thought up for her. "I want to stay here and wait for him to go away," she muttered.

He massaged her scalp, bent to kiss her. "If he goes

quickly, I'll go along with that. Otherwise I'm going to have to persuade him to leave."

"I don't want any fuss with him," Eileen said. "I don't need that and neither does Aaron. He's got some crazy notion about getting back into our lives. He could make it really difficult for us if he keeps popping up."

Angel kissed her ear and said, "Whatever it takes, I'm going to make sure he doesn't do that."

He almost made her believe he could do anything. He also made her apprehensive. That hint of violence was there again and it terrified her. There were still parts of Angel she knew nothing about but she wondered how she would feel about them.

"Angel—" Her voice stuck. Chuck had stepped inside Angel's house. "He's gone in and he didn't even ring the bell," she said.

"Don't come out of here," Angel said, his voice toneless. "Please. I'll go and explain about trespass. He'll be gone soon enough."

She stood with the rain beating on top of her head. The tracksuit was soaked. When Angel slipped away, the wet skin on his torso glistened in the dappling of shadow and light through the leaves.

Eileen shrank back until she stood close to an oak with a barrier of bushes in front of her. Cold struck up through her feet and her teeth chattered. The thought of a terrible fight paralyzed her. She didn't know if she was more afraid of Angel being arrested for killing Chuck, or of Chuck managing to hurt Angel.

Gun in hand, Angel stepped from the undergrowth and

walked directly, if lightly, toward the door. He slowed when he got close.

Chuck appeared in the doorway again, saw the gun and raised both hands. Eileen was too far away to hear what was said. She did see how Chuck turned his palms up in a submissive attitude and actually heard him laugh. The sound made her feel creepy.

She worked her way through the bushes. No way could she hide out and not hear what was being said. It was her business.

Now she could make out Chuck's car, a Ford Taurus in a light shade.

Angel put the gun into his waistband and Chuck dropped his arms. He leaned on the doorjamb. Eileen had noticed earlier that his sideburns were turning gray. Still fit, still good-looking in a hard-jawed, watchful-eyed way, he'd kept himself in shape. She wondered, not for the first time today, why he'd left the rigs. He had always liked the chunks of money he made and the weeks off between stints out there, when he could hang around, turn her into his slave and drink too much.

When he drank, the whites of his eyes turned bright red and his face flushed and seemed to bloat. Once he had wrapped an empty bourbon bottle in a towel and used it to beat her back, her bottom, the backs of her legs. Afterward she'd stretched out flat on her face as much as she could. The bruises swelled like purple blossoms filled with blood, one running into another.

Eileen felt tears mix with rain on her cheeks.

The two men continued to talk as if they weren't standing in a downpour. She saw the way Angel's back straightened and squared off. He was neither relaxed nor happy.

Angel inclined his head toward Chuck's car but didn't get any response, other than Chuck settling harder against the doorjamb.

That was enough. Eileen emerged onto the grass verge, too aware of her bare, wet feet, and walked purposefully toward the house, her gun deliberately evident. Chuck pushed away from the door as soon as he saw her and Angel looked at her over his shoulder. He shrugged, which suggested he'd known she was bound to come sooner or later.

"There you are, babe," Chuck called, and Eileen shrunk a little. "Couldn't get any information out of your friend here but I figured you were somewhere around—given your van." He nodded toward it.

"What are you doing here, Chuck?" she asked.

"What d'you think? You and I need some time alone."

Eileen appreciated that Angel didn't interfere. "Now?" she said. "I'm not talking to you now." Or any other time if she could avoid it. "I don't know why you're back in Pointe Judah. There's nothing for you here."

He lifted his chin and she was close enough to see the familiar sneer he could summon whenever she stood up for herself. "What's going on out here, anyway?" he said. "Some new game? Running around in the dark and the rain with guns? How weird is that?"

"It's none of your business," she said, as loudly as she could.

"Is this your new boyfriend?" he asked, looking Angel over, which should be enough to make most men feel inferior.

"I'd like you to leave," she said.

"Don't be like that. We've got too much in common to be snippy with each other. Angel? It is Angel?"

Angel nodded, but he kept his eyes on Eileen.

"That Sonny's your boy?" Chuck asked.

"My nephew."

"He's got Aaron under his thumb. He stood behind him at the door and kept telling me to get lost."

Eileen felt a surge of liking for Sonny. "They look out for each other." She'd never expected to say something like that.

"I finally got some information out of Aaron, but not without the other one trying to stop him every time I opened my mouth. He slammed the door in my face in the end. My own goddammed house and he slammed the door," Chuck said.

"It's not your house anymore," Eileen said, mortified that Angel was a witness to all this.

"That Sonny kid's got a nasty mouth on him."

Angel looked back at the other man. "Not unless he's pushed."

"He thinks it's pushy if a man asks his son where his mother is?"

So that's how Chuck knew where to come. He had played on Aaron. Helpless anger weighted Eileen's body.

"Don't worry about it," Chuck said, not sounding like the Chuck she knew. "Boys will be boys and they all have their little acts they play to look tough.

"I plan to settle down in Pointe Judah. I like it here. I didn't know how much until I moved away. And Aaron needs me."

The weakness Eileen felt in her limbs had nothing to do with her health and everything to do with the peace of mind she'd just lost.

"You shouldn't leave Aaron on his own at night," Chuck said to Eileen. "He's still on parole, isn't he?"

Rage bubbled to the surface. "No," she said. "He's not. And sixteen-year-olds don't need babysitters."

"From what I heard, he's been through a lot of bad times and needs keeping an eye on." He walked toward her. "Aw, hon, it must have been so hard and a good part of it's my fault. Let me help. I can be here for him. It's time we got to know each other again."

She couldn't speak, didn't dare look at Angel.

When she found her voice, she said, "We're doing fine. We did fine when you supposedly lived here before but only showed up when you felt like it, and we're doing fine now. Aaron doesn't need new confusion in his life."

Chuck looked away. "I shouldn't have come here tonight. I was wrong. Funny how a man never stops thinking of a woman as his own. You were mine for a long time, Eileen. It got to be a habit—a good habit. Love doesn't die easily."

Eileen couldn't believe the words were coming out of Chuck's mouth. She didn't want to think about the things he'd said to her before he let her know she'd been replaced by another woman as far as he was concerned.

Angel cleared his throat and she looked at him. His eyebrows were raised in question. All she'd have to do was give him a sign and Chuck would be out of here. And she could have more trouble than she was prepared to deal with.

She shook her head slightly. "Your judgment's as bad as it always was," she said to Chuck. "I'd like you to leave now."

"Okay."

Surprised, she stared at Chuck. He separated himself from the doorjamb and walked toward her.

Behind him, Angel distributed his weight evenly and Eileen had no doubt about how fast he could move if he wanted to.

"Will you let me say just a few words to you?" Chuck said to Eileen. "Then I'll leave. I promise."

She expected Angel to protest but he still kept silent, and he moved far enough away to let her talk to Chuck in private. Eileen couldn't stop the deep shaking in her body or the horror that came with shadowy memories of past "talks" with Chuck.

"Okay, say what you came to say. But do it right here," she said.

"You've got it." He kept walking toward her until he stood only a couple of feet away. Quietly, he said, "I've been wrong. I don't expect it to happen overnight, but forgive me, baby."

She swallowed the desire to tell him not to call her baby.

"I've shocked you, showing up like this. I was afraid if I let you know I was coming, you wouldn't see me."

She didn't respond.

"Think about taking me back."

Eileen breathed through her mouth and shook her head. Her stomach rose and she thought she might vomit.

Chuck stared at her and she could see a sheen in his eyes as if he were close to tears. He looked her over slowly, from wet hair hanging around her shoulders, to the clinging red sweat suit. She hated it that she felt so revealed.

"You're beautiful," he said and bowed his head. "You always were. And now I don't even have the right to look at you. You shouldn't be out here in this rain."

Chuck was rough and tough and always had been. She didn't remember a time when he was gentle with her. Tears prickled in her own eyes, not for him but for the horror he heaped on her for years. She cried for herself.

"Going to the house was hard," Chuck said. He raised his

arms and let them fall. "I let it all slip away, didn't I? What a fool I was."

"Sometimes we have to let the past go," Eileen said.

Chuck looked at her and frowned. "That other kid's no good, Eileen. He's got a foul mouth and he's no good for Aaron. Aaron said he was his best friend."

"He is," Eileen said, her throat stiff. "And he's a good boy. He grew up where it's tough is all. He's learning." Now she was defending Sonny again. She couldn't get over her reservations about him so easily, but if he helped get Chuck off her property tonight she owed him her thanks.

She looked past Chuck. Angel leaned on the front of her van.

"What do you know about him?" Chuck asked, indicating Angel.

"That's not your business."

"It's my business if it affects my son." He squared his shoulders and took a step closer to her. "Don't imagine I won't do what's right for Aaron. If I think he needs more attention than he's getting—"

"I don't know what your talking about." Eileen stared at him. "Aaron's learning to make his own decisions now. He's doing a good job of getting things together. He'll finish high school and go to college."

"He needs a father around." He came closer. "I need to make things up to him."

She barely stopped herself from falling back a step.

Chuck put his hands over his face. "I didn't come to make your life harder. I want to be where I can make sure you're okay. I was so damn wrong. I don't know what came over me. Please forgive me. I don't expect you to take me right back, but gimme a chance to show you I'm different. We had a great marriage once."

"Chuck—"

"Aaron misses me. I could tell he does."

"Our marriage was hell," Eileen managed to say.

Chuck thrust his chin the slightest bit. "You've made too much of everything. And now you believe the stuff you've dreamed up. That's not good for Aaron, either."

"Aaron is doing very well," Eileen said. The muscles in her legs shook. "He's really getting there."

"He's not sure of himself yet. He's going to take longer than most kids his age. I won't get in your way but I'll be here if I'm needed. And you can't feel bad if I get to know my son again. He needs that and so do I."

She didn't care what Chuck Moggeridge needed, but she wouldn't make even more of a scene here, in front of Angel, who could easily decide to help Chuck leave.

"You're working too hard," he said and reached for her arm. She backed away. "You look worn out. I should have thought about it before but it isn't right for you to be running around in that Oakdale parking lot on your own at night. Don't do that again."

She drew herself up. "Thanks for your concern. Now go."

"Is that what you really want?" He raised his chin. "Are you sure you wouldn't be better off following me back to your house? You shouldn't be here."

"That isn't for you to decide."

He smiled at her. "For better or worse," he said. "Isn't that what we told each other?"

She felt herself coming apart. "You're the one who changed your mind about that, not me. Good night."

"Remember what I said before. I don't want you to worry about Aaron's future. If something happens to you, I'll make sure he doesn't want for anything."

"Why would something happen to me?" she whispered.

He smiled, narrowing his eyes. "I can't think of a reason, can you? Relax. I've rented a place off Main Street. It's behind Sadie and Sam's. Nice place, too. I want you and Aaron to feel you can come there whenever you like."

Eileen wanted to scream.

"Damn. I promised myself I wouldn't come on too strong. But I have. I'll get out of here." He gave her another tight smile and started toward his car, but turned back as he passed her. "Honey, please remember what I said about the other boy. He's tough. Aaron's not—he's a country boy."

"Good night," Eileen said.

Chuck pulled a piece of paper from his pocket. "That's my phone number and address. You know the place. Through the alley beside Sadie and Sam's."

When she didn't take the paper, he pushed it into her hand. He touched her chin and she jerked away from his touch.

"Okay," he said. "How can I blame you? Just remember what I said. Stay out of that parking lot at night. You never know who could be waiting for you."

She gave him a level stare.

"Eileen, you are not to worry about anything," he told her and he held his mouth in a tight line. Sincerity shone in his eyes. "Not money. Nothing. You aren't alone. You'll never be alone again. And remember this, Aaron will never want for anything."

12

Angel knew Eileen was on the very edge. Only her intention to get rid of him the instant they reached her place stopped her from doing something crazy. He didn't know what that was likely to be—didn't want to know.

But he doubted if he would feel better afterward.

She hadn't said a word while he put down the back seats of the van and hoisted his Ducati motorcycle into the back, held the passenger door until she got in and walked around to climb behind the wheel.

Neither had he.

Whatever he said would be the wrong thing.

Eileen put her hands over her face and rocked. He heard her rapid breathing.

"Eileen?" He stroked her back, but she shook him off.

"Okay," he said softly and concentrated on the road ahead. He tried not to feel the waves of rage coming from Eileen— and started planning Chuck Moggerdge's upcoming decision to leave Pointe Judah, fast. He congratulated himself for not having grabbed the man and stuffed him back in his little car when he'd arrived in the driveway. For the sakes of the people Angel cared about, Moggeridge needed to make his own decision to leave town.

"I'm sorry you had to go through that," he said when he finally had to speak again.

Nothing.

"Don't start putting blame on yourself because your creep of an ex-husband decides to come crawling back."

Not a thing.

"Open up with me, Eileen," he said. "Too much has happened, too fast. We need each other. Don't shut me out now."

"You mean you think I need *you?*" she said, her voice shaking.

"Is that supposed to make me mad?"

"I didn't ask you to talk to me."

He tried to hold her hand but she jerked away and said, "I was wrong tonight. I knew where I belonged and that was with Aaron, not...not being selfish."

It was a start. "You mean it was selfish to be with me because you wanted to?"

"I married that *creep* of an ex-husband." She was crying, choking out her words.

"And?" he said.

"Aaron makes my mistake worthwhile. But I chose Chuck. Don't you think that should make me question my judgment?"

That was a loaded question. "Most of us make some bad decisions along the way."

"That doesn't excuse mine." She leaned forward, her hands screwed into fists on top of the dash. "And it doesn't excuse how long I stayed with him. He made me miserable, but worse still, he wasn't a father to Aaron. I should have been out of that as soon as I saw how wrong Chuck was for us."

"Why weren't you?" He sucked air through his mouth and cursed a careless tongue. "Don't answer that."

She made an odd sound. When he glanced at her, she held her mouth open as if she couldn't breathe and her eyes glittered in the dash light.

"Eileen—"

"Don't. You're right. Finn was right. My parents were right. I should have left Chuck early. I didn't have the confidence. Does that make any sense? I didn't believe I could make it on my own with a child and no college education. Now it's different. Now I know what I can do and how well, but I didn't then. And I was ashamed. Can you grasp that?"

She turned her face toward him. He looked at her again and was grateful the darkness hid some of the pain she must feel.

"I'm sorry," he said. "Chalk it up to inexperience. I said the wrong thing because I'm feeling my way with this. You know what they say about men? We don't think like women and we sure as hell communicate differently from women. You don't owe me any explanations."

She turned from him and gripped the rim of her window as if she wanted to push it open and escape.

"Here we are," he told her. The house she and Aaron shared stood at the end of a cul-de-sac in a small subdivision a short distance north and east of the center of town. "Eileen, could we talk before you go in?"

Before he finished asking, she stumbled from the van. She stood there for a few seconds, then hurried to the front door. She hammered it with her fists.

Angel recognized disaster speeding his way.

He approached Eileen's back, clearing his throat loudly.

Aaron opened the door and fell back, his dark eyes huge. "Mom?" he said.

"You opened that door without knowing who was here,"

she said, not sounding like the woman Angel knew. "How many times have you been told not to do that?"

"We looked through the window," Aaron said. "I saw the van."

"I don't mean now. I mean earlier." Shocking Angel, she thrust a forearm into Aaron's chest and pushed him out of her way. Inside the front door, she passed him and stopped. "Did you look out of the window when your father came?"

Sonny appeared. "Eileen—"

"Get your things," she said to him, nothing more, and Sonny turned back toward Aaron's room.

"Dad knocked on the door," Aaron said. "He called out for me."

"So you let him in? He could have been anyone, but he called your name so you let him in?" She coughed; her arms wrapped tightly around her middle. "What were you told? *Don't answer the door. Phone us if anyone comes.* But, no, a man called your name and you let him in."

"He isn't just a man," Aaron said. "He's my dad. I know his voice. He wanted to talk to me."

Eileen hunched over. "No, he's not just a man, he's the one who had no time for you from before you were even born."

Angel walked into the house and put a hand on her shoulder. "Don't do this to yourself," he said, and thought about the damage being done to Aaron. "That man isn't worth it. You've got a life now and so does Aaron. Chuck doesn't, otherwise he wouldn't be here. Remember that."

"If he has his way, everything I've worked for will go away," she said, throwing off his hand. "Only I surely won't let that happen."

After her fear and anger were through, she would hate

thinking about losing control like this. "No, you won't," he said.

"He didn't do anything wrong, Mom," Aaron said and Angel felt sorry for the boy. "He's in town for a bit and he wanted to see me. He told me he felt bad for not spending more time with me when I was younger."

"Softening you up!" The words rose. "Softening you up. Getting you ready to turn against me, and you fell for it. You want him. You always said you didn't miss him, but you're a liar. Just like him. *A liar.*"

"No," Aaron said. "I'm just telling you what he said. I don't want him. It's always been you and me."

Eileen looked at her son and Angel saw how her lips were drawn back and tears coursed her face. "When you heard him at the door, you were glad, weren't you?" She gathered the neck of his T-shirt into her fist and gave him a short push. "He offered you candy and you took it."

"No, he didn't. Honestly—"

"I'm not talking about candy in bars. I mean candy like something new you've always wanted. And why shouldn't you? Kids have a right to want love from their parents."

Flinching at every few words, Aaron closed his eyes and turned his face away.

Sonny came down the hallway with his backpack. He looked at Eileen, then at Aaron. Sonny from Brooklyn didn't seem so tough. His face said he was shaken and helpless.

"Go to him, then," Eileen said to Aaron. She scrabbled in her pocket and found the piece of paper that Chuck had given her and now she took one of her son's hands, opened it and folded his fingers around the crumpled wad. "That's where you'll find him. *Go.*"

She went toward the stairs.

Sonny hurried outside.

"Get the bike out of the van," Angel said to him before following Eileen. "Be careful."

Holding tight to the bannister, she climbed slowly.

"Honey," he said. "This has been a hell of a night. For you and for Aaron. For all of us. Let me help you, both of you."

"I know what my responsibilities are," she said. "I won't make the mistake of forgetting them again."

Aaron stood on the back steps of the house. The walls of his room had started to close in on him. He needed to be outside in the fresh air where he could think.

He didn't know what time it was but dawn hadn't shown in the sky yet. Fog boiled, a chill boil, across the earth and into the trees behind the house.

He only felt the cold when he heard his teeth chatter and remembered his stinging hands and feet. After all she'd done for him, he'd hurt his mother. He'd made her cry. Behaving like a stupid kid happy to see his dad after a long time, he had betrayed his mom the way he never wanted to.

When his dad used to come back from the rigs, for the first week, maybe just the first few days, he'd wrestle on the floor with Aaron. They'd laugh. He took him fishing a couple of times—Aaron would never forget that.

When school was in, sometimes his dad used to show up outside when classes were over. He'd give him some money and maybe…yeah, he always gave him candy. Aaron remembered how he felt then, how he didn't think of anything but his dad wanting to see him, too. It was never for too long, but Aaron would try to find ways to make him stick around longer.

When he came to school it was usually right before he'd disappear—not coming home for night after night, like he always did after he'd been with them in Pointe Judah for a week or so.

One time his dad had looked at Aaron's shoes and asked him if they were big enough. Aaron had shrugged. He'd been taught not to let anyone think he wanted something from them. His dad had told him to get in the car and then he'd driven them to buy a new pair of shoes. He bought two expensive pairs of sneakers that all of Aaron's friends turned green over, and some loafers.

Afterward he dropped Aaron at the house. "You comin' in, Dad?" Aaron could hear his own voice, so much younger then. "Not this time, son. Here, give this to your mother and tell her to get herself something she wants. What she wants, mind, not what she needs. Y'hear?" And his dad had given him a twenty-dollar bill.

And he'd driven off while Aaron stood and watched.

Maudlin. That was the word for the stuff he was dredging up. Men stuffed down the kid memories, the soft trash that got in the way of being strong. Maybe women did it, too. He thought his mom had—until a few hours ago when he made a dumb mistake.

Would she go back to being sad and not talking like she had sometimes when he was little? He'd learned what he should and shouldn't say to her, or do, so why had he forgotten tonight? This one time was all it took—he'd known he could destroy her happiness. And she had been happy for a long time now.

He walked away from the house, rubbing his hands together and grateful for his windbreaker. Once in the trees, the fog rose around his thighs and he went slow so as not to trip over something. The fog roiled. A fresh breeze kept the world around him moving. A Christmas sort of night. He almost expected the smell of cane smoke in the air, but that wouldn't come as long as the fog hung around.

The rush of air across his face eased, but not the swirling sounds that filled his ears.

Yards ahead, more distant than he should have been able to see, an inverted cone of bronze leaves and twigs appeared, twirled, rose, and fanned wider until it disappeared.

Aaron drove his hands into his pockets and raised his shoulders. His heart beat harder.

He could be sick. Chuzah had told him not to repeat anything that had really happened in the swamp, but he had also told Aaron he might not feel so good for a few days.

Go home.

"What?" Someone had spoken, hadn't they? He hadn't told himself to go home.

Go home quickly.

Many times when Aaron had been small, his dad had told him he was weak, usually because he cried when the wrestling started to hurt. His dad had been right; he was weak. He got scared for nothing. No wonder his father hadn't wanted him.

Tears on his face scalded. He was ashamed. He was a man and men didn't bawl.

The fog shifted in front of him, changed shape. Flattened into ribbons, it shifted back and forth, faster and faster, and the noises grew louder than ever.

Crack!

Aaron jumped. He tried to turn around but couldn't move.

A tree limb must have broken off to his left. That hadn't been a gunshot. No, not a gunshot.

Too far away to be distinct, but very real to Aaron, a shape formed. An animal. Silver. Sailing over the fog with the low, long-limbed stride of a wolf on the hunt. Only this creature didn't travel out of sight.

It whirled, pawing the vapor around its feet. Eyes that shone stared at Aaron, then away, in the direction from which that sharp snap had come. The creature hunched, poised to spring. It opened its mouth and great teeth glittered.

It *was* a giant wolf.

Aaron wanted to move but still couldn't.

From the left, in the area of that loud sound and where the animal stared, a crashing set up. Crashing, brush breaking. Loud at first, it continued, becoming less distinct until Aaron couldn't hear it anymore.

He looked back toward the creature.

Gone.

Once more the fog bowled over the ground.

Every hair on his back rose.

He ran back to the house and as he closed the door, an animal howled.

13

"Look at those two dance," Sarah Board said. "They're making me dizzy." She leaned on the bar at the Boardroom and watched Rusty Barnes whip Gracie Loder around the floor in a snappy two-step.

Sabine Webb, the red and green beads in her braids exchanged for white crystals, popped olives into three martinis and wiggled to the rhythm of the Boardroom Boys. "Not bad," she said. "I never did see that stick of a Rusty dance at all before. He's as good as anyone out there." Sabine could dance most people to collapse.

"Well he's getting practice somewhere." The club buzzed and Sarah felt good. Buying and opening this place had been a gamble, even with Delia's investment, but it was paying off.

"That guy Barnes makes Gracie want to puke," Leland Garolfo said. He worked at The Willows site as a foreman for Duhon Construction and when he'd had a few drinks he got loud and pushy. "Just because she lives at his place, he thinks she owes him more than rent. I'm gonna have to spring her."

"I don't think that's a good idea," Sarah said. She ran her fingers through short, white-blond hair, making sure her spiky do looked its best.

"Why's that?" Leland said, all belligerence.

"Leland," Sabine said, leaning across the bar but unfortunately having to look way up at tall, rangy Leland. "You can be an ass, know that? You've got the hots for Gracie and everybody knows it. She's not interested in you. Suck it up."

Sarah whispered, *"Sabine,"* even though she didn't expect the other woman to take any notice.

"Anybody tell you what a big mouth you've got?" Leland said to her.

Sabine puckered up her lips and frowned in thought. "Mm, nope, not that I remember. But I'll take it you're breaking my run of good luck, hot rocks."

Shoot. Sarah waited for the exchange to blow. It didn't. Leland shrugged and pushed his glass toward her for another shot of Wild Turkey. She poured and turned immediately to fill an order for Bea, one of the waitresses. Bea filled in on Gracie's off nights and this was one of them. Last night they'd been slammed and Gracie hadn't got off until two in the morning. She needed downtime.

"Know what you need, Miz Sabine?" Leland said. He slurred his words. "A man. That's what you need, girl, a man. You're a frustrated—"

"Whoa," Sarah said. "If you don't want to be outside that front door, Leland, you'll cool down." The guy who doubled as security and bouncer didn't get enough practice for his taste. Sarah didn't want that situation to change, but he was there to be used if necessary.

The Boardroom Boys swung into "You Ain't Gettin' My Lady" and Rusty ushered Gracie from the floor.

"Lookee here," Leland said when the dancers arrived. "A couple from the Bolshy Bally." He pulled Gracie into the crook of one arm and kissed her on the lips. Gracie pushed him away.

"Bolshoi Ballet," Sabine corrected him promptly.

Leland, who had definitely had one or two more than was a good idea, faced the bar and raised his glass. He was quiet, but not for long enough. "Did y'all hear about Emma Duhon having a turn over at Ona's last night? They reckon she flipped out in the parking lot."

Busy filling orders, Sarah listened while she ran back and forth. Sabine did the same but she skidded to a halt at Leland's question. "A turn? She was attacked. And she didn't flip out, she was just scared."

"Not the way I heard it. She said a bunch of stuff happened only it doesn't look as if it did. No evidence, is what I heard."

"Rusty," Sabine said. "You were there. You saw what happened. Emma was under a truck and all scraped up."

"Yeah," Rusty said. "The police are looking into it. Less said before they're finished, the better."

"A whole bunch of us saw it." Sabine's voice rose and her cheekbones grew ruddy. "When's the last time you were pregnant and someone knocked you under a truck, Leland Garolfo?"

"Ah, don't come on with that stuff. We all know women get funny when they're pregnant. They imagine things."

At once, Sarah dropped the cloth she'd been using and put an arm around Sabine's stiff shoulders. "Don't waste your time with him," she told her. "You're an idiot, Leland."

"I'm just tellin' it like it is," he said. He laughed and swayed and tossed down the rest of his drink. "Whips, I heard. She said he went after her with whips." His empty glass shot across the bar at Sabine and he threw down more money.

Sabine picked up the glass and Sarah quickly removed it from her fingers. "You don't want any more, do you, Leland?"

"You bet your sweet tush, I do, don't I honey?" Honey was Gracie, who got treated to a pinch on her rear.

"Keep your hands off me," Gracie said.

Sarah glanced at Rusty who watched the pair with no expression on his face. She checked to see where the bouncer, Ron Labeaux, was and saw him observing, jiggling slightly on the toes of his rubber-soled shoes.

The place was loud and getting louder. Good music, good eats, good times—just the way she had planned for it to be. But tonight was the first time she'd felt there could be violence and Sarah's heart beat too fast and hard.

She caught Rusty's eye and he must have seen her nervousness. He took Leland's Stetson off and grinned at him when Leland's head jerked around. "I wouldn't want you and the Gracie getting into a scuffle," he said. "'Sides, the show's gettin' a bit heated for us small-town folks."

The light in Leland's eyes turned purely mean. He straightened up and wiped the back of a hand across his mouth. "You sure you want to mess with me, Barnes?"

"No. But if I have to, I will," Rusty said. He had dark red hair, green eyes, a cool expression, and a reporter's unshakable persistence when he needed it. "Looks like you're forcing yourself on Gracie. Maybe she doesn't like bruises on her butt."

Sarah held her breath. From the corner of her eye she saw Rob Labeaux move a little closer.

A man came through the door and pushed his way toward the bar. Maybe six-foot even with the kind of brawny build that came from physical labor, he had thick and curly dark hair, graying at the sideburns, and one of those hard-jawed faces that was all-American pleasant, but forgettable. He reminded Sarah of someone but she couldn't think who.

Of the cluster at the bar, Rusty Barnes was the only one whose attention focused as if he knew the man. Rusty frowned and checked around the room as if someone else should be interested in the newcomer.

Sabine looked up from polished the bar and smiled at the man. Just as fast, the smile dissolved. "You eating, or just drinking?" she asked, her face turned away from him. There were a dozen or so tables ranged around the dance floor and the kitchen put out what the menu boasted were "Big bites and bigger bites," a spicy selection of local food.

"Okay if I have a snack at the bar?" the man said. He shot out a hand. Sabine ignored it. He looked at his palm, shrugged and said, "Chuck Moggeridge. I've been away a couple of years. Don't know who remembers me and who doesn't. I see some familiar faces. Hi, Rusty."

There was no doubt that Sabine remembered him and she surely didn't look happy about it. The rest of the group checked him out and Rusty said, "Yo, Chuck. You still on the rigs?"

"I'm takin' at least a year off from the Gulf," he said. "Time to get to know my family again."

"What family?" Sabine said, swinging around to look at him. "You and Eileen are divorced."

Chuck ignored this and said, "You got Turbodog?" to Sarah, who nodded and poured his beer.

"I remember you," Sabine said, tightening the corners of her eyes. "I'd have thought you'd stay away."

"This place is nice," Chuck said, indicating the club, and as if Sabine hadn't spoken. "Who's the boss?"

"I am," Sarah said. "We've been open a few months."

"I bet you get everyone in town in here," Chuck said.

"Pretty much."

"You know my wife, Eileen?"

"She's not your wife," Sabine said. She looked tense. "What're you really doing back here, Chuck? I thought you'd gone on to bigger and better things."

He looked at her fully for the first time since he arrived in the club. "A man doesn't always grow up quick enough to make the best of what he's got," he said. "I finally figured out I left the best things I ever had behind."

"Sweet," Sabine muttered. "All you're going to find here is trouble. Eileen's got someone else. She's also got a good business and she's doing nicely without you. She isn't going to want you hanging around."

Sarah had grown really warm under the collar. One of the things she and Delia had discussed before signing on the line for the Boardroom was that there would be nights like this, when the drink was in and the wit was out and things got nasty.

On the dance floor, the crowd swung and stepped, each couple with their signature moves, but all doing forms of the same dance. Colors shifted all over. Laughter came from every direction. A rack of men's undershorts—Sarah's answer to a suggestion that the Boardroom be decorated with women's bras—stretched across a space behind the band. All donated warm, they bore the owners' names and were up for sale—all proceeds to charity.

People had a simple Louisiana good time there. Sarah turned from the glaring match between Chuck and Sabine, and tried to let herself enjoy the spectacle of a successful venture.

"I'll be going to the little girls' room," Gracie said. "You thinking of going home any time soon, Rusty?"

Sarah's attention shot back to the crabby gathering around the bar.

"You bet," Rusty said. "I've got to be at work early."

"I'll be glad to take you," Leland said to Gracie. "You take off, Barnes."

Gracie faced Leland with her hands on her hips. "You're pushing it," she said. "Quit. I'm not interested in you."

She edged between people, sideways, and Chuck shot out an arm to stop her.

He smiled. "You're a real looker. How come I missed you around town?"

She turned red. "I guess you got unlucky. Excuse me."

Sarah met Rusty's blank stare again but then noticed a subtle change in his expression. His regard turned speculative.

For now, all she wanted was a break in the poisonous exchanges happening in front of her.

Gracie left for the ladies' room and Leland looked after her with hot, possessive intent.

"You need to remember that Gracie does her own thing," Rusty said to Chuck. "She's not a woman who responds to crude approaches."

Chuck shrugged, tipping his beer glass. He closed his eyes in appreciation. "I'll try to remember that," he said.

"Can I get anybody anything?" Sabine asked loudly. "We've got a lot of empty glasses around here."

"I'm leaving soon," Rusty said.

Leland rocked his glass back and forth a few times, considering, then pushed it toward Sabine. "Same," he said.

"How about a shot to go with that beer, Chuck…Mogge-ridge, is it?"

"Yes, please. And, yeah. Chuck Moggeridge. Call me Chuck."

"Moggeridge isn't a name from around here," Leland said.

Chuck shook his head. "Sure isn't. My dad worked on the rigs before me. We moved to Mississippi from Arkansas when I was a kid. I ended up here. Nice place."

Chuck shrugged, tipping his beer glass. He closed his eyes in appreciation.

"You just hanging out in Pointe Judah?" Leland asked Chuck.

"I want to find something to do. Money goes soon enough if all you do is spend it."

Leland looked him up and down. "Done any construction?"

"Some."

"Come out and see me at The Willows in the morning. Know where that is?"

"Sure," Chuck said. "Everyone around here does."

"Come to the office in the morning. I'll find something for you."

Sabine gave Sarah a poke in the back and whispered, "Don't they call that an unholy alliance?"

"Mmm." Sarah smiled.

Sabine nodded at two men who had just walked into the Boardroom and shouldered their way to the bar. "What'll it be?" she said.

"You available, blondie?" one of the guys asked. Blond himself, twenty-something and built like a fireplug, he doffed a sweat-stained tan Stetson and waggled his heavy eyebrows at Sarah.

A happy smile on her face, Sabine said, "Careful what you say to Sarah, she's a chemist, y'know."

"And I'm a Cooper," came the rapid reply. The man slapped his knee, guffawed and elbowed the man beside him who had an equally good laugh. "Ron Cooper, ma'am. You ain't so bad yourself now I take a good look at you."

Grinning to herself, Sarah turned back to unloading clean glasses. Sabine could take care of herself and if they ever had trouble, there was Ron and enough brawny regulars to handle things.

"Hey, blondie chemist," the comedian bawled. "I wanna buy you a drink."

"No," Sabine said. "It's not her name, it's what she is. She's a chemist who happens to own this place. All day long she cuts up specimens. I hear you're short of those, hey, Sarah? Specimens to cut up, that is."

Sabine had her own sense of humor.

Sarah was a chemist at one of her adoptive mother Delia Board's labs just out of Pointe Judah. She worked on whipping up cosmetics formulas. Animals weren't used in the process. She'd never thought of dissecting humans but now she took a good look at Cooper with his sagging grin, the idea developed appeal.

"You're joshing me," Cooper said. "Chemists don't look like you, blondie. You're a looker."

Apparently he liked her short, spiked hair and the makeup job she felt was her duty, given her occupation.

"She's too tall for you," the other man said. "Too thin."

"Nice eyes, though," Cooper said. "Nothing like a pair of big blue eyes, unless it's a pair of big casabas." He stared at her chest.

"She's got those," his analytical buddy said. "I like more hip, myself, though."

"Okay, boys." The group hadn't seen Matt Boudreaux come in with Angel. "Order what you want—politely—and move away. Or leave." He wasn't in uniform, but Matt assumed typical cop stance, feet apart, hands on hips.

Matt was a commanding man. He and Angel made a formidable pair.

"We was just joshin'," the blond guy said and winked.

Angel leaned forward and caught Leland's eye. The man straightened up and cleared his throat. He gave what passed for a respectful nod.

"Aren't these two of ours?" Angel said, indicating the newly arrived jokers. He looked at them. "You out at The Willows, boys?"

Both men nodded and Sarah expected them to start pawing the floor with their boots.

"Get home and sober up," Angel said. "If you work for Duhon, you work sober and smart. You be on the job that way first thing. Got that?"

"Yessir," they chorused and almost fell over each other getting out of the place. They didn't even notice Gracie when she passed them on the way back to the bar.

She glanced at Matt and Angel who both nodded. Once she passed Angel, she craned her neck to look over her shoulder at him, and he must have felt her eyes on him. He stared back at her and frowned.

"Time to go," Rusty said, and left with Gracie.

Angel turned back to Leland. "Was Bucky Smith on the job today?"

Leland shook his head slowly. "Don't even know who he is."

"You sure?" Matt said.

"Yeah." Leland pursed his mouth. He turned around and pulled Chuck Moggeridge forward.

And Sarah held her breath. Sabine lifted her heavy braids off her neck with both hands and muttered, "Matt knows about him. Does Angel?"

"No idea," Sarah said. "Poor Eileen. I never met this creep before, but he's a loser."

"Big-time," Sabine said. "He just about ruined Eileen's life."

"We could use more hands, couldn't we, boss?" Leland said to Angel.

Angel had hooked his wallet from a pocket and was taking out some bills. He looked up and saw Chuck—at just about the same time as Matt's eyes settled on the man.

"Moggeridge," Matt snapped. "What are you doin' here?"

"The henhouse got left open," Sabine said under her breath. "Get ready to collect feathers."

Angel and Chuck locked eyes. "It's a free country," Chuck told Matt. "I like Pointe Judah."

"This is Chuck Moggeridge—"

"I know who he is," Angel said, interrupting Leland, and placed money on the counter deliberately.

Leland had the slack, careless appearance of an oblivious drunk. "We could use him, boss," he said to Angel. "He's been on the rigs, so he knows how to work. Done some construction, too."

"What is it?" Matt said to Angel suddenly. "What's goin' on here?"

"Sixth sense," Sarah said to Sabine. "He smells bad apples. I guess that's why he's the police chief."

Sabine giggled, but stopped abruptly when Angel ignored Matt and took a step toward Chuck. "Here it comes," she said.

"Nice to see you again," Angel said. "You ever worked construction? For real?"

"I have. Framing."

Angel's cool gray eyes narrowed. "We've got plenty of framing to be done, right Leland?"

"Right," Leland said cheerfully.

"Report for work first thing in the morning," Angel said. "Leland and I run a tight ship."

Chuck let his breath out in a whistle. "Why would you hire me?"

Sarah raised her eyebrows. The guy had a funny way of responding to a job offer.

"You can't think of a reason?" Angel said. When he crossed his arms and flexed his shoulders he was even more intimidating.

Chuck's eyes moved from Angel's chest, to the floor, to the ceiling and back at Angel. "No."

"Maybe there doesn't have to be one," Angel said. "Except we need the hands and there aren't many spare ones in these parts, not if they're skilled and they want to work. And I put business before pleasure. Fair enough?"

"Yessir."

"'Night, Moggeridge," Angel said.

Chuck took an instant to process his dismissal but eventually nodded, and gave a mock salute. When he'd passed Angel, he looked back and hatred surfaced briefly in Chuck's face. Then he left, his gait unsteady.

"Are you gonna tell me about all that?" Matt said. "I didn't know you knew the guy."

"Later," Angel told him. He turned back to Leland. "The guys who share a place with Bucky came to me."

"They'd already been to me," Matt added. "I'm not a happy man. I've already got enough trouble around here."

"With that Emma Duhon and her phantom whip man?" Leland said, sniggering. "I was telling the ladies how wigged-out they get when they're pregnant. I'd put that one to bed if I was you."

Matt's sixth sense helped him out again. Making a move toward the bar, he stepped between Leland and Angel. "Less you say on that subject, the better," he told Leland in a even voice. "Angel and the Duhons are tight."

Leland, on delay, looked aghast. "I know that. What I said was just a guy thing. Just a joke. Maybe I'd better get going."

"Go," Matt said. "But we've asked around and nobody remembers seeing Bucky Smith since he was at Ona's last night."

"Not my problem," Leland said.

"Sure as hell is," Angel shot at him. "If we've got workers missing from shifts, it's your problem. Playing babysitter to the crews is your job, not mine. Now go dredge him up from wherever he's been sleeping it off. When you find him, tell him this is his free one. If he messes up again, he doesn't have a job anymore. Duhon's doesn't carry any deadweight."

14

Early the next afternoon, Finn and Angel hovered near the private elevator in Finn's suite of offices at the old Oakdale Mansion.

"Matt'll be on his way up shortly," Finn told Angel. "No heroics, okay?"

Angel was uncomfortable with Finn's plan to tell Eileen it had been he, not Angel, who wanted to call in the cops. "Coming clean with Matt was my idea."

"I agreed with you," Finn said. "And I didn't mention how pissed he's going to be because you didn't tell him everything days ago."

"You have now." Angel had to smile.

"Listen up," Finn said. "I know my sister. She's hard-headed. Like you said, she wanted to contact Matt herself but you talked her out of it. She's likely to blow if she thinks you've gone to Matt on your own now. So when she gets here we'll say I sent for him. It's true."

"She's been avoiding me for two days," Angel said. He didn't add that he'd moved on from feeling lousy, to feeling mad and lousy about Eileen shutting him out. "I usually stop by at closing time, but she's making sure she isn't there.

Before I came up here today, I went to the shop to see her. She bolted into the stockroom and wouldn't come out. I had two choices—make a fool of both of us in front of her customers or leave."

"She did that?" Finn cleared his throat. He had the kind of sharp, hazel eyes that snapped when he was amused and he was amused now.

"Don't you damn-well laugh," Angel said, smiling himself. "She won't come up here, either, not once she figures out I'm around."

"She won't figure it out until she's here," Finn said. "But Matt's going to arrive first. She'd be too embarrassed to make a fuss in front of him."

Angel inclined his head. "Seems sneaky. She's going to pick up on that."

Before Finn could respond, the elevator bumped to a stop and the doors slid open to reveal Matt, in uniform and looking much too official. Or should that be, officious? He also looked like a man who hadn't slept recently.

"Afternoon," Finn said. "Thanks for coming."

Matt had taken off his hat and the impression of the band flattened a circle in his dark, curly hair. He walked between Angel and Finn and carried on through the foyer toward Finn's office.

Finn and Angel looked at each other briefly before following. As far as Angel knew there was no reason for Matt to arrive with a burr under his saddle.

Angel noted how Matt looked over the tangerine walls and animal prints on furnishings. Everyone did. Emma was responsible for the bold decor.

"Coffee?" Finn asked.

"Yeah," Matt said. "And I didn't get lunch so if there's any food around, I'll eat it."

Coffee was always ready in Finn's office. The same went for Angel's. He had his own quarters here although he rarely used them, preferring to work from home or be out in the field.

"I'll get the coffee," Angel said. "For you, too, Finn?"

He got a grunt in return and filled three comfortingly stained mugs. Finn started hauling plates out of a refrigerator behind a paneled door that made the appliance look like part of the wall.

"Half a corned beef sandwich," Finn said. "That place down by Poke Around does good stuff. They bring up a selection. Ham and Swiss. A slightly stale muffuletta. There's some gumbo I can heat in the microwave. And a couple of different sausages. Then there's apples and an orange—"

"Ham and Swiss," Matt said, curling his lip at the mention of fruit. "Don't heat it. I'll eat it like it is." He sat behind Finn's desk and hunched over the vast sandwich. He ate big bites between swallows of coffee. He emptied his mug and Angel got him a refill

"It didn't sink in until after you took off last night," Matt said when Angel put another steaming mug in front of him. "What the hell made you agree to hire Chuck Moggeridge?"

"We're shorthanded."

"Don't give me that," Matt said. "You do know who he is?"

"Sure. Eileen's ex-husband."

"So you hate his guts, right?" Matt said.

Angel didn't want to consider Matt's attitude toward Moggeridge when it obviously sprang from feelings for Eileen. "Okay. If you're going to push the issue. I want the man where I can watch him, or have him watched for me. I want to be sure he doesn't get anywhere near Eileen."

Matt grunted. He swallowed his coffee and turned his attention to Finn. "I'm not in the mood for any crap," he said. "So go easy, if you don't mind. I'm not responsible for what other people say. And I can't help it if we've got malignant gossips in this town."

Angel wanted Finn to lure Eileen up here before they got into any discussion, but Matt's rapid-fire announcements were delaying the plan. What was he talking about now?

From the distracted way Finn replaced rejected food in the refrigerator, he was as stymied as Angel.

"We didn't find anything," Matt said around a mouthful of his sandwich. "We searched. Shit, I've had everyone I could spare going through that parking lot and there's not a thing there that doesn't belong. It doesn't help that the purse and notebook were found inside Ona's. But that doesn't mean I approve of big mouths suggesting Emma's having some sort of breakdown because she's pregnant." He pointed at Finn. "I'm doin' my best, so stay off my case."

Angel withdrew a distance with his coffee. He'd been told Leland Garolfo made some comment about Emma at the Boardroom a couple of nights earlier, right before Matt and Angel had arrived. "Lets move on," he said, hoping for a lucky break.

He didn't get one. "What the hell are you talkin' about?" Finn said. "Who told you that? When?"

"I can't divulge my sources," Matt said. "You want to take numbers and kick ass? Make your own list—without me." He hadn't encountered a razor in too many hours and the dark stubble on his jaw gave him a dangerous look.

Finn walked to stand over Matt. "If someone's suggesting Emma made something up, I want a name, or names."

"Hey, hey," Angel said. "It's not worth it. These people don't have enough to do with their time, so they gab."

"Emma's all scratched up and bruised. Mitch Halpern wants her to take things easy. And some light-brain calls her names, says stuff about her? Oh, no, no, I don't think so."

Matt pushed back from the desk, his mug cradled in both hands. "I want you to forget about this, okay, Finn? I don't have any evidence that Emma was attacked. Nothing other than what she says." He glanced into Finn's eyes and held up a hand. "I believe her, of course. I won't stop askin' questions and keeping my ears open."

He set down the mug, leaned to put his elbows on the desk and scrubbed at his hair. "I know you've got this Bucky Smith on your minds, too. Someone has to have seen him in three days but we can't find a trace of him."

Finn and Angel shared another look. This was their business, but not what they'd had in mind when they called Matt. "I know he's not back," Angel said. "When he does show up we'll just fire his ass, so why spend time on him?"

Matt looked up, his face deadly serious. "That place where he lives. All of his stuff is there. Not his wallet or credit cards. But his car and the keys are there. He got a ride to Ona's."

"Did he?" Angel got a nasty sensation deep in his belly. Again no real and sinister evidence yet. But he had something he wanted to share with Matt about bullets through a skylight. There was evidence of that.

"Think," Matt said. "Who does Bucky Smith hang out with?"

Angel thought about it. "I can't tell you because I don't know."

Matt looked at Finn, who also shook his head.

"If I didn't have to cope with all the interference in this town, I could move things along faster," Matt said. "What I've got here is a big, fat nothing being made into something by Lobelia Forestier and gang. They're getting in my way. Lobelia's got everyone asking if Bucky could have done the number on Emma, then ducked out of town."

"Well, could he?" Angel asked promptly.

Matt didn't look pleased. "If we could find him I could pursue that line of investigation, couldn't I?"

"Could I have a little silence?" Finn asked. He pressed a button on his phone, switched to Speaker, and after two rings Angel heard Eileen pick up. "Sis?" Finn said. "Could you do me a favor?"

A pause. "Depends on the favor."

"You got any help down there so you could leave for a few?"

Another pause. "Yes. What do you need?"

Angel looked at the other men's faces. Matt appeared entertained. "Er, Emma's going to come up later this afternoon. I want her to rest up here where I can see her."

Matt looked irritated at being held up. He turned his palms up and made small "come on, come on" signals with his fingers.

"This place doesn't look one bit like Christmas," Finn continued. "Emma loves Christmas. This year she's not up to doing what she likes to do, so I'm going to have to fill in for her. Do you have something I could put up here to cheer her up? One of those arrangements with all the berries and junk? The ones you women think smell nice. Or an angel with the little lights in the wings? How about…I saw something…"

He looked engaged with his subject. "A big snow globe. Doesn't matter what's inside. The kind you switch on to keep the snow moving and the music playing at the same time."

A suspicious little croak came from the speaker. Then Eileen said, "Leave it to me. Give me half an hour to get something together." She hung up.

Matt shook his head slowly. "Thoughtful of you, Finn," he said. "Are we finished here then? You understand I'm doing my best with the parking-lot thing and your missing guy. I'll get back to you."

"No," Angel said. "Yes, about the parking lot and Bucky. But if Emma says she was attacked, she was attacked and you'd better get whoever did it."

A long, blunt fingered leveled at Angel. "You don't get to tell me my duty. Now, if you'll excuse me." Matt got up.

"Matt, Angel means that's not why we asked you to come here," Finn said quickly. "We're not trying to be offensive— even though we're making a good job of it. We've got a lot on our hands here."

"Really?" Matt dropped back in his seat. "Oh, good. Just tell me if you really think we've got nothing more sinister than a crazy running around town cooking up rumors just when we're expecting folks to come from all around for the fair. If that's the case, I'd like to know it because you'd be saving me a lot of headaches and I could turn the thing over to Clemens or Sampson to practice on. But I'll still have to figure out if and what happened to Emma and if it had anything to do with Bucky going missing. It was the same night, for God's sake. And as far as we know, Bucky was last seen at Ona's."

"I don't see how those two things could be tied together," Finn said.

Angel agreed. He wanted to spin this out so Eileen could be there and hear what was said about the shooting at his place the other night. If she witnessed the conversation, she wouldn't second-guess the message.

"Angel and I have been talking," Finn said. "We decided we needed to fill you in on something."

There was no way to warn Finn to slow down the telling, but Angel sure wanted to.

Matt turned to him. "You and Finn? What's the big mystery?"

"Just let me think my way through it," Angel said, avoiding Finn's eyes.

"Maybe you could have thought your way through it and stopped by the station?" Matt did look tired.

"Angel's been having problems with Eileen, and—" Finn closed his mouth.

Matt checked his fingernails.

Angel said, "What Finn means to say is we'd like Eileen to be here while I talk about this and it's easier, and less stressful for her, if we meet here. We haven't told her you're here. That way, she can't get uptight ahead of time."

"Really?" Matt's tongue slid around inside one of his cheeks.

"There was a shooting at Angel's place," Finn said, his face growing tight as it tended to do when he was losing his temper. "You aren't here to referee some lovers' tiff—this is serious."

Angel couldn't believe what his friend had just said.

"A shooting," Matt repeated. He turned his face up to Angel. "At your place?"

"Yes," Angel said. "Three nights ago."

"And you're just getting around to reporting it? At least you could have told me last night."

"Y'know, Matt. It's probably not the right way to be, but when you've been doing your own dirty work for a long time you can get in the habit of taking care of things."

"Only this time you didn't manage to do that?" Matt said, his tone innocent.

"Okay," Angel said. "Lay it on me. Let me have it if it makes you feel better." He wouldn't mention that since he was protecting Sonny, he still had his own official capacity, even if it didn't exactly fit this situation. "Here." He dropped a small plastic bag containing two slugs on the desk.

Matt bent over them, looked from Angel to Finn. "These are in bad shape," he said of the bullets. "They won't do us much good, but the casings surely could. Either of the bullets do real damage?"

"Just to my bathroom," Angel said.

"Someone shot through his skylight," Finn added.

"I went after him but I was too late," Angel told Matt. "I did find the one casing in a gutter after it got light."

"The other one probably rolled off the roof," Matt said. "The yard needs to be searched."

"Already has been," Angel said. "It could be there, but he might have taken it with him, too."

"Someone climbed on your roof and shot through a skylight? Probably some fool kid."

"The fool kid was aiming at me."

"Angel was in the bathtub," Finn said.

At least he was the only one who knew Eileen had also been in that bathtub—underneath him—Angel thought.

"Sick bastard," Matt said. He pushed to his feet and went

to a window where he could look over the Oakdale Mansion Center. "Do either of you have any ideas about either Emma's encounter, or this shooting?"

"No," Finn said promptly. "Except they're not connected."

The silence that followed went on so long, Finn said, "They can't be, can they?"

"This isn't a big town," Matt said. "There doesn't seem to be anything to tie the two things together, except time frame. Or maybe it was just the full moon."

The intercom buzzed and Eileen's voice answered Finn. He got up to go meet her at the elevator.

Left with Matt, Angel met the other man's dark eyes squarely. They both knew they were thinking about their relationships with the same woman. Matt was the first to look away. An admission that he knew he'd been the loser.

Voices and the sound of wheels approached and Finn pushed a handcart into the office. A small but fully decorated Christmas tree, its stand wedged into a box and weighted with bricks, stood on the bed of the cart. Eileen steadied the tree trunk with one hand but stared at Angel as if he were one of her so-called shapeshifters. That look carried accusation as well as shock. She was too bright not to know he'd at least helped set her up to run into him.

"Will you look at this?" Finn said. "My sister doesn't do things by half. I asked for a snow globe and I got an entire decorated Christmas tree. Emma's going to love it. Will it be too tall on that table by the chaise?"

Eileen didn't answer. She continued to stare at Angel with an expression suggesting betrayal in her dark eyes.

"Eileen," Finn said. "On the—"

"Yes," she said quickly, turning her back on Angel.

"There's an outlet for the lights over there, too. It'll be a good idea for you to have Emma come up here with you. Maybe she'll stay in one place a bit more then."

"What d'you mean?" Finn straightened. "She's been at home."

A cornered look crossed Eileen's features. "Yes, yes. I just meant that if she's here with you she can really rest."

Clearly Emma hadn't been staying at home, but Finn was too oblivious to concentrate on the clue. He hauled the tree from the box and Eileen hurried to drape some thick white cotton on top of the table. She covered the stand with the same material. Finn plugged in the tree and was the only one to look delighted with it. "It's great, sis," he said. "Emma's going to love it."

"Good. Well, I don't want to interfere with your progress here, so I'll be off."

"Don't I even get a *hi,* Eileen?" Matt said.

She said, "Hi," and gave him an abbreviated hug. Angel got a jerky little wave and a nod. Darn it, he would get her alone and they'd hammer this nonsense out. He hadn't spent months coming to care about her, to want her, and finally get her—more or less—only to have her steal herself away from him again. He relived holding her in that tub—frequently.

"If Sonny feels like it, he's welcome for dinner tonight," she said, with not the smallest smile.

If *Sonny* feels like it. She wasn't inviting Angel, but he wouldn't have expected that anyway. It would be good if Eileen relented toward Sonny who was a much better kid than he got credit for.

"'Bye." She walked determinedly toward the foyer and Angel felt his temper rise with the level of his disappointment.

"We need you here," Finn said. "Angel's been worrying about the shooting at his place. He was trying to deal with it himself—big idiot—but I called Matt in. We've been talking about it, but since you were there at the time, he'll have questions for you, too."

Geez, Angel thought, he was an idiot. He had been going to let her walk right out of here.

Finn fussed with the tree, moved ornaments from branch to branch, checked to make sure the trunk was straight in the stand.

And Angel discovered the true meaning of being hung out to dry. Eileen, her eyes sharp, shot nonverbal accusations in his direction. Why did she think any of this was his fault?

"There's a lot of weird stuff going on in this town," she said. "Other people must have mentioned that to you, Matt."

He looked blank. "Weird? You mean in addition to someone accosting Emma? And someone firing through the skylight into Angel's bathroom? That had to be a shock."

She turned so red, Angel made fists to stop himself from going to hold her. Not that she was likely to let him get that close.

"It had been a stressful day," she said. "With the boys going missing like that and us finding them in the swamp with Chuzah."

She must think I've already told Matt about it. Angel settled and resettled his elbows, all but flapping them in an attempt at sending a semaphore. *Please don't say anymore.*

"Keep 'em away from that kook Chuzah," Matt said. "As far as I know, he's a stranger to everyone in town, but that doesn't stop a lot of folks from being scared of him. Some of the older ones have a lot of tales to tell, but for all their talk, they go into the swamp whispering and come out with little bags of stuff in their pockets. Folks say he's high up on the food chain." He paused and raised his brows. "You know what food chain I mean? They also say folks have disappeared in that swamp and nothing was ever found of them later. Not as much as a bone. Boys are going to push things like that, but impress on them they shouldn't go near the man again."

"That's what I thought," Angel said. He wondered how Matt would take it if he told him he thought Chuzah might have healed a bullet wound in Aaron.

Matt turned to Eileen. "You don't think Chuck could have had anything to do with what happened at Angel's—"

"It wasn't Chuck," Eileen said abruptly. The pink had gone from her face, replaced by an unnatural pallor. "He did come to Angel's house right after that other man was on the roof, but he didn't try to do anything bad to us. He thinks he wants to get to know Aaron again."

Matt hooked his elbows over the back of his chair. "I wondered what Moggeridge's angle is for being here. I guess I still do. Nothing was ever simple with Chuck. Be careful around him, Eileen, and don't hesitate to pick up the phone if you need my help. Anytime, day or night, mind."

"I'll be careful." She sounded breathless.

Eileen would not be needing Matt's help, Angel thought.

Matt's eyes sharpened and Angel could almost hear his mind moving. "Someone did get on the roof, though," he said.

Angel tried to send warning glances at Eileen but she was deliberately not looking at him.

"Chuck doesn't like heights," Eileen said. "He's afraid when he's on the rigs. Only money makes him go."

Shoot, Angel hated to hear her make excuses for the bastard.

"Whoever did it wanted to frighten us," Eileen said.

Us. There it was again and Matt was no dummy, not that it mattered if he knew Angel and Eileen were lovers, or it wouldn't if Eileen wasn't likely to be mortified to have the tub event spread around.

"How many bullets do you think were fired?" Matt said, in the most gentle of voices.

"Two," Eileen said promptly. "One hit the edge of the tub and bounced away. It shattered one of the wall mirrors. "If Angel hadn't moved so fast, I think the second shot would have got both of us."

"Interesting," Matt said. "How do you think that would have happened?"

"It would probably have gone through Angel's back and into me, only Angel got us out of the tub too fast for the guy to get the next shot off properly. I expect the skylight was steamed up...too."

She paused with her lips pushed forward and her eyes very wide open. No one responded.

Eileen cleared her throat. "Angel's got great reflexes. We hid in the shower so the...the angle was too hard for the man on the roof to get us."

Angel closed his eyes for an instant. As the saying went, more or less, it was hard to stop a speeding train once its brakes gave out.

"But he did intend to hit us with that second bullet," Eileen said. "He shot a hole in the bottom of the tub. Water went everywhere."

15

Rusty Barnes's house stood a short distance from Bayou Nezpique about twelve miles south of town. He owned the house and kept it in pretty good shape. Neighboring houses were visible but not close.

This was Gracie's afternoon off and she arrived home planning a long soak in the tub later, a nail job and maybe a nap—unless something on TV interested her. But first she'd attend to some business. Gracie always attended to business.

She parked at the side of the house, got out and walked to the back. It worked well, living with Rusty. Mostly their hours separated them. They had their habits and kept to them. He used the front door, she climbed the steps to the gallery overlooking the bayou and went in that way.

At the edge of a sloping, waterlogged lawn, willows dipped their branches into the slowly moving bayou. She saw a pirogue, its single inhabitant standing in the narrow wooden boat to navigate his way upstream. He wore oilskins and looked like a man from any place but Louisiana where heat was what they knew best.

Gracie opened the screen door and let herself into the house. Rusty had added her rental apartment on to one side of the structure. The rest of the house was his domain although she was at ease wandering around there when she felt like it. He had a main floor and a loft. The loft was her favorite place and Rusty had told her to use it as long as he wasn't there.

No loafing around in the loft this afternoon. This evening she was working at the Boardroom and she had her reasons for wanting to look her best.

In the apartment, she made a rapid pass-through, picking up in the living room, the kitchen and eating nook, and the bedroom. Most of her time in the apartment was spent in the bedroom, which she'd made into the hideaway she'd always wanted. She had picked every item carefully: a blond wood four-poster bed with frilly white organza drapes and a matching spread, heaps of soft, embroidered pillows and a white carpet she'd talked Rusty into since she was the first tenant and signed—almost in blood—that she'd be responsible for any damages.

She kicked off her shoes and sighed at the softness beneath her feet. Worth signing in anything Rusty wanted to ask for.

Shedding clothes as she went, Gracie grabbed her fluffy, white terry robe and hurried into the bathroom to take a rapid shower. The bath would come later. For now she enjoyed drying and mussing her short curly hair, smoothing jasmine-scented lotion over her skin and wrapping herself in the robe.

Back in the bedroom she could see fog forming over the bayou and the shapes of the willows turning smudgy beyond rain-splashed windows. Being in her own little place on a day like this was heaven. After all the rotten things life had sent her way, she was finally her own woman. Standing on her own feet, making her own decisions, she had learned how to get what she wanted. Men didn't push her around anymore.

She got a glass of chilled white wine from the kitchen, pulled her wicker chair in front of the windows and settled into the plump, floral cushions.

From here on, Gracie Loder would call all the shots.

It was payback time.

Just faintly, she heard a car engine. It gradually grew louder, then stopped near the house.

Gracie smiled and sipped her wine. Sure her tummy flipped around a bit, but tension excited her.

Soon footsteps jogged up the wooden steps to the back gallery and her intercom rang. She took her time getting up. When she opened the channel, she said, "It's not locked, I'm through the door behind the staircase to the loft," and cut off at once so she had time to return to her chair.

Looking down at herself, she crossed her legs, let the robe fall open all the way past her hip. A little loosening of the belt and her cleavage, which didn't need any help, was impossible to miss.

He came into the apartment and closed the door. The carpets dulled his footsteps. "Gracie?"

"Straight ahead," she called. "In the bedroom."

Very quickly and lightly, she smoothed a hand under a lapel and over one breast. The nipple stood erect and she shuddered. So she liked sex—nothing wrong with that.

He came in, closing the door again, and walked immediately up behind her.

Without a word, he kissed her neck and whispered, "Hi, Gracie," in her ear. She offered him her glass.

"You've been in town more than a week," she said. "What took you so long to come and see me, Chuck?"

"I've got to play things smart this time."

She sniffed. "We played things smart before. You played it so smart I didn't know you'd left town till someone told me. You wouldn't be here now if you hadn't run into me at the Boardroom."

"Yeah, and you were a good girl that night. You kept your mouth shut—and you'll keep it shut. I'm a nice guy so I let you know I was coming back to town. I didn't make any promises."

She was going to close him down before he got started pushing her around. "If you want *anything* from me, you'll treat me the way I want to be treated."

"You asked me to come here today…no, you *told* me." Chuck bit a fingernail, never taking his hard eyes from her face. "We can have a nice chat about old times and be friendly, or I can walk out. Either way, I'm not listening to your bitching. When we were together before I never offered you anything. I didn't have anything to offer. You knew the score."

His tone surprised her. "Not when we met, I didn't." She had hated him for that.

"History," he said shortly.

"I hear you've taken a job with Duhon's," Gracie said. "You'll be working for that Angel DeAngelo. Why do that when you can see he hates your guts?"

"The money's good."

"Of course," she said. "Money." With Chuck it had always been all about money.

He rested his fingers on either side of her neck and gradually slid them along her shoulders, knocking the robe down until it showed off a lot of flesh. She didn't try to change a thing. "Let's go at this another way," she said. "Why would Angel hire you?"

Chuck laughed. "To keep me under his nose and thumb

probably. I don't give a shit why. He won't stop me from getting what I want."

Her heart beat faster. "What's that?"

Again, he laughed. "Everything I've got coming. Don't worry your head about it."

He took the wine back, drained the glass and threw it on the floor. It bounced against the wall and broke.

"Gaddammit," Gracie said, enraged. "Why d'you do that?"

"Because I could. Nice bank shot, huh? I want you to remember, every day of your life, that there's nothing about you that I can't break if I want to."

Sudden changes in his mood were all too familiar. She started to get up but he grabbed her arm and swung her to her feet in front of him. His smile didn't disguise the mean gleam in his eyes.

"If I were you," she said, keeping her voice down, "I'd be real careful how you treat me. If you want to make a good impression in this town, you won't give me any ammunition. And don't doubt I'd use it."

He laughed, pulled her painfully close and kissed her full on the mouth, pushing his tongue into her throat.

Why, even after all her promises to herself, was he still able to excite her? Already she was slick and throbbing. She would have to keep a tight hold on herself because her intention was to make him regret what he couldn't have anymore, not to give it to him.

Chuck raised his face and stared at her. "If you could have sunk me, you'd have done it years ago."

She curled her lip. "If I could have done it without hurting myself in the process, you mean? You are so right." She spat in his face—didn't mean to, but couldn't control the urge.

He wiped the back of a hand across his cheek. "That was stupid. But you are stupid. Now it's time to get everything straight." With one forefinger he unhooked her belt and pulled it from the loops. The robe, already precariously balanced, fell to the floor. She loved the hunger in his eyes.

"Remember what we used to like so much?" he asked, advancing, passing his tongue over his lips. "I bet you're still a little acrobat with flying feet."

"You wrote all that off when you walked out on me," Gracie said. "There's just one thing I want from you—respect. When you see me around this town, you'll treat me like a lady, understand?"

He shook his head and the look on his face was incredulous. "*Lady?* Don't make me laugh."

"Laugh away. If you've got some idea of wheedling your way back into Eileen's good graces, you'd better make sure there's no reason for anyone to think we've got a past."

He passed a forefinger from one of her collarbones to the other. "You don't have to worry about me. All you have to do is remember that I can't afford wagging tongues. And neither can you."

"Keep your mouth shut and listen." She swallowed past a dry throat. He'd always been one to turn nasty, but she could control him. "I get along with everyone in Pointe Judah and I want to keep it that way."

He slapped her, suddenly and hard across the top of one arm. She fell back, rubbing the skin.

"Are you getting my message?" he said. The expression disappeared from his face, just the way it used to when he started into his games.

She shouldn't be naked with him. She shouldn't have deliberately made sure he got turned on. Keeping her eyes on him, she ducked to pick up her robe.

Chuck yanked it from her hands and threw it on the bed. And his hand connected with her bottom, so viscously that tears sprang into her eyes. She held her ground, stood tall and felt grateful her heavy breasts showed no sign of drooping.

He walked around her, briefly touching the place where his hand had connected. "Feel good?" he said. "Does the sting still sex you up?" Another blow landed on her other buttock and she tightened the aching flesh between her legs. She looked at him over her shoulder, glaring, baring her teeth. How easy it was to slip back into the old behavior.

"Stop it," she told him. "I'm respectable. I've got friends. You'll get run out of town if anyone finds out about this."

"This?" He smiled, dipped his head and bit her left nipple until she beat at his head.

He released her and said, "If you see me—anywhere— you'll nod, got it? Just like we're acquaintances. And there was never anything stronger with us than a meal together now and then." Chuck stripped off his shirt.

"Get out," she told him. She'd fantasized about having him here in this room, doing the things they used to do together. The way he was today, she still wanted the sex but he made her nervous. She had so much to lose this time—but she wanted him. However, she intended to be the one who called all the shots when Chuck came running.

He kicked off his shoes and his pants followed his shirt. Black bikini briefs stayed where they were—even if they did have a life of their own.

Gracie trembled. A pure thrill heated her. She put her hands on her hips.

Chuck grinned and started a slow hand clap, alternately slapping her breasts lightly between each beat. "You always did know how to make the best of everything you've got," he said. "I didn't know how much I'd missed you till I walked in here."

"I want you to get out of here," she told him. "And I mean it, Chuck. If you give me any trouble, I'll mess things up for you."

"Oh, sure, you'll mess things up for me. And it'll go both ways. People will find out what you did behind Eileen's back and you'll be on the outside, just like you used to be, and just that fast."

Her eyes stung, but anger made her strong. "When we met you let me think you were single."

"I didn't see you go running when you found out I was married."

Working on the rigs had made sure he stayed hard-bodied. Today he was hard all over and the purpose in his stance didn't mean he would walk away quietly without getting what he needed.

"Are you really here just to be around Aaron?" She had a good idea what Chuck wanted but she wanted to hear him spell it out.

"No," he said. "I've got much bigger plans."

She just bet he did.

"Eileen's made a real success of things," she said. "You didn't expect that to happen, did you?"

His face darkened. "Sure I did. She's a smart girl. I should have given her more credit."

"Is that what you think you're going to do now, give Eileen credit? Do you think you can wheedle your way back in and get your hands on what she's built up?"

A blow to her midsection, just under her diaphragm, stunned her. She fell to her knees, winded, gagging, curled over.

She fought through the pain and expected him to hit her again. When nothing happened, she looked up through eyes swimming in tears.

"It's a hell of a thing," Chuck said evenly. "You just look better and better from every angle."

"Pig," Gracie said through her teeth. She dragged herself to her feet and crossed her arms, keeping her face down. "I want to forget about all of it."

"But you can't forget what you like, can you?" Chuck said. He closed in, spun her around and slid his hands beneath her arms. Holding a breast in each large hand, he walked her to stand beside the bed. He turned her to face him. "And you can't forget who can give you what you like and do it the best anybody can do it."

"Leave me alone."

"Hit me," he said.

Gracie's skin turned cold. Then she heated up inside.

Chuck took her by the throat and hauled her against him, dragged her breasts back and forth across the hair on his chest. "I told you to hit me." He let her go and took a step backward.

A beat set up in Gracie's temples, she felt it in her throat, heard it in her ears. She rubbed her hands together, then pushed him.

His body didn't shift. "This isn't the woman I knew," he said, sneering at her. "The woman I knew could hit hard enough to make me mad. She made me mad enough I had to take her apart. And we both enjoyed that."

"I like to make you happy." She crooked a strong leg and jackknifed her heel into his ribs. He flinched, let out a sharp breath, but didn't try to touch her. A gradual smile took over his expression.

All the saliva in her mouth had drained away. She sweated. And she slapped him with her right hand, then with her left, the fingers spread, the impact shooting through her wrists. Both blows landed just above the waist, at his sides. There would be marks. Gracie looked into his face—that's where they never made marks. Any bruises must be where clothes covered them.

She toppled over, knocked off balance by a single, unexpected shove. On her knees, Grace lunged at his legs with her fists.

Chuck grabbed both of her wrists and stood with a foot clamped on either side of her knees. "You know what to do," he told her. "Do it."

He thrust his pelvis against her face. His erection forced against black cotton briefs…and Gracie's mouth. And she glanced up only once at the way he threw his head back and the veins strained in his neck.

Nipping, sucking, she worked over him until the cotton was sodden and Chuck breathed in sobs. She felt him start to go over the edge and thumped her mouth against him.

Abruptly, he released her arms, stepped back and got rid of the briefs, then he lifted her, rotated her, dropped her on the bed and opened his mouth on her. Gracie shuddered, twisted her hips. "I can't," she panted. "Come here, Chuck." She had never met another man with a tongue like his.

The first ripple of her climax started. Grinning, Chuck lifted his head and flipped her onto her belly.

"Don't stop now," Gracie cried.

He slapped her bottom; slapped it again and again. "I won't stop, baby. We've only just started."

Gracie teetered, awash in the one pain she welcomed. "I'll help you get what you want," she cried. "You tell me what to do and I'll do it. I'll always do what you want." Agitation built until she thrashed around, reaching for him.

He stopped her with one stab of hot, hard flesh. "Now we're singing the same song. It's all about Chuck because you like it that way. Now move with me," he said on a hiss, and their rhythm set up as perfectly as if no years had passed since the last time.

Gracie's laughter came in jagged shrieks.

16

Time to change the balance of power.

He who thinks he calls all the shots needs an attitude adjustment.

Once Eileen left Finn's third-story offices in the Oakdale Mansion, she rode his elevator to the ground floor, then ran up a single flight of stairs to the open balcony surrounding the second floor. A few specialty shops, small professional offices, a coffee shop and a bistro occupied the commercial spaces there.

From a table by the balcony railing outside the coffee shop, she had a good view of both the entrance to the building and Finn's elevator door.

Visions of how she'd blurted out details of the shooting at Angel's, and where she'd been when it took place, brought blood rushing into her face yet again.

She seethed. Angel and Finn, or probably just Angel, had set her up.

Angel's motorcycle stood in a parking spot in front of the mansion. Convenient. She could see it from where she was and if she had to sit outside the coffee shop until morning, she didn't intend to leave until she had confronted Mr. DeAngelo, alone.

He was too sure of himself. All that silently observant, distant confidence—his face for the world—brought him the respect of most. Well, Eileen was confident, too, and with the way he must have talked Finn into getting her to the Duhon offices today, he'd stepped over the line.

He would wither under her cleverly controlled rage. She'd make sure he knew it was there, but she'd practice a little poker face of her own.

She kicked a balcony railing, hard, and grabbed for her foot. Damn it, now she'd probably broken a toe.

The waitress, Mary-Jo, refilled Eileen's coffee cup. "I love this time of year," the woman said, wiping her free hand on her bright orange apron. "The place looks like the North Pole. And I never get tired of the music."

A decorated tree stood in the center of the main floor and lighted garlands draped the balcony handrails. Tinsel and glitter adorned every spare inch.

"It's pretty," Eileen said, grateful for the diversion.

"The fair's next weekend," Mary-Jo said, a big smile brightening her round face. "I'm lookin' forward to that. I saw your boy over on Main Street working on the decorations. It's really going to be a show. They're putting up a Christmas village."

"Emma Duhon's in charge so it'll be something," Eileen said. "I'm glad Aaron picked up some extra hours over there. He needs new shocks on that old Impala of his. I'll never be able to complain that he isn't a worker."

"He's a nice boy." Mary-Jo patted Eileen's shoulder and her look communicated that, like everyone else in Pointe Judah, she knew Aaron had been through his troubles but he was okay now.

"Thanks," Eileen said.

"He's a looker, too, and mature. Looks older than sixteen or seventeen. It's a good thing he takes after your family. He could be Finn's brother."

Eileen didn't say, *much younger,* or mention that Finn didn't wear his dark, curly hair slicked back into a tail. "Don't you tell Aaron that. He's already got a big head."

Mary-Jo moved to another table. Aaron was doing well. What did worry Eileen was the possibility that Chuck could shake their son's determination to get best education he could. "Get through high school, then go on the rigs," Chuck used to tell him. "More schooling is a waste of time when you can be making good money." Not for the first time, she puzzled over Chuck being in Pointe Judah on a so-called break when he had lived for his big paychecks and to throw money around with cronies, for so long.

Emma Duhon pushed open the front door on the floor below and came in. Eileen hoped she got pleasure out of the tree that worm, Finn, had used as bait to get Eileen to his suite.

Emma glanced up and spotted Eileen. What were the chances? Eileen didn't feel much like talking and shrank back a bit, but it was too late, so she reversed directions and waved.

Promptly, Emma climbed the stairs. Her honey-colored hair stood out in tight curls. She looked healthy. She looked happy. And she looked very pregnant.

"You shouldn't be climbing all those stairs," Eileen said, leaning to kiss Emma's cheek when she arrived. "You've had a shock."

Emma's expression turned serious. "That's a problem. I'm still looking over my shoulder everywhere I go. But I'm as healthy as a horse—no thanks to that pervert. I need some coffee before I face Finn's hovering."

"Hovering, huh?" Eileen smiled. "It isn't easy to think of that big, tough brother of mine hovering over anything—except you. You make him so happy."

"He makes me ecstatic," Emma said. "He fusses too much is all."

Mary-Jo came with her carafe and a mug and poured for Emma. Eileen didn't miss the curious glance Mary-Jo gave Emma. The rumor machine had been working overtime.

"Did you see that?" Emma muttered as soon as they were alone. "The way Mary-Jo looked at me? Everyone thinks I made it up about that man. I won't argue about it, but I'm going to track him down."

Alarmed, Eileen put a hand on the other woman's wrist. "Please, let Matt take care of things. Finn won't let this drop."

"Mmm." Emma didn't look convinced. "We'll see."

"Aren't you going to ask me what I'm doing here?" Eileen said. Emma was the closest friend she had and they shared most things.

"Sure I am. What are you doing here? Are you rolling in so much dough you can afford to close Poke Around for an afternoon in the middle of the Christmas rush?"

Eileen laughed. "Suky-Jo is working for me full-time now. And one of the nice things about having old friends move their salon next door to the shop is that it's easy for Frances or Lynette, or one of their girls, to keep an eye on things if both Suky-Jo and I have to go out." A walk-through had been built between the gift shop and the hair salon and the arrangement worked well. It certainly increased business for both shops.

Originally Lynette had opened a nail salon in a tiny group of shops off Main Street. That had been years earlier and business had boomed. Then Frances, a hairstylist, became her partner and the business eventually outgrew the space. Moving to the much bigger shop next to Poke Around had been perfect, even if Eileen didn't always love the music they tended to "share."

She felt Emma watching her and looked up.

"You haven't said why you're here," Emma said.

Eileen gave a brief explanation, skirting the bathtub details but including the way she'd been ambushed by Finn and Angel. She didn't mention the surprise tree.

"Whoa," Emma said and left her lips parted. She leaned forward. "Hold it right there. A shooting at Angel's and you were there? This is the first I've heard of it."

Eileen's brain moved fast. "Angel's been in law enforcement. But you know that. He wanted to do some investigating himself before the place was overrun, so he kept quiet about it."

"And told you not to say anything?"

She felt trapped. "I could tell it was important to him to buy some time."

"Threats to me, a shooting at Angel's. Could they somehow be connected?" Emma said.

"I don't know. But this isn't a very big place so I wouldn't be surprised."

"You must have figured Matt would have to know eventually," Emma said. "What got you so mad about being there when he was told?"

She breathed deeply. "I didn't like being brought to Finn's without knowing Matt would be there."

"Why?"

Why? "I just don't like being manipulated." She'd die if the sex-in-the-tub story became town gossip. How they would all love it!

"You've been avoiding Angel," Emma said.

"How do you know?"

"Finn and Angel talk about most things."

Eileen didn't think that was a comforting idea. "Do they? Did anyone mention to you that Chuck's decided to turn up again and make trouble?"

"I know he's here and making nice with you."

"He says he wants to be a father to Aaron. At the same time he tells me I should stay home to be there for Aaron—as if his son was seven rather than almost seventeen. And he more or less told me to stay away from Angel. Can you believe the man's nerve? I don't know why he's here. We're divorced and that's never going to change. He's out of my life."

Emma settled her hands on her belly and Eileen could see the baby moving. "He may think he can get back together with you," Emma said.

"Don't say that," Eileen told her. "It makes me sick to think about it."

"Okay." Emma moved her chair closer to Eileen's and looked her in the eye. "Do you care for Angel?"

Eileen swallowed and pursed her lips.

"Don't give me the silent treatment," Emma said. "Tell me the truth."

"Yes, I do. But that doesn't mean I'm not worried about that, too. I haven't always made… Oh, I might as well be honest. I've made poor choices in life. I don't want to make another one."

"You think Angel would be a poor choice?" Emma's eyebrows rose.

"*No*, probably not." Eileen tried not to think of the night at his place, and failed. "Anyway, who says either of us are thinking of doing any choosing? We're mature people. We'd think carefully about anything like that—if it was ever a question."

"Right," Emma said, her glance sliding away. "So, I'll ask my question in a different way. Why are you sitting here?"

"I'm having coffee."

"Don't be smart with me, girlfriend. You don't sit around in this place. In fact, I don't think I've ever seen you here before."

"Okay. But if you tell anyone I said so, I'll deny it. I'm waiting for Angel to leave the offices. He's got a lot of explaining to do."

Emma smiled and the effect was wicked. "The gauntlet is going down. Goody. That's a great start. Our house is empty if you want to go there and talk." The switch to an innocent air wasn't convincing.

"I'm sure Finn would love it if we took over your place," Eileen said. "But thanks, anyway. I do wish there was somewhere we could go and be sure we wouldn't be interrupted. It's hard to be anonymous and private in a town this size."

"You could get a suite at Damalis's on Rice Street," Emma said, grinning now. "Of course, there would be questions about that. Then there's the Roll Inn, but—"

"Stop," Eileen said, chuckling. "The day hasn't come when I seek out motels with hourly rates. Thanks for the idea anyway. You'd better go to Finn before he sends out a search party."

Emma wrinkled up her nose. "I know. Shall I tell Angel you're waiting for him here?"

"Don't you dare," Eileen said.

"Well, if you don't get down there, he'll be on his bike and you'll miss him."

Eileen looked through the railings, saw Angel leaving the elevator and shot from her chair. "Later," she called back to Emma. "Behave yourself. Love you!"

17

She raced down the marble steps and across the wide foyer, dodging shoppers and office workers as she went. For an instant she lost sight of Angel and almost panicked.

She broke through a clot of people near the front door and cannoned into him.

"Eileen, love," he said. "What's happened?" He took her by the shoulders and examined her face as if he expected to find bruises or blood.

"Nothing's happened," she said through her teeth, carefully extricating herself. "I was trying to catch up with you, that's all."

"You were?" He took her by the elbow and, rather than make a scene, she let him steer her outside. "I was going to come looking for you."

Eileen had made a personal pact to avoid smart comebacks. For now. "This worked well then," she said.

They stood on the sidewalk in front of the bike.

"What did you have in mind?" Angel said.

Eileen frowned at him.

He had the grace to look uncomfortable. With his hands stuffed into the pockets of his jeans, he drew up his shoulders and grimaced. "That didn't sound so good, did it?"

She shook her head. "What I've got in mind is to give you hell." Eileen kept a straight face. His awkwardness made it hard to stay as angry as she wanted to be at him.

His mouth turned down and he nodded slowly. "I was afraid of that."

She stepped out of the way of people on the sidewalk and Angel took her by the hand. He stood in the gutter by the bike and urged her down beside him. "We can't talk here, cher," he said.

Eileen pried his fingers from hers. "Sure we can as long as we're quiet about it."

He smiled faintly. "I don't suppose you want to come back to my place."

"No. I wouldn't. Isn't it a crime scene by now?"

Angel winced. "They'll have tape everywhere and cops tromping all over the house."

She nodded. "Then you'll understand why I pass on that idea. We could go to the library."

"Now you're being funny."

"What's wrong with the library?"

"Grrr." He looked at the overcast sky. "We'd have to whisper in the library."

"So?"

"Forget the library," Angel said. "Tell me one thing. Are you mad at me?"

"Yes, very." She crossed her arms. "You owe me an apology."

"I apologize."

"Oh!" Eileen glanced around and lowered her voice. "That's a general apology. Not good enough." And he was doing a creditable job of taking some of the steam out of her arguments.

"Okay," he said. "Let's go. We'll walk."

This would be easier if she didn't weaken each time she looked at him.

"You don't like the idea of walking?" he asked.

They could walk and talk, as long as they didn't take so long and go so far that getting back became a problem. "I do," she said. "It's fine."

Once out of the main Oakdale complex, they started off toward the south. Minutes passed, stretched to many minutes before she said, "You set me up."

"That wasn't my intention. You wouldn't talk to me—I was ready to do anything to get in the same space with you. Remember me coming to the shop? Remember what *you* did to *me?*"

"I told you we shouldn't see each other for a while."

He bent his head until she met his eyes. "You made it sound like you didn't want to see me again. Period," he said.

"So you had me walk into a trap with Matt because you figured I wouldn't make a fuss in front of him." She stood still. "And look what happened. I've never been so embarrassed."

"I didn't know you'd say that, did I?" he said. "It went that way is all. Finn and I figured Matt had to be filled in and that you needed to be there."

She looked up at him. When he looked back, his gray eyes darkened. He stared.

"If you had let me know first—let me know what you intended to tell him—I wouldn't have made a complete fool of myself. He didn't need to know about…you know."

"Yeah, I know." Slapping a hand onto the trunk of a young sycamore, he swung slowly around the tree. He managed a collision and made an unnecessary effort to steady her. "I do know, Eileen. I wouldn't deliberately do anything like that to you."

She wouldn't allow herself to soften toward him.

"We were interrupted that night," he said. "The timing was the worst. Don't you think we should do something about that?"

Eileen made fists on his chest and prepared to tell him what she thought about *his* timing. She sighed and let it go. There was something almost wonderfully childlike about the psyche of some males—or maybe that should be about the way some males blurted out exactly what was on their minds.

"What is Matt going to do next?" she said.

Angel shrugged and frowned. "We'll see. So far he hasn't turned up a thing about the attack on Emma."

"I don't think he believes she was attacked," Eileen said. "That makes me mad. I've known Emma a long time and she's the most sane woman I know. Do you think these events are tied together? Whatever happened to Aaron, the guy in Ona's parking lot and the crazy at your house?"

"This isn't a big place. All the potential victims know each other. Sure, I think there's a connection. But I don't know what it is, yet."

Eileen looked at her hands on his chest and dropped them. She was allowing him to lull her into his corner. Well, it wasn't going to work. "You need to apologize to me properly."

"I already apologized."

"Not after I told you how you embarrassed me." The anger freshened.

"I'm sorry about that."

"Nothing's changed. I know what my responsibilities are and I won't be neglecting them again."

Angel pulled her against him and there was no softness left in his eyes. "Don't be a little fool. Your son isn't a child anymore. You don't have to be there to put sandwiches in his lunch box or to make his dinner or to wash his clothes."

"He washes his own—"

"You know what I'm saying to you," Angel told her. "He's going to move on as soon as he's through high school."

Now she was really mad. "You keep tabs on Sonny."

"You can't begin to imagine how different that is."

She wondered if she ought to know exactly how different. "Is Sonny a danger to Aaron?"

He snorted. "I figured out almost at once that you thought Sonny was too worldly for Aaron, but I didn't think that you were afraid he was dangerous." Angel closed his mouth. His eyes moved away and he rubbed her arm absently.

Eileen tipped her head to one side. "What is it?"

"Hmm? Nothing." His expression suggested otherwise. "I've already told you why I have to keep an eye on Sonny, but I don't think he's a danger to Aaron. I think he's more likely to take care of him. Not that Aaron needs that, but having a friend who knows the score isn't a bad thing."

"What did Matt think about the shooting near Chuzah's place?"

He put a hand on either side of her face. "I didn't tell him."

"Finn must have, then."

"I didn't tell Finn, either."

She didn't understand. "Then how is Matt supposed to investigate what's going on? You've already said there's got to be a connection here."

"I still think there is." He sounded too reasonable.

"The police can't do their job with only part of the evidence."

Angel, looking at her mouth with a distracted air, wound her nerves tight.

"Angel?" she said.

"I think Chuzah could be a good man to have on our side. He doesn't like cops."

"That doesn't make it right to hold things back," she said. "It's a miracle I didn't mention the bayou shooting. I did say the boys had been out there."

Angel's expression sharpened. "What else do you think we ought to tell Matt about that night?"

"The whole truth." She snapped back at him.

"Sonny and Aaron thought they heard someone following them in the swamp," Angel said. "They did happen to be pretty shaken up because they were lost, but we'll discount that."

"Darn it, Christian, I'm going to Matt right now to tell him everything. What are you planning to do? Keep things to yourself about Aaron until someone does shoot him?"

"You just answered your own question."

"What?" He stood too close and she gave him a push. "You think we should wait until Aaron gets shot, maybe killed?"

"That's not what I said. Aaron wasn't shot. There's no solid evidence that anyone followed him."

"But they heard a shot. And he collapsed."

"What did they hear? For sure? Do we know why he collapsed? He wasn't wounded. There's no bullet."

Eileen felt very cold and sick. "So what are we going to do?" she asked quietly.

"We can't lock those two boys away, can we?"

"No," she said. "What then?"

"We're going to be careful, make sure Sonny and Aaron continue to be careful, and we're going to be vigilant. Finn's in when we need him and Matt'll be all over anything he can get his hands on. He might get a make on the bullets I gave him from my bathroom."

She spread her arms. "This feels like doing nothing."

"Kind of," he said. "Only not quite. This guy's been having too much fun. He'll try something else. When he does, we'll be waiting."

Her scalp tightened. "So we're putting our money on luck? We're betting on him messing up again?"

"No. Just betting on him showing up again—and catching him."

18

"We're gonna regret this," Sonny said. "I've got this feeling and I'm not into that sort of thing."

"Having feelings?" Aaron said. "That's what you'd like everyone to think. This is my decision. The other time we came, you were the one hot to get here. This time I'm going to see Chuzah and that's it. I don't want you with me. I *told* you I don't want you with me. Say the word and I'll let you out of the car."

Sonny slid deep in his seat beside Aaron in his Impala. "If you're going, I'm going."

Rather than grin because he was glad of Sonny's company, Aaron sniffed and frowned hard through the windshield. "I need to talk to him on my own. At least for a bit. You gonna make something out of that?"

"Uh-uh." Sonny shook his head. His head needed a shave and the sharp point at the center of his peaked hairline showed clearly. "He could be somewhere else. If he is there, maybe he won't feel like letting us in."

Aaron had already thought about that. "I'm not leaving till I do see him." He had issues he couldn't discuss with anyone but Chuzah.

The ancient Impala he had bought from the lady who played the organ at St. William's Catholic Church moved regally, like a ship through a slight swell. His shock absorbers were shot and the vehicle undulated over every dent and crack in the road. The road to Chuzah's kept the car in constant motion.

Aaron had painted the car bronze-orange, or so the paint had been called. Everyone hated it except him. He guessed he was the one who mattered.

That lady organist had bought a retractable hardtop Miata, yellow, and it took longer for her to get in or out than she probably spent driving. She smiled a lot more, though.

Sonny grabbed the back of his neck when they hit the next bump. "You're gonna give me a whiplash." The black garb settled around his thin body in folds. "You know we don't have to ask permission to do what we want, don't you? We're adults."

"Sure, I know," Aaron said. "But I can't afford to get in any trouble. I've got to stay clean and get through school. I'm not doing anything to mess with that now. Mom stuck with me through everything. She smothers a bit, but I can cope." He thought his mom was pretty cool. She'd stuck with him even when he told her he didn't want her.

Sonny put his elbows on his knees and propped his chin. "I don't want any trouble, either. It's just I'm sick of being treated like a kid on curfew."

"You aren't," Aaron said. Sonny in one of these moods could be a pain in the ass.

"We don't have to do what anyone else tells us," Sonny said, like his brain had gotten stuck.

Aaron was already tight all over. "I know what I can and

can't do," he said. "But I don't see what it has to do with anything."

"If we want to hang out together in our spare time, we can. We don't need Eileen's permission—or Angel's."

Now Aaron got it. "Parents overreact sometimes. Let it go." He pointed to a broken-down shed. "That's where we left the bikes last time."

"Yeah, I didn't expect to find them when we finally got back."

"We wouldn't have if people didn't stay away from here. Who wants to drive on this when there's a good road going the same way? Keep your eyes open. It can't be more than a couple of miles to where I want to go. I haven't been there in the daylight."

"D'you think Eileen's done thinking I'm the enemy?" Sonny said.

Aaron considered. "Could be. She had a shock that night, what with my dad showing up and everything. You're right about one thing."

"Like?"

"She's gotta let go a bit. Not that I don't want to be around her."

Sonny blew out a long breath. "But you want her to trust you?"

Aaron glanced sideways at him. "Maybe." He knew that was it. He wanted back where he used to be and everyone thought he could be counted on to do the right thing. "I like it at Sadie and Sam's. Never thought I'd get off on sellin' cheese. And I keep getting odd jobs like I did before, so its pretty okay again. How about you? Sadie and Sam say their deli-sandwich sales go up over the weekends when you're there."

They both had jobs at the shop.

"Yeah." Sonny laughed. "New Yorkers are deli-sandwich experts, didn't you know that? I've got 'em all fooled. Sam told me he's thinking of doing the sandwiches at lunchtime every day of the week."

"Brilliant!" Aaron said and laughed. "More money."

"Miranda was in yesterday," Sonny said. "You haven't forgotten her, have you?"

"Hell, no. I've been a bit busy, in case you haven't noticed."

Sonny snickered. "She said you look like Johnny Depp but she didn't know if that's because you wear your hair in a tail and look a bit like a pirate."

Girls thought Johnny Depp was cool. "She said that, huh?"

"Yeah." Sonny drew up his knees and his laugh got louder. "She doesn't like him."

Aaron gave him a good dig in the side. "I hope something important to you falls off," he said. "That's what liars deserve."

Sonny chuckled on, then cleared his throat. "I told Sam we should try bagels and lox. I thought he wouldn't know what I was talking about, or he'd laugh me out. But he said it was a good idea. We're going to do it. He's also thinking about putting in an espresso machine. Sadie says that's caterin' to loiterers."

Aaron slammed on the brakes and the car shuddered to a slightly sideways stop.

"What?" Sonny hollered. He pulled himself up straighter and looked out. "What d'you do that for?"

"Over there," Aaron said. The hair on his arms stood up. "Locum."

"Huh?" That got Sonny's full attention and he located the

Weimaraner, hovering at the side of the road with one front paw raised. "He came out that night I went for Angel and Eileen. To guide us in."

Aaron watched the dog who stood motionless, looking back at him. "Yeah, so you said. Only this time, Chuzah doesn't know we're coming."

"Creepy," Sonny said. "Let's turn around."

"I'm wrong," Aaron said.

Sonny rubbed his palms together and checked through the back window. "What d'you mean? We're gonna get rear-ended if we stay here."

"When was the last time you saw another vehicle on this road today?"

Sonny glanced around again. "I haven't seen one."

"I'm wrong because Chuzah does know we're coming," Aaron said. "Don't ask me how he knows but he sent Locum to show us the way. The dog wouldn't just come."

Sonny made a strangled noise.

"Settle down," Aaron said. "Chuzah didn't hurt us before and he won't now."

"It's the creepsville stuff with the dog and with the guy knowing we're coming that I don't like." Sonny straightened his back. "That's all garbage. The dog must have gotten out."

Ignoring him, Aaron drove forward slowly until he was parallel with Locum. The dog dropped his paw and walked ahead, repeatedly looking at the car over his shoulder. Aaron followed until Locum stopped, raised his head and gave a single bark. Where he stood the grass was long but looked bent and broken. There was a wide-enough space between at least the first trees for the Impala to pass through.

Aaron checked his mirrors and made stately progress from

the road onto the faintly marked track that almost instantly took him into the cover of tall trees.

"Shit," Sonny said with feeling. "This is it. I recognize it now. Last time we left the cars by the road and walked in, but this is where we came after you that night."

"I'd rather not leave the car by the road," Aaron said, watching Locum, who continued his obvious guide-dog routine.

"Why not? Because you don't want anyone to have a clue where we've gone?"

"We're okay," Aaron told Sonny. "You aren't carrying, are you?"

"Nah."

Aaron grimaced. "You are. Chuzah won't like it."

"Chuzah won't know."

"Wanna bet?" Aaron slowed even more. Ahead, the track ran to an opening between trees and tall bushes. He put on the brakes and switched off. "Stay here. I'll come back for you."

"No way," Sonny said. "I don't believe in any of this magic crap. I'm only coming with you because I think the guy's missing some gray cells and you may need backup. You've got to stop thinking about him. We don't belong here."

"Remember my side?" Aaron said, automatically touching his ribs on the left. "Even the bruises are gone now."

"I made a mistake, that's all," Sonny said. "There weren't any shots. You weren't hit. We got worked up out here and imagined a bunch of stuff is all."

Aaron got out and approached the break. Locum gave what looked like a smile and ran ahead. His paws hammered on the wooden stairs up to the cabin and he sat at the top, his tongue lolling.

It really would be better if he'd come alone, Aaron decided. Not that he could change anything now. Sonny walked slowly along behind him.

The Morgan was parked in its place. In daylight rows of growing things hugged the ground, and crosshatched canes supported vines.

"I don't think those are flowers," Sonny said. "Or any vegetables I've seen before."

Aaron gave a short laugh. "You're building it all up, buddy. You're from Brooklyn. You wouldn't know a carrot from a cornstalk."

"We got carrots in Brooklyn," Sonny said, deliberately broadening his accent and waving his hand. "We got *cawn*. There's grocery stores all over. Believe me, those ain't no vegetables."

Aaron sniggered.

They stood side by side and looked up the steps to the front door. It was closed. The colored lights were on in the window but were not real obvious in the afternoon light.

"Now what?" Sonny whispered.

"Chuzah," Aaron yelled, and Sonny jumped. "Chuzah, it's Aaron and Sonny."

Sonny clutched his chest. "You about killed me," he said. "Yellin' like that."

Locum stood, his ears perked, and stared at the door.

"Shit," Sonny muttered.

The dog crossed the gallery, planted a foot and pushed the door open.

"Holy, crap." Sonny's voice disappeared up the scale and he held Aaron's arm.

"You here finally?" Chuzah's voice, not as loud as before,

came from inside. "You sure take your time. Come on, come on, I don't got the whole of my life to wait for you."

Aaron broke away from Sonny's hand and jogged up the steps. He went into the house without looking back. "I've got to talk to you alone," he said in a rush. "Sonny's here, but I've got to talk to you first."

The inside looked just as it had before, except Chuzah was stretched out on one of the couches and he didn't wear a turban. His robes were as voluminous as ever, but more subdued, mostly in shades of brown. Short and oiled, his tightly curled hair showed off a perfectly shaped head. Aaron didn't know a whole lot about these things, but he thought Chuzah would be considered very handsome. The bridge of his nose was narrow, his lips sharply defined, his eyebrows arched and a bit winged above his black, uptilted eyes.

Aaron looked closer. "What's wrong?" he said and his stomach made a turn. "You look sick. Are you sick? Do you need a doctor?"

Chuzah laughed, dropped back his head and showed his very white teeth. "I am all the doctor I need. Chuzah is not sick. A little tired, perhaps, but that will soon pass. It's the time for it to pass now. Already I feel stronger."

Sonny crept into the room and stood just inside.

"The quiet boy," Chuzah said, holding a long hand, with its silver-tipped nails, out to Sonny. "Come here, quiet boy. You haven't had many friends, or so you think, but I am your friend. Just as Angel is your friend and this fine Aaron—and even Eileen who sounds like the shrew sometimes. Forgive her, she worries too much."

Sonny gave Chuzah's hand a horrified glance, sidled forward with his face averted and reached until they touched fingers. This brought a memorable Chuzah laugh and he clasped Sonny to give a hard shake.

Immediately, Aaron offered his own hand and he and Chuzah locked fingers. Aaron looked into the man's face and saw joy, but also fatigue.

"Locum needs to run," Chuzah said, looking at Sonny. "Would you take him for me? He doesn't need a leash, just company."

The dog's head, Aaron noticed, jerked sharply to one side. *Locum doesn't need company.* Chuzah was paying attention to Aaron's request for privacy.

"Out there?" Sonny said, hooking a thumb over his shoulder. "In the swamp?"

"No, no, boy. Use your head. Back the way you came in, between the trees. He likes that. Then he'll make sure you get back."

Sonny narrowed his soft eyes. "This is to get rid of me. Fess up, Aaron, you told him you wanted me out of the way."

Chuzah pulled himself to sit up and set his feet on the floor, he stood, like a great tree. "It was I who asked the favor, not your friend. And you have your weapon to keep you safe."

Sonny's olive skin turned sallow.

Backing away, Locum following, Sonny left and they heard his footsteps on the stairs.

Chuzah approached the altar where candles burned. He took a small bag from the folds of his robes, opened it and sprinkled what appeared to be dust on the open flames. At first they dimmed as if they would go out, but then burst to brighter light.

He couldn't make himself ask, but Aaron wanted to know what the man was doing.

Once the bag was closed again, with a length of twine wrapped tightly around it and tied, Chuzah held it out to Aaron.

He looked into the man's eyes, stepped closer with his hands behind his back. The beat of his heart was a drum in his chest and a rhythmic plucking at his temples.

Aaron could see only Chuzah's eyes, the darkness—the distance—a pulling force.

But the force promised strength, not peril.

Chuzah put the bag on the palm of his hand and brought it closer to Aaron, who took it. Held it tightly in a closed fist.

"Good." Chuzah nodded. "Keep it with you at all times. Be careful you are not parted from it, Aaron. Will you promise me this?"

For moments Aaron hesitated, looking at his own hand, then he nodded. "Yes." He slid the bag into a pocket in his jeans. "What is it? What's it for?"

"Don't concern yourself with it," Chuzah told him. "Consider it a remembrance from a friend. When you touch it, think of strength and safety."

Chuzah frowned. He rubbed first one elbow, then the other, and when he saw how Aaron watched him he said, "I have exercised too hard. I am stiff. Sit. We'll have something to drink."

When the man walked, the faint jingling sounded from his ankles and the heavy belt of bones slung loosely at his waist.

"I want to ask some questions," Aaron said. If he waited any longer, he would completely lose his nerve. "About the dog. About Locum."

Standing beside a cabinet, pouring orange fluid from a flask into two glasses, Chuzah paused and faced Aaron. He raised his eyebrows. "What about him? He is looking after Sonny now."

"Yes," Aaron said. "But does he always stay here, or wherever you tell him to be?"

"I don't understand."

Aaron considered how to talk about his experience on that early morning outside his house. "I think I saw him three days ago—early in the morning. He looked at me. He wasn't close, but I could see he was bigger, like he had made himself much bigger. But I knew his eyes."

"You," Chuzah said, pointing at Aaron, "are too imaginative. But you have experienced more than you should have at your age. That is the reason."

And that, Aaron thought, was not an answer. "The dog was large. Like a large wolf. It ran fast without moving." He paused, watching for signs that Chuzah was laughing at him. He saw none. "And when the shot came, the wolf-dog howled."

Slowly, Chuzah approached. He gave one glass to Aaron and drank from his own. "Orange juice," he said. "For energy. You're sure you heard a shot?"

"I think so." He was sure now even if he hadn't been at the time. "First crashing sounds, then the shot. The dog howled and there was crashing again. As if someone was running away. Just like…like the sounds in the swamp." He touched his brow and felt sweat running freely.

"And you think what you saw was Locum? He was there to help you?"

"Yes. To protect me."

"Drink your juice. If you saw the dog, then the dog was there and he frightened the enemy away. That was good. But now it's over."

"He did look more like a wolf, except for his eyes."

"Then perhaps he chose to look like a wolf to be more fearsome," Chuzah said. "And perhaps you were dreaming." He nodded and smiled, like a parent over the bed of a child waking up from a nightmare.

He could have dreamed it. Chuzah's answers remained non-answers. He was, Aaron decided, supposed to make his own interpretations of what he had seen…if he had seen anything.

The scratch of claws climbed the outside stairs, and footsteps followed. After a knock on the door, Sonny put his head inside. "I've got to tell you something. You'll know it soon enough anyway."

Chuzah poured another glass of juice and gave it to Sonny. He didn't press him.

"The police are at Angel's house now," Sonny said. "He called to tell me. I had to tell him where we are and all he said was for us to stay here if we're okay."

"You are okay," Chuzah said. "You shall both eat until you're told to go back."

"Three nights ago, late in the evening, someone shot out a skylight in Angel's bathroom," Sonny said to Aaron. "It happened when I was at your house. It must have been while Angel was showing Eileen the renovations."

Aaron swallowed. His throat dried and he drank the sweet juice. "How could it have been that night? They didn't say anything when they came back."

"Sometimes people try to protect others," Chuzah said. "This happened late, three nights ago?"

"Yes," Sonny said. "Angel just said so."

Aaron looked from Chuzah to Sonny. "Why did the police take so long to investigate?"

"I don't think they knew about it until today," Sonny said.

"And you didn't, either?" Aaron said.

Sonny shook his head. "Nothing. Remember how your mom sent me home? She was mad and she sent me home."

"She was upset," Chuzah said.

A skylight shot out. And only hours later, there had been the sound of another shot—in his own backyard. Aaron let a breath out slowly. He smiled and felt lighter. "A hoax," he said. "This is all a silly joke."

Sonny sat down suddenly and drank his juice in earnest.

"It's good to hear you so confident," Chuzah said. "Will you share your thoughts?"

Aaron leaned against the cushions in his chair. "Someone is shooting, just to shoot. Three times, they've done it. No one could miss three times if they really wanted to hit someone."

19

Angel let the door swing shut behind him and stood at Eileen's shoulder. The police station lobby was empty—almost. A gray tabby cat overflowed the seat of a metal folding chair, one of a row of similar chairs. A green eye gave them the once-over and closed again.

"Where is everyone?" Eileen whispered. "Shouldn't it be busy?"

"We're not in church," Angel whispered back, and bought himself a narrow stare. "I hear voices in Matt's office. He is one angry man these days."

Eileen didn't comment, but she nodded and leaned her elbows on the reception desk.

"I always expect to see Carley out here, but I guess she has other things she does," Angel said. "She's probably gone home." The female officer seemed like the glue that held the place together.

Since Eileen remained silent, he did what he had always been able to do, he put his body in neutral, relaxed, and breathed deeply even while he was aware of the physical power coiled inside himself.

He listened to Matt's voice until it became a drone and melded with the overhead fan.

A cool current wove across Angel's skin. He felt still, inside and out. His mind, quiet, calm, drew away and he recalled, faintly, other times when this separation of his mind and body had imposed itself.

He focused on Eileen's back, the way she crossed one foot over the other, how her ankles were narrow beneath cropped, yellow linen pants. She felt a long way from him but he could reach her the instant he had to.

Her hair rippled, lifted a little as if a breeze passed.

There was no breeze.

She was in danger. A fleeting image of dark eyes came and went and he felt as if he'd been winded. Whose eyes were they? How were they connected to Eileen being in danger?

I have seen those eyes.

Startled by his thoughts he said, "Stop," almost under his breath, and he physically shook himself, stretched his fingers. The coldness remained, but he was completely present to himself again.

This, these manifestations, had left him when he turned his back on the work he'd once done for the CIA in South America. He'd come away from it all and gone into ATF because he didn't want to see what others couldn't anymore. *The best interrogator in the service.* That's what they had called him because he had taken men who had endured everything but death and not talked, yet when Angel DeAngelo finished with them, they had revealed every secret and would have told him more had there been more to tell.

Angel breathed again, deliberately, and went to stand beside Eileen. He put an arm around her shoulders.

Matt stalked into the hallway. He gave them a two-fingered, thumb-cocked, point. "I'll get to you shortly," he said, then walked deeper into the building and out of sight.

"Did you hear that?" Eileen said. "Give a man a little bit of power and he goes mad."

Angel decided to let the comment pass.

The front door opened again and a guy with more gray hair on his face and exposed chest than he had on his head walked in. He went directly to a coffee urn on a card table in one corner, helped himself to a paper cup and filled it to the brim. It stopped. Bending over, flapping the wet fingers of his free hand, he slurped from the rim of the cup until the coffee just about stopped running down the side.

"Good coffee?" Eileen said, surprising Angel.

The man gave her a dark-toothed leer. "Gotta come in this place for my coffee after the bank closes and they finish serving at the shelter. I'd rather be over there at the bank. They got better chairs." He sat down.

Eileen turned to Angel. "So why did we have to come over here *right away?*" she said quietly. "You can see how much of a hurry Matt's in. I'd have told him to hold his horses."

Once more Angel didn't choose to respond. He and Eileen had still been walking near the Oakdale Mansion Center when Matt's call came in. The light had been fading, but they had so much to say.

"I still can't believe you told Aaron and Sonny to stay at that madman's place in the swamp," Eileen said. "You don't know what he's capable of. They've been there for hours. He could be a pedophile."

"Who you callin' a peedophile, lady?"

Angel swung around. The coffee-drinker, little finger

sticking out from his cup in a queenly parody, glared at him. "We aren't talking to you," Angel said.

"I don't want to be here," Eileen muttered.

"Who does?" He needed to put her mind at rest about the boys. "Chuzah's okay. I know we don't have to worry about the boys being with him." The one thing he couldn't tell her was that his instincts about people had saved lives, had saved *his* life.

She turned a little pink and shook back the long black hair that made his fingers want to play. "Maybe Chuzah is okay, but he's not suitable."

"Gimme a break," Angel said. He did love looking at her. She'd looked particularly good in his bathtub—before that fool arrived on the roof. "They were going to stay and have something to eat there and then leave. They could be on their way home by now."

Eileen looked at the ceiling. "What were they going to eat? Bone soup?"

He laughed and she took a deep enough breath to turn him hard. She had beautiful breasts.

And he should be concentrating, something he usually found easy.

She touched his arm, which didn't help him stay focused. "Just ignore me," she said. "I don't know why I can't keep it together. Every little thing sets me off. I embarrass *me*."

A current, hard and fast, brought back the sensation that there was something he already knew. He'd forgotten something. But he'd seen what he needed to know. For a second, a stick figure jerked before his face—like the ones he'd finally left behind in South America. It shook him so badly he gasped. A stick figure wearing a dress. Then a raised hand fell and the figure disappeared.

Please, God, not this again.

"You okay, Angel?" Eileen asked.

Very quickly, he kissed her earlobe.

"Christian," she hissed, but she was smiling. The smile straightened out. "Do you have any sort of feeling that something's about to happen? I don't mean something big. Just anything."

He raised his chin and looked down at her. "Lack of evidence is a big problem. How do you make progress with a case when there's no evidence other than a couple of mangled bullets, a casing but no weapon?"

Eileen wiggled her nose. "We've got to be grateful those things didn't have to be dug out of our bodies. Our *dead* bodies."

"Nice," Angel said. "Now, there's a thought. Maybe Matt's going to tell us they've already got a make on the ammo." And that was wishful thinking. Finding a match that quickly would be a miracle.

"So for that Matt called us in here as if the place was on fire?"

Angel frowned at her. "I'm getting a nasty idea. He could ask what I carry. He could ask if you've got a weapon and what it is. What d'you bet he starts asking questions about what I carry and if you carry? He's shouting and glaring around the place because he's out of ideas. Hell, he didn't have any in the first place. Maybe he's going to suggest we've been doing our own shooting."

"He wouldn't do that. That's insane."

Angel inclined his head to look at her. "What is sane about any of this?"

Matt appeared in the hallway again, then came all the

way out to reception. "Hi, Joseph," he yelled to the coffee-drinking visitor.

Joseph said, "Eh?" so loudly the cat jumped off its chair.

"He's deaf," Matt said. "We used to try kicking him out till we figured he couldn't hear what we were saying." He flicked up one corner of his mouth.

Deaf? Angel smiled at Eileen with his eyes. And he caught a knowing smirk from Joseph, who cupped a hand around one ear.

"Let's go," Matt said and they followed him back to his dismal office with his battered metal desk and the faded carpet where he rested his feet when he sat there. As they entered, he said, "How many bullets does it take to kill someone? That's what I think my guest is here to ask."

"Not exactly," Chuzah said.

Angel stared. If he'd been asked who was least likely to be here, now or at all, Chuzah wouldn't even have been on the list of possibilities.

He heard Eileen gasp and sympathized. And this was not the Chuzah they were used to: Silver-gray silk slacks, white silk shirt open at the neck, one dark, highly polished loafer resting on his opposite knee, and a nonchalant attitude worthy of any successful citizen dropping in for an afternoon call. He sat near Matt's scarred desk and for once he wasn't smiling.

What the hell was this all about? "Why are you here?" Angel asked Chuzah.

"I popped over to bring in some items I thought Matt might find interesting. He wanted you here to discuss these things. I need to get back to my pad quickly."

"How many bullets?" Matt repeated, and tapped Angel. "To kill someone?"

"Depends on who's pulling the trigger," Angel said. He wasn't amused that he and Eileen had been told, not asked, to appear at the police station when they were in the middle of an important discussion. Finding Chuzah, not looking at all like himself, didn't help a thing. "I talked to Sonny and Aaron a while back. They said they were at your place," he told the man. "Did they leave?"

"Nope. Still here," Chuzah said. "And they are in exceptionally good health. We decided against the bone soup in favor of fried oysters in cornmeal. When I left they were enjoying my latest shipment of Swiss chocolate. Later—with your permission, of course—I shall start teaching them mah-jongg before they go home. I'll await your instructions on where that might be, the home they're to go to, I mean. If there is one."

Eileen was too busy with one of her blushes to take umbrage at Chuzah's cracks. "What I said about soup was just a joke," she said, giving him a dimpled smile.

So fast, Angel almost missed it, Eileen gave him an amazed look. "How did he know what I said about soup?" she asked Angel. "It was out there, way out there, and I whispered."

Chuzah lowered his eyelids a fraction. Angel didn't miss the appreciative male inventory of a sexy woman. It pissed him off. The guy was too good-looking, even Angel could see that. "My hearing must be exceptional," he said, turning a bone-melting smile on Eileen.

Angel wanted to know a whole lot more about Chuzah, man of many faces.

"So what is it we have to look at—right at this moment?" Angel asked Matt.

"Sit down," Matt told him. "You can have my chair, Eileen. It's more comfortable."

Eileen hesitated as if she'd refuse the offer. She nodded and walked to sit behind his desk.

Matt slid a single piece of paper from the desk. "This is very preliminary, but they think the weapon used at Angel's house is old. Probably an old Colt. Can either of you think of where I could find a weapon like that?"

"Not me," Angel said.

"No, sir," Chuzah said.

Eileen shook her head. Then she said, "There must be guns like that all over."

"I'm finished with nice," Matt said, and threw the paper to the desk. "Now I want you two to open up and start telling the truth—all of it."

Angel stopped smiling. "What does that mean?"

"I can help with some of this," Chuzah said. "Aaron—"

"I want to hear it from Eileen and Angel," Matt said. His face was tight and furious. "Finally I get called in but I'm only told part of the story. Why bother to tell me anything? What's going on here?" He spoke directly to Angel.

"Aaron didn't want to tell you he was shot at in the backyard," Chuzah said rapidly.

"Whose yard?" Eileen and Angel asked together.

"That would be yours, Eileen," Chuzah said. "He was feeling a trifle unsettled and went out back to take the air. That would have been in the early hours of the morning several days ago. He heard a shot and hurried back inside. He did assume someone was firing a weapon at him."

"As soon as I heard about this, I sent out what personnel I have available to your place, Eileen. They did knock but you weren't there."

"I work," Eileen said.

"You weren't at work, either," Matt said, his expression smooth. "I spoke with Suky-Jo, who told me she doesn't give out personal information about you to anyone. Fortunately Frances Broussard at the salon wasn't so difficult. She said she'd seen you go out for a walk with Angel."

"My friends only want to do what's best for me," Eileen said.

"Your house is a crime scene," Matt said.

"Great," Eileen snapped. "Angel's house is a crime scene. And now my house is a crime scene. But there's still no progress in the case."

"I'm releasing your place, Angel," Matt said. "But as long as someone keeps shooting at you two—or anyone else, there are likely to be a lot of crime scenes."

"Until we get hit," Eileen said. She didn't look as flippant as she sounded.

"I should give you this," Chuzah said, getting up and pulling an item from his pocket. He dropped a bullet casing into the hand Matt hastily extended. "That one came from the swamp not far from my estate. My dog sniffed it out. He's good with those things. Do you think it'll match the other one you have?"

"Is this from Eileen's house?" Matt said.

"No," Chuzah said. He took a casing from his other trouser pocket and handed it over. "This is the one from Eileen's backyard, from the trees there on that lot next door." He bowed to her slightly. "I hope it was acceptable for me to go there and see if I could be of help. Aaron seemed to think it would be."

This man, Angel thought, either knew how to get around fast, or… Or what? He was…a shape-shifter? Angel almost laughed at himself.

Matt gave the evidence a glare and muttered, "So much for getting fingerprints." He indicated the first casing again. "This was found near your place? What do you mean?"

"Not exactly near my place," Chuzah said. "In the vicinity. I'm not sure how it came to be there but decided to bring it to you since it resembles the one from Eileen's property."

The rhythmic nod of Eileen's head suggested she'd stopped taking any of this in.

"How could you find this second one?" Matt said to Chuzah. "How did you know where to look?"

"Oh," Chuzah said. "With Aaron's help, of course. And my dog always knows where to find whatever is lost."

"Why didn't you give me these when you got here?" Matt said.

"I knew you'd want Angel and Eileen here for that," Chuzah told him.

From the color of Matt's face, from his gritted teeth, Angel could tell he was about to blow, but then Chuck Moggeridge walked through the door.

"Where's Aaron?" he said to Eileen, walking directly toward her. "I've been looking for both of you. I decided to walk in here and see if they knew anything that would help me. It looks like Aaron should move in with me—that way I can make sure—"

Eileen shot to her feet. "Aaron will do what he wants to do."

Matt's phone rang and he reached to turn off his speaker before picking up.

"I think you should get out of here," Angel told Chuck. *Hate* was a big word but it definitely described how he felt about Chuck.

Barking one-word answers, Matt's tone cut through the tension. He looked at them but obviously didn't see them. Then he hung up. "Angel," he said. "I'd like you to come with me to the landfill."

20

"You'll stay in the car when we get to the landfill, Eileen," Matt said. "I only let you come because I couldn't leave you there with Chuck hanging around."

Seated behind him in the cruiser, she looked at the back of Matt's head. "Thanks for that." She caught an over-the-shoulder glance from Angel. His frustration with the situation showed but he smiled at her.

They headed north through town, passed buildings Eileen had looked at all of her life. They got to the trailer park and she noticed the streetlights were on. Day was getting squeezed out.

"Are you going to explain what this is all about?" Angel said to Matt.

"We'll be there soon enough. I don't have all the facts myself. That Chuzah's a case."

"He's all right," Angel said.

"He's very thoughtful and kind," Eileen added. Chuzah was on his way back to his "estate" where he would suggest Sonny and Aaron remain until they were contacted.

Matt barked out a laugh. "He's a wolf in sheep's clothing," he said. "Thoughtful and kind? What have you been drinking? Look at him. He's a mystery and I don't have any way of figuring him out—yet. That really gets to me."

"Why would you want to figure him out?" Eileen said, annoyed. "He hasn't done anything wrong."

Again, Matt laughed aloud. "As far as *you* know."

"And you know better?"

"I know the guy's a chameleon," Matt said. "There's a whole lot of people in Pointe Judah who would as soon swim with cottonmouths and gators as get any attention from Chuzah. If you saw his place, you'd know what I mean. I don't get why you'd let those boys be out there."

"We've seen his place," Angel said, without inflection.

"It's interesting," Eileen said. Matt Boudreaux wasn't going to back her into a corner.

"You've seen it? Why? Why would you go there?"

"Angel and I like new experiences," Eileen said, feeling silly. "And Chuzah invited us in." That wasn't a total lie.

"You didn't have to go."

"We wanted to," Eileen said. "Most people around here are boring. He's not."

Matt grunted but didn't ask if he she counted him among the boring. "Don't you wonder why he's living out there when he has money? He's got to have money. Look at him today—he didn't buy those duds with green stamps. But you like him, Eileen?"

"I do," she said staunchly. Angel trusted Chuzah and she trusted Angel's instincts.

"He is a handsome guy. Film-star material is what Carley calls him."

"That's not why I like him," Eileen said immediately.

Matt applied his brakes for a stop sign, then started out along the winding road she could drive with her eyes shut. The landfill was at the end of a dirt track that ran from the switchback road where her parents had built their house years ago. Part of her wished she could still go there and visit the memories, but money from the sale had changed her life for the better. Thanks to Finn's generosity.

"This is it," Matt said and took a left. The dirt track ran between dense trees. "Get ready for the stench."

A wide metal gate stood open in a tall wire fence. Eileen winced at the smell seeping into the car even though the windows were shut.

Just ahead, Officer Sampson leaned on the side of another cruiser with a shiny-faced new member of the force. Eileen didn't know the woman's name but she was small and pretty—and eager from the way she bounced on the balls of her black lace-ups.

Sampson saw Matt's car before it drove past the gate and into a turnaround.

Matt stopped, cracked the windows open about an inch, and got out of the car. Angel followed him. "Hang in there, Eileen," was all he said.

Patronizing piece of male arrogance, she thought. "And now I sit here like a good little girl." What made this scene suitable for a female kid cop, but not for Eileen?

She had thanked Matt for letting her get away from a potential confrontation with Chuck, not for telling her to stay in his car. Bowing her head, she listened hard and Sampson's loud voice carried to her easily. "It's back this way, Chief. I didn't call for more backup. Thought you'd want to make up your mind what's next."

They walked away and she lost sight of them when they went along a path between towering heaps of refuse.

She counted to five and slid out, then ran to the point where the *grown-ups* had turned. Holding her nose, she stood against the nearest mountain of garbage and peered around the corner. They were heading straight back through the lot and moving fast.

Eileen scuttled past the opening to the next break and turned in there. Jogging to make up time, she moved rapidly until she heard voices again. She couldn't imagine how anyone could work around this place unless they wore a gas mask.

Ahead lay an area of more open ground. When she reached the last patch of decent cover, Eileen stopped to listen more closely. The rest of them were fairly near and she dared a peep.

Angel stood with the other three and what appeared to be two landfill workers, not far from a fresh-looking rubbish mound. Several high-powered lanterns, set on the ground, gave off garish light.

Both workers stood with one foot on a shovel and their wrists balanced on top of the handles.

Sampson, brilliant flashlight in hand, pointed at something. Eileen had no idea what, but her stomach turned.

"Damn," Matt said. "Who would know the poor devil?"

Angel spoke up. "You brought me here to look at this?" he said. His voice was steady but too somber. "Still want me to look, or have you made up your mind it's pointless?"

"You're a cold son of a bitch," Matt said. "I was reacting to the obvious. He's a mess. Sure I want you to look. If it's who we think it is, you should be able to ID him."

Eileen stepped from her place, she couldn't help it. She wanted to be with Angel. She didn't want him to be alone and facing something awful, even if he *was* a strong man.

While she walked, unnoticed, toward the group concentrating on him, Angel got close to the garbage and knelt down. He turned his head sideways but didn't say anything.

"I'm already here so don't you start with me, Matt Boudreaux."

Matt looked at her as if she were a phantom. Then he shook his head and said, "You're going to regret not doing what I told you to do." He turned away again.

"Don't come any closer, Eileen," Angel said. "You don't need to see this."

She hesitated but then approached a little closer.

"What do you think?" Matt said.

"I think someone killed him and tried to burn him," Angel responded. He looked again. "He's been scalded. Look at his skin."

"We need a full team," Matt said.

Sampson turned to his female companion and said, "You know what to do. Isaacs, call it in."

"You should have done that as soon as you saw this," Matt said. "Holding off just wasted time."

Sampson turned red. "Sorry, Chief. I thought you'd want to see first."

Matt said, "Thanks. Don't do me any favors next time. Is it Bucky Smith?" he added to Angel.

"I don't know him," Angel said. "You'll need to get Leland Garolfo in here—and the guys he shared quarters with."

A face, or what had been a face, showed between layers of junk. Eileen sucked in a breath. Acid rose to her throat and she put a hand over her nose and mouth.

The eyes were open but coated milky white…as if they'd been…cooked. A deep breath didn't help her. The eyelids were completely gone. She took another step, drawn to the corpse by pity. It had been a man but she seemed to be the only one remembering that fact. His hair, an unrecognizable color but flattened to his head in stiff strips, had hunks of things caught in it.

"What's in his hair?" she asked. "It looks like food."

Matt made a move as if he'd cut off her view. He changed his mind and got closer to the dead man instead.

"It *is* food," Angel said. "Shrimp tails, among other things. God—it's fried."

"I thought it was," Eileen said. She arrived immediately behind Angel. "Where was he?"

"In a Dumpster," Matt said. His nostrils flared.

"I figured that," Eileen told him. There was no point in getting touchy. "But where was the Dumpster?"

"That's going to be something we'll have to find out," Matt said.

One of the workers punched the point of his spade into the rocky ground. "We know where each new load comes in from. This is from Ona's."

21

Eileen walked into the original Mansion building ahead of Angel. It felt strange to be there so late.

Colored lights sparkled on the Christmas tree in the soaring lobby, but low security lighting, turned on for the night, still cast eerie shadows behind the marble pillars and in the doorways of businesses.

"Home sweet home," Angel said, although he knew any attempt at humor would fall flat. Holding Eileen's hand, he walked to the private elevator, set down her overnight bag and pressed the button. The door opened immediately and they stepped in. He'd had a hard time persuading her to come here after she was told she couldn't be in her house until the police had finished with it. At last she'd gathered enough clothes to get by with over the next day and come with him.

In the small elevator, they leaned on opposite walls. Eileen couldn't look away from Angel's eyes. He touched her with his stare. They had been through hell together today and she felt even closer to him. The breath she took was too shallow. Her heart beat fast and hard.

The elevator bumped to a stop and the door slid open.

Neither of them moved until the door started to close again

and Angel slammed out a hand to make it stop. He'd rather not move at all.

"Here we go," he said, and smiled at her.

Apart from a single lamp in the foyer, the suite was in darkness. Eileen stood in front of a black console table with brass feet and the portrait of a woman in a period riding habit sitting sidesaddle on a black horse. The rider's serene eyes stared straight ahead from her gilt frame.

Coming up behind, Angel rested his chin on her shoulder and she jumped. "Cute, huh?" he said. His hands settled at her waist.

"I don't think she would have understood that compliment." The urge to lean against him almost won. "Just point me in the right direction. I promise I'll be gone before you and Finn get here in the morning."

That was supposed to be a good thing? "The bed's in a small room, but it's private. You can get up when you feel like it." He watched the way she turned her head sideways to look at a Sèvres vase and cachepot.

He held the back of her neck under her hair and ran his thumb back and forth. She shuddered, and he smiled. They were both caught in the same thrall and he hoped she didn't want to break it any more than he did.

They moved through the suite and he turned the lights on low as they went.

"You do think it's the right thing to let Aaron and Sonny stay at Chuzah's tonight?" Angel asked. "You think it's safe?"

"I believe so. Chuzah will call us, and Matt, if he thinks there's a problem."

She tried to take her bag from him but he wouldn't let her. "I'm not helpless," she said. "But, thanks. Mah-jongg. Who'd have thought they'd be interested? I think you're right—our suave swamp man is okay. I like him."

He likes you, too. He probably enjoyed any sexy female, after all, he was all man even if he did hang out in kaftans a lot. Angel knew there was nothing to fear from Chuzah, at least not for the boys. "I'm glad you feel the way I do. It makes like easier. I like having Chuzah on our side—anyone who wants to get at the boys now will have to go through him." He stepped in front of her, tilted up her chin and kissed her mouth quickly. Just as rapidly, he returned to her side and guided her through the suite.

"What was that about?" she asked, knowing perfectly well. They both wanted to touch, to taste.

"You needed a kiss," he said, smiling to himself. And when she widened her eyes at him, he said, "So did I. Do I." Suddenly he didn't feel like smiling anymore. Being with her, now, was like carrying a grenade—pull that pin and everything would go up.

The room he used when he worked so late he didn't want to go home was at the end of a passageway between Finn's office and Angel's. He went into the very small space and put Eileen's bag on a chair. "There's a closet," he said, sliding a mirrored door open. "And the bathroom's over here." He opened the door and put on a light.

Eileen puckered her brows together. The one thing missing was a bed.

With his hands on the hips of his dark pants, his khaki shirt open at the neck to reveal dark hair, and a pleased grin on his face, Angel looked devilish. He was, she figured, waiting for her to ask about the bed.

Wait on, buddy.

His chest expanded and Eileen enjoyed the view. She

glanced downward and away. Some things a man couldn't hide. Her heart began pounding again.

"This is great," she said. "I'll be just fine. I'm glad you'll be back at your house tonight."

He wouldn't, Angel thought, contemplating absenting himself until the pain she created subsided—if it did. "How about a little brandy first?"

From her frown, he thought she'd refuse.

"Okay. But I'm aching to take a shower, so we should be quick."

"You take your shower," he said at once. "I'd like to look through the rest of my mail, then I'll get the brandy. And you might like to have this for later." He pressed a paneled wall and caught the edge of a platform bed hidden there. When it pulled down there was almost no extra space in the room.

"We could have the brandy now," she said, turning pink over her cheekbones. Eileen had slightly olive skin and a blush was charming.

"No way." He wanted her soft and warm and ready for bed. He wanted to torture himself some more. "You go ahead and get comfortable. Anyway, if there's a call I need to return I can't wait any later."

She wanted to tell him it was already too late for business calls, but didn't. "Okay, I won't be long." The bed beckoned and she'd like to flop onto the mattress, preferably with Angel beside her. Her life was complicated enough without this "falling in love" thing.

Angel pulled the door shut behind him.

Eileen stood where she was, a fine tremor passing beneath her skin. The idea that she could love him wasn't new. Contemplating being in love with him was.

Armed with her nightgown and robe from the case, she took toiletries and went into the bathroom. She shut herself in and stripped. When it came to bathrooms, Angel definitely favored mirrors. She gave herself a jerky downturned smile in one of those mirrors, turned on the fan and figured out the shower.

Steam billowed and droplets settled on her already tingling body. She took a towel and wiped one of the mirrors. The fan took hold and the clear spot she'd made with the towel widened quickly.

She'd had Aaron when she was nineteen. Mostly she didn't think about her age; thirty-six seemed a good number of years and she'd been blessed with a healthy body.

Assessing that body now, she felt detached. Her legs were long and smooth. Regular exercise took care of any problems there and at her hips and belly. She knew her hips and bottom were rounded, but that was her build and nobody had ever complained. Her waist remained slim, and her breasts weren't moving toward her bellybutton yet. She chuckled.

Then she cupped her breasts and studied them. She inclined her head. Sensation awoke in her flesh. Slowly, Eileen passed her thumbs back and forth over the tips of her dark, already budded nipples. She sucked in a sharp breath and almost closed her eyes. Other parts of her throbbed. Without giving herself more time to get into trouble, she got into the shower and let hot water beat down on her head and shoulders.

Washing her hair usually distracted her. Not this time. While she let the water stream through her hair, dashing rivers of lather over her skin, she touched her breasts again, pulled lightly on her nipples and made herself stop when she wanted to stimulate herself.

Panting, she leaned against the wall and this time she did close her eyes. She had been vulnerable to Angel before, but not like this. Eileen needed him.

She toweled off and pulled on a pink cotton nightie. The dark, rigid tips of her breasts showed through. Anxiously, she tugged on a matching robe and tied it tightly at the waist. The suggestion was still there but not noticeable if you weren't looking for it.

Getting a brush through her hair wasn't easy and she hadn't thought to bring a dryer. She found a smaller towel and wound it around her head. Another glance into the mirror didn't reveal a scrubbed-looking innocent. A voluptuous, flushed woman, who looked ready for a long night without sleep, stared back at her.

She returned to the bedroom, steadied herself, and walked out into the passageway.

Angel walked back and forth at the other end. He saw her and smiled, and his gray eyes turned black, thrilling her, tensing her body all over.

"I thought I'd have to come rescue you," he said. He'd had to stop himself from going in there. "Five more minutes and I'd have been in on my charger."

She flipped him an arch look as she walked by. "Where do you want me?"

"Anywhere I can get you," he said before sanity took over again. "In my office. To the left."

Eileen heard what he said but pretended she hadn't. Angel's office wasn't at all like Finn's. Emma's decorating touch hadn't entered here. White walls, a single good Chinese rug in shades of red, a desk, credenza and bookshelves, a whole wall of crammed bookshelves. Apart from two deep cane chairs with gray cushions, that was it; although pale coffee-colored grass shades were lowered over the windows.

She looked at the chairs. "Should I sit in one of these?"

"Yes. They're more comfortable than they look—or so I'm told. I never use them."

As soon as she was seated, he gave her a brandy and dropped to sit, cross-legged, in front of her. Eileen hiked her legs sideways onto the chair—they had to be cramped—and tucked her bathrobe around them. She looked into the brandy as she swirled it. "Thank you for letting me use the bedroom here. I hope they're finished with my house by tomorrow evening."

Her lowered eyes made him think she was trying not to look at him. "At least they let you get some things. Matt was in such a mood, I was afraid he'd refuse."

"He's got a lot to deal with." She sipped from her glass and puckered up. "Mmm, that's good, but it's strong. This was a horrible day."

"Not really so horrible until later," he told her. "I thought our walk had promise."

He got a piercing look. "It had promise of turning into a row and don't pretend you didn't know that. You and Finn ambushed me with Matt. Not that it matters now."

"Matt's going to have to question a lot of people. He'll have to just about take this town apart and people aren't going to like it."

"No." Her expression turned sad. "That poor man. No one deserves to die like that."

When the crime-scene team had arrived and set up their lights and paraphernalia, all too soon the full extent of what had happened to the dead man, at least on the surface, was revealed. Angel frowned at Eileen. She'd taken what must have felt like multiple punches to the gut and kept calm. A lot of men as well as women would have passed out, or at least thrown up when the layers of garbage were carefully removed from above the body and the damage was laid open.

"I think they'll get whoever did that to him," Angel said. "The Dumpster was picked up today, it shouldn't be hard to pin down the window of time when he could have been put in there. And the medical examiner will have plenty to say."

"I've been thinking about Ona, too," Eileen said. "She'll be devastated. He was probably killed in her kitchen, wasn't he?"

There was little doubt that the guy had been shoved, head-first, into the deep-fat fryer. Angel looked away. "Probably." Gently he smoothed his fingers up and down her shin and rubbed the tops of her feet. "Try not to keep thinking about it. We can't change anything."

She shook her head no.

"Chuck's going to keep on being a nuisance. I think that worries me almost more than anything—other than the bullets flying around." Flopping back into the chair with her glass balanced on her thigh, she stared at the ceiling. "Can you believe we're talking about these things? Only days ago I was looking forward to Christmas. Now all I'm looking forward to is keeping all of us alive—if we're lucky."

"Do you think Chuck's capable of killing someone?" he said, thinking aloud as much as asking the question.

Did she know the answer to the question? "If he was, he wouldn't take potshots at his son. Or are you talking about Chuck killing that man? Oh, Angel, he—"

"No, I'm not. I do want to know if that's Bucky Smith. I couldn't identify him."

She shuddered. "Senseless violence."

"Hang in with me," he said. "Would Chuck want to kill you?"

"I don't know anymore." She stared at him and her eyes filled with tears. "Why would he? He left me, not the other way around. Surely, I intended to divorce him, but he got there first."

"Either someone wants to get rid of Sonny and me, or you and Aaron. With that shot in your backyard, Aaron chalked up another arrow in his direction."

"In the bathroom at your house, you must have been the target. The more I've thought about it, the more convinced I've become that whoever was on the roof didn't know I was there."

He raised his brows. "What would he think I was doing in that tub? I wasn't washing my back. And you're one distinctive woman, Eileen. You were seen."

"And the first bullet went off the rim of the tub right beside my head," she said, gradually pulling the towel from her wet hair. "Why would someone want to kill me?"

"I don't know," he said honestly. "There's nothing logical about it. Have some more brandy."

She did, and she observed the way his throat moved when he followed suit. Whatever happened, she would not be a ninny and lean on him.

He had strength, both physical and mental. Leaning on him didn't sound so bad.

"Nothing much gets done till someone dies," she said and heard the flatness in her own voice. "I mean, it's like when someone's missing. You have to wait first to make sure they don't come back. Then it's just as likely they're never found and if they aren't there's no body and the killer gets away—"

"Yes," he said firmly, rising to his knees. He rested his forearms on the arms of the chair and his face was very close. "Don't forget I'm here. This isn't the first time…I've had some experience with criminals. They come in all shapes and sizes and they're always mean and often stupid. I don't mean completely stupid, just that they make mistakes and get caught."

"But not till after they kill someone."

Fury surged through him. He wanted to get his hands on whoever was doing this. "Often they get caught before they pull anything off. And this one's not a pro." Best not to tell her that was the reason he had become certain she and Aaron were the targets rather than either Sonny or himself.

"I'm okay." She was whining too much. No one liked a whiner. "A good night's sleep and I'll be a new woman."

His grin let her breathe again. He didn't have her pegged as a scared, would-be victim. She swallowed more brandy and savored its aromatic burn all the way down.

Angel really was close to her. His thighs were a scant inch from her legs and he didn't make any attempt to back off, even when he tilted his glass. He lowered his brandy and peered through it. "I like being with you," he said. "A lot. More than a lot." He put his glass on the floor and played his fingertips over her collarbones. "I'd like to stay here with you tonight."

Her stomach flipped and that tingling she'd begun to know so well started all over again. "Mmm. You're going back to your place."

"No, I'm not. Matt's got a cruiser going up to the house regularly. If someone wants to find me, they'll call."

Eileen glanced at his mouth and away. She fidgeted in the chair.

Angel leaned slowly until he could kiss her and when their lips finally parted again she was breathless. She looked at the open neck of his shirt, at his chest.

"Look at me," he said.

She shook her head no.

"Why?"

"Because I want you." She covered her mouth and mumbled, "I can't believe I said that."

Neither could he, but he'd handle it. "I'm glad you did," he said, preparing to kick himself if she agreed and backed off.

"Me, too," she said, and returned his kiss, slowly, deeply.

Angel held her by the shoulders and gave as good as he got. Better.

She muttered into his mouth and he arched his head back.

"Brandy," she said, her eyes huge, dark and shimmering. "My glass."

He smiled and took it from her to set beside his own. "Don't they say good loving is a cure-all?" Homing in, he nipped at her bottom lip, sucked it lightly into his mouth. "I think they do. And if they don't, I do."

They kissed for a long time. Eileen knew she couldn't do anything to stop what would happen. She didn't want to.

Keeping hold of her shoulders, Angel studied her. She looked kissed. She looked sexy, but not the relaxed sexy of aftermath. His lady was on alert as much as he was.

Briefly, he considered how deep he was getting with her. Only very briefly. The answer was—real deep, and he was okay with that.

She didn't try to stop him pulling her legs from beneath her, sitting on the floor and massaging her feet. Each touch made her jump, and not because she was ticklish. He rubbed the bottoms of her feet with his thumbs, worked toward her ankles and smoothed softly but firmly over her calves and shins. The brush of his fingertips behind her knees zapped her nerves.

"It's getting late," she said.

"You sound hoarse." He gave her another heavy-eyed, provocative grin. "It must be almost time for bed."

"I didn't know you were so traditional," she told him. This new woman she'd discovered in herself was a little wild, at least in comparison with the old Eileen.

"I like the pink," he said and she didn't doubt he could see her nipples, hard inside the soft cotton.

His hands traveled her thighs. Her bottom slid forward and he smiled that knowing smile. Fingertips in her groin sent her against the back of the chair again and she grabbed at his hands.

"You don't like that?" he said.

A slow throbbing contraction and rush of dampness made her hot.

"Don't you know?" Angel said and spread his fingertips over her belly. His thumbs settled in slick folds. "You still don't know if you like it?" His voice sank low.

"I like it," she told him.

With her lips parted and her breath coming in short spurts, she undid the buttons on his shirt. Leaning just a little nearer to him intensified the pressure on her clitoris. She couldn't concentrate. The buttons slid through the holes by feel. She bowed her head and tugged the shirt open, kneaded his pecs and used her fingernails on his flat nipples.

"Gimme a break," he said. "Let me…hell, that's good. You feel so good, so sweet. You're wet, honey. You're driving me mad."

Eileen panted. His thumbs moved harder and faster and she hung on the edge, waiting to tip over, urging him to tip her over.

He took one hand away to open her robe, and fastened his teeth and lips on a nipple. The erotic pulling through wet fabric speared her.

Pushing to the edge of the chair, gripping his shoulders, Eileen whimpered when release broke over her. She all but fell on Angel and he held her while her climax wracked her in waves, and while she tore her robe and nightie over her head.

"My God," he said. Looking up at her he pinched his thighs together, willed himself not to come like that. With her hands above her head, her breasts swayed, full and rounded, the nipples distended. Big, dark, distended nipples. He covered them, reared up and flicked them with the tip of his tongue. Every sound she made drove him wild.

On his feet, he shucked his pants and lost the shirt fast. He twirled her around and sat on the chair, pulled her down astride his hips and sank into her so hard he watched her face for signs of pain. Eileen's eyes were closed and she smiled.

Angel tensed every muscle, pushed on her knees to get as close and as deep as he could. Eileen caught him around the neck to keep her balance and do her part to drive them both to a mad seeking.

He jerked, jerked and poured into her. His grip on her slackened as his head fell back against the chair and he flowed into hot, dark mindlessness.

"Angel," Eileen moaned, her voice high. "Don't stop." He felt her body locked around him and bent toward her again.

He felt her rapid build, the convulsive urging in strong, slick places. She tried to kiss him and Angel opened his mouth against hers. He took her sobs into his throat and with one last, huge effort, stood up, staying inside her, and half ran, half staggered the length of the corridor to the small bedroom.

They landed, locked together, on the mattress, and immediately climaxes shot through them. Through a haze, Angel wondered if either of them would survive this in one piece, but Eileen was already pushing a hand between them, touching him again.

"Are you a sex addict?" he murmured into her ear. She nodded and he said, "What a relief."

22

The back of Eileen's neck was soft and smelled of soap. They lay on their sides, her bottom tucked into his pelvis, on the bed in the room where he'd only slept alone before. Holding her in his arms, smoothing the undersides of her breasts, he decided he never wanted to face the bed again without her.

Warm, soft, she revolved to face Angel and held him. In the darkness he could see the glitter of her eyes. She kissed him. Angel rose over her and took her face in his hands. He made the kiss leisurely and explorative. When their mouths parted, she trailed her tongue to his ear and nipped at the lobe.

"How do you feel?" he asked.

"Grateful," she said, and chuckled. "Mmm, I didn't mean that to sound the way it did."

"You didn't?" He liked her rapid comebacks.

She thought about it. "Yes, I did."

"Me, too."

A cell phone rang, hers, and they fell together in a heap on the mattress.

Angel kissed her. She traced the outline of his mouth with the tip of her tongue.

The phone rang a third time and they kissed hard, clung together as if they would never let go. Eileen pulled away and went for her phone. "It could be Aaron," she said as she flipped it on. "Hello?"

She listened and repeated, "Hello."

"Who is it?" Angel asked.

"I don't know. They hung up on me."

"It could have been a wrong number," Angel said. "If it was Aaron and he wanted to reach you, he wouldn't hang up like that."

He was right. "Mmm." Eileen snuggled into him again and he held her. She felt safe.

She felt sleepy. "Are you tired?"

"Exhausted," he said and she felt him smile against her shoulder. "But getting stronger. And stronger." His head slipped beneath the sheet and he kissed her breasts with little kisses and big, open-mouthed kisses—closer and closer to, but never quite touching, her nipples.

"You're a tease," she said. "I'm not tired anymore."

Her phone rang again.

On the fourth ring she answered, "Yes?"

"Hi, darlin', please don't hang up."

"It's too late for calls, Chuck."

23

If he was a nice guy, he'd leave the room and let her talk to her ex in private.

Angel didn't like nice-guy odds.

Sitting on the edge of the bed, Eileen hadn't said a word since she'd told Chucky boy it was too late to be calling. She found the switch that turned on a nightlight and threw an indistinct beam across the sheets.

He got up and walked to the only window. Fumbling, he lifted one side of the shade and peered out. Over the rooftops, vapor lights let him see the back of the parking lot in front of Eileen's store, and a new condominium complex. Fog gathered, almost obscuring the colored lights looped around the entire perimeter of the property and festooned in every tree and shrub. It was past time when anyone was moving about in that eerie world that seemed to mock any celebration.

"Are you drunk?" Eileen asked abruptly.

The corners of Angel's mouth twitched. Chuck Moggeridge was taking too long to get the message that Eileen didn't want him.

Turned half-sideways, he studied her. Her hair still looked damp and it fell past her shoulders in dark tangles. A frown pulled her fine brows together and downcast eyes threw the curved shadows of her lashes onto her cheeks. He couldn't seem to get enough of her.

Eileen felt Angel looking at her. He smiled. She didn't. "I don't think you believe a word I say," Chuck said to her on the phone. And he did sound as if he'd been drinking. "I don't have any rights. Don't deserve any. But I'm still askin', will you marry me again, sweetheart?"

She kept her eyes on Angel. Big, solid and very real, having him with her was keeping her sane while Chuck babbled.

"Eileen," Chuck said softly. "I love you, baby. I've paid for my mistakes. Look, I'm only working for Duhon's because I don't like too much time on my hands. You know I'm a doer. I've got plenty of money. If we need to be together all the time for six months…a year, to really get to know each other again—" he laughed "—we can afford to do that. Let me take you away somewhere. You can hire someone to look after the shop. Hell, that brother of yours worships the ground you walk on, let him take care of things. You love it here and I like it, too. But we could go to one of those places in the Caribbean for a week or so. Or to Hawaii. Sun, sand. You and me and a chance to—"

"No!" She found her voice and heard the way it croaked. She couldn't believe he'd suggest such a thing. "We're divorced."

He sniffed.

Please don't let him cry. Chuck had always been tough, especially with her, and she wasn't sure she could take it if he shed tears, not that she'd believe they meant anything.

"I want to be a father to Aaron." He choked on the words.

"I was lousy, ever since he was born, but I love him and I know how important a good father is to a boy. Especially now when he's had trouble and could go either way."

Eileen closed her mouth before she could tell him that Aaron was only going one way—up. The hellish times were over for him. She sighed. *Let it all be over, including the shooting spree someone was waging against them.*

"Eileen," Chuck said. "Forget I mentioned getting back together. It's too soon. Sure it is. Too soon. Just remember what I've told you about looking after you if you need money. You and Aaron. I've got to find a way to make it all up to you."

A shooting spree against them. The enormity of the thought smacked Eileen. How could she even walk around knowing that bullets had already been fired at Aaron and at her, at Angel, probably at Sonny, too?

"You still there?" Chuck was saying.

"Yes. But I don't want to be," she said sharply.

"You've gotta do this for Aaron," he said. "And for us, but mostly for Aaron. He never had it good before."

Angel's gray eyes had turned black, as they did when he thought deeply. His tanned body glistened from wide shoulder to narrow hip and from his muscular thighs to his feet. A paler band swathed low on his hips. He'd been hard the whole time she'd been talking. He'd been hard while they cuddled in bed. She straightened her back and pressed the heel of a hand into the juncture of her legs. A quick tingling response caught her off guard. So did the possessive stare he gave her.

"Eileen," Chuck said. "Talk to me."

"There's nothing to say except stay away from us. I'm going to hang up now."

"Wait! Just hear me out. I had to go to the medical examiner's office a couple of hours ago," Chuck said rapidly. "Leland Garolfo—he's the foreman at The Willows—he asked me to go with him because he couldn't find any of the other guys. I think he just wanted moral support."

"Get to the point, Chuck."

"They wanted him to identify a body."

Eileen shivered. She didn't need to ask which body he was talking about.

"It was that Bucky Smith. They already knew because of his ID being on him, but they needed a visual, or so they said. God, what a mess. His eyelids were gone."

Chuck didn't sound horrified enough to Eileen. And she didn't need his laundry list of the insults to that poor dead man's body.

"They know it's Bucky Smith?" Eileen said, meeting Angel's eyes and swallowing. "I wonder if he has any family."

"I think he was a loner," Chuck said, conversationally. "Leland said he never talked about anything personal. I don't know about this stuff, but I bet shock took him out before the boiling oil."

"Yes," she said.

Angel suppressed an urge to take the phone from her and tell Chuck to get lost. He might do it if he could predict Eileen's reaction. She liked to do things her own way. He settled a hand low on his belly, the side of his small finger pressing into his penis. He locked his thighs. How the hell would he ever get past this erection without homing in on the object of arousal?

He wasn't a stranger to cold showers.

Movement outside the window caught his attention. He looked through the glass at thickening shrouds of fog. The vapor lights had sunk into soft halos of gray. The movement was beyond that. He frowned and got closer to the window. A long shadow bounding along the road?

Shadows didn't bound.

There wasn't anything there.

"Matt Boudreaux said you and DeAngelo were out at the landfill when they found the corpse," Chuck said to Eileen.

"No. After they found it. Matt thought Christian might be able to identify the body. He couldn't."

"Who's Christian?"

She was tired of this. Sleep was all she wanted, sleep and Angel. "Good night, Chuck."

"Please don't hang up," Chuck begged. "I don't have anyone else to talk to. Leland knew the man, even if he did look like boiled pig. All he needed was an apple in his mouth."

"Damn you," Eileen said. "Speaking of pigs—"

"I'm sorry. I'm sorry, okay? Some people say inappropriate things when they're upset. You can't look at a thing like that and not be upset."

Eileen thought Chuck sounded like a ghoul who relished being on the inside of this one. "That *thing* was a man. I've got to go now."

Whatever he saw wasn't that far away, Angel thought. He tried to listen to Eileen, but his skin had become cold. Inside he turned absolutely quiet. His mind had stilled. No, not now, he couldn't have a disconnect now.

A shadow took shape—long, a head, a tail, and outstretched legs. Where trees should have lined the road, the fogbank hovered like a pale canvas behind the apparition instead.

"Look," he heard Eileen say. "I appreciate you sharing this with me, but—"

"Cher," Chuck said to Eileen. "They think they narrowed down the date when the killing happened. There were newspapers on top of him. Whoever did that wasn't thinking. Unless he didn't care if everyone knew the time line."

Two shining, polished slits glowed in Angel's direction. He couldn't have closed it out if he'd wanted to. The perspective was all wrong. If the glowing slashes were eyes, and they seemed to be, he shouldn't be able to see them so clearly.

The thing faded, or snuffed out.

Angel turned his back on the window. If he hadn't had the experiences that plagued him while he was a CIA operative, he'd dismiss the whole thing.

The auras were back—the second sight, the visions of figures that foretold things to come.

"Angel?"

He wanted to look over his shoulder.

"What's the matter?" Eileen asked.

"What was all that?" he said, dodging her question. She'd put her phone aside. "You're really upset. I've got to get rid of that bastard."

"Don't talk like that," Eileen said. "There's been too much violence already." Tears hung in her eyes. She slid down into the bed.

"What did he say to you?" Angel asked. His spine tightened. Even if there had been some kind of a creature out there, it couldn't have seen him from so far away.

He didn't know how far away it had been.

He didn't know how big it was.

He didn't know *if* it was.

She had hauled the sheet all the way over her head. Angel sat beside her and found his way to stroke her naked back.

"Speak to me." They had gone from a simple friendship, even if he'd always known he wanted more, to a complex entanglement.

"Please go and check on Aaron and Sonny."

"What's happened? What did Chuck say to frighten you?" He snatched the sheet from her head and pushed her hair away from her face. "Eileen!"

"You didn't hear what he said. I didn't think… I don't know what I think. He said things about Bucky—and Emma." Her voice rose.

Angel kept rubbing her back. He couldn't begin to see what Bucky and Emma had in common. He kissed Eileen's forehead. "Settle down. It's okay."

"It's not. Chuck reminded me how I got to know Emma. We both belonged to a club for women called Secrets. It was just to support each other and share problems, and good things, too."

"A women's club?"

The interest had left his voice and manner at once. "Don't dismiss it like that," she said, sitting up abruptly with the sheet held to her breasts. She detested talking about Secrets. All of them had tried to forget about it. "Other people dismissed it as silly. Then one of the members died. It was horrible."

He listened closely again. "What does the club have to do with things now?"

"I don't know. I hope it doesn't have anything to do with it. Chuck said Bucky was probably killed the night Emma was attacked in the parking lot at Out Back."

Angel didn't see any connection with this club she'd mentioned and said so.

"Chuck said the club made a lot of men mad because it changed the women who were in it. We got pushy, that's what he said. And it was Emma's fault that I changed because she was the one who got me to join."

He had to let her make her way through this.

"Chuck and I would still be married if it hadn't been for Secrets. That's what he said."

"Take it easy." He tried to recall if he'd talked one-on-one with Chuck. Had they looked at each other directly? He couldn't remember, couldn't visualize the other man's eyes other than their being very dark, like Aaron's.

"No wonder someone tried to hurt Emma outside Ona's," Eileen said, breaking down. "He shouldn't have said that. He's had too much to drink and he's stupid. I'm sorry to make a fuss. I feel so shaky."

"Don't worry about it." He pulled her into his arms. "The guy's mad because you aren't buying what he's selling, so he's lashing out."

"He's Aaron's dad and Aaron wants to spend time with him. But I don't want him to."

Angel felt out of his depth. "I guess that's all normal."

"I shouldn't want to keep my son from his father. They should be able to get together and Aaron's hoping for that. I know he is. I could ruin that for him."

Her ex-husband might be smashed, Angel thought, but he still knew what strings to pull. Eileen and guilt were old friends and Chuck was using the fact. "If Chuck wants to be a good father to Aaron, he will be. If he wants to use Aaron to get to you, he's not a good father or a good man." He screwed up his face. "I'm way off base interfering. I told myself I wouldn't go there. I don't know beans about being a father—or a husband."

But he knew a lot about being a real man, Emma thought. She couldn't stop herself from trembling. "Chuck as good as said it would have been a good thing if Emma died that night. He wonders if something went wrong and she was supposed to be the one in the landfill."

24

"Gracie!" Emma shouted. "Get out of that tree. You'll kill yourself."

Matt walked toward the woman hanging strands of bells from branches high up in a sycamore tree, bracing himself to break her fall if necessary. That wouldn't be an altogether unpleasant experience—as long as she didn't kill him on her way down.

"Tell Gracie to get out of there," Emma told him. "She climbs trees like a boy."

"I do not," Gracie said. "I climb like a woman who can climb trees. Don't you go setting your own kind back that way, Emma Duhon."

Emma spread her hands to Matt. "She's fearless. The bells don't need to go so high."

"That bark's gotta be like glass. Gracie," Matt said, eyeing the late-morning drizzle, "slipping would be easy."

"Go find someone who needs your help," was all the thanks he got.

Tonight the fair started. The preview and Santa party as they called it. The original plan had called for a morning opening tomorrow, but Emma decided it would be prettier and more lucrative with an early evening kickoff. Fortunately the fire chief had okayed the barbecue, the boiler—and the brazier that promised to be roaring tonight. The fragrant scent of frying crabs, crawdads and shrimp would make every mouth water.

Buzz, who owned Buzzard's Wet Bar just up the street, had actually applied for a license to sell beer. Matt was impressed. Buzz hadn't been so careful on previous occasions. The Boardroom had a lock on frozen daiquiris in plastic cups. Couldn't call a celebration a celebration till the gutters were clogged with those red and green cups.

Matt was expected to make this walk-through during the final preparations and show an interest, but his mind and heart weren't into checking out safety compliance on Main Street, or dealing with Lobelia Forestier.

Lobelia had popped up front and center. "Did you think about what I told you to do?" she said. He hadn't noticed before how the broad tip of her nose separated into two distinct bumps.

"What was that?" he said.

"Setting up that stuff for terrorists."

He tried to concentrate on her. "Stuff for terrorists? Are we expectin' a whole lot of those, Miz Forestier?"

She huffed. "We shouldn't be finding bodies in the landfill or havin' our citizens attacked on the way to their cars, but it all happens right here in Pointe Judah just the same as it does in New York. When that big old glass ball comes down—" she paused, frowning "—or goes up. One or the other. The one in Times Square on New Year's. They put up barricades, they search bags, and they don't allow any backpacks. All we need are checkpoints either end of the block. Your officers can check everyone comin' in."

Hammering sounded all around as stalls went up. The hundreds of bells Gracie Loder had already hung tinkled with every breeze. Hoover, the large, bearlike Bouvier belonging to Aurelie Board, a lawyer in town, snuffled back and forth, gathering mouthfuls of whatever got dropped on the street. Suky-Jo was in charge of setting up a stall for Poke Around and must have wound up each music box and snow globe as she unpacked them. "Jingle Bells" fought with the "Hallelujah Chorus" and a lot of other tunes that just made noise.

"Did you hear me, Matt Boudreaux?" Lobelia said. *"Terrorists."*

Lobelia was a terrorist, but Matt didn't want to tell her so, not right now. "Relax," he said. "This is a little holiday street fair in Pointe Judah, not Times Square on New Year's Eve. But we'll be on our toes, don't you worry."

She wasn't moving. "We know about the man in the landfill, y'know."

"So you already said." Rusty, who owned the town newspaper, hadn't even had a chance to put out the weekly issue, but Lobelia and her cronies could rival a champion team of homing pigeons for spreading news.

"We've got big trouble," Lobelia persisted. "We can't be too careful."

"And we will be careful," Matt said patiently, poised to act as Gracie's foot found the top rung of her ladder. She ran to the ground and moved to the next tree. Gracie had a nice body, he thought, but she wasn't his type.

Eileen was his type, but he'd managed to blow that.

Sarah and Delia Board huddled with the musicians who played at the Boardroom, most of whom looked as if they had hangovers. Matt wandered that way. In truth, these guys never slept much, so their eyelids were always at half-mast.

The Bouvier passed Matt and plodded over to sit at Sarah's feet.

"Matt." Delia waved. "Tell me we won't blow anything out here when we plug in the amplifiers." She gestured dramatically and her orange silk dress, which almost matched her hair, flipped around her calves.

"You won't blow anything," Matt said.

With Sarah in tow, Delia separated from the men and took Matt by the arm. She guided him to stand in front of Sadie and Sam's. "What's going on?" she asked him in a low, theatrical voice. "Lobelia's twittering all over the place. Of course we all know about that poor man who got fried at Ona's." She shuddered. "Dreadful. But *who* was he?"

"Someone who worked for Duhon's. We don't know much more than that yet. If you put the amplifiers out here now, what will you use at the club tonight?" He didn't care but wanted to change the subject.

"They won't be out here if the band's not out here," Delia pointed out.

Matt realized Sarah was smirking at him, and that she knew he was just trying to make conversation. He saluted her, scratched Hoover's head and turned around to look down the disaster that was Main Street. Vehicles picked their way cautiously between the stalls.

Angel DeAngelo's silver GMC truck wasn't a welcome site. He was the only person around to own one of the crew-cab monsters, which he usually left behind in favor of the motorcycle.

With the truck parked at the curb, Angel got out and did a

visual of the area. He quit searching as soon as he sighted Matt, who had figured the other man could be looking for him.

Matt separated from Delia and Sarah and walked slowly toward Angel. The man had one of those loose strides that covered a lot of ground fast. Did he, Matt wondered, know everyone looked at him when he passed? Coming right down the middle of the street, the gap narrowing between them, Matt recalled scenes of shootouts in western towns. All they needed was spurs.

Now, he wasn't a fanciful man. The pressure around here must be getting to him.

"Chief, hold up!"

He paused to let Sabine Webb catch up with him. "Hey, Sabine."

"Hey. I need your help."

"You've got it."

She grimaced. "With Lobelia."

"Maybe you don't have my help," he said.

"I'm going to tell fortunes tonight and she's having a fit. She says fortunes don't have a thing to do with Christmas. But people like it and it's fun, so where's the harm? Lobelia isn't complaining because someone's coming over from Toussaint to read dogs' minds, but she's giving me a bad time about fortunes."

Matt rotated his shoulders. "I'm thinking Delia might—"

"She said you'd tell Lobelia to butt out."

He thought fast. "Emma's in charge. She'll fix it."

Angel arrived and grinned at Sabine. "Good morning, gorgeous."

She was gorgeous but she still blushed, turning her dark

face even darker and making it glow. "Have you seen Emma yet?" she said, giving him a great big smile back.

He said he hadn't and Sabine took in the situation fast. The two men weren't going to be an answer to her problem right now.

"I've seen her," Matt said. "She's riding herd on Gracie. Over there. Gracie's up that tree."

Sabine looked doubtful but went in that direction.

"I think you should question Chuck Moggeridge," Angel said as soon as they were alone.

"Why would I do that?"

"He's saying some weird stuff."

"Yeah?" Matt said. "He should fit in real well around here."

"I don't like the way he keeps bothering Eileen," Angel said. "He needs to get lost."

"So he's saying the weird stuff to Eileen? I can't arrest someone just because you don't want him hanging around your girlfriend." He wasn't proud of the way that sounded.

Angel gave him one of his emotionless stares. "Chuck went with Leland when he identified Bucky."

"So I heard." Matt kicked at a stone and squinted heavenward. "If it rains on this lot it's gonna be one miserable evenin'."

"Santa will just have to wear rain gear," Angel said, smiling a little. He sobered. "We could get a tent from Delia. She's got them at Place Lafource. Uses them if she gives a big party. If we put one up down here, the kids could visit Santa in there."

"That'd make it real easy on traffic," Matt said.

"It's going to have to be diverted anyway," Angel pointed out.

"Yeah. I'll talk to Delia." Matt scrubbed at his face. "I'm short of personnel. Have been for more than a year. We're spread too thin. What I need is a real qualified backup who can keep the place going if I'm off. Seven days a week gets old. Of course, with the right man, we could be more-or-less a team. The money could be better, but I'm hoping that'll happen before long."

Angel made a sympathetic noise. It wasn't the first time Matt had made pretty pointed overtures for Angel to show interest in working as a small-town cop. Hell, there were days when Angel almost felt like taking him up on the offer, only chances were he'd be moving on one day. He'd never stayed in one place too long.

But he'd never before cared for a woman the way he cared for Eileen, either.

"Who would tell Chuck they thought Emma was supposed to be the one murdered and put in the Dumpster that night?" Angel asked. "Last night he was flapping his mouth about it."

Matt hooked his thumbs into his gun belt. "That's a pretty wild conclusion. Did he come up with it all on his own?"

"Partly, I think. He blamed Emma for causing the rift between him and Eileen. Something to do with a women's club."

"Secrets," Matt said promptly. "Some of the women in town got together to gossip and share recipes or somethin'. Things happened. It wasn't the club that was the problem though, not really. A personal agenda got in the way."

"Sounds as if Chuck's mad at Emma because she introduced Eileen to Secrets."

"He's lookin' for something or someone to blame," Matt said. "The guy's an ass who can't keep his zipper shut."

"Look," Angel said. "I'm wondering if Chuck was mad enough at Emma to try to frighten her."

"Could be, if he's spent the last couple of years working up a rage over her. But I don't really think so. He's back here trying to get back into Eileen's pants is all."

Angel gave Matt a hard look. "I wish you hadn't said that."

"I call it like I see it," Matt said. "You know how to keep your mouth shut, don't you?"

Muscles jerked in Angel's cheeks. "Yes, I do."

"Does yellow paper under Bucky Smith's fingernails give you any ideas?" Matt said. "Yellow paper and a wiry, gray hair."

Angel frowned at him.

"Start with the yellow paper," Matt said. "I'm not playing party games. I've got my ideas, but backup always helps. I'm waiting for reports, but something's obvious to me."

Automatically, Angel looked around to be sure they weren't overheard. "Could have been from the papers Emma lost?"

"Reckon so."

"So unless Bucky had a reason to pick on Emma... He wasn't around Pointe Judah when the little Secrets club was operating, was he?"

"Nope." Matt shook his head slowly from side to side. "He's only been here a few months. Came for the work."

"Poor bastard," Angel said. "Wrong place, wrong time, then."

"Yeah," Matt agreed. "But what was he doing in Ona's kitchen?"

"Beats me. What would you bet he got in a tussle with someone who didn't want to be seen or remembered there? Like whoever *did* go after Emma?

"Her purse ended up back in the restaurant—and her notebook. All the women agreed she took them with her when she left. What if the guy who attacked her grabbed her stuff and ran in through the side door of the kitchen to put it back and make it look like Emma's losing it? Delia and the clan were in the parking lot by that time. He must have watched and known the restaurant was empty. So in he goes and Bucky sees him and gets the paper under his nails when they struggle. Then, dead Bucky."

"Real helpful," Matt said. "Too bad dead men don't talk."

Angel laughed. "It'd wipe murder off the map if they did. Put you out of work."

"Nah," Matt said, grinning. "They'd still need me to watch for terrorists at the Christmas fair each year."

Angel scratched his forehead, but didn't ask for an explanation. "If anyone's going to find out if Chuck's more than just a nuisance around here, it's going to have to be you. Glad to help, but I can't be up front about it."

"No." Matt looked thoughtful and Angel braced himself for another job offer. "Does Finn keep you busy?"

Angel almost laughed. "He sure does. Sometimes I feel like a Little League coach sorting out a bunch of kids, but I'm okay with the job. I figure you already know this, but we didn't have any major trouble in town before Chuck showed up—not recently anyway."

"I did notice." Matt squared his shoulders. "He's on the radar. One piece of solid evidence pointing to him and I'll take him in."

Angel nodded. "I'm glad we're on the same map."

"If you ever get tired of it, let me know. I could really use you, Angel."

"Thanks," Angel said, admiring the other man for not allowing personal issues, like both of them wanting the same woman, to get in the way. "If anything changes, I'll let you know."

"You coming to the fair?" Matt said.

"Wouldn't miss it. I'd better get on now."

"There's something else you'll find interesting. They may have traced our gun."

That got Angel's undivided attention.

"I got the news this morning. They traced it to Toussaint of all places. It was used in a murder there—several years back."

"They got the killer?" Angel said.

"Yeah. But that's not what we care about. I talked with the sheriff over there, Spike Devol. Good guy. I've dealt with him before."

Angel knew he had to keep his mouth shut and be patient until Matt got wherever he was going.

"You know all about rifling, the marks on the ammo and so on, so I don't have to explain."

"The F in ATF *is* for firearms," Angel said. "Gives a guy an edge in that department. So, are you going to tell me they know who's got the gun now so we can all start sleeping at night?"

Matt looked really miserable. "Turns out the gun got stolen from evidence and they're not sure when."

"Yeah," Angel said. "I wonder how I figured out you were going to tell me that."

They both screwed up their eyes.

"Matt Boudreaux." Lobelia Forestier hurried up. "I don't know why I didn't think of this before. Your officers should stay put during the fair to make sure no one misbehaves."

"Miz Forestier—"

"More important than that. They can search every bag on the way out, too. Things always get stolen. If they check receipts against what folks have, they can catch anyone breaking the law."

25

"You know I don't like you in pants," Chuck said. He leaned against the wall in the farthest corner from the door. "I like to see your legs."

Gracie shook a finger at him and closed the door to her apartment behind her. "You wouldn't have wanted me in pants this morning," she said, grinning. "I was running up and down ladders on Main Street. Nice to see you're making yourself at home."

One thing about a woman like Gracie was that she didn't know how to cover up her weaknesses. He, Chuck thought, was her major weakness. He'd earned the right to use that.

She had known he'd be at her place when she got back from town and had given him the key to let himself in. He intended to keep the key for when he came back. Next time she wouldn't know he was coming.

Gracie locked the door.

"You expecting Rusty back?" he asked.

"No. I'm used to taking care of security. A woman alone has to do that."

"When are they expecting you back at work?"

"I've got my shift at Buzzard's before I work the fair for Sarah."

She never got straight to the point. "So how long do we have, darlin'?" he asked.

"A couple of hours." She kicked off her sneakers, took off her pants and went toward her bedroom. "I'm going to put on a skirt—just for you."

"Just for me you'll stay the way you are," he told her. Gracie had girlie legs, the kind he liked—one of the kinds he liked, all curves even if he did know how strong they were. He smiled to himself.

She folded the pants and put them with her purse on a straight-backed chair.

He patted his lap and held his arms out to her.

Gracie dipped and said, "Will I be safe?"

"No, I promise you won't."

She all but leaped onto his thighs and hugged his neck before kissing him. Gracie knew a lot about kissing and he felt her smile against his mouth when she felt an uprising in the south.

"Mmm." He set her firmly where she couldn't distract him any more than she already had and tilted her head back onto his shoulder. "What do you want from me, Gracie?" Every word he said had to be thought out first.

"You know what I want. I want you. I've always wanted you."

"But it's never been easy for us, has it?"

"No," she said. "I thought I'd lost you but you've come back. We're going to get back together, aren't we, Chuck?"

"We surely are. But you're going to have to help me. We've got to talk about things I don't want to remember and I wish to hell I could wipe out of your mind."

She shifted her head till she could look up at him. A faint

flush warmed her features. Sex did that to her, even thinking about sex.

"We want to be together," he said, looking back at her. She nodded, her lips parted, her breath coming in little pants. "If that's going to happen, we'll have to help each other."

"Whatever it takes, we can do it," Gracie said. She put her hands on his neck. "Together, Chuck. We'll do whatever it takes."

Chuck slid a hand under her blue T-shirt and pulled a bra strap from her shoulder. Her eyes glossed over when he fondled her breast. He spent time bringing her pleasure.

He felt her body tighten and could guess she was confused that he wasn't getting right to it, the way she was used to. Chuck had his reasons.

"I love you, Gracie," he said against her forehead. "I want to do something about it. I've waited too long."

"Oh, Chuck." She had tears in her voice. "I love you, too."

"I'm scared is all," he told her, keeping his eyes on hers. "It's going to take time to do everything we want to do. I know it'll work out in the end, but it'll be damned hard on both of us."

She sat up, rested her arms on his shoulders and kissed him again and again.

Chuck unhooked the back of her bra and covered both of her breasts. "I'm going to be with you," he told her. "And I'm going to get what's coming to me—for the two of us. I want it from Eileen. She kept me poor the way she spent before she decided she wanted a career. Only she didn't go after the career until after I'd left and we were divorced. She still wants me, Gracie."

Her eyes fixed on his. "What does that have to do with us?"

"You're going to help me get what we've got coming. If it hadn't been for her, I wouldn't have left town in the first place. I only did it to save her feelings."

Her mouth trembled. "To save her feelings?"

"The Duhon family's looked up to around here. Her father was police chief in this town for years and they still talk about him like he was a saint. If it had come out about you and me and the way we made a fool of Eileen, she'd never have lived it down. I didn't want to do that to her."

"So you made a fool of me, instead."

This was exactly what he'd expected. "Baby, folks didn't know about us. When I left Pointe Judah, no fingers were pointed at you."

She flattened her hands on his chest and rubbed up and down. "You still thought about her first."

"I shouldn't have," Chuck said. He'd say whatever it took. "I got so confused I ran. That was wrong, baby. But it's going to work out better for us in the end. When I left, she had nothing. Now she's got plenty. She's got too much for one woman to handle. She's rolling in it and you and I both know it."

At least Gracie nodded. She also pouted.

"I've got to tell you the whole thing. I haven't told anyone else because I've been trying to put it behind me." He hung his head and shook it slowly from side to side.

"You can trust me, honey," Gracie said, ruffling his hair.

Chuck sighed. "Yeah. I intended to come back for you earlier but I got in trouble on the rigs. Some bastard set me up and I was kicked off. It took me a while to decide what to do. No woman wants a man who can't take care of her. When I found out Eileen was in fat city I knew there was a chance I could make it good for the two of us, you and me."

She lay against him, her face in his neck.

Let him get through this, he thought. Let him persuade her to do what he wanted. If it worked, he'd stick around long enough to get a fat little stake then move on—or not. That depended on how good he could have it right here in Pointe Judah.

Playing Mr. Nice took it out of a man. "Maybe you won't be able to pull it off, Gracie."

"I can do whatever you need." She looked into his face again.

"If I can get Eileen to marry me again, we'll—that's us, baby—we'll have it both ways. We'll have each other and we'll have money."

Gracie's stare shook him. It wasn't going to work.

Tears slid down Gracie's face and he wanted to yell at her to grow up. "Why are you crying, babe?"

"I work hard. I can work harder. I've never had any trouble getting jobs. With you at Duhon's and what I make, you don't need Eileen. I'll make sure we have what we need."

He got up, let her overbalance backward and fall on the carpet. Standing over her, he breathed hard. "You think I want you to keep me? I want to be the one to make a good life for us. What do you think I am? Some mama's boy who needs her to do for him?" He shifted like he was going to step over her. "Forget it. I understand what I've asked is over the top. Sometimes we just have to move on. You deserve a different kind of man from me."

"What do we *need?*" she cried. "This place is plenty big enough for both of us. We'll do okay. Don't leave me again, Chuck."

He looked away, then thudded back into the chair and put his head in his hands.

"She never worked a day when she was married to me," he muttered. "All I want is a share of what came to her when she could have been making things good for us."

"I don't want you to marry her. She's seeing that Angel anyway and I bet they're real tight."

Thinking about Eileen with friggin' Angel sweating over her didn't thrill Chuck, but he couldn't let it get in the way. "She wants the best for Aaron. Having his folks together, Mr. and Mrs. Small-town America, is what she always said he needed. Now she can get it for him."

"Aaron's not a little kid anymore," Gracie said.

"He's at an impressionable age," Chuck told her, barely managing to keep the lid on his temper. "His parents still matter."

She had swung her legs to one side but remained sitting on the floor. "So I'm supposed to stay out of the way and watch while you get together with Eileen?" She wouldn't look at him now.

"Just help us get what we want. Make sure she never guesses we were ever together."

"And if she does find out?"

At least she was thorough. "She won't as long as you don't tell her. No one knows about the baby, do they?"

"Chuck, don't talk about the baby."

"I'm sorry, but we've got to get through this. Did you tell anyone about the abortion?"

He might have guessed it was time for more waterworks and this time he didn't say anything or try to make her stop.

"Our baby's gone," she managed between sobs. "There wasn't anyone who knew but you, and you didn't want a baby. It was hard, Chuck. It still is."

"Sure it is and I'm sorry you had to go through that."

"I didn't *have* to—if you'd done the right thing by me."

He knew better than to get mad. Women were weird about these things and they had to work them through. But she was taking too long over it. "If I could turn the clock back, I would. I can't, baby."

She looked down and nodded. "What if Eileen does find out and she tells people? I live here. I have to work here."

From her voice, he couldn't tell if she might be threatening him.

"You don't work for Eileen and she's not going to embarrass herself by blabbing about how I made a fool of her." His restraint was cracking. "But she'll never find out."

He took her by the wrists and pulled her in front of him, onto her knees between his thighs. He undid his belt slowly and pulled it from the loops. Then he unbuttoned and unzipped his pants

"But *if* she did hear something, she'd only hate you more," Gracie said, watching what he was doing.

This time the threat was obvious. If he didn't give Gracie what she wanted, or enough to keep her happy, she would make sure Eileen heard the whole story. He grunted and pushed his pants halfway down his thighs. "That feels better," he said. "We need to make sure we understand each other. You're a woman. You know better than I do what it takes to make a woman mad enough to go after a man, just to hurt some other bitch—and the man."

"Yes, I do."

"I could use a little help here," he said, moving his hips just enough to set things in motion. "Just trust me. I'll make sure you're glad you're on my side. You will never want anything to hurt me."

Gradually, her gaze fixed, Gracie bent over and took him in her mouth.

His balls contracted and he sucked in his belly. Sex would keep her in line.

26

THE BOARDROOM BOYS, playing "Here Comes Santa Claus" with Bugbelly Pitts grinding the words through his callused throat, set a wild tone. Aaron wondered if they played this loud at The Boardroom. Playing in front of the thirty-foot, glittering, flashing Christmas tree Mayor Patrick Damalis had arranged as a personal gift to the town, the Boys had replaced their Stetsons with Santa hats and wore red, green-and-white-striped vests.

"You people have weird ideas about music," Sonny told Aaron. "My grandpa used to say I couldn't carry a tune in a bucket, but I reckon I could do as good as that Bugbelly."

Aaron smirked. "Shows what you know about Cajun music," he said. "You've been here long enough to learn, but maybe it's your ears that still need workin' on." He punched a booted foot into the surface of the street, keeping time.

The shops lining the street were closed but had their interior lights on low. Holiday strands twinkled in most windows. Smells from a giant pot of crab and shrimp boil, sausage on a barbecue, and frying beignets drew crowds to the food stands. Aaron saw Gracie Loder serving up daiquiris in plastic cups for the Boardroom right next to Buzzard's Beer Garden.

"That's one great tent," Sonny said, pointing to what looked like an acre of green-and-white canvas.

Aaron watched children running in and out of an open flap.

"It's called a marquee. Delia uses it when she has a party out at Place Lafource. I guess the food goes in there. She lent it to the fair in case it rains. They've kids' games in there."

"How come you know that and I don't?" Sonny said.

Aaron shugged. "Maybe they don't have garden parties in Brooklyn?"

"Garden parties?" Sonny laughed. "You're jerking my chain."

Two local cops wandered by looking relaxed. Everybody had heard how Lobelia requested searches for possible terrorists. Aaron grinned. Apart from folks who had come in with stalls of stuff to sell, he figured he knew everyone there.

"I didn't know these people had it in 'em," Sonny said, rubbernecking in all directions to take in the scene. "Did you see that Wazoo, or whatever she's called? The woman from Toussaint who reads dogs' minds?"

"Cats', too," Aaron said, laughing. "Reckons she's an animal psychologist. Maybe we could borrow Locum to get a look inside her tent."

"You borrow him," Sonny said. "I like Chuzah a lot, but I'm not going all the way out to his place—not in the dark."

"We've done it before and you liked it once we were there," Aaron said, looking away and frowning. Chuzah was special and he was the only one Aaron knew who didn't expect anything from a person. "Just be," was one of Chuzah's favorite sayings. He wanted to *just be,* Aaron thought. His mom only wanted things to make his life better, but she still didn't seem to understand how a guy needed space and quiet and time to think.

"You okay?" Sonny asked, elbowing him.

"Sure." Aaron flashed him a grin. "I'm great, just taking it all in. Nothing much happens around here so when there is a shindig it takes some getting used to." He liked having Sonny around.

"It's cold," Sonny said. "It's not supposed to get this cold in Louisiana."

"Who says? Just be grateful we don't get snow here—or almost never do. You want to go see the animal woman? There's got to be someone who'd let us use their pet." At that moment he saw Hoover, Aurelie Board's big dog, hanging around Sarah Board. "I bet Hoover's head would be worth a look inside."

They sauntered up to Sarah who said, "Hi," with a big grin.

"Okay," Aaron said. "I'm just coming right out with it. If we promise to take care of Hoover, can we borrow him to take to the animal lady?"

The music had grown even louder and Sarah took the boys aside. She made them repeat the request then said, "Miz Wazoo is an animal psychologist. It says so on her sign. There's a long line for her but if that's what you want to do, be my guest. Hoover could use some analyzing. His leash is draped around my mother's neck. Tell her I said you could use it."

Delia Board not only gave Aaron the leash, she also insisted on tucking money for the "consultation" into his hand with a request, "Ask her if she knows why he sucks up and chews everything he sees. Food, plants, pens, socks, everything. If she can cure that, it would be a nice homecoming gift when Aurelie and Nick get back."

When they got close to a black tent outlined with blue fairy lights Sonny said, "Look at the line." The sound of barking didn't quit and some owners wrestled to control their animals. "You sure we want to do this?"

Aaron held Hoover's leash. The dog's huge tongue lolled out of his mouth and what could be seen of his eyes through shaggy black bangs looked adoringly at each of them. "I think he likes being with us," Aaron said. "Look at him sitting right there. He likes the leash."

"Why don't we take it in turns to stand in line, then?" Sonny suggested. "You go first and I'll stay. You're supposed to check in with Eileen."

Reluctantly, Aaron agreed and took off to find the Poke Around stall. He saw his mother before she saw him. She was laughing with Frances Broussard who owned the salon next to Poke Around at the Oakdale Mansion Center. Angel stood with his arms crossed and the closest thing Aaron had ever seen to discomfort on the man's face. Rusty Barnes from the newspaper was taking a picture of them. He finished and hung with Angel, gesturing and talking.

"Hey," Aaron said, planting himself front and center. "I need Christmas presents, lots of 'em. I've got all these people to give totally unique stuff to."

Angel chewed the inside of a cheek and rocked onto his toes and back.

"Unique is unique," Aaron's mom said.

"That's what I said. Totally unique stuff."

"It's already totally. Unique means the only one of its kind—"

"Give him a break," Angel said and grinned. "Will you look at this?" he said to Rusty. "She's got me playing shop boy. I have to check the price on anything I sell and if the customer doesn't pick it up and give it to me—if they just ask for something—I don't know what they want."

"How much are those?" Rusty said. He pointed at the laden stall. Angel followed the direction of the finger for an instant before landing a backhand on Rusty's chest. Rusty winced and pretended to stagger. "Almost had you there," he said.

Eileen finished wrapping a bunch of crystal icicles in tissue paper and took money from Frances. "You know what Angel's anglin' for, don't you?" Frances said, lifting her mouth to Aaron's ear. She had about a million long but tiny twists in her black hair. The twists left the ends loose and they were bleached light gold and curled up. He thought it all looked cute.

"You know, don't you?" Frances said.

He started. "I like your hair. What are those called?"

Frances patted her head as if she couldn't remember what her hair looked like. "These are Michael twists. Any time you feel like makin' a statement, you come right on in and I'll give you a whole new look. Now, you gonna answer my question?"

Fortunately, he remembered it. He grinned at Frances and turned to Angel. "I wish I could take over for you, man, but Sonny's waiting for me. We're in line with Hoover to see the animal woman—I mean psychologist. Miz Delia Board wants us to ask some questions for her." That wasn't a lie.

Frances laughed, a rich sound that got everyone around them chuckling, too.

She moved off with her icicles and Eileen said to Angel, "Suky-Jo sold out those sachets she makes so she's gone home for more. She'll be back to spring you soon—after I get some fresh stock from the van."

Angel turned to her and said, "You will not be going to the van on your own."

Aaron's mom started to say something, but he saw her change her mind about what that was going to be. "I'm sorry you hate doing this," she said. "You did volunteer, Christian."

Angel scrunched up his face. "She calls me Christian when I'm in trouble. Right now she's pissed off—"

"Christian!"

"Yeah, well." Angel crossed his arms again, but his instant smile slowly left his face and he turned toward the next booth. He held very still.

Aaron almost asked what was up but thought better of it.

"It's about time Santa showed up," Rusty said. "I hear we're all in for a surprise."

"Who's being Santa?" Aaron asked.

Rusty said, "Now, how would I know? It's a well-kept secret. Smell that barbecue. I'm going to get something for dinner."

"I'll go for you," Angel said, reaching for his wallet. "Just tell me what you want. All you have to do is watch the booth."

Rusty laughed. "I won't know what I want till I see it. I'll scout around first." He wandered off.

"I should get back to Sonny so he can look at stuff. He wanted to eat, too."

A hand landed on his shoulder. "Hey, Aaron. How's it going?"

He turned toward his dad's voice and got pulled into a bear hug. Hugging back came naturally, and it felt good. "I'm great, Dad," he said when they stood back. "You enjoying the fair?"

"Better now I see you. Bought anything?"

"Not yet." He dropped his voice. "I've seen a necklace I'm gonna get Mom as soon as I'm sure she won't see me."

"Sounds good. Expensive?"

"It's worth it. I don't spend on anything much."

"Here." Chuck pulled out his wallet. "This'll help."

"No," Aaron said. "Honest, I've got enough."

His father stuffed some bills into Aaron's pocket. "Maybe there's earrings or a bracelet, too," he said and hugged Aaron again. "I miss you, son," he said quietly.

Aaron's throat got tight and he nodded.

"Evening, Chuck," Angel said. He sounded too calm for Aaron's comfort.

Chuck turned to the stall and said, "Good evenin' to both of you. How's business?"

Aaron's mom hadn't left yet. She was putting a painted metal penguin with legs made of springs into a tissue-lined box. She kept her attention on her customer, and smiled too brightly, laughed too loud. Once the transaction was completed, she moved immediately to help the next in line and Angel actually said, "Anything I can sell you, Chuck?"

Aaron grew hot. He felt a little sick.

"Sure," Chuck said. "I'll take one of those penguins like Eileen just sold. Make it two. I've got to get my shopping done."

"Bye Mom and Dad," Aaron said and added, "Bye Angel." But he knew what he'd said and how it sounded and his stomach turned over again.

He fled back toward the animal woman's tent but did stop at Lori's Gems, an out-of-town seller, to buy the jade necklace he'd seen earlier. He added both a matching pair of earrings and a bracelet and discovered the money his father had given him covered everything.

"Sonny," he shouted when he got close to Wazoo's tent. "Your turn."

"Woohoo," Sonny said, handing over control of Hoover's leash. "I just about passed out from hunger."

"Are we next?" Aaron asked. Sonny and Hoover were at the front of the line. "We *are* next. You can't go for food now."

"You'll do fine," Sonny said. "I've had enough of dogs and cats for one night. When you're through, come to the food tent. I'll still be there." He took off, then ran back. "Chuzah's in there with her. I saw him take Locum in while I was way back in line and he's stayed there for everyone who went in since."

"Yeah?" Aaron grinned. "Maybe he reads animal brains, too."

This time Sonny did meld in with the crowd, going in the direction of the food vendors.

"You sick of waiting, boy?" Aaron said, rubbing the area between Hoover's ears. The dog got closer to make it easier for Aaron to scratch him.

The tent flap opened and Cyril from the hardware store walked out with a black lab. "She's great," Cyril said to Aaron in passing.

A bell rang and the woman behind Aaron said, "That means you're to go in."

He realized his hand had turned sweaty on the leash but in he went, pulling aside the flap and letting it drop behind him. Getting used to the gloom took a moment.

"Come to Wazoo," a dark-haired woman said, looking directly at Hoover. "A Bouvier de Flandres and a very handsome fellow. Sit by me."

Aaron let go of the leash and Hoover went at once to sit beside Wazoo. He looked up into her face.

Slightly behind Wazoo sat Chuzah with Locum who cocked his head and stared at Aaron. "This is a friend of mine," Chuzah said. "Aaron Moggeridge."

Aaron met Chuzah's eyes. The man's stare held first question, then, after a few seconds, emptiness. Tonight he wore an orange Hawaiian shirt and loose, white cotton pants. The clothes shouldn't be warm enough but he looked comfortable—all the way to his long, silver-tipped nails.

"You should tell Wazoo how Hoover shows his troubles," Chuzah said.

"He, er, isn't mine," Aaron said. "He belongs to some people who are out of town and I'm bringing him for their family. I was asked to tell you he, er, sucks up everything. Anything he can get to. He chews it and gets into trouble. His grandma wants—I mean a member of the family that owns him wants to know why he does it and what to do about it."

Wazoo rested a cheek on top of Hoover's head and her long hair fell to cover her face and cascade over the dog.

Aaron thought the lady was beautiful and mysterious, like an Egyptian princess in a long, black-and-purple lace dress. Not that he was sure how an Egyptian princess was supposed to look.

Silence went on for what felt like forever. Each time Aaron looked at Chuzah, he met the same dark stare but wasn't certain the man saw him at all.

"How can this work with another dog in here?" Aaron said suddenly. He hadn't thought about how quiet and watchful Locum was, or that Hoover didn't react to him at all.

Chuzah raised one finger to his lips. Looking back at Wazoo and Hoover, Aaron felt as if he'd been told off.

Flinging back her hair, Wazoo lifted her head a little. She

spoke to the dog in a voice too low to be heard and Hoover rested his big head on her knee. Aaron thought the animal's eyes were closed.

"He is shy, him," Wazoo said. "He steals things—"

"*Steals* them?" Aaron said.

"They don't belong to him, no way," she told him. "He steals things to make him feel like he's the important one. Him, he likes touch, likes hands on him. When he steals, he gets those hands real quick. You got two choices with this boy. Don't you take notice of him and he'll steal and chew and give it up in the end—probably die in some corner of a broken heart. Or put your hands on him a whole lot when his mouth is empty. You're welcome."

After seconds passed, Aaron figured that was it. He was out of here. "Thank you," he said, pulling Delia's money from his pocket and holding it out.

Somehow Wazoo's fingers moved so quick and smooth it felt like no bills had been in Aaron's hand in the first place.

Chuzah stood. He said, "We'll meet again," to Wazoo and left. Not a word to Aaron.

"You and Chuzah are old friends?" Aaron said.

Wazoo massaged Hoover gently. "Nope. We just made acquaintance. A courtesy from the gentleman. A welcome to share his place." She gave Aaron the end of the leash, and rang a shiny bell she had on the ground beside her.

With Hoover a little wobbly beside him, Aaron went out into the din, the sparkle, the whirl of people and colors. He found Delia and told her what had been said about the dog—and got an odd look from her. "Is that so?" But when he got a few yards away again and glanced back, she had crouched to give Hoover a hug.

"Here you go, young man."

He automatically took the pamphlets Miz Lobelia Forestier thrust into his hands from the bulging canvas bag she carried. She had moved on before he'd seen that she'd given him a list of emergency services in Pointe Judah and a map of the town.

A man passed him, running, dodging when he had to, but going fast. Uncle Finn. People stopped to watch him.

Carley from the police station hurried by, then Matt Boudreaux overtook her. Something was definitely up.

Aaron started to follow, but looked over his shoulder at the same time. Emma walked toward him, slowed down by the baby, and she looked like she was trying not to cry. He went to her and awkwardly patted her arm. "Don't cry," he said.

She grabbed his hand and squeezed harder than a lady should be able to. He wanted to wiggle his fingers loose but Emma walked on, still holding his hand.

"What's wrong?" Aaron asked, and she let go of the tears. She shook and made choking sounds. "You're gonna be ill," he told her.

They were passing the band and Aaron wondered vaguely why they stood there with instruments silent. Bugbelly saw Emma and hurried to her with a chair. "You sit there, Miz Duhon," he said. "You can't help. We all need to wait and see what they want us to do."

Emma sat but she didn't let go of Aaron's hand. "Your mother's going to be fine," she said. "She can't have just disappeared. Or her van. Eileen must have decided—" she paused to swallow "—she took a drive somewhere. That's what she did."

27

All those things broke.

She was damp. Cold. Her eyes wouldn't open.

Angel?

Sounds, louder and louder. Frogs and things squeaking, rustling, creaking. Popping, sucking, popping, sucking. Water really close.

That man, Bucky Smith, died of a heart attack. They said that. A heart attack when he got pushed in the fryer.

"Help me." She heard her voice. "It's Eileen."

Her head ached, it thumped inside. And the side of her forehead, the side on the ground, stung. She should turn her face.

"Two," the man had said. That was all.

He breathed loudly, in short breaths. Like he was frightened?

She was warmer now, and the ground, the little stones turned softer.

"Angel?" she whispered.

28

Delia's marquee had been turned into Matt's operations center. Things moved fast and there were already volunteers from law enforcement in other towns on their way. The FBI was standing by. They had already started work on Bucky's murder.

Angel, flanked by Sonny and Aaron, watched as maps were pinned to standing boards. The professionals were cool and efficient, moving rapidly through a protocol they had applied too many times before.

Outside the striped canvas, shadows of fair-goers passed, some hurrying, some taking time to look in the marquee. Most of these people were friends of Eileen, or at least they knew her; many had already congregated at a designated meeting point, waiting for search instructions.

"The darkness is going to make it tough," Matt said. "A miracle would be welcome but I don't guess we'll be makin' much progress before dawn."

Angel knew all about the dark. He wouldn't be waiting for dawn. He took a few steps backward.

"Mom can't be out there in the dark alone," Aaron said. The temperature might have been cool, but sweat shone on his face. "Do you think she went for a drive?" He looked at Angel as if he had all the answers.

"She is out there," Angel said, gripping Aaron's arm. "And we're going to find her. I need you to be calm. I know what I'm doing and we're not wasting any more time here."

"Gotcha," Sonny said. This kid had already seen and been through too much for his age, and it gave him an edge tonight.

Chuck Moggeridge pushed his way into the marquee. He'd have to be Oscar material to look as frantic as he did if he wasn't on the verge of losing control.

Dropping all the way back behind the throng, Angel led Aaron and Sonny outside.

A crowd had assembled there and they weren't talking. On either side of them people—most of them with children—scurried to clear the area.

"Go to the right," Angel said. He saw Dr. Mitch Halpern hovering, alone and watchful. "We could use you," Angel told him and the man fell in immediately.

"Where do we start?" Mitch asked.

"Thank God for someone who thinks we should get started," Angel said. "Scratch that. I've got to learn that I can't run every show."

Mitch chuckled. "You can run any show like this one for me."

The boys were too quiet, but Angel didn't have time to do any counseling. "I've got a radio," he said. "I registered it with the cops so they can get to me—and I can get to them." He didn't mention that he also had his Glock. "Start close and work outward makes the best sense. The first thing is to check out where Eileen's van was parked and then go over the surrounding area…for clues," he added rapidly.

"Or Mom," Aaron said, breathless when they'd hardly started. "Mom could be around here."

"Sure, she could," Mitch said.

"She's dead," Aaron said. "If she wasn't, we'd know it."

"Don't you do that," Sonny said loudly. "Panic plays with your brain. You can't think straight. So shut up and follow orders."

Grimacing, Angel didn't try to soften what Sonny had said.

They ran down an alley between the shops toward the area of open ground behind where everyone parked when Main Street was full.

Cars left the field in a nose-to-tail stream. Angel went to the spot where the van had been parked and said, "Damn it. Why wasn't this taped off?"

A pale-colored, rusty pickup was parked there.

"This is what happens when the local police are short-handed and someone doesn't act on an order," Angel added.

Two men jogged to the pickup and opened its doors.

"When did you park here?" Mitch Halpern said.

One of the men laughed. The other said, "What's it to you?"

"Was the spot empty when—" Angel stopped himself. His gray cells were starting to stick together. "Sorry to break in on you, but was someone pulling out of this spot when you got here? Did you have to wait for them?"

More laughter.

"It's important," Angel said. "There was a van right here and we think someone could have been carjacked in it."

"No *shit*," the guy on the driver's side said. Both men were probably in their late twenties or early thirties and Angel thought he'd seen them in one of Duhon's construction crews.

"It was empty, man. We only took a drive through just in case. Looked like the place was full."

"How long ago was that?" Angel said.

He got twin shrugs before the driver said, "Maybe fifteen minutes. We just had to stop in at Buzz's for somethin'. Here—" he ripped a scrap of paper from a brown bag he carried, pulled a pen out of his shirt pocket and wrote "—our phone number. I'm Jim Pence. That's my little brother, Ace."

"You work for Duhon's?" Angel asked.

They did and he took the paper feeling secure about getting in touch with them again if he had to.

Mitch got some powerful flashlights from his car and he and Angel started to search the parking space. "Lanterns are part of a doctor's kit in these parts. It doesn't happen often, but I've been called to more than one place where they used oil lamps. Try delivering a baby using only oil lamps."

"I'll pass on that," Angel said.

"There isn't anything to see," Aaron almost shouted. "Why are we wasting time here?"

"To make sure there's nothing," Sonny told him. He thumped Aaron's shoulder. "We gotta keep going. We can't let down now. Eileen needs us. She's out here somewhere. Either someone's driven off with her, or she's driving around on her own. Hey, Angel, did you two have a fight?"

"A what?" Mitch Halpern said.

Angel wanted to cuff smart-mouthed Sonny but that could come later. "Eileen and I didn't have a cross word."

"Not even when you didn't like being at the stall?" Aaron said, shoving his hands hard into his pockets and giving Angel a glare.

"We weren't fighting.... Ah, hell no, Aaron. C'mon, I want this field looked at. Sonny'll go with you, Mitch."

"We're looking for clues," Aaron said. He rested a fist against his mouth. "Things that might lead to finding Mom's body."

"You're with me," Angel said and took Aaron by the arm. Immediately, the boy flung him off and stalked away, looking around in the dark. Angel caught up with him and started moving his flashlight beam back and forth over the gravel and grass.

Aaron turned away again, and Angel followed.

They walked side by side then, all the way to the end of the field. When he flashed the light toward the undergrowth and bushes, he heard Aaron choke off a sob.

"All I'm doing is working a grid. We'll gradually move out until we've covered everything here. It's not big." He put a hand on Aaron's shoulder and felt the muscles and tendons jerk like steel cable. This time he didn't get shaken away.

The radio crackled and he tuned in. "Angel, here," he said into the collar mike he wore.

"Where are you?" It was Matt.

"Searching the overflow parking area," he responded and controlled the urge to add that the job should already have been done, that the slot where Eileen had been parked should be taped off.

"I thought that was already done," Matt said, the connection buzzing and breaking up.

"What's up?" Angel wouldn't waste effort shooting the breeze.

A short period of sounds like a road drill bouncing on rock followed.

"Matt, you there?" Angel said.

"Yes. We've found the van. It was just called in."

Sonny and Mitch had returned and the four of them stood in a close group. "And?" Angel said. He stuck his teeth into his bottom lip to stop it trembling. His mouth was trembling, dammit. What was wrong with him?

"She's not in it, Angel. It's in a cul-de-sac out at The Willows site. In Division Five."

"Nothing's been started in Five, yet."

"No," Matt said. "That's why the van was spotted. I'm on my way there."

"So am I." Angel ran for the exit from the lot. Footsteps pounded just behind him all the way to the corner of Cotton Alley where he made a left toward Main Street. The others kept coming, too.

He'd eaten dinner at Ona's and she insisted he leave his truck there and walk to the fair. Parked on the first end he came to, the crew cab shone in lights from the windows. Out Front looked empty inside. A murder on the premises, in the kitchen, could dampen appetites that usually ate there.

"We'll all fit," Sonny said, and added, "Good thing you didn't come on your bike."

Angel unlocked the doors and the four of them piled in.

They drove south a way, then up through the high-rent district around the golf club. He'd been told Emma used to live there when she was in a bad marriage to a former Pointe Judah mayor, before she and Finn met.

Several miles and they reached the First Division at The Willows. It was all built up and there was plenty of evidence of occupation.

"It's good you know your way around here," Mitch said. "I'd be useless."

"Yeah." Angel leaned forward, peering ahead.

"Cop cars," Sonny said. He gripped the back of Angel's seat. "Loads of 'em. See the flashing?"

"We'd have to be blind not to," Aaron snapped back. "Why'd you let her go to the parking lot on her own, Angel?"

"I didn't, God dammit." His gut felt like it slammed against his spine. "I went to the bathroom. Suky-Jo was back and I told Eileen to wait for me before she ran to the van. She didn't wait. She told Suky-Jo she needed to get something and she'd only be gone a second."

He reached the row of cruisers, three of them, and an emergency-aid vehicle. And he saw the van where floods were being erected and the white glare came on.

Throwing open his door, he jumped out and approached fast.

"Watch it," Matt said when he saw him. "You boys stay back."

"It's my mother you're looking for," Aaron yelped.

"Do as you're told," Angel told him. "We don't want to mess with any evidence."

Aaron passed him and Angel grabbed him back. "Evidence to find the murderer, right?" Aaron said. He crumpled and almost fell before he staggered back the way he'd come.

"Stay with him," Angel told Sonny. "Matt, what are you seeing?"

"Forensics—"

"Sure, they're taking over." He watched the team going through a drill that looked like it had been performed many times.

"A whole lot of stuff in the back's broken," Matt said. He

put some distance between himself and the van—and Aaron. "This is just guesswork right now, but we think someone was thrown in the back of the van on top of everything," he told Angel and Mitch.

A woman swathed in white got closer to the back of the abandoned vehicle and took pictures. From the way she pointed the camera and moved it only fractionally, Angel could tell she was shooting one area from different angles.

Angel narrowed his eyes but couldn't make out any details. "What's she so interested in?" he asked.

Matt took a very long time to draw in a breath and say, "There's a dent in the left rear door. Looks like there's some blood there. And maybe a hair or two."

29

Eileen felt a warm weight pressed against her side, resting on her shoulder. She opened her eyes, or the right one. The lid on her left eye wouldn't work, and it hurt to try.

Pain.

Thumping in her head, like before. When was before? She let her open eye move over rocks and plants silvered by the moon. There had been another time when she'd woken up— earlier—she didn't look at anything then. But she heard sounds, as she heard them now, only there were more of them all the time.

She moved the fingers of each hand, bent her left elbow, and shifted her head slowly to look down—and opened her mouth to scream.

An animal lay there, its head on her shoulder, its bright eyes looking into her face. Eileen choked down the noise rising in her throat. Wild animals didn't strike if you held really still. No, that wasn't right. Wild animals ate dead things.

She shuddered and the creature got up, sat beside her. It lowered its face closer to hers and she did scream, and close her eye tightly. The hammering in her head felt as if it kept pace with a heart that beat so hard it ached. Her whole body ached.

Breath crossed her cheek, then the animal licked her and licked her again. It's cold, wet nose met her skin and sniffed. And then, more licking.

Eileen dared to look again, and she saw how the moon made the animal's eyes silver, too, and its coat.

Locum. "Locum?"

She got another lick.

Slowly, Eileen curled around and pushed herself up to sit. Locum stayed where he was, watching. She held out a hand and the dog nuzzled her palm.

The sound of water intruded again. Not far away, she thought it must be Bayou Nezpique, but supposed it could be just about anywhere. She sat among shallow puddles with clumps of rough grasses and creeper vines running in every direction. The area she could see fairly clearly was small, then as she raised her chin, recoiled from the immediate crash in her brain, and glimpsed the contorted upper branches of cypress trees, black against a paler sky. Heavy beards of Spanish moss swayed.

This was swampland.

Two was all the man said as he'd thrown her into the van. Small boxes made of thin cardboard had collapsed beneath her and she'd heard her stock crack and shatter. But she hadn't heard any more. A film had coated her vision and she'd felt herself slip away.

Locum came closer. He raised a paw and she held it, but there was urgency in him now, Eileen felt it. She also felt how sodden her jeans and shirt were, but at least her sneakers were still firmly tied on her feet.

After nudging her again, he withdrew a few feet, pointed his body away and looked back at her,

"Don't go," she told him and he ran back to butt her with his head. Away he went again, not far, and turned his head to stare at her with his light eyes. He was trying to get her to follow him.

Gradually, she rose on shaky legs and chafed her arms, nervous about attempting to walk.

Thoughts came faster. "How did you know where to find me?" she asked Locum, who kept staring at her. Prickling ran rapidly up her spine and the hairs on her neck stood up. Goose bumps covered her, but being cold and wet could account for that.

Gingerly, she started to walk. Her only injury seemed to be on her brow and inside her head. But whatever had hurt her face could make her brain painful. Locum repeatedly ran a little and returned. At last he sat again, but not near her this time.

She tried to smile but her left eye stopped her. Very carefully, she touched that eye and found it hugely swollen. Crusty matter lined the opening. More crust clung to her forehead but when she pressed it lightly, she felt fluid on her fingers and peered at them. Blood, there was no doubt of that.

"Okay, lead on, Locum," she said.

He led and she followed, watching the dog, watching the ground, afraid of tripping and afraid of coming upon a snake or a rat. Things struck and killed around here and death didn't come easily.

They went over fallen trees, Locum jumping, Eileen putting down a supporting hand and climbing carefully. In places she squelched into mud and faltered, nervous that she'd slip down.

With each passing minute, she thought more clearly. She

remembered the fair, and Angel trying to persuade her not to go to the van until he could go with her.

She should have listened to Angel, she should always listen to him. And deliberately sneaking off while he wasn't there had been wrong. A frown made her cry out, "Ouch," and Locum returned to her side. She stroked him and he set off again.

Listening to Angel all the time wouldn't work. He didn't always get everything right—just most of the time.

He had said something about a bad *feeling* he'd had, but she didn't believe in those things.

An owl hooted and Eileen slapped a hand over her heart. Without Locum she just knew she'd die out here because she wouldn't know where to go or have the guts to risk the things she could encounter.

The next time Angel got one of his bad feelings, maybe she'd take more notice—whether she believed in such possibilities or not. When she'd pushed him about what he'd meant, he looked distant, the way he could when he had decided he didn't feel like talking about something anymore. That habit needed fixing.

She shook her head—not a good idea. Angel DeAngelo wouldn't change anything about himself unless he wanted to.

Locum stopped again and she caught up with him. A tinkling sound came to her, as if the breeze jostled little bells. In the distance she thought she saw the sheen of light high up between trees and leaned against a cypress, fighting panic in case she was losing consciousness again.

Sudden baying from the dog shook her. Locum raised his head and howled. If she could, Eileen would hide.

Someone or something came in her direction. The dog sat

quiet, sniffing the air. Rather than just the tinkling bells Eileen continued to hear, dull clacking and the jangle of different bells joined the cacophony. The noise approached her. She couldn't move at all, could only stare in front of herself and wait, unable to take a breath.

A figure appeared, shifting through tree trunks, walking as if the way were smooth with no obstacles in its path. "Don't be afraid," a great, deep voice called. "It's Chuzah."

Relief made her weak. She swayed, but bent over until blood returned to her head. Now she saw him almost clearly. What rattled was a belt of tiny bones and bells fasted loosely around a voluminous kaftan. He wore a tall turban and when he was close enough, his white teeth showed in a wide smile.

On his hands were tight white gloves, and white socks were his only footwear. Eileen thought that out-of-character for a man who liked to go barefoot out here and who delighted in showing off his dramatic fingernails.

"Thank you for coming to help me," she said and worried she would start crying and never stop. "Locum found me."

Chuzah nodded and took a final stride, bending to pick her up at the same time. "I will take you home. It's close. Then we will let everyone know you are safe. Those who wish you harm are still abroad and we must all be watchful."

"What do they want?" Eileen said, happy to be carried.

"They confuse me," Chuzah said. "I mean the possible motives for what's going on confuse me, but you might have died in the swamp. Whoever left you there made no attempt to ensure your eventual safety."

Her teeth chattered together. "No," she agreed.

Chuzah fell silent and rapidly covered the way until he broke from the trees near to his house on stilts. The fairy lights shone in their uneven loops and a glow showed inside the windows. "You will soon feel much improved," Chuzah said.

"I already do."

"There are things I must deal with to make sure there is no real damage," he responded. "And then I have more work. I hope I have the strength or someone else may not be as fortunate as you. The next victim might die."

30

Matt's office felt stuffy. Jalousies on the high windows were open but air wasn't circulating. Voices bounced between angry people; each had a point to make, for or against. Most were for Angel taking Aaron and Sonny and going out to Chuzah's to pick up Eileen. But they were also against anyone going without Matt and Officer Sampson and even more backup.

And Matt demanded to go in first, in case they met with force.

Matt was ready to arrest Chuzah for attacking and abducting Eileen.

"We'll go alone," Angel said, not for the first time. He was incensed by Matt's hasty judgment. "We know Chuzah and he cares about people—he doesn't look for ways to hurt them. Eileen said Locum found her and barked until Chuzah came to see what was up. How do you get from there to Chuzah being a criminal?"

"Chuzah shows up wherever there's trouble." Matt banged a fist on his desk. "You're not thinking. You don't want to face the probable truth. Chuzah is crazy—I told you that already. We know how he supposedly found Aaron out there and made sure he was okay. Now it's Eileen. He—or his damn dog, for God's sake—found her. This time it was Eileen who was unconscious and came around in time to be rescued by that voodoo peddler. Know what I think? I think this is all a publicity stunt. The man's reputation must be slipping, so he's doing this stuff to grab the limelight."

"Have you finished?" Angel said. "If so, I'm leaving."

"I agree with Matt," Chuck shouted angrily.

Angel hadn't seen him come into the office. A glance around showed there were a number of people Angel hadn't realized were there.

He bent over Matt. "Can we get rid of folks who don't need to be here?"

"You can't blame the town for getting riled up. We've had a lot of events that scared people pretty badly."

Using Matt's pen, Angel jabbed at the pages of an open notebook. "There's been a murder," he said, keeping his voice down. "That was the same night Emma got pushed around. Have you figured out if that killing was connected to Emma? Or if it could be connected to what happened with Aaron and Sonny, then Eileen and me? Or to Eileen tonight?"

"Have *you?*" Matt glared at ink dots all over his notes and yanked the pen out of Angel's hand.

"No, I haven't," Angel said. "But I asked you first."

"We're pursuing leads." Matt tossed down the pen. "I'd like the room cleared," he said loudly.

"In other words you've figured out squat and now you're grasping for anything that could make sure you're not accused of failing on the job. And you're finally agreeing to getting rid of the rubberneckers in here because you don't want them to figure out you haven't made any progress."

"If you and I were on our own, I'd make you wish you hadn't said that," Matt told him.

Angel didn't doubt Matt would make a serious opponent, but he was darn sure the cop wouldn't win.

"We're leaving," Aaron said, standing in front of Matt. "Now."

"You should have sent that Chuzah packing years ago," Lobelia Forestier said. "He's the one who's causin' all this trouble."

"That's all hearsay," Angel said. "Old wives' tales. People love to pretend there's all kind of stuff going on and then say Chuzah did it. Drop it. It's getting old."

"Miz Forestier, you go ahead and leave now, please," Matt said. "And the rest of you. We've got work to do. Let's all be grateful Eileen's okay."

"I'm coming out there with you," Chuck said. "Eileen's my wife."

Angel whirled to look at him. "She *was* your wife, Moggeridge. *Was.* Stay away from her. Take a hint. She doesn't want you around."

"Hey," Matt said, shooting to his feet. "Break it up. Moggeridge, *out.*"

Matt watched Chuck struggle with wanting to stay where he was, and then bottle his anger. He didn't say anything else before he left.

"If you want to talk to Chuzah, I'll invite him to come in," Angel told Matt. "Let's go, boys."

A welcome breeze drifted through the window propped open by a skull. Eileen got her eyes fully open. She didn't remember falling asleep on the comfortable couch or having pillows placed behind her head and a soft, light blanket spread on top of her. The deep blue blanket seemed to be made of hand-spun angora.

This, Eileen thought, was a peaceful place as long as you didn't dwell on some of the decor. Even the incense burning on the candlelit altar spread a sensation of calm.

She really did like the herb cabinet that covered most of one wall. One of those would make a great conversation piece if she could ever move into a bigger, less conventional house.

Chuzah's kaftan was lime green and shiny. A kind of silk. The turban was the same color, but striped with bright yellow. He was possibly the kindest man she'd ever met. At the moment he was talking to Locum, or making sounds the dog listened to while looking into his master's face. Dishes, one of food and one of fresh water, were put down.

"How do you feel?" Chuzah asked without looking at Eileen.

"Good." But she had no inclination to sit up. "How long have I slept?"

"Not so long. Angel and the boys will be here to pick you up soon." He came to sit in a chair beside her. "Do you have pain?"

"Almost nothing. I woke up when I was in the swamp— before Locum came—and my head hurt so much I didn't think it would ever stop." Very carefully, she put fingers to the left side of her brow. "It hardly even stings anymore and it's a big wound."

"When Angel takes you home, you should have that Dr Mitch Halpern put in sutures. He is a good man. Running from something, but ready to have more than medicine in his life."

Eileen looked at Chuzah with interest. "Mitch running from something? He seems fine to me."

"He is fine, because he keeps busy and doesn't allow himself to think too much. One day he'll stop to evaluate and then he— Enough. As I said, he is a good man and he'll do a good job with that." He indicated Eileen's forehead.

She might have pushed him to say more about Mitch but was sure it would be a waste of time. Once his mind was made up, Chuzah wasn't a man to be pushed.

"I can tell you are strong," he said. "You'll be yourself in no time, and whatever happens, trust that you are never alone."

He made comments that were unusual, but generally un-remarkable. But what did he mean when he said she could trust she'd never be alone? How could he begin to know that? She'd been alone plenty of times.

"So quiet?" His smile had it's usual warming effect on Eileen. "You may be a woman who analyzes everything too much. Sometimes it's best to accept and move on. Never be foolish, but be confident."

"Yes," she said. He wanted her to be strong and deal with whatever came her way. She hoped she could.

"Move your head from side to side. The instant you feel any pain, stop. Never move beyond pain because it means that you have moved enough."

Dutifully, Eileen moved her head from side to side, then up and down. "My neck is a bit stiff, that's all."

"The injury wasn't bad, other than on the surface. You were suffering from being cold and damp—which makes you feel so much worse. Now you are warm and safe again."

"I should get out of your hair and go home."

His bass laughter filled the place. "Out of my hair, hmm. Getting into my hair would be too difficult for you to have to get out. Relax until your man comes." Tilting his head, he regarded her intently.

Eileen felt herself blush. She sank deeper beneath the luxurious angora blanket.

Chuzah's eyebrows rose and he laughed again. "What did I say to embarrass you? And don't tell me you aren't embarrassed."

"When you look at me like you just did, I imagine you can see inside my head."

He cleared his throat. "I was sensing is all." He got up and walked to the window. Locum loped to his side. "We shall have company," Chuzah said.

"Angel's here? And Aaron and Sonny?"

"They are on their way." With that he returned to the kitchen and moved so languidly that when he returned with a plate of cubed cheese with walnuts, and a mug of something hot, Eileen couldn't help thinking the man could do anything, and do it faster than anyone she knew, without appearing to hurry at all.

Cautiously at first, but quickly gaining confidence, she scooted to sit up. Chuzah put the plate on her lap and turned the mug so she could take it by the handle. "A good green tea," he said. "My own blend."

She drank, and it was so good, and ate with a feeling she had never been more hungry. "Thank you," she said and looked at her watch. If Angel had been close to this house when Chuzah said he was, he'd have been inside for several minutes by now.

"There have been some unusual events leading up to what

happened today. The shots at Aaron in the swamp, and behind your house, I know about. And I understood there was another shooting at Angel's house. I'd like you to tell me all about that, and anything else you think might help in solving this puzzle. You fell asleep when you started to talk about how you got from the fair to the swamp."

He put a finger to his lips and listened. "We will talk of this later perhaps."

The footsteps of more than one person climbed the steps outside and a solid knock landed on the door. Chuzah boomed, "Come right on in."

Eileen grinned at the sight of Angel. "I can't tell you how glad I am to see you," she said, putting her mug on the floor and holding out her hands to him. He looked tired and anxious. "I'm fine, really I am. Thanks to Chuzah."

As if he didn't hear a word she said, Angel crossed the room and grasped her hands, knocking what remained of her food to the floor. He didn't notice that, either, but a snap of Chuzah's fingers brought Locum to deal with the cheese.

"Hey, Mom," Aaron said from behind Angel. "You okay?"

"Yeah," Sonny said. "What happened?"

"I'm great," Eileen said, chuckling. "Boy, what a woman has to do to get some real attention." She swung her feet to the floor but gathered the blanket about herself again.

"She was very cold and damp when I found her," Chuzah said. "Getting warm and dry made her feel human again."

Angel sat beside her and held her face gently in his hands. He smiled a little, catching her off guard. "This needs stitches," he said looking at the wound near her hairline, "but wait till you see your van."

"It's bad?" she said, not amused.

"The damages will probably be best paid out-of-pocket, if you don't want your insurance rates to go through the roof," Angel said.

"Stinkin' creep," she said with feeling.

"They're everywhere," Sonny said in his slightly nasal voice. "If you got any sense, you only drive a junker in New York. A few bullet holes in it don't hurt. Nobody wants to steal a thing like that."

"I'll remember that next time," Eileen said. "Maybe I won't have the van fixed. Maybe I'll mess it up completely instead."

Angel pulled her close and eased her head onto his shoulder. "I don't think you should be getting excited over all this. Do you, Chuzah?"

"Nope. Good call. She does feel really good but she needs a couple of days of taking it easy. And when you get back, see if you can get Mitch Halpern to put some stitches in that head."

"Looks like you got beaten up with a baseball bat, Mom," Aaron said.

"Thanks. I already know it feels bad but I haven't looked at it yet."

"You hit the back of the van real hard, Eileen," Sonny said. "Matt said a whole lot of stuff inside got broken."

"Terrific. Any more good news?"

Angel kissed the corner of her mouth and stroked her shoulder and upper arm. "Hush. Getting upset won't change a thing. Relax. I'll take you home soon. Could you run through what you remember first?"

She didn't feel like repeating everything she'd already told Chuzah but did it anyway. Angel's gray eyes never left her face until she talked about Locum. At that point he and the boys stared at the dog who lay at Chuzah's feet.

"He's a sweetie," Eileen said.

"Careful he doesn't hear you saying soppy stuff like that," Chuzah said. "He's all male."

She felt Angel's fixed attention again and felt his breath on her cheek. If they'd been alone she would have suggested they go to bed—only to cuddle, of course.

"I'm glad," Chuzah said suddenly.

Eileen and Angel stared at him blankly.

"That things are working out," Chuzah continued and Eileen noted he was speaking to Angel alone. "A lot of that anxiety is gone. You know, what I talked about before?"

Angel knew. Who could forget Chuzah's straight talk about how Angel and Eileen should consummate their relationship. The man's comfort with discussing really personal things blew Angel away.

"Any thoughts about who we're looking for?" Chuzah asked. "Seen anything worth going after?"

He meant: had Angel come to any conclusions about who was turning Pointe Judah into a one shaky, frightened town? And he also hinted, unless Angel was completely mistaken, that he might be able to see things others didn't. Or it could be that Angel was putting ideas in the other man's head.

"We need to talk," he told Chuzah. "I learned a thing or two about myself when I was in the CIA. I thought all that was behind me, but I was wrong."

"What are you talking about?" Eileen asked predictably.

Angel fished around for the right words to explain himself without really explaining himself at all.

"The CIA teaches how to use perceptive powers and

Angel's probably thinking some of them may be trying to come back," Chuzah said.

Turning sideways on the couch and pulling up her legs, Eileen waited until Angel looked back at her. There was no way out for him. "What Chuzah says is true. I'm starting to think like an agent again." He smiled but Eileen didn't look convinced. She also didn't pursue the topic.

"We've still got some work to do," Chuzah said.

The door blasted open. If the hinges hadn't been strong, the entire thing would have fallen in.

"Okay?" Matt said stepping inside. "Everyone okay here?"

"Very okay, thank you, Matt," Eileen said. She couldn't believe the way he was behaving.

Chuzah got to his feet, smiling a little tightly at Matt and at Officer Sampson who had followed him in. Both had drawn guns.

"For God's sake put those things away," Angel said, surging to his feet. "Someone could get hurt."

Matt's expression showed nothing. "Not if everyone does as they're told."

"Why don't you boys find a couple of seats," Sampson said. "It's been a long day. You've got to be tired."

Wordlessly, Aaron and Sonny backed to another couch and sank slowly onto it.

"Read him his rights," Matt said to Sampson who droned them out to Chuzah.

"If there's something you want to ask," Chuzah said, "ask away."

Matt frowned. "First I want to know how Eileen is." He gave her a piercing look. "What happened to you? What do you remember?"

She told him slowly, trying not to leave anything out, but he still looked ferocious.

"How did you know where to find Mrs. Moggeridge?" Matt said to Chuzah.

Eileen wanted to tell him to get rid of the act. She didn't.

"My dog found her. He led her toward this house and barked until I went out to meet them."

"Quite a dog," Matt said, his skepticism accentuated in each word. "Does he usually run around the swamp at night? Aren't you afraid the gators'll get him?"

Eileen drew a shaky breath. She'd thought about gators while she was out there.

"Locum knows the swamps," Chuzah said. "He needs to run and he takes good care of himself."

"Interesting," Matt said. "You got cold hands?"

"No," Chuzah said. He wore white gloves and Angel didn't know why he hadn't noticed them before.

"What's with the gloves then?" Matt said.

"Occasionally I like to wear gloves," Chuzah said, but Angel thought he saw the slightest flicker of uncertainty in the man's black eyes.

"You surely don't need them indoors," Matt said.

Chuzah didn't wait to be told to take them off. He pulled them from his hands and tossed them aside.

"An altar," Matt said, moving slowly closer to the raised, screen-backed place where candles flickered and, as before, something sizzled. "What's cookin', sheep's eyes?"

"Take a look," Chuzah invited. "It's not sheep's eyes."

Matt bent to take a closer look but quickly straightened. "It's a baby thing. Is it a cat?"

"Cats are...no, never a cat. It's a rat fetus. I like the smell."

He got a questioning gaze from Matt who said, "Enough messing around. I'm going—" He closed his mouth and stared before pointing to Chuzah. "Turn both of your hands over. Palm side up."

Showing no emotion, Chuzah did as he was told. His palms and the tips of his fingers were red, blistered and covered with small cuts.

Matt took handcuffs from the back of his belt, slapped them on Chuzah's wrists and said, "Should be interesting to hear you explain those away. We're taking you in."

31

Five o'clock in the morning and Gracie heard the faintest sound. She recognized a key turning in a lock, no matter how quietly done. When Chuck let himself into her apartment and walked into the kitchen, she held her ground and returned his glare with an oblivious smile.

"Good morning. Did you lock my door?" she said, and took the kettle to the sink to fill.

No reply.

She hadn't expected one, but she wasn't going to let him know that he was scaring her. "I'm surprised you're here—you never were a morning person," she said. She hoped Rusty's ears weren't as good as hers. "I'm making some instant coffee. I want to work out this morning and I don't have time to brew any. Do you want a cup? I've got some yam bread I can toast. Chuck, sit at the table."

No reply, and she didn't hear him move.

Heat exploded inside her. Rage made her face burn and her teeth clamp together. "Fuck you, Chuck Moggeridge." She slammed down the kettle and faced him. "What do you think you're doing, sneaking in here when you're not expected. Rusty could have heard you. And why are you looking at me like that, like I've done something wrong? I've got a lot to do. Get out."

He took a step forward and slapped her face. "If I get out, I won't be back," he said. "Is that what you want?"

"Yes!" Gracie held her face, covered it with both hands. "Go, freak. I don't hang out with men who hit me in the face." She wanted to be alone. She wanted to cry alone. Why did everything have to go wrong for her?

"You agreed to stay away from Eileen."

"I have!"

"You called to check up on how she's doing, damn you. You called Matt, then you called her place."

She touched her stinging face again. "How do you know?"

"I was told by someone who thought you were *nice*. Damn you, Gracie. You're staying close to her in case you decide to make trouble for me."

"We never talked about me not calling her," she said.

"You should have known better."

"What am I, a glass ball?"

He came in closer again. "You're a spoiler, that's what you are. You don't want to help me with Eileen."

"I don't want to help you marry her? No, I don't. How is that goin' to bring you and me close?"

Chuck grabbed her wrists. "You didn't believe what I said when I told you I'm doing this for the two of us, for you and me. I only want Eileen because she's got money now. And my chances are best while Aaron's still here. I can tell he likes having me around and I'm going to use that, too."

"Yeah. So where would I figure into anything?"

His face had whitened. His lips were white and rigid. "Maybe you don't."

Prickling in her eyes shamed her. She looked away.

"Ah, Gracie, you know you do. Without you, none of this would be worth it. It was because of you that I came back. I've felt bad about us ever since I left, but I couldn't figure out how to put things right. Now I have and it's going to work for us, baby."

"Is it?" The thought she had was new. It could be better for her to cut her losses with Chuck. "I've got to think this through. Without letting emotion get in the way."

With his eyes lowered, Chuck said, "I understand. I don't know what made me snap. All the fuss last night, I guess. And I saw Aaron."

Gracie studied him through narrowed eyes. "You love him a lot."

"I didn't know how much till I came back this time. He's a good kid. I want to know him and for him to know me. After Eileen went missing, he looked like he was falling apart but he kept on going. Aaron's strong."

"It's nice to love a kid that much."

He looked at her sharply. "Gracie, believe me. I wish I could turn the clock back so we could have our baby. I was so wrong to do what I did, to turn my back. I felt trapped. That's not the explanation you want to hear because it's not good enough. But it's all I've got. And now I want to make it up to you."

It wasn't easy to say, "You can't bring our child back." The pregnancy had been early when she found out she was going to have to go through it alone. "He would have been going on two now."

"I'm sorry." With a smile that softened his face, Chuck said, "If you want, we can have another one."

Making big decisions wasn't going to happen fast. "We'll see." Her anger toward him did dampen.

In a rapid move, Chuck pulled her terry robe loose. In fell open. She was naked underneath, just as he'd known she would be. He knew her habits too well.

She put her hands in the robe pockets and made no effort to wrap it around her. "It was normal to call about Eileen. We're supposed to be friends." God, how she hated the woman.

Chuck thought about that. "You're probably right," he said, looking her body over. "Can I come over tonight, baby?" Chuck said softly. He stroked both of her breasts and used his rough thumbs to incite the very ends of her nipples. "I need to be with you. Don't worry about when I get back with Eileen. She doesn't have what you have. I'll just put up with her to get what we want, but it's you I'll be comin' home to just as much as I can."

She loved what he could do to her and right now she felt like taking him to the shower with her and really getting it on, but she said, "I hope you mean every word you say. Ditch me again and I'll make sure it's you that suffers this time. I'd ruin everything for you, Chuck. I promise you."

He laughed. "You can sound so tough." He caught her around the waist, under her robe and started licking a line from her collarbones down between her breasts.

Gracie stopped him when he reached her navel. "I've got to get to my workout," she said. "It gives me the energy I need to deal with all the long days."

"Mmm." He fastened his teeth and lips on her breast and nibbled, sucked. He paused to say, "I'll give you all the workout you need. You're so hot, you burn me. C'mon, let's get somewhere comfy."

No woman would miss how badly he needed sex right now. Gracie sensed it because he'd turned off anything else he'd been worrying about. This was about the two of them and an itch they scratched so well together.

She couldn't give in to him. "Come on up and let me see your face," she said, making her voice purr. "Come on, look at me. You're a big boy. Oh, yeah you are such a big boy. I want you, Chuck."

"Of course you do." His moist mouth stayed open and his eyes weren't focused. "We've got something special."

"What time will you come back tonight?" she asked, holding the lapels of her robe together. "I'll cook you dinner. We can talk about whatever happens today, and then it'll be playtime, big boy."

His mouth turned sharply down. "I want to play some now."

"Petulant," she said, laughing quietly. With hasty motions she retied the robe. "I guess I'll have to be strong for both of us. Tell that magic pole of yours to take a nap till tonight."

For a moment the dark frown returned, but it went just as quickly and he managed an imitation of an amused smile. "You're one hard woman," he said. "Okay, I know when I'm beat. Can I at least watch you get dressed?"

"No," she said and didn't smile. "Go about your business and let me get to mine. I'll buy something for dinner and cook it for you. What time?" she asked again.

"Seven or eight." He backed off and retrieved his light jacket from the back of a chair. "I know it's a bit late, but they're pushing us on the job. And the overtime pay's good."

Gracie said, "Fine," and shooed him toward the door.

After giving her a serious kiss, he let himself out into the living room Rusty never used, but Gracie stopped him from shutting her door. "You take care now, y'hear?" she whispered, moving into the main room of the house behind him. She waved as Chuck went out the front door and closed it.

The strain was getting to her. She pushed fingers into her eyes. The past couple of weeks had been crazy. It was time to get through with this part and move on. Chuck had mentioned another baby, but he hadn't even mentioned that she'd called the child they could already have "him." That was because he didn't even pick up on it—or care.

Men weren't as observant as women about some things, she thought. She needed to hurry to get to the gym before work.

The slightest movement above her, barely noticed, jolted Gracie. She looked up and saw nothing above the loft wall. She started breathing again.

Then she heard the sound of a door, Rusty's bedroom door, closing softly.

Half an hour later Gracie, dressed in a loose, cropped T-shirt and cotton shorts, climbed the stairs to the loft in Rusty's house. She had thought of and discarded a string of things to say to him. Now she thought she had the perfect lines.

"Where are you going?"

Gracie blinked rapidly, reacting to a jolt that went all the way to her toes. Rather than being in his bedroom, as she'd expected, Rusty sat on a wicker love seat, his heels resting on the edge of the faded floral seat cushions.

"I thought you'd be in bed," she said and coughed, checking all around her. "I was going to knock lightly on your door and see if you were awake."

"You saw me up here right after Chuck left and you panicked," he told her evenly. "While you were deciding what to do, I figured I'd better come out here so I wouldn't miss anything. Do you blame me for wanting to keep an eye on what happens in this house?"

"I've always been an easy tenant, Rusty. Never any trouble."

He rested his head against the back of the seat, all the time staring into her eyes. "That's not what I asked you about. I didn't say you weren't a good tenant. I asked if you agreed that a sensible man makes sure his home isn't being used for the wrong things."

Gracie swallowed several times. Her throat remained dry.

"Do you?" Rusty's green eyes were so cold, she folded her arms tightly to stop herself from trembling.

"You'd be wrong not to be careful," she said. "I wouldn't feel safe here if you didn't. I just want to explain about Chuck."

Rusty took a hard candy from a bowl on a table beside him and put it in his mouth. He sucked hard, never looking away from Gracie. He had dark red hair shot though with some gray strands, a sharply defined nose and his mouth was wide. A good-looking guy, Gracie had thought from the day she met him.

"Could we have a chat?" she asked. He could blow everything for her and Chuck. "What I'm most worried about is your feelings about me. I'm hardworking and respectable. You wouldn't have rented to me if you hadn't known that."

He cracked through the hard shell of the candy. The love seat and two tables with lamps were the only furnishings in the entry to the loft—other than a table, with a laptop on it, pushed against a bookshelf on the opposite wall.

Gracie needed to sit down so she didn't have to keep on feeling like an unruly kid in the principal's office. Even the chair usually in front of the table wasn't there this morning.

"What are you looking for?"

"Somewhere to sit," she said automatically. "It doesn't matter, though."

"There's room here." He scooted close to the right arm of the seat and concentrated on selecting another candy while she sat beside him. She should have worn a bra, and something other than skimpy shorts that crept into her groin and showed her belly button between a low waistband and the bottom of her short T-shirt.

Rusty tossed a red candy into his mouth. "Want one?" he said.

"No, thanks. I've been lonely a long time, Rusty. When Chuck came back to Pointe Judah, he called to see if I wanted to go out for a meal. We used to know each other a bit so I went and we had a nice time."

"What does that mean?"

Where had the nice Rusty gone? "It means we had dinner together and talked. What came out was that we're both lonely and a man and woman can have a friendship without it leading to sex. That's what you're thinking, isn't it? That Chuck and I are sneaking around having sex."

"Why would you have to sneak around?" He turned toward her, adjusting his position. "He's not married. You're not married. Some folk are married and still have sex with other people. None of my business."

"But we haven't," Gracie said, trying to sound insulted at the idea. "We aren't interested that way."

"I still say it's your business." Finally he lost interest in her face and gave her body a long study. Then his gaze returned to the tops of her legs, to her crotch, before her breasts got a thorough visual massage.

Gracie needed him to say he believed her, not that it was okay for her to get in the sack with Chuck. Rusty could blow everything for them with a casual remark that got back to Eileen. Gracie wanted Chuck's plan to work. She was on board and if they didn't pull it off, it wouldn't be her fault—unless she allowed Rusty to keep on thinking she and Chuck were intimate.

"You're lonely, Rusty," she said, careful with every word she said. "You have to be. All you do is work like crazy to keep that paper going and then grab a few hours sleep. It makes me feel bad that you don't have anyone special in your life."

"Don't waste your bad feelings on me," he said and again she got a thorough inspection. Rusty glanced at her face. "You're a lovely woman. You shouldn't feel lonely. There must be guys out there who are aching to date you. You meet a lot of men."

"Not any I want."

"Do you give anyone a chance to get to know you?" Rusty said.

"No, and I won't unless I know them first. Which means I'm on my own. But I'm just fine with it. I'm making my way nicely. I don't suppose Chuck will stay here long. He's a traveler. When he goes, I'll miss him."

"You never can tell who might come along to make sure you don't have to miss him." Rusty smiled a little and touched her beneath the chin. "You hang in there. You'll be okay."

"Thank you." She looked down and felt good when she saw

his erection. "But I want to know you believe me about Chuck."

"I believe you."

"Thank you." She felt her lungs deflate in a rush. "I'm going to make dinner this evening and Chuck's coming. Why don't you come, too?" She felt brilliant.

He raised his eyebrows. "I'm grateful for the invitation, but I'll be working. You know how late I get in."

She managed to look disappointed and gave him a quick kiss on the cheek. "I'm just going to have to wait up for you one of these nights," she said.

"Maybe," Rusty said. He got up and pulled her to her feet. "Feel okay now?"

"Oh, yes." When he released her hand she gave a little wave and walked toward the top of the stairs. Looking back quickly she caught him with his eyes on her fanny. "I feel fine, thanks to you. Go get some sleep."

He nodded, but waited while she ran down the stairs and until she couldn't see him anymore.

She didn't feel fine. And she didn't know if he'd told the truth when he said he believed her story about Chuck. Rusty wanted to get her in bed and that could help stop him from throwing out any dicey remarks.

Telling Chuck about any of this was out of the question.

32

Bringing Eileen to his place had made sense. She'd been there since Mitch Halpern cleared her at the clinic early in the afternoon of the day before. Aaron and Sonny were out at Chuzah's, keeping an eye on the place and making sure Locum was okay.

"Eileen?" Angel said quietly, pushing the door to his bedroom open. "I'm home." He looked heavenward. That sounded like something a husband said.

When he saw her, she sat cross-legged on the faded blue carpet, wearing a red blouse and navy pants. She faced the door and her smile was the kind that heated him up all over. Her cell phone rested beside her. "Hi," she said.

Having her there when he walked in the house was special. It felt unfamiliar but right. "Hi. Look at you. The bruises on your forehead are already disappearing. The cut's perfectly closed. Mitch is a genius."

"He sure is."

"How about the headache?"

"It never came back. I feel normal. I've got more energy than usual. Maybe that knock on the head helped wake up some extra brain cells."

He laughed. "I've always thought you were in command of all those cells."

"Thank you, sir. I spoke to Aaron and Sonny. They're well-settled. And they're actually looking forward to their second night out there. Locum's skittish, though."

Angel sat on the floor where he could look right at her, and crossed his legs. "The dog's bound to be missing Chuzah," he said. "I couldn't get anything out of Matt today except that it's going to take a couple more days for Chuzah's DNA results."

"They won't match anything. How can they? They'll get the results of the samples taken from my van, too. And I don't see how Chuzah could have had anything to do with that."

"Matt thinks he does."

Eileen shook her head. "Poor Matt. He's desperate for a break in the case. When he saw the blisters and cuts on Chuzah's hands, he must have thought about the boiling fat in Ona's kitchen, and Bucky."

"He said there was a lot of broken glass in the van," Eileen went on. "He's wrong to think Chuzah had anything to do with what happened to me, but I'm sure he does. Matt only wants to keep his town safe."

"He's pandering to the opinions of ignorant people," Angel said. "Old superstitions hang around this place like pus in an abscess."

"Nice picture. Very poetic." She turned her face from him.

"So you're completely on Matt's side in this? Chuzah's been good to us, but that doesn't count for anything with you?"

She rested her elbows on her knees and let her hands hang. "Chuzah counts for a lot, but I'm not going to blame Matt for doing what he thinks is right."

Anger was something Angel had learned to control, but he felt a major slip coming. "Even if you know he's wrong and he's thrown an innocent man in jail?"

"Once he finds out Chuzah's innocent, he'll let him go," Eileen said.

"Oh, my God." He scrubbed fiercely at his hair. "So if one of us, you or me, Aaron or Sonny, get picked up by nice-boy Matt, you'll say he's doing what he thinks is right?"

"He would be."

"He damn well wouldn't. What's the matter with you? Have you ever been in a jail cell?"

"No, Christian, have you?"

She could be so infuriating. "Yeah, you're hanging out with an ex-convict. And I wasn't guilty of anything, either, other than being on the wrong side the way a bunch of rebels saw things. In a place like that, all you want is out—and a chance to get some justice."

"You're mad at me. I've told you my opinion, that's all. But I'm not supposed to have one, am I?"

He flung himself backward and spread his arms on the floor. "Why are you so stubborn?"

"Now I'm stubborn because I won't say I think Matt's a creep who doesn't know what he's doing. I won't because I don't believe that. This isn't some sort of jungle justice. No one's going to get tortured. That's what you did, isn't it? You tortured people for information, so you think the police in small-town America might do the same thing."

Now *he* had a headache. They'd disagreed before, but never like this. "I was in intelligence, but I didn't actually torture anyone."

"But you had some sort of hand in it."

The headache left him. Cold quiet replaced it and he felt blank. Awareness, like he'd felt at the Christmas fair, and other times, came back. Weaker this time. The same pulsing aura, this one greenish, formed half of an arch, then it faded and left him irritable, anxious to know why the arc had been incomplete. Then he understood. The arc was still forming— and at the other end there would be trouble. Someone was lying, pretending, and they were deadly.

"You don't want to answer," Eileen said.

He heard her clearly but took a few seconds to answer. "Don't talk about things you don't understand." He sat up. Premonitions of danger had left him for so long he had begun to feel free of them. If they continued he would start making psychic connections again. The possibility chilled him.

"Angel? What is it?"

Quickly, he forced his mind to see only Eileen's face and to concentrate. "You're a civilian. The only information you have is what you've heard from other people. And most of them say what they think will serve their cause best. It's people like me, on the front lines, who really know. And the only reason anyone suffered out there was to save innocent lives."

She rocked slightly, her mouth quivering. "You're right. I don't know anything about that. I don't want to. I wish you didn't, either."

"If all the good guys ran away when things got tough, the bad guys would win. For some of us, making sure they don't is important. I'd still be down there if I hadn't decided it was time to get out."

"Why did you?" Eileen said.

He searched for an answer to satisfy her while he stayed

away from what he wasn't ready to talk about and probably never would be. "I was tired," he said. "I was ready to move on."

She nodded. "But you still think it was wrong for Matt to jail Chuzah?"

"I see the connection you're trying to make. I don't believe Matt does things out of malice, or because he's only interested in his own reputation, but he made a wrong move this time," Angel said.

"I don't believe he did," Eileen said. "There was evidence against Chuzah."

"Are you still in love with Matt?"

Her eyes filled up with tears. At the same time, bitterness gave her the face of a stranger. Finally she said, "How could you?" in a whisper.

"You keep defending him," Angel said and sagged while fury drained away. "I don't get it, you taking his side when it's me you're supposed to care about."

"That's childish. It's *stupid*. Matt's a friend, but even if he weren't, I'd want to be fair to him."

Staring back into her wet eyes, watching her struggle not to cry, he felt sheepish. What he'd said and suggested *was* childish, dammit. Partly childish. But she'd pushed him. "You are fair," he told her. "But you throw out statements without explanations. What am I supposed to think when all I hear is how Matt's right and I'm wrong?"

Those tears overflowed and Eileen let them go without attempting to wipe them away.

He leaned toward her and brushed at tears with his hands. Hanging on to fury had never come easily to him. "Look at what we're doing to each other. I'm sorry. I'm so mad about

Chuzah being in that place I'm not reasoning as well as I should."

She cried again, quietly sniffing and finding a tissue in her pants pocket.

He had to let it go, Angel decided. If he could, he would force Matt to let Chuzah out. That wasn't going to happen until Matt was ready.

"Were you up here all day?" he said to Eileen.

"Most of it, except when I was raiding your kitchen." She gave a wobbly smile. "I've been reading."

"Reading what?" He'd already noted how much she read and he liked that.

"One of my favorites, Elizabeth Guest." She turned her head sideways to see the spine of a book resting on top of the bed. "*Night Life.* I'm really getting into some of this vampire stuff."

He lifted his upper lip to reveal his teeth. "I've been meaning to explain about my fangs."

"I know all about your fangs," she said, but deliberately shivered. "You sexy beast."

"Mmm, sexy beast? I like it. I like you, so much. Forgive me for coming on strong."

Eileen supported her weight on her hands, with her elbows rigid. She looked down, then quickly knelt and kissed him. "I love you," she said. At once, she sat down again.

It wouldn't be hard to think he'd only imagined what she said. But he hadn't, and she wasn't the kind of woman who tossed important words around. He wanted to say the right thing. What was the right thing so he didn't sound like a cliché? He smiled at her. He stroked her cheek.

Eileen blinked and more tears slipped down her face.

"I'm a very lucky man. Somehow I found the perfect woman and I don't deserve you." His chest actually felt tight. "I'm not letting you go, though."

"Do you see me running anywhere?"

"Uh-uh." He couldn't drag his feet anymore; he had to tell her about the message he'd received. "Eileen, I've got some good news." A man could never be sure how a woman would take something, but he hoped she would be pleased.

She waited for him to go on.

"I was contacted today—about Sonny. Or about the guy we were afraid could be after Sonny."

Eileen dug her fingernails into the flattened pile of the carpet. She appeared puzzled. "What guy?"

"I don't get to talk about names. He was in jail, on death row. You know how long it takes to go through the appeals process. A month ago he escaped from a courthouse. I don't know how. I've been pretty stretched out about it. But they've got him again, thank God."

Eileen took far too long to say, "Why didn't you tell me about this before? I would have insisted Aaron stayed away from Sonny. I don't want anything to happen to Sonny, ever. I'd do what I could for him too, if I could help."

"I was taking care of them both." It stung that she didn't believe in him.

"Is this the man who killed Sonny's father?"

"Yes."

"A gang-type or something?" Her mouth thinned. She stood.

Angel looked up at her, felt the rage building in her. "Something like that."

"You said Aaron wasn't in any danger, but he was. You put him in danger."

"No—I didn't," Angel said, struggling not to explode.

"Did he work alone—the man?"

"No, of course not."

"The others are all in prison?"

"Not all of them, but they're small potatoes, lackeys." He got up and she took a step backward.

"Lackeys? They don't have guns?"

His thoughts stumbled around. It wasn't reasonable to expect her to understand, but he had hoped she would accept that he was a professional and didn't leave things to chance.

"I asked you a question," Eileen said. "I guess you can't answer because—"

"Don't second-guess my motives."

The blood had drained from her face, but she raised her chin and looked up at him; her expression dared him to push her too far.

Dammit, she ought to feel safe with him. She should believe he would take care of all of them. Sonny did.

"I think I should leave," she said very quietly.

"I think we should talk," he told her.

"We're only going to get angrier. You risked my son's life, but you told me whatever happened in the swamp was nothing to do with Sonny. Now you announce that someone horrible has been roaming around."

"But he wasn't the one who took a potshot at Aaron out there. I explained to you that if it was, he wouldn't have missed."

"You lied to me by not explaining, Christian."

He took her by the shoulders and gave her a single shake. "I didn't lie. I work from my own experience and I know exactly what I'm saying. I wouldn't lie to you."

Eileen caught at the sleeves of his shirt with hands that shook convulsively. "You don't scare me." Everything about her screamed that *she* was lying. The brave words came out small and ineffectual.

"I don't ever want to scare you. But I want you to trust me, you hear? Trust is a big deal to me."

"You haven't trusted me enough to let me know exactly what's happening." She clenched her fingers in his sleeves.

"Stop it, Eileen. You've gone too far. Congratulations on getting what you wanted. I'm mad and I feel guilty at the same time. Why should you be able to do that to me when I haven't done anything—except—"

"Except what?" Her face didn't thaw a bit.

"Operatives have been plastered like invisible paint everywhere those boys have gone. They're watching Chuzah's place now."

"I can't cry anymore," Eileen said, but she did cry. "If I'd known that, I wouldn't have worried."

"I'm sorry I've hurt you," he told her. Sometimes he thought he was too jaded to be around normal people.

"You didn't mean to. What were you going to say when you stopped yourself? Why should I be able to do anything to you when you haven't done anything except—except what?"

"Love you." Saying the words felt so strange. "I've never said that to anyone before."

Her hand went to her throat. "But you're so angry with me you could spit. I never wanted to do that to you. I'm sorry, Angel."

"I'm not angry," Angel said. "But I want you to believe in me and believe in yourself. Can you take that in? Do you get that this is all something that means so much to me?"

She closed in on him and he didn't attempt to make any move himself.

When she started to unbutton his shirt, he closed a hand over hers. "You aren't ready for this." But he wanted her. He wanted her every day, dozens of times a day, whenever he thought about her.

"This is what I want to do," she said. "Someone hit my head, not…" The bemused crunch of her features made him chuckle.

"I feel serious," Eileen said and resumed unbuttoning his shirt. "This is about you and me. Everyone's safe, I believe you." She looked toward the ceiling. "Unless someone's on the roof with a machine gun this time."

"They're not." He expanded his lungs.

Eileen had completely undone his shirt and pulled it out of his jeans. "Have I told you what I think about your butt?" She put her fingers over his mouth, although he'd had no intention of answering. "It's hard. How does a butt get that hard? It feels good to the kiss, too."

"Mmm." He didn't embarrass easily but a little heat turned his ears red. "That appeals to me, too." He slid his hands down her sides and over her hips to hold the cheeks of her bottom firmly. "Mmm."

She rested her face against his neck and giggled. "Maybe we can bottle and sell the feelings you give me."

"If I bottled mine I'd get arrested."

"Is it okay if I feel you up?" She ran her fingers up and down his back. Her breath was soft and warm on his neck. He grunted and she pushed a hand into the back of his pants.

"I believe you," Angel said. "You like butts."

"Your butt."

"Cher, what I want is to tear off our clothes and play target practice somewhere. Instead, I'm going to cuddle you in that bed until you fall asleep."

"Target practice where?" Eileen said. Eileen unsnapped and unzipped his jeans.

"Don't get excited," he said. "It's not good for headaches."

"I don't have a headache. What's target practice?"

"You don't know? How old are you?"

She narrowed her eyes and gave him a punch in the gut. From her grimace she suffered a whole lot more than he did. "That's not nice. I'm old enough but not so old I'm out of touch. You make it all up as you go along."

"Phew, just wanted to make sure you weren't underage. The point of target practice is to hit the bulls-eye. You have to be lined up properly to do that."

Her red shirt landed on the seat of the nearest chair. She looked edible in a low-cut black satin bra with a lace edge that didn't cover the tops of her nipples.

The navy pants followed and he feasted on a wispy lace thong. Long legs, smooth hips with a perfect curve all the way up to the tiny black band at her waist. All of her was woman, not girl. Lush, that was the word.

"You're in a hurry to go to bed," he said.

Eileen wasn't talking.

She turned her back on him and his breath escaped slowly. Speaking of butts...

It only took a step to stand close behind her and run his hands over her satiny rear. He kissed her shoulder and looked down at her breasts. *Served up perfectly* was the thought he had before he slipped his hands around her waist and upward to cup her breasts. He softly passed his fingers over the fine white skin and firm flesh above her bra. When he dithered, returning again and again to her rib cage, her breathing grew shallow. She arched her body and rested the back of her head on his shoulder.

Angel smiled, he blew against her ear, kissed her cheek and gradually worked toward her mouth. With one hand, he turned her face up to his and kissed her, a long kiss that cost him. His body stood at attention and began to actually hurt.

Smoothly, he pressed his way down, down to the triangle of lace between her legs, over it to the warm moistness that waited there. It waited for him. Her eyes closed and her knees made a jerky dip. She twirled in his arms, bent over a little and backed away, her chin up so she could watch him with an intense smile.

"Are you teasing me?" Angel said.

"Well, I surely don't see any other men around here and I am teasing someone."

He made a growling sound and grabbed for her.

She jumped away, shaking her finger at him. Then she pulled herself up to sit on a long, low chest of drawers. A pile of Angel's folded clean clothes flew from the shiny top of the chest and scattered across the floor. "Shall I pick them up now?" She sat on the very edge, swinging her feet, her hand gripping the wood between her legs.

"No. I want you right where you are." He shucked his pants.

Eileen pointed to his shorts. "I like you better without those."

Obliging her, he stood there naked, every blood vessel pulsing.

Without warning, Eileen hopped to stand on top of the chest

and made a runway walk along the top, turned perfectly and sashayed back. Then she giggled and turned pink.

She made him smile. She thrilled him.

He'd had it with the games.

"Come right here." He crooked a finger at her and she obliged but remained on her feet, swaying gently and looking first into his face, then down the length of him, almost the length—halfway. "It isn't nice to stare," he told her.

"I think it's nice."

Angel caught the crotch of her thong and tore it apart. Immediately his head was assaulted by open-handed swats. "You ruined these," she said, laughing, breathless. "Don't think you'll get away without replacing them."

"You can have as many as you like."

He settled his teeth on her pubic bone and she shrieked and rose to her toes. "That's nice of you," he said and clamped her hips still to allow him to seek out the sweet spot. She had perfect rhythm, worthy of his agile, hard-hitting tongue. Almost at once, she went stiff, cried out and slumped in his hands.

"Look at that," he said, sitting her down. "Almost a perfect lineup." Kissing her, tenderness overtook him. "You are perfect for me."

"So are you for me. Will you listen to me? I can hardly scrape up an original thought or word."

He looked into her face. "You don't have to say anything. You're original all on your own." He discarded what was left of the thong, unhooked her bra and took it off, and held her hips again.

Without giving him a chance to take complete charge, Eileen took him in her hands and pushed him inside her.

Angel's legs turned weak, before he locked them and tried to hold himself back.

"Angel," Eileen said, her voice breaking. "I want you all the way. Come on, please?"

Watching her face, breathing on her white breasts, fighting his need to grab and impale her again and again, Angel nodded at her. Smiling would take too much energy.

Eileen thrust herself forward, slammed against his pelvis with his penis as deep inside as it could go. They gave and took, and he sweated, heard his own sobbing voice. His climax all but sent him to his knees and she cried out as she shuddered.

They panted. Eileen pushed him away and got down to stand on the floor. Angel reached for her but she stepped backward quickly, held up a hand that told him to stop.

With each moment he grew stronger and began to stir. She watched him, watched his body, smiling faintly. The look she gave him was suggestive. A moment later she stood with her back to him, leaning against the bottom of the bed. Slowly, she bent forward, supported her weight on the mattress and moved her feet apart.

Angel layered himself over Eileen, made sure she didn't take his weight, and held her breasts. He kissed the back of her neck, her spine, bone by bone. Up he came again and pushed her farther over, settled his elbows on the mattress and crossed his arms beneath her, held her.

She was so wet. Sliding between her legs was so easy. The last easy moment. By the time he had penetrated her three times, Eileen's head hit the bed and she did all she could to help him. He wanted to make her part of him forever, never to let the exquisite pain stop.

The night wouldn't be long enough.

33

Tonight would be their third night in a row together. Beyond the windows of Angel's truck, the afternoon was gray and fading.

Now she knew what it meant when a woman said she felt like a queen. Eileen tingled. As she sat beside Angel, she felt weightless and a long way off the ground. She'd better not open the window because she would blow away. Her chuckle wasn't soft enough for Angel not to hear and turn on a major-watt grin.

They knew why they were having moments of perfect, if jumpy, peace. It almost seemed as if their cells were reaching out to blend again. That would be fine with Eileen. This happiness ate her up and she loved it.

"You're really okay with stopping by to see Chuzah, if he's still there?" Angel asked.

"Of course. He must be there or we would have heard. Then, and I really don't want to, but I've got to get to Poke Around and see what's happening with Suky-Jo. She's more capable than her manner suggests, but there's too much to do for one person."

"She seems capable to me, just a bit "out there" when she's not concentrating."

"Suky-Jo would do anything for anyone. I think she's learned how to disengage when she needs to. Anyway, Frances is keeping an eye on the shop for me and not much gets past her. But when I talked to her last night, she told me business was booming. I know she wanted to make me happy, but she's got the salon to run and that's busy, too."

Angel drove sedately onto the area around the police station. The cracked and subsiding concrete should have been replaced several years earlier.

"Too bad Mayor Damalis didn't put his gift money toward this lot instead of the Christmas tree," Angel said. "Putting lights in a sycamore made everyone happy last year, but I guess a donation earmarked to resurface this wouldn't be so public."

"Patrick is a player in a very small group of Pointe Judah players," Eileen told him. "He's always looking for a way to puff himself up."

They parked and got out. Despite a bright sun, the temperature was low. Shrubs looked peaked. The people at the police station had forgotten to turn off the Christmas lights surrounding the front door and there was no point now since they would only need to be turned back on in an hour. Eileen had the thought that welcoming decorations on the front of a police station might not be considered tasteful by some. She liked them just fine.

When they got inside, Matt wasn't there but Carley took them back to the jail where another officer with a familiar face let them in. Chuzah was in the first cell and the officer had been sitting on a rickety wooden chair, watching him.

"I guess this is supposed to be maximum security around here," Angel said.

Eileen's stomach did a little flip at the sarcasm in his voice.

The officer only laughed and motioned them forward while he locked the outer security door again. Immediately Eileen saw Chuzah's back. He lay facing away from them, curled up on a bottom bunk. Apart from him, the cell was empty.

"You've got visitors, Mr. Chuzah," the policeman said. "A lovely lady and her friend are here to see you."

Chuzah raised an arm to motion them in. He didn't turn over.

"Consider yourself honored," the cop said as they passed him on their way into the cell. His identification said he was Officer Fisher. "He's refused to see anyone else." He stopped a moment and frowned. "How weird is that? He didn't take a look to see who you are."

Angel pushed the door all the way open and went in with Eileen. "Hey, Chuzah," he said. "This stinks."

"I'd say it does," Chuzah said, his voice perfectly clear and controlled.

"They'll have the DNA results by tomorrow and let you out," Eileen told him. "It's silly that you're here at all." She met Angel's eyes and shrugged.

In one fluid motion, Chuzah rolled over and got to his feet. "Excuse my manners," he said to Eileen. "These have been disconcerting days."

"Do you have a lawyer?" Angel said.

Chuzah drew himself up to his considerable height. He wore a white T-shirt, cleverly stamped Jail front and back, and a pair of jeans that didn't touch his feet. "I am still considering my course of action. It seems likely that I will be released as soon as their little test results come back. In which case, why hire a lawyer?"

"It's a good idea to have one," Angel said. "You'll probably want to sue the socks off the authorities when you do get out."

Making dismissive motions, Chuzah began to pace. He flung out his hands repeatedly and sent intense glances at his visitors.

Eileen tried to think of something to say. "I'm glad they didn't cut off your fingernails" was the best she could manage.

He looked at them and laughed. "At least they do not contain my bodily strength. And my hair is already short. You will remember the story of Sampson and Delilah. She cut off his hair and he was left a helpless man." He laughed again, with real mirth this time, and patted his head.

Fisher cleared his throat and when Eileen glanced at him, he shrugged one shoulder in a way that suggested he thought Chuzah's sanity was questionable.

Frustrated, Eileen raised questioning brows at Angel, but he didn't respond, or even look as if he'd noticed.

Chuzah came to a halt. "How are you, Eileen? Do you feel well?"

"Yes, thank you."

He resumed his pacing, pointing his face toward Angel with each pass. Once more he stood still. "Our gifts do not touch," he said very softly and with a deep sigh. "Such a pity. But you push yours away, so it must be that you do not want them at all."

"What's going to happen?" Angel said. He straightened as if he'd been resting. "What's going on?"

Chuzah gave a sad smile. "You should have been encouraged to develop, Angel. You should have sought help as soon as you knew about…" His voice faded away. He shook his head.

"I didn't waste anything," Angel said. "I used it well, but now that's over."

"What are you talking about?" Eileen asked, really frightened now. "And don't say *nothing.*"

"You must trust your man now," Chuzah said. He appeared to see into her thoughts. "You two have truly become one, and whatever hurts either of you will hurt you both. Allow him to explain these things to you in his own time, or not at all if that's what he thinks is best for you."

She wanted to accept his advice but every free-thinking bone in her body rebelled. "Okay, Chuzah. But can you tell me what you mean about your own gifts?"

"Hush," Angel said. "None of this is a big deal. Forget about it."

Once more Chuzah laughed. He slapped Angel on the shoulder. "You still do not understand women, my friend." His hand dropped and any amusement left his features.

Eileen slipped a hand into Angel's and he squeezed.

"I have to get out," Chuzah said. "I have to get free now, before it's too late."

Angel gripped the man's arm. He kept his voice too low for Fisher to hear. "Tell me what you're worried about."

"You can't do it," Chuzah said, tearing away and resuming his measured step from one side of the cell to the other. "Could a lawyer get me out?"

"Possibly," Angel said.

"Then get me a lawyer. *Now.* He can get them to release me at once. I need to go *now.*"

"I think Aurelie Board may be back. She does general law

now. If she isn't here, the only other attorney I know and trust is Joe Gable over in Toussaint. He could be here in under an hour."

Chuzah closed his eyes and shook his head. "It will all take too long." He raised his chin and grew absolutely still, all but the heavy rise and fall of his huge chest.

"Everything okay?" Fisher's chair creaked as he got up and came to the cell. "You doin' okay, Mr. Chuzah? Can I get you anything?"

Not a word came from Chuzah.

"He thinks he needs a lawyer," Angel said. "We'll call one for him."

"Wait," Eileen said, her agitation growing. "He's making up his mind what he wants."

"I have to leave this place at once," Chuzah said, staring at Fisher. "If you let me out I promise to return. I will not try to run away."

Fisher's light eyes became round and his Adam's apple jerked when he swallowed. Fisher was a very thin man. "Can't do that, Mr. Chuzah," he said and Eileen saw how his hand hovered near his handgun.

He was afraid Chuzah would try something. She checked her friend out and decided Fisher wasn't dumb to be cautious.

Angel went close and whispered in Chuzah's ear. He shook his head and said, "Make them let me go. It's not for me."

"Look," Fisher said. "I know what we'll do. I'll get Chief Boudreaux in here to talk to you. He's a decent guy and he has the power to make a decision like that. Could be he'd say that as long as you take a couple of guards with you, he'll go along with it."

Chuzah looked hard at Eileen, then Angel. He sat on the bunk and rolled to lie, facing the wall, in the fetal position.

Angel took Eileen's hand and stood by the door while Fisher let them out.

Matt entered the station and went directly to his office. He'd come back in to interview a possible new deputy chief. The in-basket overflowed and he'd bet good money the e-mail was close to overloaded. Officer Fisher came slowly to stand just inside the room.

"Who's watching the prisoner?" Matt said.

Fisher cleared his throat. "That would be Lieutenant Vasseur, sir, Simon Vasseur."

Matt faced the man, staring. "Simon Vasseur who's here to interview for the deputy chief job?"

"That would be him, sir. I was running around looking for someone and he volunteered."

"Oh, my, God," Matt said. "Everyone around here really pulls together to make sure we look professional, don't they?"

Fisher's thin face set hard. "Sorry, Sir. We're shorthanded."

"We're always shorthanded," Matt roared. "And we're goin' to do somethin' about that. Go relieve Vasseur at once."

"I'm here to ask you something," Fisher said.

"Then ask. And then get the hell back where you're supposed to be."

"Mr. Chuzah is asking for, er, a release. He says he'll come right back. That was a promise, he said. He's got some serious business to attend to."

Matt processed the man's words slowly, then ran through them again at a normal pace. "Are you mad?"

"Not the last time I checked, sir. Mr. Chuzah's talking

about court action because he's been wrongly imprisoned. Seemed like a good idea to bring this request to your attention. Maybe something can be worked out to make Mr. Chuzah happier with us. Mr. DeAngelo and Miz Moggeridge visited, and I think they agree with me."

"I give up." Matt hit the intercom and told Carley he wouldn't be in his office for a few minutes. "Come on, Fisher. I'm going back there."

Matt walked fast enough to leave Fisher and his deliberate plod behind him. Metal toe and heel caps on the man's shoes clacked on hard floors.

"Simon," Matt called when he entered the corridor to the cell block and saw Simon Vasseur. "Glad you could make it. Sorry you got put to work, though. My officer didn't know who you were."

A red-faced Fisher caught up.

"Why should he? I'm fine here. Sitting and having nothing to do for a few minutes is a novelty."

"You're too generous," Matt said. "Fisher, take Lieutenant Vasseur to my office and come back. I'll talk with Chuzah while you're gone."

He took Fisher aside and asked softly, "Did you leave Chuzah alone while you were looking for me?"

Fisher nodded miserably.

Matt took the keys from Simon Vasseur and locked the door behind him and Fisher. He couldn't remember the last time he'd felt so angry.

Sorting for the right key, Matt went to Chuzah's cell at once. He found the key and shot it in the bolt.

Keeping his hand close to his weapon, out of habit, he entered but stayed close to the door. "You wanted to talk to me?"

The lights were off. Chuzah had a heap of blankets on top of him. Matt threw these off. "Get up, please."

The blanket and one taken from the upper bunk covered two pillows.

"God dammit!" He ran into the corridor and sounded the alarm.

Back in the cell, he examined the other side of the lock. It was so scratched up, who would know if Chuzah had tampered with it?

He looked at the lower bunk again, then the upper.

The clothes Chuzah had been wearing were neatly folded at one end of the mattress.

34

"They won't leave me behind," Betty Sims reminded herself. She was sick of being herded on and off that old tour bus. Tours had never appealed to her and she wouldn't have come from Lafayette on this one if she hadn't wanted to please her son. He was always looking for ways to get her out of town—probably because that bitch of a wife of his hated her.

They'd blown the whistle for them all to get back on the bus. She'd heard it for the first time at least half an hour earlier. It screeched away every five minutes or so. She couldn't ignore it forever or they'd come looking for her.

Smiling to herself and making the best of her two arthritic knees, she leaned heavily on her cane as she left the big foyer at the fancy Oakdale Mansion Center. Instead of turning left to find her way back to the parking lot and the bus, she went right and started making her way around the back of the big building.

Young people might call her stubborn or difficult. Others could laugh and whisper behind their hands. That happened at home with that woman and her friends. Betty knew they were making out she was going into *dementia*. Betty had heard that daughter-in-law of hers pushing that notion, and she'd heard the woman's raised voice harping on how she wasn't going to be no nursemaid to a "drooling old fool."

The last laugh would be Betty's. Surely, it hurt to know you weren't wanted. They could say what they liked, but they wouldn't manage to get their hands on a penny of what she'd spent her life saving if they tried anything. She wasn't putting up with no caretakers who took over what was hers and locked her in the basement.

Lordy, she could hear that woman right now, telling her friends how hard she worked to take care of Betty, but how it was her duty. That woman never came down the stairs if she could help it. That was fine with Betty. What some people didn't realize was that there was a whole lot of satisfaction in being old and wise and having enough money in the bank to keep them at least pretending to consider her feelings.

She was old, but she wasn't dead yet and didn't intend to be anytime soon. There were too many books to read first.

Her grandchildren would inherit whatever was left after she'd gotten through spending it, but not till each of them reached twenty-five. Betty loved them a whole lot and it was the right thing to try to help them when they were just getting started. Very soon she'd be showing the will to her son and daughter-in-law. They wouldn't like it but they wouldn't want to risk an inheritance for their children by mistreating Betty. They also wouldn't like it when they read that she had to be tested by two disinterested but qualified experts appointed by the court if any attempt was made to declare her incompetent.

Enough about them. Even if she didn't like buses, she went to some real nice places and she enjoyed most of them.

It was pretty here, she'd give them that. Tomorrow would

be Christmas Eve and she had begun to feel in the mood with all the colored lights and wandering elves giving out candy canes. She'd snagged a dozen of those to take back and keep in her basement room. The grandchildren would like them when they came downstairs to visit. Which didn't happen often if the bitch had her way.

They'd put white lights way up high in the trees all around the central building, with spiky colored balls on low branches. Each path into the place was lined with illuminated snowmen looped together by strands of unlikely-sized foam popcorn. A semi-circle of men and women dressed in Victorian style sang Christmas carols and one of those contraptions blew artificial snow over them.

It really was ever so lovely.

Betty was grateful she'd already taken several trips to the bus with packages. She had gotten a haul at that Poke Around shop and everything was unusual, which meant the bitch wouldn't like it. Fine, that way Betty would gradually get it in the basement. At a shop inside the mansion she had found an antique ship's clock for her son and some lovely old children's books for the kids. The pastry shop had been her undoing. She ate a plate of hot apple fritters all herself with plenty of tea. Then she had bought some of just about everything to take home.

The place was starting to empty. People flowed toward the parking lot.

That nasty whistle blew again.

Betty continued to trudge onward, a heavy bag of candy dragging at her on one side. She liked getting away from the crush and being on her own. The far side of the building was a bit dark for her taste but she'd be back at the bus in no time.

To her left, where a fence closed the property off from whatever lay beyond, someone started to cry out, but the noise cut off real sudden.

Betty pulled back against the wall. Now she wished she had one of those cell things so she could call for help. She looked right and left and didn't see a soul.

Slowly—she was getting more and more stiff—she stepped off the sidewalk and went toward the fence. It was quite a long way.

The whistle blasted several times. The driver was getting desperate.

But a good woman couldn't just walk away if she thought someone else might be in trouble.

The closer Betty got to the fence, the more definite the thumping and struggling noises became. She wasn't afraid of people, never had been. She had her stick and wouldn't hesitate to use it.

A gate stood open with a padlock and chain hanging from a hasp. Betty gathered herself, held the stick firmly, like a club. Tall grass grew on the other side. It was a big piece of land with trees and brush here and there but no buildings.

She limped along slowly, careful not to trip. The light failed fast and a dark gray shroud settled wherever she looked. There was another thump and she turned quickly, almost losing her balance.

Someone was there.

Betty saw the shape of a man struggling with someone he held by the back of the neck. Betty put a hand over her mouth. The person being held stopped fighting and hung limp, as if they were…dead.

She turned and shuffled through the grass as fast as she

could, heading for the fence again. Night had crowded in, thrusting the last of the day aside.

Too soon she heard a man's voice yell from behind her, "Stop. You'll hurt yourself in here, hurrying like that. Let me get to you and I'll help you out."

Fierce banging started in Betty's head. She'd worn an old but warm coat because these evenings were cold, but she was too hot now and sweat made her feel slimy.

Driving her cane in to steady her steps, she pushed through the grass. She could hear the rapid flop of her heart, which wasn't so good anyway. The worn-out membranes in there would be doing a shimmy. She felt how they speeded up and her head started to buzz.

"Hold up, lady. You're not in any danger."

She surely was. Betty got closer to the gate.

Cast in deep shadow, the man appeared in front of the open gate. He reached behind to pull it shut. It closed and she couldn't see a thing anymore.

Betty cried out. She staggered, barely keeping her balance. "Help!"

It was so quiet, except for the sounds of grass riffled by the breeze. She looked ahead, searching for the end of the fence, or another way through it, but saw no way out.

Before she could turn, her cane was wrenched from her and the crook, hooked around one of her ankles, jerked her from the ground and she fell, hard. Betty had to grit her teeth not to scream.

"I'm trying to get to my bus," she said. "I got lost." She could only make out a bulky person in clothes that blended into the background. "Could you help me?"

The handle of the cane, smashed into her glasses,

embedded pieces of wire and plastic in her face. It ground into her eyes, the pain so huge she couldn't cry out.

"It's too bad when old people wander off and hurt themselves," he said.

Betty could only mumble.

The stick came down again, this time crushing her nose and breaking her teeth. When she screamed, the only noise was a gurgle. Blood filled her mouth. *Pretend you're dead.* Flopping into the grass felt better, despite her pain.

She swallowed blood, tried not to make a sound. Her face pounded and the stabbing, burning sensation rolled over her again and again.

"Silly old bag," the man muttered. "You'll be glad I put you out of your misery."

Betty's eyes hurt, but she could still screw them up and see. But she couldn't make out anything familiar about him.

While this pig gasped to catch his breath, the full moon got higher. The silver gleam hovered behind him, burying him in an even deeper shadow.

An awful howl, high and horrible, came out of the deepening darkness. A death howl. Betty closed her eyes, then slit them open again. Blood on her lashes, already gummy, almost prevented her. She'd known a whole lot of pain and she forced her lids until she could see. The man stood beside her. He'd raised her cane again and she flinched, braced for the next blow.

He didn't move because he saw what also caught her attention. Leaping so high and long it seemed to fly, an animal approached, silent now but for the solid thumps of its feet briefly hitting the ground between bounds.

The animal leaped again, his great breaths rasping. Betty

made herself watch. If this was her end, she wanted to see it come.

A wolf. Betty couldn't believe it. The biggest wolf imaginable, so long he seemed endless. Over her he soared, and he landed on the attacker just as the man realized what was about to happen and tried to run.

The next howl came from the man, and with it the harsh sound of fabric ripping. Betty saw his neck stretch as he tried to turn his face away.

Then the wolf was gone, and the man, hunched over, staggered away.

Betty let her eyes close.

35

Lights shone in every window of the single-story clinic.

It wasn't much past dawn. Eileen joined Angel in front of the truck and he put an arm around her shoulders.

"Frances is going to be okay," he said. "Matt said she's got some broken bones and she's banged up, but she'll recover just fine."

"You don't know that," Eileen said, shivering.

Frances had been seriously beaten and left in a field behind the Oakdale Mansion complex. She would still be there if Lynette hadn't noticed her car was still in front of the salon and she couldn't find Frances. They looked for her for hours.

Roused from sleep before five in the morning, by Matt calling her cell phone, using the flattest voice she'd ever heard from him, she felt unsteady. "I'm not ready for this," she said.

"No. But we need to be there for Frances."

"I know. Matt called my cell and asked the two of us to come here. He was fishing to see if we were together."

"That, or he just expected to find us that way," Angel said. "Feels good to me."

Eileen gave him a very tight smile, then the smile relaxed.

"Well, he didn't embarrass me, so he can forget any little triumph he expected to get." Eileen meant it. What sane woman would be ashamed to be with Angel?

At five forty-five, there was a definite hint of frost on bowed-over plants and grasses. When they walked over a strip of grass between rows of parked vehicles, the ground scrunched under their feet.

"Feels like Christmas Eve," Angel said.

Eileen held him tightly around the waist. "I'd forgotten it was. I hope tomorrow's a better day. I want to call Sonny and Aaron quickly."

"While you were getting dressed, I did that," Angel told her. "They're having a ball. I got the impression that, much as they love Chuzah, they hope he won't come home too quickly. I also talked to my contact operative and he said there's been no suspicious activity, except for Locum lying on the top step with his paws hooked over his ears."

Eileen turned her face toward his.

"I don't think he's big on rap," Angel said. "I didn't know Aaron and Sonny were into that now."

They reached the front doors of the clinic and walked in. Eileen stopped at once and Angel crowded up against her back.

"Lobelia's over there," Eileen said.

He propelled her far enough inside to let the doors close.

"Lynette, Delia, Gracie and Ona," Angel said. "Could we get back out before they see us, and find another way in?"

"You poor darling," Delia said in ringing tones. She had spotted Eileen and came over, arms akimbo in the drapy sleeves of a citrus-yellow and green-silk knit dress.

"Hi, Delia," Eileen said, bracing for impact.

Delia swept in and folded over Eileen like a brilliant bat. "Just let me hold you a moment. I need to feel how real you are. What a shock you gave everyone. We thought you must be dead."

"My head still hurts a bit." Gently, Eileen made herself bigger, lifted her shoulders and, when she'd made enough space, patted Delia's slender sides.

Delia pulled away just far enough to look closely at Eileen's forehead. "It's an ugly color, but really, darling, it looks remarkably better than I expected. People do blow things out of proportion, don't they?"

"Morning, Delia," Angel said, and Eileen caught a glimpse of his amused smile. "What are you ladies doing up to so early?"

Delia straightened to a considerable height in her high-heeled yellow sandals, held on by a web of impossibly skinny straps across her toes. She said, "Good morning, Angel," without looking at him. "We were getting together for an early meeting before these girls have to work—to finish arranging the Christmas party for the kids and dinner for the families in need. Lynette called and told us to come here, instead."

"Let me know what I can do to help with the kids," Angel said.

Delia gave him a measured look. "You can be Santa Claus. A few pillows in front, a wig and beard and you'll be perfect. Thanks, that's one less thing to worry about."

Before he could protest, Delia returned her attention to Eileen. Her voice dropped, "Did you see him, dear? You know who I mean, that beast who tried to kill you."

"No," Eileen said promptly, wishing Angel would bail her out. "Have you seen Matt or Mitch?"

"Did Mitch Halpern put in those stitches?"

"Yes. He's very good."

"He certainly is," Delia said. "And I hope he doesn't get stolen away from us by a town that can pay more." She looked momentarily dreamy. "Hmm, yes, we'll have to make sure he doesn't want to go anywhere else."

"Once that wound heals completely, you'll hardly know anything ever happened. I always liked Chuzah. He's…interesting, a true individualist. He has such style."

"But?" Angel said behind her, his voice dangerously soft.

"Lobelia let us know he's safely in jail now—and why—and I must say, it's a relief in a lot of ways. But I'm still sad about Chuzah."

Lobelia must have heard her name, not that she wouldn't already have been straining to listen to the conversation, but she stood, a floor light beside her raising an orange aura around her tight, dyed curls.

Eileen smiled at her and looked determinedly away again.

"Matt's done a good job," Lobelia said. "Putting that crazy monster away in the jailhouse. They'll have the experiments done today."

"She means the DNA matches," Delia said. "I guess I hope they've got the right man so we can all start sleeping at night again."

"They don't," Angel said, and compressed his mouth. "They've made a mistake and while they're congratulating themselves on having someone locked up, the real threat is still out there, planning his next moves."

Delia stared at him.

"We think Matt came to an obvious conclusion," Eileen said quickly. "But it couldn't have been Chuzah."

"Nicely done," Angel said. He gazed into the distance. "You're a loyal woman."

Moments like these made her wish she didn't get those feelings every time she looked at him. Darn it, she didn't even have to see him, thinking about him started a heated fizz where a person shouldn't fizz at all.

"You're wrong," Delia said and turned at the squeaky sound of Ona's approaching feet. "We shouldn't discuss this subject anymore. Ona's really suffered because that man got fried in her kitchen."

"He died of a heart attack," Ona said, sounding weary. "I told you that before. At the autopsy the medical examiner said there had definitely been a heart attack."

"After he fried?" Lobelia suggested helpfully.

"No," Gracie Loder said, and Eileen appreciated the woman's firm tone. "It happened before his head went in the fat. It's perfectly possible he had the attack then fell over the fryer."

"Don't you bother about it, Ona," Sabine said. This morning her many braids, the thickness of fine yarn, were looped back from her face with candy-cane clips, the long ends wrapped together in a tail that fell between her shoulder blades.

Ona seemed frozen in place.

Sabine came to her, rubbed her back. "It's all been too much. People are unkind because they're silly. They just don't think."

"They found all sorts of stuff under Bucky's nails," Lobelia announced triumphantly. "I bet they've had those results for days. They'll tell a story when there's something to match them against."

"Are you thinking there's something there to tie all this to Chuzah?" Gracie asked. "You'll be disappointed if it doesn't because I figure that'll put everyone back where they started. Too bad they've stopped looking for other possibilities."

"You've got that one right," Sabine agreed. "The real killer could be out of the state by now. Out of the country, even." Even at this ungodly hour, Sabine's skin glowed deep bronze and her eyes were alert—as, evidently, was her mind.

"I can't see Matt putting all his eggs in one basket," Angel said and took a look at his watch. Irritation showed in the tightened muscles of his face.

Eileen saw how Lynette slumped in a chair and hurried over. "Frances had a bad experience," she said. "But we've been told she'll get well again."

"I should have realized she was missing earlier," Lynette said. "She was in that cold, wet field a long time."

"Why don't you all find a chair?" Angel said. "Mitch is bound to be along soon. Better yet, it's going to be a while before Frances can see anyone. Why don't you go to Ona's or somewhere you can be comfortable and we'll call when we're told Frances can have visitors."

With obvious disappointment and muffled grumbling, Lobelia and the group did as he suggested and straggled toward the front doors.

Eileen excused herself and went to the bathroom.

She left the stall to wash her hands and Lynette stood there, or rather leaned against a wall.

"Hey," Eileen said. "You following me?"

"Sure am," Lynette said with a wan smile. "Did anyone tell you how Frances left the salon to run over and drop some money at the bank in the mansion? I don't like it that she does that. She shouldn't go alone."

"No," Eileen said, thinking about how many times she'd done the same thing herself. She gripped the edge of the basin with slippery hands.

Lynette's eyes seemed to sink back. "I've never been so scared. Trouble is, she often takes a long time because she talks to everyone. You know how she is. The sweetest woman."

"I do know," Eileen said with fervor. She loved Frances. "Please say what you're going to say. I can't take this." She held her dripping hands over the sink and watched Lynette in the mirror. She felt incapable of moving.

"She's going to be all right. But she's so beaten up."

Ignoring the water that ran down her face, Eileen slapped a hand over her mouth. She wanted to scream.

"She said she heard a dog barking back in that field and you know how she is about animals." Lynette closed her eyes. "He started to strangle her, but stopped. Just stopped when she was losing consciousness. Then he beat her head into a tree. He was so vicious. He dropped her and kicked anything he could reach until she passed out."

"My God, what are we going to do here? You saw her, though, and she's going to be fine?"

"So they say," Lynette said, fixing her gaze on a corner of the room.

"Are you staying, or going with the others?" Eileen said.

"I can't leave Frances," Lynette said. "I'm the closest she's got to family."

"Yes," Eileen said. "I'll see you back in the lobby. Thanks for filling in more details."

Lynette nodded and Eileen left the bathroom. A voice called to her softly and she saw Gracie at once, hovering nearby.

"Hi, Gracie," Eileen said. "I think it's great how you get involved in all the town events."

"I don't have a family of my own around here," Gracie said, with no sign of self-pity. "It's fun to be around kids at Christmas. And it feels good to do something for folks who wouldn't have much otherwise. You wouldn't believe the donations that are coming in."

"Did you clear good money at the fair?" Eileen asked. She wanted to get back to her Angel, but she felt guilty that her own nasty episode might have interfered with the success of the fair.

"Wonderful," Gracie said. "People were in the mood to buy. That Wazoo from Toussaint made a bundle and she split it with us. That was nice. We only asked for twenty percent. Everyone was generous."

Relief made Eileen a little giddy.

"Eileen?" Gracie dropped her voice lower. "This is going to be one of the hardest things I've ever done, but could I talk to you privately later today? Between my shifts at Buzz's and the Boardroom? Around four?"

The request caught Eileen off guard. She couldn't imagine what she and Gracie might have to talk about on their own.

"Absolutely," she told Gracie. "Where?"

"How about my place? I rent the apartment at Rusty's. He'll be at the paper—he always is at that time."

She didn't want to drive out there but she smiled and said, "Yes. I'd better go now."

"Thank you," Gracie said behind her.

Eileen couldn't think of anything Gracie would have a problem discussing with her.

When she caught up with Angel, he pulled her aside. "Have you figured out what all this means?" he asked.

"Sure. Matt's got to be squirming. There's been another crime and he's got Chuzah locked up."

"You said it," Angel said. "He's got the wrong man in jail, just like we told him."

"But I do hope Matt's got people scouring every inch, both in town and outside," Eileen said. "This guy seems to prefer doing his work in areas people don't visit."

"Except for what he did to Emma," Angel pointed out. "Mitch Halpern's got her in the clinic now, too. I meant to tell you earlier but I forgot. Early labor, although Mitch said it wasn't that early. Apparently she's a hard woman to keep down. If Finn takes his eyes off her, she sneaks off on some mission. Their house looks like a Christmas shop. She gets more decorations whenever she can. Decorations and baby things."

Eileen smothered a smile. She recalled her own compulsion to get away and be busy while she was expecting Aaron. But it was Gracie Loder's request that kept niggling at her. She could have sworn she saw fear in Gracie's eyes.

"You're quiet," Angel said. "Lots on your mind, I'm sure. I know there is on mine."

Should she tell him about Gracie?

Not yet. He might either try to stop her from going or insist on hanging around outside in case she needed him. Eileen had nothing to fear from Gracie Loder.

"I've got to get out to Chuzah's place and check on the boys," she said, feeling guilty for not telling him everything on her mind.

"Chuzah will be going home once he's released," Angel pointed out. "He may even be out there by now."

"He wasn't when you called," Eileen pointed out and Angel nodded. "I'm really worried about Frances. A broken leg and broken fingers. And right at their busiest time of year. Christmas and New Year is a mad time for them. The mortgage on the new salon is much higher than the place off Main Street."

"Don't worry about that," Angel said. "I'll talk to Finn about it."

"You are a kind man."

"Nah. I'm mean. All I do is take the path of least resistance. More comfortable that way."

Mitch Halpern's face was a welcome sight. He walked rapidly from a corridor toward the reception area, his white coat flying.

"Hey, Mitch," Angel said. "How is Frances?"

"Surprisingly good," Mitch said, "given the broken leg and fingers. Where's Matt? He left about an hour ago and said he'd be right back."

"We expected to meet him here," Eileen said. "So far we haven't seen him."

"He'll be here," Mitch said. "It's amazing how well the older woman's doing, too. We don't want to move her again yet, but she's going to need more than we can offer here. Dr. Max Savage from the plastic-surgery clinic near Toussaint will be over to take a look at her as soon as he's out of surgery. She doesn't have a good heart, but it's holding up okay. She's a tough lady. We do have to watch her for shock, though."

"Who is this woman?" Angel asked.

"She's Betty Sims from Lafayette. She was at the Oakdale

Center with a bus tour. She's eighty or so, and she's got enough guts for a battalion. And a sense of humor."

Angel figured they'd find out the reason for Matt holding back soon enough.

"Can we see Frances?" Eileen asked. "Then, if it's okay, I'd like to see this Betty Sims. Poor woman. How did she get hurt?"

"Wrong place, wrong time," Mitch said. "She was in the same field where they found Frances.

"An old lady?" Eileen said. "Coward, whoever hurt them."

Mitch nodded and led the way.

Eileen followed Mitch into a cubicle.

Angel hung back to collect himself. He wanted a private word with Matt, and he didn't want to persist with the draining sense that there would be more trouble, not in front of an audience.

Minutes ago a premonition had begun. The shapes that came with it were more formed this time and it sickened him. He didn't want to go back to all that. And this is exactly how it progressed. With each of the events, he saw more shapes and suggestions of shapes. And the stick figures were back. If he was really unlucky they'd become more or less clear in the end. A few episodes of that in South America had been enough. He couldn't argue with the successes he'd had with prisoners who fell apart once he started telling them things they thought only they knew. But there wasn't anyone here he had to shock into breaking under interrogation.

The feeling could be about Frances and this woman they didn't know yet. The black premonitions were not always accurate in their timing. What was this? He concentrated on Frances, but felt no fear. He hadn't met the other woman and his mind didn't react to her at all.

He stood upright against the wall, watching for Matt.

His head buzzed, not badly, but he wished the discomfort would go away.

Matt walked in, a grim expression carved into his face.

"Have you been in there yet?" Matt asked.

"Thought I'd wait for you," Angel said. "You're ticked off big-time. Why, if it's not just the attacks?" He didn't mention that he figured Matt's stuffing was knocked out by learning that Chuzah shouldn't have been arrested.

"This is the biggest mess I've ever had on my hands," Matt said. He leaned a shoulder on the wall beside Angel. "Remember we started out with someone taking potshots at Aaron and Sonny, then at you?"

"And Eileen," Angel said. Might as well put it all out there.

Matt sighed. "And Eileen. Then the shootings stopped and we got women being beaten up, a murder and what looks like an attempted murder."

"Betty Sims, you mean?" Angel said tonelessly. "How come you didn't mention her on the phone?"

"I've had a bad night," Matt said. "And this is turning into a bad day. I don't feel like I have control over anything. I should have remembered to tell you about her."

Angel slapped his shoulder. "Forget it. We're all walking on nails."

"There's more."

Just then the front doors opened again and Finn Duhon came in. He took off a slicker and shook it. "It's really coming down out there," he said, hooking a thumb over his shoulder. "Sky just opened up."

Angel grinned at him. "You gonna put that wife of yours in restraints? Maybe Matt's got a spare pair of handcuffs."

From the look on Finn's face he was too wound up to take anything seriously—or notice a joke. "Mitch thinks it won't be more than another couple of hours. Her blood pressure's up so this is the right place for her. I'm not letting anyone take my pressure about now." His wide smile made him look like a teenager.

"You might as well hear this, too," Matt said to him. "You know all about Frances and the older lady?"

Serious at once, Finn nodded. "Whoever's been doing these things has to be crazy." He leaned forward for a moment. "I'm going to stick around here until things settle down. There needs to be someone on guard."

"Thanks," Matt said. "There will be two officers here, too."

"Any ideas about who we could be looking for?" Finn said.

Angel was glad he could be a bystander on this one. He didn't want to be asking Matt all the touchy questions.

"Yes, I know all too well," Matt said. He needed a shave. Dark streaks under his eyes showed how tired he was. He looked up from beneath the brim of his hat with an expression of defeat.

"Who?" Angel said when he couldn't wait anymore.

"Chuzah," Matt said, and held up his hands to ward off the barrage of questions. "He escaped late yesterday afternoon—as near as we can pin the time, anyways."

36

The patient lounge hadn't been furnished from Sotheby's, or even an upscale thrift shop. But the square, sagging couches covered with worn gold fabric felt blissful at the moment.

Matt and Mitch were both there with Eileen and Angel. All of them had their legs stretched out and had that "after the steamroller passed through" look about them.

"Chuzah didn't have anything do with this," Mitch Halpern said.

"How would you know?" Matt looked as if he'd like to bite Mitch's head off—or just punch him.

"I've known him for a couple of years. He's very spiritual and very smart. He wouldn't do harm to another human being."

"Another human being?" Matt said and Angel could hear the sneer in his voice.

"What does that mean?" Eileen said.

"Whatever you want it to mean," Matt shot back. "But he's escaped and more people have been attacked."

Angel had just about had enough of Matt Boudreaux. "You don't need to speak to the lady like that."

"She needs to watch herself," Matt said. "Just because you got through one attack, Eileen, doesn't mean there won't be another one."

"Thanks for that," Eileen said. "You've got a mean streak, Matt. And when you're pressured, you hurt people, whether you mean to or not."

The lady could obviously take care of herself in any war of words. Angel met Matt's eyes, noted the faint flush on the other man's cheeks and didn't feel sorry for him.

"I've got to get back to the station early," he said. No attempt at an apology, Angel noted. "I'm interviewing the man I want as deputy chief. Simon Vasseur. You'll probably remember him from the Board case. It's taken all this time for him to get completely free of the Lake Charles sheriff's department. They were fine as long as he was only on loan. I guess they never thought about anything permanent. Too bad."

It was obvious the man was talking for the sake of talking. "I hope it goes well," Angel said.

They had visited with Frances who drifted in and out of sleep, no doubt with some medicinal help. Her face was cut in multiple places and big bruises had formed, some filled with blood. Splints and bandages hid her hands and the bedclothes were arranged over a cage that covered her left leg. She'd repeated the word *three,* several times and Lynette explained that when she'd first got there, Frances was more lucid and told her that's the only thing the man said when he attacked her.

He said *two* to me," Eileen said.

"You're shaken up," Angel told her. "Put your feet up and I'll ask for a blanket. It's cold in here." He caught Matt's annoyed expression and the smile that flitted across Mitch's face.

"I'm just fine," Eileen said.

He went for the blanket anyway, returned and stood over her until she pulled her legs up sideways on the couch and he could cover her.

"Frances told me about *three,*" Mitch said. "I really hate the way this man goes for the head and face."

"It's obvious what all this is about, though," Eileen said.

Matt rested his head back. "It is? Well, it isn't to me."

Or to Angel.

"Emma was number one, I was number two and Frances, number three. Secrets, that was our club I told you about. We all belonged and so did a bunch of other women. It looks like he's counting us off," she said to Angel. "Men really hated Secrets, especially if their wives were members. It was bologna, but they said the women got above themselves and were difficult to handle. It didn't help when several of us went after divorces."

"I bet they didn't like it," Angel said.

"Those guys had it coming," Matt said, catching Angel off guard. "I wish Chuck Moggeridge would get lost again. He gives me the creeps."

The pain in Eileen's eyes didn't please Angel.

"You and me both," she said to Matt. "He keeps working on Aaron. I don't know why. He never had any time for him when he was younger."

"He's trying to get to you through Aaron," Angel said. He didn't like the way the thought made him feel.

"What point would there be in that?" Eileen said.

Matt and Angel stared at one another, but Angel let Matt respond. "He's figured out what he's lost and wishes he could get you back."

"Chuck came back to Pointe Judah around the time the

trouble started," Angel said. "I don't suppose my opinion of him counts for much, given the circumstances, but how can I help wondering if he's involved?"

Matt put a hand over his mouth and played his fingertips on his cheek. He dropped his hand and said, "I think he's such an obvious suspect, it hurts to think about not jumping on the guy and hauling him in, but there's no evidence against him."

Eileen pulled the blanket up to her neck and didn't look at anyone.

"We're continuing to watch him," Matt said.

"What else did the Secrets members do?" Angel asked. "Rob banks? Steal husbands—not their own? Sacrifice little children?"

"It's all on record," Eileen said shortly. "The statements from the time are on file at the police station. Read about it. We tried to gain strength from each other. They gave me the strength to ditch Chuck—or I would have if he hadn't beaten me to it. And Emma, she managed to get up the courage to get rid of that horrible Orville LaChance. Sometimes I can't believe we were so scared of them."

"And Frances?" Mitch asked.

"Frances just supported the rest of us and we did our darnedest to find her a man. Think of that. We were shedding men and Frances wanted one. Women are strange."

"You said it." Angel realized there had been a male chorus and didn't manage to hide a smile before Eileen saw it, but she smiled back.

"Most men in this town weren't thrilled with Secrets," Matt said.

"Because their wives got balls?" Eileen asked.

"Something like that." Matt's mouth didn't even move in

the direction of a smile. "It's only a thought, but there could be someone with a grudge."

"Why not Chuck?" Eileen said.

Angel was thinking the same thing.

"Does Chuzah have any reason to bear a grudge about Secrets?" Matt said and Angel didn't like it that the man avoided looking at any of them.

"No, he doesn't," Eileen said and she sounded angry. "Why go back to him again? None of this has anything to do with him."

"He escaped yesterday afternoon," Angel said. "Late."

"So now he's suspect number one again," Eileen said, sitting up straight. "This is plain laziness. Chuzah's convenient so why not blame him? He's odd, isn't he? What is it, Matt? Are you past doing a bit of honest police work?"

Angel barely stopped himself from groaning. Matt continued to stare at the ceiling but his mouth turned down sharply. And Mitch looked as if he'd rather be somewhere else, anywhere else.

"I'm sorry for that, Matt," Eileen said. "I stepped over the line."

He shrugged. "We're all stretched thin."

A male nurse tapped on the door and stepped in. "Miz Betty Sims is asking to speak to you," he said. "All of you, from what I gather. Anyone to do with the case, she said. And that woman is determined."

They all got up at once. "She can't mean me," Eileen said. "I just got hit over the head."

"Oh, she wants you, ma'am," the nurse said. "If you're Eileen, she does. Someone told her you were in the middle of things."

37

Outside Betty Sims's cubicle they stopped and looked at each other.

"How old is she?" Angel asked quietly.

Eileen bristled. "I know lots of sharp old people. Just because you're old doesn't mean you're stupid."

He shook his head. "No, no, I didn't mean that. She's been through a lot, is all, and I'm trying to be ready for what we'll be dealing with."

"Eighty-two," Mitch said. "She was conscious and lucid about everything by the time she was brought in. And mad as a wet hen."

"Mad?" Matt said. "She wasn't mad when I saw her."

"She wasn't conscious when you saw her in that field," Mitch reminded him. "Now she wants to get back at whoever set on her like they did. She wants to do it for herself and for Frances. Betty says she's taking a gun because it'll be in self-defense."

"Good for her," Eileen said. She had never stopped getting riled up over male delusions of superiority. Not that she didn't like the idea of getting a hand, a big hand, in tight situations.

Mitch pushed open a swinging door and walked in. The rest of them followed and stood at the foot of Betty Sims's bed.

"The assailant broke her glasses," Mitch said. "She's got a lot of contusions, but the eyes themselves are functioning well enough."

The woman in the bed reclined on pillows and also had a cage over a leg, the opposite one from Frances. Looking at her face made Eileen want to hunt down the wimp who beat her up with her own cane.

"I'm Betty Sims," the woman said, more clearly than might have been expected when her jaw was wired shut. Her eyelids, top and bottom, had swollen to look like two over-size plums, but with splits in the middle through which Eileen could see the faint glitter of Mrs. Sims's eyes. Her arms were crossed.

"We're very sorry, Mrs. Sims," Matt said.

"Call me Betty. Don't worry, I'll get the bastard for you—and for poor Frances. I've already visited with her. Imagine that, breaking her fingers so she can't work at the busiest time of year. Tells you something though, doesn't it?"

"Yeah—"Angel began.

"He knows her, or knows about her," Betty continued. "He knew she was going to the bank. She goes there same time every day—only she won't in the future. Damn fool behavior. Advertisin' you're carryin' money. Not that robbery interested him."

Betty Sims wore her white hair short and brushed back at the sides. Eileen saw that, although her fingernails were broken, they were buffed smooth. "He didn't take that rock you're wearing," Eileen said of a large diamond Betty wore on her ring finger.

"Wasn't in no shape to take anythin' by the time he ran away. Now, I want to know all about what's been going on in Pointe

Judah. There have been crimes. You can bet The Bitch knows all about them, but we don't talk and she wouldn't tell me anyway. She's going to be so disappointed."

A silence followed.

"Of course you don't know what I mean," Betty said. She parted her lips and showed the broken tips of her teeth. "The Bitch knows everything that happens everywhere. She probably hoped I'd get knocked off while I was visiting Pointe Judah."

Matt cleared his voice. "The bitch?"

"Will you listen to me?" Betty said. "I ought to be ashamed. Only I'm not. My daughter-in-law hates me. I'm not so fond of her, either. Makes sense she'd send me here for a day and hope I never got back."

Mitch took one of her hands in his and explained evenly what had been happening in Pointe Judah. He finished by pointing out that Betty's daughter-in-law couldn't begin to guess if, or when, there might be a problem in town.

"Hmm." She frowned, sucked in a breath and smoothed out her expression. "Sounds logical, I must say. Forget what I said. Hate's like worms, it can eat your brain."

Eileen hid a smile. She liked this woman.

"Has your family been contacted?" Mitch said.

Betty shrugged.

"Which means?" Matt stood on the opposite side of the bed from Mitch.

"It means they'll be called when I'm ready," Betty said. "They know where I am. The bus company found out and they will have told my son." She looked around the room. "I don't see him, do you? Of course, his wife's probably got a meeting at the church, but she'll come over afterward."

"Give the word," Angel said, "and there's plenty of room for you to recover at my house."

Eileen wanted to throw her arms around him. He never stopped amazing her.

Betty managed a smile. "Might take me a long time to recover," she said.

"Betty," Matt said. He pulled a chair beside her and sat down. "Let's talk about last night."

The glint in Betty's eyes disappeared.

Matt glanced at Mitch who shook his head slightly, and they waited quietly.

"Would you like us to wait outside?" Eileen said, suddenly aware that Matt might prefer to get rid of any audience.

"You stay right where you are," Betty said.

Matt cleared his throat again. "Last night," he said. "You went into that field because you heard something?"

"Nothing's changed since I told everything to Dr. Mitch," Betty said. She beamed at the doctor. "Someone started to call out, then the noise stopped. I thought there was trouble, so I went to try and help out. Pretty stupid when you're as old as me, but it's habit, I guess."

"Let's move on to the accident—when you fell."

"Accident?" she squeaked. "Is that what you call it when someone uses the handle of your cane to pull you off your feet? Then clobbers your face with the stick?"

"I don't think so," Matt said. "Earlier I didn't actually ask you what you saw. Do you feel up to talking about that?"

"Does she need a lawyer?" Eileen said.

Matt took a deep breath. "No, Eileen, Betty's not being charged with anything and she's made a complaint—justly so. But if you'd like a lawyer, Betty, that can be arranged at once."

"Thank you, dear," Betty said. "I'm not paying for a lawyer. I haven't done anything wrong and I don't believe in suing people."

"Of course not," Matt said rapidly with a challenging glance at Eileen. "The sooner we get this dealt with, the better. Can you tell me about anything you saw, Betty?"

"Yes. That man was shaking someone like a rag doll. I didn't find out about Frances till later. Her arms started swinging and I thought she was dead. It was awful. But she's going to be just fine."

"Yes, she is," Eileen said. "I've seen her."

"What can you say about the assailant?" Matt said.

"He was tall."

"Yeah," Matt said. "Really tall?"

Eileen saw Angel's hands tighten—he'd be all over Matt if he tried too hard to get a description of Chuzah out of Betty.

"When you can't see over a five-foot fence, most people look tall to you."

"Yeah," Matt said, forcing a laugh. "But you know what I mean. Was he basketball-player tall?"

Betty backed off from another painful frown. "Maybe six-foot."

Matt looked decidedly disappointed. Chuzah was pushing seven. "Did you see his face?"

"Just about," Betty said, her voice rising. She repeatedly patted a tissue over her mouth. "He was going to look my way but something…caught his attention," she finished in a hurry.

"What?" Matt said, leaning closer. "What caught his attention?"

Betty snuffled into the tissues. "Oh, I don't know." There was no missing a new attitude here. Betty was being a bit cagey. "I guess he was just listening. I couldn't tell anything about him really."

"Not anything? Not a thing?" Matt watched her intently.

"No."

"So you couldn't tell his ethnic background."

"Are you supposed to ask that?" Betty said, sounding shocked.

Even Matt rolled in his upper lip to stop from grinning. "Let me put this another way. Was this a green man?"

Betty gave his hand a smack. "You shouldn't make fun of injured people. That man was whiter than I am. I know because I saw his neck."

38

"Do you think Matt's decided we're hiding Chuzah?" Eileen said.

"I've been wondering the same thing," Angel said. "He's making a lot out of us visiting Chuzah in jail."

"He could have asked us questions at the hospital."

Angel snorted. "He wants us on his official turf. Don't be surprised if he goes completely cop and separates us before asking each of us the same questions."

Eileen gave him a sick look. "I'm getting Aaron and Sonny back from Chuzah's as soon as I can," Eileen said. "It's Christmas Eve and they should be with us. If Chuzah's still hiding out somewhere, Locum can come with us, too. We'll feed him turkey. If I ever get a turkey cooked."

Angel followed her over the cracks in the police station parking lot. He shouldn't feel so complacent, not when there were major issues still to be cleaned up, but there was something about the way Eileen said *us* that felt right.

"I think the boys should stay where they are until Chuzah shows," he said. "If we have to have the big feast tomorrow, so what? A lot of people eat their meal on Christmas Day."

Eileen stopped, just stopped dead and waited for him to

catch up and look at her. "What's the matter?" he said. Her thunderous expression didn't bode well.

"Tradition," she said. "Christmas Eve is when we eat turkey."

"Did you buy a turkey?"

Her eyes slid away and she looked vague. "Of course I did. I picked it out at Sadie and Sam's just like I do every year." A frown settled in. "Didn't I? I told Sam exactly what I want and he said he'd make sure it was there for me. One of the boys runs it out here."

"Which boys?"

He barely held on to his laughter. Eileen got a sudden, panicked look. "They have several people who do the odd jobs over there. It isn't just Sonny and Aaron, is it? My goodness, if it is they must be having fits. And they wouldn't say a word to me when they know what's been going on with us. That's it. Come on. We finish with this, then make sure the boys come back. I've got to go to Poke Around and Locum can come there with me."

She didn't wait for any reaction from him, just rushed ahead and inside the station. "Where's Matt?" she asked Carley who, as usual, stood on a box behind the reception desk because she was short.

"You don't want to get in his way," Carley said. "He came in here like a tornado. Probably in his office. Everyone's out looking for Chuzah. We've got folks over from Toussaint and Lafayette—everywhere. Not so popular on Christmas Eve, I can tell you."

Angel went ahead toward Matt's office and found it empty. He bumped into Eileen on the way back out. She raised her eyebrows.

"He's not there. Look, Eileen, I think we'd better calm down and take a look at what we've got here. Chuzah's gone missing and it's great we know Matt couldn't have been more wrong about him. But there's been a murder and a string of attacks and as far as I know all Matt's got are a few bullet casings. Oh, yeah, and no gun was used in any of the attacks."

"So what are we supposed to do?" she asked. "We have to get on with our lives. Y'know, I think I'll go right to Poke Around as soon as we get away from here. I'll get the turkey on my way back."

"I agree we should get on with our lives," Angel said. "But we don't have to be careless or behave like a piece of turkey will put everything right."

She snapped her fingers. "The turkey."

"Forget the turkey," Angel said. If he didn't know better he'd say she was hysterical. "Seriously. Sonny and Aaron are being watched. I'm not worried about them—just everyone else. Who knows where Chuzah's gone? He thinks he can't show up around here without getting arrested."

"Matt came in here," Eileen said. "If he went to the bathroom, he can't still be there. At least, I don't think so."

Angel walked along the corridor outside the offices. The door to the room that was used by the deputy chief stood open and he recalled Matt talking about finally hiring someone to take the place of the guy who left last year.

"Matt?" Eileen yelled suddenly and Angel jumped.

"What is it?" he said. "You scared me."

"I'm the one who's scared. Where is everyone? Matt couldn't just disappear." She passed him and trotted ahead toward the cell block.

He caught up with her at the gate. It stood open. Inside,

Officer Fisher sat on the chair where he'd been the last time they came.

Angel stepped through the gate and saw Matt inside the cell Chuzah had occupied. Matt and the guy who had filled in for the department last year, Simon Vasseur, stood side by side.

"If I believed in things like that," Angel heard Matt say, "I'd be buying a spell or two to ward off spirits."

Lying on his back, Chuzah was stretched out on the bunk. His feet hung over one end. He appeared to sleep.

39

"Don't leave so fast," Angel said to Eileen. They'd driven straight to her place from the police station and all she wanted to do was get her keys and leave again.

"You said you were going out to the construction sites," she reminded him. "That was early this morning and you're still not there."

"That's why you hire good help," Angel said. "Anyway, everything's wound down for the holidays so I just want to check around and see where we are on our schedule. We've been ahead for several weeks."

She couldn't risk his reaction if she told him she only intended to make a brief stop at the shop then go to see Gracie. He'd wonder why, not that she didn't. But he'd read all kinds of stuff into something simple and try to tag along.

"Eileen?" The front door had slammed shut behind him. "Give me a few minutes, please."

With the keys in her hand, she left the kitchen and retrieved her mail from inside the front door. "Of course." She smiled at him. "What's on your mind?"

"You wouldn't ever consider getting back with Chuck, would you?"

She turned cold and her fingertips pricked. "Where did that come from?"

"Just from what was said earlier. About Chuck realizing what he's missing now he's lost you."

"The answer is *no.*"

He stood in front of her and rested a forearm on each of her shoulders. "I hoped you'd say that."

"Maybe I'm insulted you ever doubted it. We both know he's unstable."

He bowed his head, then looked her in the eyes. "I know Chuck was unfaithful, but you suggested other things. You've told me he was physical with you. You used the word *violence.* Was it worse than you've said?"

"Yes. But why are you asking this now?"

"Because I know damn well that Chuzah hasn't been beating up women, including a little old lady, or sticking a man's head in a deep-fat fryer. So who has been doing these things?"

Eileen took a shaky breath. "I don't think Chuck would do that. Everything has always been about him. None of those people were likely to do him any harm."

He bent and kissed her slowly and softly and then not so slowly and softly. His hands held her head steady while he made sure that when he'd finished, she'd know just how much she'd been kissed. Being without her, the thought of it, weakened him. For the first and only time a woman, this woman, had crawled right inside his skin and taken up residence. She fitted in there very nicely.

The thought of being so close to Eileen that there was no beginning and no end for them, took over and he hugged her tight to answer some of his need, and to give himself a little time to start pulling himself together.

"What did Chuck do to you—that you haven't told me about?"

"I've said plenty. Please let it go now." She clung to him.

Maybe he shouldn't press, but he needed to know if he was going to decide how much of a danger Chuck could be. "How badly did he beat you?"

Eileen rested her face on his chest. "Until I bled," she said, quietly. "Many times. He knocked me out. He made sure the marks didn't show."

Their assailant liked to make sure his blows were obvious so that didn't fit. "I'm sorry," Angel said.

"He took skin off me." She choked. "Then he made me have sex with him."

Angel froze. If he said what he was thinking, he'd scare her. He embraced her, rocked her, rested his chin on top of her head. "Okay. I don't want you to even talk to him. And I don't think Aaron should have anything to do with him. Was Aaron in the house when this was going on?"

"Yes. Sometimes. Chuck pushed my face into the bed so I couldn't be heard. He'd hold me there until I couldn't breathe, then let me go. He'd told me that if Aaron ever found out, I'd be dead."

"And you believed him?"

"Yes," she whispered. "He shot my dog to prove it."

Angel didn't say there was a big difference between a dog and a woman. Chuck had known what he was doing. He'd married a sweet, loving woman for whom all life was sacred. She must have loved the dog a lot and that's why Chuck killed it.

Angel wanted to kill Chuck. He also had the unpleasant

thought that it was said that if someone would abuse or kill an animal, they might eventually do the same to a human.

"You understand that Aaron mustn't go near him, don't you?" he said.

"Yes. But I don't want my boy to know what his father is. That's like telling him he's half monster."

Chuck had parked out of sight of Rusty Barnes's house and approached the building through the overgrown vegetation. He kept close to the siding and slipped downhill to the back of the house, then along the wall leading to the door.

He'd taken the precaution of calling the paper from a public phone, hearing Rusty's voice and hanging up.

If he had to get Gracie to let him in, it wouldn't matter. Completely surprising her would be better, but you took what you could get.

Carefully, he tried the door.

Locked. He didn't want to risk using her key unless he was certain she wouldn't notice he still had it.

He tapped lightly, waited, then tapped louder and started reaching for his pocket.

"Who is it?" came from inside. Gracie sounded cautious.

"It's Chuck, honey." *You friggin' useless bitch.*

When she opened the door she was looking at her watch.

"Am I interrupting something?" he said. He had to control himself. Control himself and make sure she knew what would happen if she didn't do as he'd told her to do.

Her false smile left the fear in her eyes. "Of course not. You come on in. You've been neglecting me."

Chuck went in and followed Gracie until she was a foot or so from the open door to her apartment.

He raised a boot, a heavy construction worker's boot, and smashed it into her rear end.

Her hips shot forward while her limbs flailed backward and her neck jerked back, too. She screamed and fell into the apartment.

Chuck went after her, slammed the door behind him. "Get up," he said through his teeth. "You fucking, useless whore, get up off the floor or I'll kill you right there. I'll put my boot on your head and stomp till you'll never be recognized again."

She crawled and dragged herself across the carpet until she reached a chair and pulled herself up. "My back, Chuck." She pressed a hand behind her. "My back hurts so much. What did I do? Why would you do that to me?"

"Because you promised me things and you didn't follow through. Now I'm runnin' out of time and it's your goddamn fault. You let me down."

"I've—"

He punched her hard enough in the stomach to drop her to the floor. She buckled over, retching and moaning at the pain in her gut. He pulled the corners of his mouth down. No fool woman was going to ruin the best chance he was ever likely to get.

Slowly, she rolled to her side and sobbed softly. "I don't know what you think I've done wrong."

"I told you what to do," he said, kneeling beside her so he could stare into her face. "Twice I told you to stay away from any opportunities to get careless and say something to Eileen or one of the others. You've been with Eileen several times since the last time we talked. You lied to me about helping make sure she never found out about us. And no one lies to me and gets away with it."

"Chuck." He hardly heard his name croak from her throat. "I haven't said a word."

He ripped her blouse open, tore the straps on her bra loose. She struggled feebly against him but she was useless. Her cotton shorts shredded in his fingers and with them, her panties.

She pushed herself to sit, unhooked the front of the bra and let it drop. Then she got rid of the rest of her shredded clothes. All the time she gave him a lopsided smile. Lipstick smeared from her lips and mascara smeared the skin beneath her eyes.

"Do it, then," she said. "Do whatever you want. I've never done anything to you, but you go ahead and punish me. *Then* I'll tell you what I'm doing with the rest of my day."

"Tell me now," he said, undressing rapidly. Her body was rich, ripe—had been since the first time he'd seen it. She had the kind of imagination that made sex a feast. And he was a hungry man.

"I'll tell you what I want to tell you, when I want to tell you. Kill me and you'll suffer for it. Show me why I should care about you."

He noticed a little blood at the corner of her mouth and cursed. He'd made an art out of leaving no visible marks. At least, not the kind that could be seen when a bitch had clothes on.

His clothes lay in a heap on the floor.

Gracie stood against the wall, beckoning him.

Chuck strolled to stand in front of her, so close he had only to thrust his pelvis and touch her with the business end of what interested both of them. He dipped his knees, drove into her and pressed her hips to his. Jogging around the room, laughing, his head thrown back, he sucked in every burning, beautiful jolt. When she cried out for him to stop, he jolted her harder. "You like it," he panted. "Tell me how much you like it. And tell me you'll never go near Eileen again—or Aaron, or anyone else you could say a casual word to and ruin my plans."

Out of breath, desperate to kneel down, Chuck stopped. He opened his eyes. Gracie's were only inches away. Her mouth stretched open, her face a rigid picture of hatred.

"Gracie?"

"In half an hour, your beloved Eileen will be here to visit with me. I'm going to make her tea and serve her cookies. She asked to come because she wants to thank me for being a good friend. Maybe I'll have something she won't expect me to tell her."

He bounced her off and pushed her into a chair. "Get dressed, you little fool. Fast." Dressing quickly, he watched her sit there, slumped, her eyes unfocused. "Shit, Gracie. Pick that lot up—" he pointed to what she'd been wearing "—and get in that bedroom. Dress down. Wash your face and put on some pale lipstick. *Do it now.*"

She still didn't move.

One arm around her waist and he hauled her into the bedroom. He threw clothes at her. "Put 'em on."

Moving too slowly, she put on underwear, a pink cotton dress and flat white sandals. He combed her hair through himself, grateful she kept it short. Then he washed her face and raked through a drawer where she kept her makeup.

"Get out of the way," she told him and pushed him aside. She put on mascara and lipstick.

Chuck gave thanks when she began to look normal again.

"Baby, can I come back in a couple of hours and see how things went?"

"You ever come near this house again and I'll have you arrested. In the future, this is all on my terms."

"Listen—"

"*You* listen. I'm going to visit with Eileen. You won't know what's happened till I decide to let you know. Now get the hell out of here."

"Please, Gracie," he said, reaching for her.

She made a wide circle around him, walked from the bedroom through the living room and out of the apartment. When he reached her, she'd opened the front door and stood outside, at a distance.

"Gracie," he said as he left the house.

All she did was point away from the house.

"You'll call tonight?"

She wasn't going to answer. Would he kill her now?

He heard the approach of a car and took off running, back through the overgrown bushes at the edge of the property.

40

Pushing the door to Poke Around open with a shoulder, Eileen staggered in under the weight of the fresh turkey Sam, at Sadie and Sam's, had produced like a magician the moment he saw her. Also in the box were all the fixings for the rest of Eileen's Christmas meal. The pies were still in the van because she couldn't carry any more.

She could hardly think about the homemade cookies Sadie had produced, flapping away Eileen's protests and thanks. "You're having a hard time," Sadie had said. "This is what neighbors do." And a Yule log got added to the collection.

Sam had asked Eileen to tell Sonny and Aaron he'd be glad to see them back at the store just as soon as their lives calmed down.

Christmas music and the tinkle of bells on many trees met her the moment she was inside her shop.

"Eileen!" Suky-Jo all but shrieked. "You shouldn't be here but I'm so glad you're looking better. You don't have to worry about a thing here. We've got everything under control."

A small woman with oversize blue eyes and a lot of very curly black hair emerged from the stock room, saw Eileen and came at a trot. "You're in one piece! Yay!" Aurelie Board said.

"This town specializes in colorful stories. I was expecting a headless woman."

Eileen laughed and slid her burden onto one of the café tables near her red Cadillac espresso machine. The array of fresh goodies in the case beneath didn't go unnoticed. This shop—her baby—was clicking over quite nicely without her.

Customers laughed and chatted among baskets heaped with eye-catching merchandise. Eileen prided herself on stocking things rarely found elsewhere, and at Christmas she went wild.

"What are you doing here?" she asked Aurelie. "I wasn't sure you and Nick were getting back in time for Christmas."

Aurelie and Nick Board had married the previous year, a love match that had seemed too dangerous to pursue at the outset. Aurelie was a lawyer but while going through a disenchanted period, she'd worked for Eileen at the store.

"I'm having a ball," Aurelie said. "Nick's out at Place Lafource, smoothing Delia's feathers because we were so late getting back from our vacation. I'm not opening my office until after the New Year, so when I heard what was happening, I came over to help Suky-Jo." She grinned. "And to buy everything in the place because I haven't had time to shop."

The music that blared abruptly from the salon next door sounded like a heavy-metal version of "Silent Night" and Eileen winced. "Where does that stuff come from?"

She didn't get an answer.

"I've got to run an errand down to Rusty's place before I go home and this is my entire Christmas dinner. Turkey, the lot. If Sadie and Sam hadn't put it together, we'd be eating Spam sandwiches. I love Spam sandwiches, especially with chili sauce on 'em, but they aren't exactly Christmas."

Suky-Jo and Aurelie shook their heads. "We've got the big doings out at Delia's," Aurelie said.

"I'll be at Ona's for a while with the kids and families, tomorrow," Suky-Jo said. "Then we're having dinner at my place. Lynette's coming and we're going to make up something for Frances at the clinic. That Betty Sims is a hoot. She said she wants Bailey's coffee through a straw."

Eileen rolled her eyes. "Will all this fit in the refrigerator?"

"Don't worry about it," Suky-Jo said. "We'll make sure it all stays cold."

"Did Betty's family show up?" Eileen asked, suddenly remembering the woman's comments.

"Her son did. Nice enough guy but a bit of a wimp," Suky-Jo said. "He didn't seem keen on taking her home when Dr. Mitch told him she'd need a lot of care for a few weeks. Said his wife's not strong."

"Won't it cost a fortune for her to stay at the clinic?"

Aurelie started unpacking Eileen's box. "Easier to fit in this way. When Betty's ready, she'll go out to Place Lafource with Delia. According to Lynette, Angel wanted her at his place but Delia's got Sabine and they can take care of things better."

She left the store and the complex. A call to Aaron and Sonny gave her the news that Delia had been out there with all kinds of food and so had Angel. Apparently Delia had taken on the town's woes and decided it was her responsibility to ease them.

The boys and Locum were coming home for dinner tonight.

How would she get the turkey cooked in time?

Hating to do it, she called the shop and got Aurelie. "I'm

embarrassed but I've got to get that turkey cooked and I don't have time to take it home," she said. "Can you think of anywhere around where an oven isn't being used?"

"Leave it to me," Aurelie said. "I know of several ovens that aren't being used. Bye."

Eileen vowed never to have another crazy Christmas like this one. If necessary, she'd leave town. No, she couldn't do that because of the shop.

She headed south toward Rusty's house. She absolutely hated the idea of going to visit Gracie when she had no idea what the woman wanted, especially on Christmas Eve. Getting away without telling Angel had been easy and she hadn't lied. She had gone to Poke Around. Now she had to get through here and get back or he would think something was wrong.

When Angel called Poke Around, Aurelie Board answered.

"Aurelie? What are you doing there?" he asked.

"Enjoying myself," she said. "That's all you have to know. And, yes, Nick and I have been away, but we got back yesterday."

He digested that and said, "Okay. Great. Is Eileen there? I'm upstairs at the Mansion. Just got into Duhon's and there's nothing going on here. You'd think we were running a rest home. I thought I'd see what Eileen's up to."

"She's running errands," Aurelie said. She thought Angel was a dish and the perfect match for Eileen. "She'll have to come back here because your dinner's here. You are eating with Eileen and the boys, aren't you?" She gritted her teeth at her own audacity.

"Yes," he said and she heard laughter in his voice. "Maybe

I'd better come down and get the turkey. We'll be eating at midnight otherwise."

What a man! "Eileen thought of everything. The people at the patisserie next door have finished baking for the day so they put your turkey in one of their ovens. Nothing to worry about."

Eileen waited while Gracie closed the front door at Rusty's.

"When does he get to sleep?" she asked Gracie, more to make conversation than because she wanted to know.

"He usually gets home in the early hours of the morning and goes right to bed," Gracie said. "At least, I think he does. I get home and pass out."

"Two jobs is one too many," Eileen said. She followed Gracie into a neat apartment that barely looked lived in. The galley kitchen was to the left and she supposed that in daylight the view over the bayou would be nice.

"It's more comfortable in my bedroom," Gracie said. "Sounds funny, I guess, but when you live on your own you tend to make a nest and it's in here for me."

The first item Eileen noticed was a tiny, artificial Christmas tree on a chest of drawers. The bed was only double-sized, a small TV stood on a wheeled cart pressed against the bottom of the bed and there were two comfortable-looking blue chairs with a polished but scarred table between them.

Gracie waved her into one of the chairs and excused herself. She returned with a carafe of what smelled like excellent coffee and two mugs. "Do you take cream?"

"No, thanks." Eileen wanted Gracie to get to the point.

The woman set down the mugs and poured coffee. She put

one mug in front of Eileen. "This isn't going to be easy," she said. "I've been trying to talk to you for a long time, but I always lose my nerve."

There seemed nothing for Eileen to say.

"Please let me finish what I need to say," Gracie said. "It's going to sound really bad at first, but everything that involves me happened years ago and it's been over a long time. I want to come clean."

"Okay." Hair prickled on the back of Eileen's neck. She saw how Gracie's hands shook. The other room would have been much better for whatever this conversation turned out to be.

Rather than sit down, Gracie held her mug between both hands and paced. She'd tried to wash off some makeup that accidentally spattered on the bodice of the pink sundress but had only managed to make more of a mess.

"I had an affair with Chuck before he left Pointe Judah." She didn't glance at Eileen. It was Chuck's fault she had to do this. He'd gone too far and now she intended to make sure Eileen never took him back. "He left because I threatened to break up your marriage by telling you. He never wanted a divorce, but I pushed him to go ahead with it. I never told anyone about us because there was nothing to gain. He's back now because he wants to get back into your life—and get your money. That's why he's been pushing you to marry him again."

All Eileen felt was cold. She was supposed to react, but she didn't feel anything. Gracie was telling the sordid truth; Eileen was certain of that. "Is that all?" she said. She didn't want to touch the coffee or anything else here.

Gracie stopped pacing and stood a few feet from Eileen. "I shouldn't have done what I did to you. I feel responsible."

"You shouldn't," Eileen said. "He's the one who committed adultery. Or are you married, too? Were you?"

Dull red swept into Gracie's face. "No, never." Her mouth twisted. "I was never lucky enough."

"You must have had your chances. Or do you only date married men?"

Gracie opened her mouth as if she would snap back, but stopped and averted her face. "Do you think this is easy for me?"

"I don't know why you're telling me at all. It doesn't mean anything to me now."

"Of course it does." Gracie actually sounded petulant. "You can't believe Chuck made such a fool of you."

Eileen couldn't speak.

Gracie began to fear what Chuck might try when he found out she'd betrayed him. "I wouldn't be surprised if he did something to himself when he finds out what I've told you. Maybe you'd better pretend you don't know."

Slowly, on legs that shook, Eileen stood. "How dare you? Chuck loves himself too much to deliberately cause himself pain." She walked toward the door as steadily as she could, grateful that her anger held back any tears.

"You always were a prissy bitch," Gracie said behind her.

Eileen kept on walking, until Gracie, her fingers tangled in Eileen's hair, yanked her backward and tripped her. She fell awkwardly, her head turned to one side. Gracie tightened the punishing hold.

Punching out with her feet and fists, Eileen strained to make contact. Gracie, always athletic, fought as if she'd done it more than a time or two before. Dropping to her knees, she pulled Eileen's left arm behind her back, forced it up until she finally got what she wanted: Eileen cried out.

"Why are you doing this?" she gasped between pants. "I'm no threat to you. I don't care about you and Chuck. He's nothing to me."

Gracie spat in Eileen's face. Eileen shut her mouth tightly. Her stomach burned. She screamed. Every attempt to struggle tore at her shoulder.

"I hate you," Gracie said. "I've always hated you. You do *too* care about Chuck. You've managed to keep him on the hook. I never knew how until a little while ago. You knew you were coming into money and once he left you, you used it to keep him hanging around. You taunted him, told him you'd marry him again and you'd share everything with him."

There was nothing sane about this. "Did Chuck tell you that?" She had to be careful if she hoped to get out of here.

Gracie pushed her onto her face. Eileen heard the distinctive sound of duct tape unrolling before Gracie wound tape around Eileen's forearm and upper arm, trussing the limb behind her back like a dead chicken.

"Don't do this," Eileen sobbed. She couldn't move. Her shoulder felt as if it would pop her arm free at any moment. She could hardly think past the pain.

Kicks pounded her sides. Over and over, Gracie kicked her, stomped on the backs of her legs. "You bitch!" Gracie screamed. "You ruined my life. I lost my baby because of you."

Grayness wound around the edges of Eileen's mind. She heard the words but couldn't concentrate.

A kick to the kidney left her gasping.

"It's your turn to suffer," Gracie hissed. She sounded out of breath. "That baby was Chuck's and mine but he couldn't be a husband to me or a father to our baby because of you.

My baby had to die. How would I bring up a kid on my own, working the kind of jobs I do?"

"That's sad," Eileen mumbled.

"Don't you feel sorry for me." A kick punctuated each word. "You're never going to get a chance to feel sorry for me again."

Gracie jumped up and ran to the windows. When she lowered the blinds they cracked against the windowsills.

Then she was back, her fingers in Eileen's hair again, twisting, tearing. "Get up," she said. "Time for your last walk."

Angel left the Oakdale Center and rode south on his bike.

If he hadn't called back to the shop and spoken to Aurelie, he still wouldn't know Eileen had gone down to Rusty's. For the third time he called Eileen's phone, and for the third time he got her answering message.

He considered alerting Matt, but about what?

Eileen couldn't stand up straight. She bent almost double from the waist, consumed by the agony in her shoulder and arm. Faintly she felt how bruised she was all over, but only faintly.

Behind her, Gracie held Eileen's tortured arm and pushed her toward another room. Once there, Gracie reached around Eileen and pushed open the door into a tiny bathroom.

"I want your clothes off," Gracie said.

Eileen's knees began to buckle and she screamed again.

For moments she was left alone beside a free-standing tub.

Eileen slipped down and hit the linoleum floor, banged her head and moaned. Why didn't she pass out? She wanted to be unconscious.

Her feet weren't bound. Struggling, Eileen rose to her knees, fighting back the urge to vomit. Too slowly she got one foot flat on the floor, then started to push up with the other. The fronts of her shoulders rested on the edge of the bath.

Hands on her shins, jerking her feet up behind her, shocked another scream out of her.

Insane with fear and pain, Eileen landed face-first in the tub. She started to scream and scream again but a piece of tape over her mouth cut off the sound.

Again she tried to move, and again blows flew at her back. "Keep still," Gracie ordered. "It'll go easier for you."

Cold, unyielding metal pressed into the base of her skull. The muzzle of a gun.

"I want this as clean as possible," Gracie said and a thick towel settled over Eileen's head.

When Angel punched in Eileen's number again, he got the canned message that the customer wasn't available. She wouldn't turn off the phone without telling him first.

Images, sparse as pen sketches, hovered before his eyes and Angel's heart took a huge, shuddering beat. He hadn't had this kind of vision since South America. They usually followed the colored auras. He'd started to see them in Chuzah's cell, but not like this. Though the psychic connections had stopped while he worked for ATF, since he'd been in Pointe Judah, there had been increasing signs that the unasked-for visions were returning.

The images faded but not his anxiety. There had never been a time when he'd seen the stick figures and they'd proved to mean nothing.

His own phone rang and he heard Chuzah's rumbling

voice. "This dangerous man has been released upon an unsuspecting world. There was no DNA match."

"Thank God. I'm heading for—"

"Rusty Barnes's house. I know. It would be better if you didn't need me this time. Days present their own difficulties for me. Eileen invited me for dinner. I'll see you there. It's very important for you to hurry, Angel."

Angel realized his mouth was open and closed it. He saw the back of a figure, only a black outline, he saw through and past it to the road ahead. The turn to Rusty's house was coming up.

The outline formed again, and it slipped, fell forward and disappeared.

Someone was in terrible danger.

He gave the bike all the power it had. The wheels all but left the ground entirely.

Angel's only thought was that the slipping figure could be Eileen. He was sure it was.

Sounds bounced around inside Eileen's brain. Loud, a broken scream—a man's voice shouting Gracie's name. The muzzle of the gun left her head. "Stay out," Gracie yelled. "Don't you come in here."

The door crashed into the wall with the sound of splintering wood. Rusty had fallen against the door and crashed it into the wall. "You've got to help me," he said, his voice barely audible. Relief poured over Eileen. He would get her out of this.

"You fool," Gracie said. "What's the matter with you?"

"A fever," Rusty said. "I'm burning up. I can't see straight."

Eileen managed a look at him. His face was splotched red.

Sweat plastered his hair to his head and ran in rivulets down his face. A cotton shirt clung to his body. He moaned, and cried out—staggered forward.

"Get away from me," Gracie said. "Go to bed."

"I'll die up there. I'm on fire," he said, coughing. He retched and bounced against another wall. "What are you doing? Is that Eileen? Is she hurt?"

"I'm going to call the police," Gracie said. "I just got home and found her in here. Lie on my bed and I'll call Mitch Halpern just as soon as I get the tape off Eileen."

Eileen tried to shout at Rusty through the tape on her mouth. He mustn't leave her alone with Gracie.

"I can't," Rusty muttered. "Can't move."

"I'll help you," Gracie said. She grunted, and Rusty wailed.

"Don't touch me," he cried.

Eileen managed to turn her head and peer upward, in time to see Rusty fall, with Gracie beneath him.

The bike's wheels howled. Angel dropped it on its side when he jumped off.

Either Rusty was at the paper or he'd put his car in the garage. Eileen's van was parked by a broken curb.

If he remembered from the one time he'd been to Rusty's, the entrance to the apartment was downhill, at the back of the house and on the bayou side. If everything was okay, there would be no reason not to go down there and ring the bell. But if Chuzah's instincts were right, and his own, he'd better go carefully and quietly.

At the back door, he tried the handle and it turned smoothly. He opened it an inch and it didn't squeak, so he pushed again and stopped. Listened.

He heard coughing, then a sound like a trapped animal.

"Fucking get off me!" The voice was Gracie's.

The howling went on, and a man groaned. He said something but Angel couldn't hear him. Angel breathed deeply, shoving the fear away. He had to stay calm for Eileen, who could be in this mess.

Once inside, Angel slipped the door shut again, afraid a current of air would alert someone to the door having been opened.

With his gun at his shoulder, he crossed the main living area of the house. The noises came from an open door into what he thought was Gracie's apartment.

Flat against the wall outside that door, he listened. The man screamed and kept on screaming. Angel knew it was a man by the pitch and the way the sound fell low and rose again. The woman shouted at him and now he heard Gracie's voice clearly.

"I don't want to shoot you, too, Rusty, but I will. Move. I'll help you."

"Can't!"

Angel assumed it was Rusty Barnes. *I don't want to shoot you, too, Rusty.*

Who else had she shot—or was she going to shoot?

He could see into a galley kitchen inside the apartment. Through the crack in the door, simple furnishings showed and no one moved.

With two fingers he eased the door open wider.

He couldn't see anyone yet, but he could tell where the noise was. Another door, in the opposite wall, stood open and the mounting sounds came from there.

Angel went swiftly across the first room and stood, gun at

the ready, where he could ease sideways to see inside a bedroom.

Gracie shouted, "Get—off—me, Rusty. You're suffocating me. Roll, you fool, roll. I can't help either of us down here."

Angel crossed the bedroom and peered cautiously inside a bathroom. Rusty, spread out and apparently close to unconscious, lay on top of Gracie whose right hand almost touched the butt of a gun she must have dropped.

But worse than that, Eileen, her left hand taped behind her back, lay in a bathtub. She clawed for the edge with her free right hand.

"Shit! Move, Rusty," Gracie said hoarsely. "I swear to you, Eileen—I'll shoot you full of holes if you keep on coming."

"So hot," Rusty said. "Maggots are crawling out of me. I feel them. All over me. Going for my eyes. Gracie, help me."

A crash sent Angel towards the bathroom. He had everything to lose by holding back.

Eileen had pulled herself up and fallen from the tub. With her free hand she tore the tape from her mouth. She struck at Gracie's reaching fingers. Again and again, she thumped them, and then she grabbed the gun from the floor.

At that moment, Gracie finally heaved enough to scramble from beneath Rusty and turn on Eileen.

Eileen held the gun steady and pointed it at Gracie's chest, but the other woman came for her, teeth bared, fingers extended to claw at her.

And Gracie grabbed the hand that held the gun and wrenched the weapon free.

Angel blasted into the bathroom.

Gracie saw him and her eyes stretched wide. He saw her start to pull the trigger.

Already aiming, Angel shot first. Gracie's wrist and hand blew apart in a bloody mass of sinew and bone.

At least he knew where he had seen those eyes that haunted him. For an instant, at the Boardroom, he had seen them when Gracie looked into his face.

41

"This clinic is busting out all over," a tall nurse said when he saw Angel and Eileen coming in. The nurse stopped and looked at them. "Which of you is the patient?"

Angel said, "Eileen is," at the exact moment when she announced, "Neither of us."

"Her arm is about dislocated," Angel said. "And a wound on her head's been opened up again."

"I can see that," the nurse said. "How's the pain?"

"A helluva—a whole lot better than it was," Eileen said. "Really, I'm fine to go home. I've got dinner to cook."

A woman in floral scrubs, a long black braid hanging forward over one shoulder, gave Angel a knowing look. "Someone else will be cooking dinner tonight, dear. If you even care after Dr. Halpern works his magic."

"I'm not taking sedatives," Eileen said.

With another pitying smile at Angel, the nurse carried on down a corridor much too busy for Pointe Judah's modest clinic.

"Eileen," Angel said, "please do whatever Mitch decides you should. I don't think he's going to be too keen on you using your arm a whole lot at first."

"I've still got one good arm." Eileen drew her brows down.

"Of course," he said, keeping an arm around her waist. She had refused to be transported by aid car.

"I've got one chance to get my licks in," she said. "Once Mitch realizes I'm here, I won't get another chance."

Angel looked at her head and wondered just how hard the blow had been this time. "We should sit down."

"You sit down," she told him. "And don't worry. I'm not into killing people, or trying to kill them. That's what she did, y'know. All that talk about me getting back with Chuck. She didn't want that. She wanted me dead, and Aaron, so Chuck would turn to her.

"What a crazy woman. If she could aim a gun, Aaron would have died in the swamp, or in our backyard. And I'd have died—" she checked left and right "—in your bathtub. You, too, probably. That skylight's a bubble— I think she saw my face and didn't know who was what. She was trying to kill *me*."

"Kind of hard to know who was what with us all mixed up together like that." He made sure not to grin, or, worse yet, laugh.

"Gracie told me it was her idea for Sonny to take Aaron into the swamp in the first place. Sonny went into Buzzard's where she's the part-time bartender and she set those boys up."

"Sonny was in Buzzard's? He's going to be sorry about that."

Eileen poked her leg and winced. "Shoot, that hurts," she said. "Everything hurts. Stay here, there's just something I'd like a chance to do. I want to ask Gracie a couple of questions. Take that look off your face. I told you I'm not a killer."

"Don't even talk like that," he said, but she ducked out of his arm and took off toward Emergency, hugging her arms close to her body.

Angel gave her a few minutes, then followed.

* * *

"Psst."

Eileen paused and saw Betty Sims, in a wheelchair, one leg in a cast and stuck out in front of her. Betty hung back inside a door. "Hi," Eileen said. "You look so much better."

"Shh," Betty said, beckoning. "I saw all the cops and heard the commotion. Did they get him? I want to look him in the eye."

"I know how you feel," Eileen told her. "They don't have him yet. But they've picked up a woman who's going to end up in jail. I don't know what she had to do with the man who attacked you. But the cops will find out, then they'll get him. I'll stop by on my way back."

Still supporting her left arm, she continued down the corridor. Deep down she knew who the man was. She didn't want to admit that she'd married a monster, and that the same monster was Aaron's father, but there was no denying it now.

There were two sets of swinging doors into Emergency, one on either side of the pharmacy. Eileen made sure she wasn't seen and sidled up to peer through a window in the closest door.

Right inside, still in his crumpled shirt and jeans, Rusty lay on a gurney, his eyes closed, obviously sedated. He had a drip in his arm. By the time the medics had got to him, he was howling and tossing on the floor.

Several other patients occupied beds beyond where Rusty lay, but Eileen noted there were two empty beds between them and Rusty—probably in case he had something contagious.

She couldn't see Gracie and crossed to the opposite door, strolling when she passed the pharmacy where a technician concentrated on whatever she was doing.

Eileen repeated the process of looking through a window. The two nearest beds were empty, the curtains drawn back, but curtains were drawn around the third. Yards farther on stood Matt, Simon Vasseur, and two men in suits whom Eileen hadn't seen before. While she watched, all four used the counter at the nurses' station to spread papers.

Shelves beside Eileen contained folded scrubs, skullcaps and booties. Past caring about modesty, she found a set of scrubs, pulled off her shirt and pants and pushed them behind the clean laundry. No one interrupted her while she managed the painful task of pulling on pants and a short-sleeved shirt over her head.

She reached for a cap, then saw a separate pile made like helmets that would cover everything but the middle of her face. With the helmet on, she pulled booties over her shoes, waited for the pain in her arm to calm down again, and pushed into the unit.

Just before the door closed behind her she heard footsteps and glanced back. Angel appeared and approached the pharmacy. Eileen turned away before he saw her.

Eileen walked to the head of the second empty bed, on the side where curtains were closed around the next one. If this wasn't Gracie, she would feel like a fool, but so what?

She looked inside the curtain. Gracie dozed on the bed. She was receiving blood and her right hand and arm were heavily bandaged.

Her head humming with tension, Eileen went to Gracie's side, close to her head, and put both hands over the woman's mouth.

Gracie's eyes flew open and Eileen whispered in her ear, "Call out and you'll wish you hadn't. I just want you to answer one question for me."

Gracie watched her, horrified.

"Was it Chuck who attacked people who used to belong to Secrets? Was it his way of getting back because that's how I finally figured out I was a human being and he was nothing?"

Gracie stared for a long time, then nodded her head.

"What happened to Bucky? Did he catch Chuck after he'd pushed Emma under that truck? Did Chuck kill him to keep him quiet?"

Once more Gracie stared at her. She didn't agree or disagree.

"If I take my hand away, are you going to shout for help?"

This time Gracie shook her head no.

Eileen removed her hand and tears poured down Gracie's cheeks. She got her mouth close to Eileen's ear and said, "He threatened me. He told me if I didn't do what he wanted, he'd let the whole town know about us."

"Once they check his DNA against Bucky's samples, and the ones they got from Betty Sims's cane, I guess the truth will come out anyway," Eileen said.

"But you'll tell the cops how Chuck threatened me?" Gracie said. "You'll tell them he was going to murder me if I didn't do as he said?" Her face twitched. "And I didn't hit anyone I shot at, did I? That's because I didn't want to. I missed on purpose." She grabbed a handful of Eileen's scrubs. "You'll stand up for me?"

"You missed because you're a lousy shot and you were scared out of your wits, too," Eileen said softly. "And that dumb little .32 needs to be screwed into someone's ear before you can be sure it'll shoot anything straight enough to hit a target."

Gracie panted.

"That gun was stolen from Toussaint, from the evidence room. It was used in some killings there several years ago. Your prints are on it and so are the other killer's. Think about that. What are the chances of a thing like that happening?"

"I bought the gun from a pawn shop," Gracie said. "I'm fine now. I'm going to go home now but I promise I won't leave town."

"Don't tell *me*. I'm not a cop." She got close to the woman's ear again. "You're going to be accused of attempted murder and I'm going to do everything I can to make sure you're found guilty. I can repeat every lie you ever told me. First I'll pass them along to Chuck, just in case he feels like coming and having a chat with you. They're really nice around here. They'll make sure you get lots of privacy while you two talk. You deserve everything you get for trying to kill my son."

Gracie shook her head.

"Nice of you to visit the sick," Matt said from a gap in the curtains at the bottom of the bed. "No surprise there, though. But you do have to watch the quiet ones, Angel, and don't you forget it. I wouldn't turn my back on that one if I was you."

Angel had come in by the same route as Eileen. He said, "Nice hat," to her.

That's when the peace of the emergency facility fractured and screams of pain reverberated from every wall.

"Stay there," Angel told Eileen and ran after Matt.

Eileen counted to five and followed. She figured Gracie wouldn't be going anywhere with a smashed hand. And from the ruckus, there was a lot going on that she wanted see.

* * *

Angel arrived on the opposite side of the unit right behind Matt and the gaggle of other officials.

Seated in a wheelchair beside Rusty Barnes, one casted leg extended, Betty Sims wielded a steel instrument, a long, narrow, tubular thing. Rusty yelled and tossed and batted the air as if a swarm of bees had assaulted him.

Nothing he said made any sense.

Rusty's shirt was already torn open. Betty had managed to poke the tube through from the inside of the garment and stab a hole in the right sleeve. Holding both ends of the instrument, she leaned away, pushed her chair back with her good foot and tore away most of what was left of his shirt.

"There," she said, her face red. She wheeled up close again. "See that?"

A nurse came at a trot and looked at Rusty's chest. Mitch Halpern was right behind and Angel shook his head when Eileen arrived.

"He's got burns on his chest," the nurse said.

Like burns from boiling fat, Eileen thought. They were open and weeping pussy fluid. The surrounding skin flamed.

"Never mind his chest," Betty said, waving the tube above her head. "It's his shoulder and back. Look at 'em. Putrid. They stink. Can't you smell that?"

Angel could smell rotting flesh.

"These are burns," Mitch said, still concentrating on Rusty's chest area. "Like he got spattered with something hot."

"Shit," Matt said. "Would boiling fat do that?"

Mitch shrugged. "Sure. The wounds are infected. Why wouldn't he have this treated?"

"Because he killed Bucky," Angel said. "Bucky grabbed at Rusty's chest and that's when he got the paper and hair under his fingernails."

For an instant it looked as if Betty would poke Rusty's shoulder but she caught Angel's eyes, smiled slightly, and drew back.

Mitch got to her side and, hardened as he was, the subtle shock was impossible to miss. "Everybody out. Marion, we're going to have to operate on this."

"Here?" the nurse said.

"He's not going to make it if we don't try," Mitch said. "It looks as if he was attacked by something. We're looking at a flesh-eating disease."

An intern with excitement glowing in his eyes all but skidded to a stop beside Mitch. "Wow," he said. "If I hadn't switched shifts with someone else I'd have missed this."

"He's the one who attacked Frances and tried to kill me," Betty said. "I'd know that whiter-than-white skin on his neck and that curly hair anywhere."

"He was engaged to Denise," Eileen said, horribly fascinated by Rusty's wounds. "She was murdered, remember, and she belonged to Secrets. She and Rusty planned to be married."

"Vengeance," Matt said quietly. "Finally he couldn't stand the sight of the rest of you living while Denise was dead. He must have blamed Secrets, I guess. Must have fallen on a rake or something to do that to his shoulder."

"Rake?" Betty said. "It wasn't what he fell on. It was what mauled him. Biggest wolf I ever did see. You should have seen his claws. And those fangs. Hoo Mama. Took that boy in his mouth and shook him till I thought he was dead. Then he looked at me and at first I thought I was wolf meat, too. But that animal—almost a block long, he was—he just smiled at me, then winked and ran off."

"I guess someone brought in that Bailey's for you, Betty," Eileen said.

Angel stood beside her. He put a hand on the back of her neck and led her from the unit. Then he faced her and said, "Aaron saw the wolf, too. And so did I."

"Yes," Eileen murmured. "Me, too."

42

The still unfinished salon at Angel's house resembled the inside of a very fancy package. Lengths of silk and satin, gold, deep blue and white, covered the ceiling and walls; and more fabric, this a silver metallic mesh, had been applied in a single, wide line up each wall as if it were the ribbon on the package. The mesh came together in a huge bow in the center of the ceiling.

No, the room looked like a package turned inside out. Angel squinted at the intricate bow woven through his antique chandelier.

Several inches of sparkling, multi-colored confetti covered the floors and Angel wondered how long it would be before he stopped finding it in other parts of the house.

"I don't know how you pulled this off," Eileen said to him. They'd barely walked in out of a chilly night. "Everyone knows Delia Board insists on a big family do at her house. How did you get her to come here instead?"

"I didn't do a thing," Angel said. "I'm as amazed as you are. Look at that woman. Where did she get all the staff this late on Christmas Eve? That tree's got to be fourteen feet tall and it's perfectly decorated."

"But you didn't have anything to do with it?" Eileen said. She longed to lie down, but no way would she put a damper on the evening. "The table looks as if it's ready for a presidential dinner."

"What I care about is what I smell," Angel said. "My mouth is watering."

Eileen hadn't been hungry, but she was now.

"All of the Boards," Angel said. "Aaron and Sonny. Matt. *Lobelia Forestier?*"

"Hush," Eileen said. "It's Christmas."

He puffed. "And two confetti snufflers." Hoover and Locum rolled in the confetti, occasionally standing up to give mighty shakes and send the stuff everywhere. They were both glittery.

"Chuzah," Eileen whispered as he swept from the kitchen in immaculate chef's garb with bells strung around his very tall chef's hat. He placed dishes on a white-draped sideboard. Eileen suspected that under the drape she could find a sheet of plywood and some sawhorses.

Suky-Jo was there, and several members of the Boardroom Boys who strummed and hummed carols around the Christmas tree.

Matt saw Angel and Eileen and came over. He was still in uniform, but with the neck of his shirt unbuttoned and his sleeves rolled up. "This is hokey, you know that?" he said.

"I love it," Eileen said. "There's only one thing better than a lot of glitter and that's even more glitter. What I want to know is how it was put together. You don't do something like this in five minutes."

"From what I hear, if Delia Board wants to do something, she finds a way. Took 'em a couple of hours is all. She had a whole staff laid on at her place and all she did was move it over here."

Delia, wearing a long, white satin sheath dress, was apparently doing what she did best: giving orders. Sabine nodded each time Delia said something to her, but did what she was already doing.

"Delia's got everyone working," Eileen said. "They came for dinner and cooked it!"

"No," Matt said. "Chuzah cooked it and allowed a few people to help. I really went off on the wrong track with him."

"You surely did," Angel said. He caught Eileen's eye and added, "Anyone could have come to the same conclusion. Too bad Dr. Mitch can't be here."

They fell silent and Angel knew that, like him, the other two were thinking about Rusty. "Does Mitch think Rusty will make it?" Angel said.

"He doesn't think he'll last the night," Matt said. "And poor Emma's still in labor, darn it. She really wanted to come to this party."

Chuzah bore down on them, a covered silver platter in hand. He managed to place himself where his back was to Matt but he faced Angel and Eileen. "You did well," he said to Angel, "but I never doubted you would. I approve of every move you make. Now, this is what we will *not* be having for dinner." He removed the cover with a flourish to reveal a black and shriveled turkey.

Eileen grimaced. "Poor thing. Everyone forgot it at the patisserie. There wasn't a fire or anything?"

"No, lovely lady," Chuzah said. "I'm told they have magical ovens that switch off if food begins to burn. We need the two of you to sit in the middle on the far side of the table. The silver napkins with bells on the rings are yours." He looked hard at first Angel, then Eileen. "We will start assembling everyone."

He swept away, paused and returned to shake hands with

Matt. "You are a good man," Chuzah said. "Misguided on occasion. Bullheaded frequently. But a good man."

Angel watched them and once Chuzah was gone said, "I'm going to have to research shape-shifters."

"Finally you admit I was right about him," Eileen murmured.

Matt returned and Angel said, "Chuck didn't really do anything, did he?"

"He did plenty," Matt responded. "Gracie's a loser and she'll spend a long time in jail, but that doesn't mean he's got the right to beat the crap out of her."

Until now, Eileen had not let herself think deeply about Chuck and what he had done to her and, most of all, to Aaron. "When Aaron finds out what his father tried to do he's going to feel betrayed all over again," she said.

"He'll get the support he needs." Angel smiled at Eileen. "We'll help him."

Matt looked into the distance. "He got away, but not for long. He'll pay."

"Good," Angel said, but his mind was elsewhere. He said, "Excuse me," took Eileen by the hand and walked into the entrance hall. "It's too hot in there. Let's take a walk in the conservatory."

Without a word she went with him to the big, empty room where the only light came from a thin moon shining through the glass ceiling and windows.

"Angel?" Sonny's voice made them both jump.

Eileen saw him hovering in the open doorway to the conservatory with Aaron lurking behind him. Angel left her side and went to carry on a short, whispered conversation. The boys left and Angel returned.

"What was that about?" she asked.

"On any other night, I could get mad," Angel said. "When did they all decide I'm too dumb to know what I'm supposed to do?"

Eileen couldn't think of an answer.

"I can't be mad tonight," Angel said. "So it doesn't matter. Could we get right to the point?"

She was glad of the gloom and hoped it hid her grin. "I'm all for getting to the point."

"How long before you think I can take you upstairs and get us naked?"

Eileen poked his chest. "That's not what you're supposed to say, and you know it."

"What a relief," Angel said. He did love this woman. "You're going to say it for me. I was starting to get flustered."

"Go ahead and get flustered. I'm not helping you out."

"If I say it, can we go upstairs and get naked then?"

"My arm's in a sling."

"I'll do everything. Just leave it to me."

"We'll still have to eat dinner first," Eileen said.

"And go through the champagne toasts and hoopla that they've got planned for those silver napkins."

"You've got it," Eileen said. "Unless you've decided you don't want to get to the point after all."

Angel felt as if he could do something stupid, like laugh, or worse yet, cry. He dropped to his knees and held Eileen's good hand.

"Get up, you fool," she whispered loudly. "Someone might see you."

He did laugh then. "I hope they do. I love you, Eileen. I didn't know it, but I'd never been really happy before we met. Do you feel like being my missus?"

Eileen bent to kiss him, for a very long time. When she allowed them a break, she said, "If you feel like being my mister."

Standing again, Angel hugged her carefully. "If that was hokey," he said, "I want to be hokey for the rest of our lives."

Epilogue

December 24

If he didn't know better, Chuck would say the sky sat on top of his car. A black sky without a sign of moon or stars. He drove north out of town on the road not too far from NezPique. Not many people came out this way, and he didn't blame them. But tonight he was glad it was deserted. He couldn't afford to meet anyone who might recognize his car.

There wouldn't be a second chance. He had made himself wait until it was dark enough to hopefully avoid getting caught before he was even out of Pointe Judah.

His father hadn't taught him much except to keep women in their place and never to trust them. Chuck thought he'd taken those lessons seriously, but this night was proof he hadn't listened nearly closely enough.

No woman would get the upper hand with him again, and he was damned if Eileen would get off scot-free after what she'd done to him. He'd make sure she suffered.

This wasn't a part of the area he knew. He didn't trust the bayou. The swampland that spread out from it in places gave him the creeps.

He switched on the radio. Darryl LeChat ground out his eerie version of "I'm Gone, And I Ain't Comin' Back." The singer managed to take any joy out of a zydeco number and turn it into a dirge.

Chuck went to change channels, but a gentle bump at the back of his car, so soft he hardly heard it, popped him forward and he craned around in his seat to look behind him.

Nothing.

He checked the wing mirror and the rearview mirror. Not one speck of light or any outline of another vehicle.

His exhaust system was probably gummed up. Once he was away from this hellhole, he'd dump this pile of trash and get him some new wheels. He had a nice stack of bills in his pocket, compliments of the job at The Willows.

Even thinking about Angel DeAngelo made Chuck's temples pump hard.

Rain slashed the windshield, or it could be a bunch of water swept from a tree by the wind.

The water kept on coming.

Something bumped the rear again. Chuck opened his mouth to breathe. That hadn't been anything to do with his exhaust. He'd been hit from behind.

One thing he wouldn't do was stop and confront whoever this joker was.

Another contact jerked him around a bit. This time it was more of a shove.

He leaned on his horn, the next second realizing that his right rear wheel was entangled with someone else's wheel. When he attempted to steer left and unhitch himself, he over-corrected.

His headlights, shining on the worn-out road, had kept

him going fairly straight. Now his headlights swung, arced to the left, and swung sickeningly downward. "Fuck!" he yelled, bouncing and banging down a bank. Trees loomed. Moss slapped the car. He turned the wheel hard one way, then the other, threading a path through cypress trunks.

Braking wouldn't do a thing but drive him deep into sludge.

He was burning up and rolled the window down a couple of inches. Screeches ate up the earlier silence.

The trees got tighter.

He was going to crash.

Wet branches caught in the open window and tore free. They crowded the inside of the car. He yelled and held a hand in front of his face.

Trees were growing in here, crushing him. He dragged a branch, saw his headlights slam into two trunks, close together, and he screamed. He jerked the wheel.

He somehow got through those trees.

More loomed.

Again, he jerked the wheel.

The nose of the car rose, kept on rising until Chuck felt his back bumper had to be resting on the soggy ground. Then the front of the car swept down again, down and down.

Water rushed at him. The headlights bounced off a rushing, gleaming black wall.

The car dove. Chuck didn't hear anything, not even the gush of stinking swamp water through the window.

The car lights went out.

He took a breath, but there was no air.

The last thing he saw was a pair of silver eyes watching him through the windshield.

POINTE JUDAH NEWS
Under New Management
Special Edition

February 1

Local police chief, Matt Boudreaux, announced yesterday that a vehicle believed to belong to Chuck Moggeridge, the missing suspect in December's murder case in Pointe Judah, has been found.

The partially decomposed remains of a male decedent were found inside the vehicle and are being examined by the FBI. Preliminary findings suggest they belong to Chuck Moggeridge.

The discovery site was a small lake in the swamp area near Bayou NezPique, just north of Pointe Judah.

Moggeridge was last seen alive on December 24. So far, there are no reports that the remains show signs of foul play.

* * * * *

Please turn the page for a preview of
Stella Cameron's next romantic suspense
CYPRESS NIGHTS
Coming April 2008
Only from MIRA Books

Toussaint, Louisiana
March 16
10:00 p.m.

"Why are you here?" Blue Labeau said. She knew Roche Savage had come to the Parish Hall meeting because she was the one giving a presentation. He couldn't have any interest in plans to build a new school.

He had come for her.

A tall, rangy man, with curly, almost black hair and the bluest eyes she had ever seen, he was in the business of fixing minds. And from his reputation, he was very successful. Somehow he must have found out her secret and she was a challenge to him now. Only one person in Toussaint was aware of the life she had been trying to outrun for more than three years, and her cousin Madge wasn't the gossiping type.

Why didn't he say something? She inched away from him.

He stared at her as if he was planning his next move.

Roche weighed what he should do. Blue's behavior had caught him off guard. The woman trying to move away slowly enough to stop him from noticing, or as if he might pounce on her, wasn't the one he'd met a couple of weeks ago over a cup of coffee. Something had happened to make her afraid of him and he wished he didn't feel so certain about what that was.

Blue was still moving. With her hair streaming in the wind, she took sideways steps up the slope from the Parish Hall to the spot where she had parked her Honda.

Keeping a tight hold on his temper and the confusion he felt, Roche didn't follow her. "Just talk to me," he said. "That's all I want. Tell me what's wrong and I'll try to make it right."

She had been the last to leave the packed meeting on plans to build a new school. Everyone else had already driven off.

And the instant she saw him, she had just about run away.

Blue's head pounded. "Please excuse me," she said. "I have to get home. Tomorrow's a full day."

What she wouldn't ask him was if he knew about her divorce, about the horrible, personal things she'd been forced to talk about in a courtroom. If he did, he was also aware of the way her ex had turned sex into something horrifying, and that she had been left with a fear of intimacy.

Yesterday the truth about his interest in her suddenly became clear. She had been looking forward to having dinner with him when she figured it out: she wasn't his type. He had another reason for wanting to spend time with her.

He picked up some of the documents and files she'd dropped when she saw him waiting for her. "You'll need these." He felt furious that he'd missed some signal she must have given him. Last night she'd stood him up for dinner, but he had put it down to preoccupation with getting ready for tonight's meeting. Obviously he had been wrong; she'd ducked out of the date to avoid him.

Damn, he was a healer of minds, a seasoned psychiatrist, not a man who terrified women in the dark.

When he looked up again, she stood like a stone, utterly still. He saw her honey-blond hair glint in the moonlight, saw the glitter in her eyes. In the daylight they were bright green, always questioning, always vulnerable.

"Thank you." Her soft words were difficult to hear in the wind.

Blue Labeau, with her unassuming air and the way she listened closely when he talked, and her passion for the job she'd come to Toussaint to do, had captured him. The passion he felt for her, the urge to protect—and possess—almost disoriented Roche.

Disorientation was dangerous. He had to be in control of himself at all times.

She couldn't have any idea of his single-minded focus on her. If she did, even this encounter would be impossible.

"I heard your presentation at the meeting," he told her. *And afterward I stood in the shadow of a wall out here, waiting for you. You and I were meant to be together, at least until we find out I'm wrong. But I'm not wrong, Blue. If someone told you I have a sexual addiction, they're right, damn them, but it'll be different with you.*

She looked from him to her car, probably figuring out how fast she could get away from him and what the chances were that he wouldn't catch up.

About zero, lady.

Blue took another small step. She felt foolish. He must be adding up symptoms to analyze later. He would be thinking she seemed afraid of him, and she was.

The only way out of this was to change the subject and

calm down. "It will be a fight to build a school here," she said. "So many people are against it." Holding her ground wasn't easy.

"Don't leave without your papers," he said. Blue had come to Toussaint to do a study on the feasibility of building a new school for St. Cecil's. The papers were important to her, every one of them.

"A lot of people are angry," she continued, her voice tight. "The money hasn't even been raised yet, but they're talking about using it for something else."

Now she was babbling. One more symptom for his list.

"Yeah," he said. "Some of them. Not all."

Roche finished gathering her things and walked toward her. The pale moon did nothing more than suggest a light all but snuffed, and his eyes looked black and fathomless.

"Some of them made it clear they wish I'd go away," Blue said.

He would have expected her to be tougher. She had been through the same type of process a number of times before. "They'll come around," he said. "Who could resist you for long?"

That had been the wrong thing to say. She turned away at once. Her breath came in loud, rough gasps.

"Blue! Damn it, why are you afraid of me?"

She had made a pact with herself that no one would frighten her again. Now the pact was broken.

"I'm not afraid of you," she lied. "I've got to go."

"Fine. Here, take these and I'll wish you good night," he said.

"You don't understand," she told him.

"No I don't. What is it about me that's suddenly disgusting

to you? Last night you were supposed to have dinner with me. You didn't call. You just let me show up at your place and find out you weren't there. You didn't forget, did you?"

"I'm sorry." The thin skirt of her dress blew back, gripping her thighs.

Roche felt the swell of anger. "You don't have to be." Her shape was sweet, curvy, all woman.

"Goodnight, then," she said.

The old wildness attacked him. Blue hadn't gone two steps before he reached her and settled a hand on her shoulder. "Look at me." Her pause let him know this could go either way, but then she turned toward him. Roche stepped up beside her. "I'm not a threat to you," he said.

Blue couldn't hide her spasms of shivering. "Roche," she whispered. "I don't know you. You don't know me."

He knew himself. This was a test and it wasn't going well. He had decided to prove he could be alone with a woman he wanted desperately and not make the kind of move that might turn her off.

"It's time we did know each other," he said. He didn't give her a chance to argue.

He kissed her, and her body tensed.

It had been so long since she had felt this—invaded. Yet Roche didn't intend to violate her. Her eyes closed and she tried to relax. With the tip of his tongue he made soft, sleek and persuasive passes until her lips parted. Where they touched, she tingled. Her muscles softened and she leaned closer. A tightening low in her belly stole her breath and her attention. Downward between her legs it went, sharper and sharper. *"Then she felt wet. Women are weak. They need saving from themselves."*

That voice she thought she had forgotten, the one from her wasted years, sounded so clear that she braced for the shove, the fall to the bed and the punishing pressure of a big man's body.

"No." Blue jerked her head away from him. "I don't want this."

Roche held her firmly, wrapped his arms around her and pressed her face into his shoulder. "Hush," he said, wishing the damn paperwork wasn't between them like a shield. For a little while she had started to respond to him, but she was rigid now.

Careful. Don't push too far.

He used his thumbs to raise her chin, and he brought his mouth to hers again. Holding her against him with the pressure on the back of her head, he emptied her hands and leaned them both sideways to put the pile on the ground.

She kissed him in return, but not like a woman who had done a lot of kissing. With his mouth and tongue, turning her head with his fingers, delving deep, he showed her that this wasn't about putting one mouth to another. It was a connection, and could be a prelude, a small, erotic promise of a close joining.

A promise wasn't enough.

Already hard, he strained against his pants.

"You're safe with me," he whispered, leaning away.

No, she wasn't, but he had a logical mind and he worked to make it heed him in situations like this one, where lust had taken him over the edge in the past.

His heart thudded. Slowly, gently, he put his hands beneath her arms. Her body was warm, the bodice of her dress made of a silky stuff.

His palms settled on the sides of her breasts.

Again she stiffened in his arms.

He rested his forehead in the curve of Blue's neck. Tonight he felt leaden but even that didn't dampen his drive to make love to her. Nothing had ever dampened that drive.

But he could change, or at least keep some instincts under wraps.

"You feel so good," he whispered, his lips against the soft skin of Blue's neck.

"I don't…I'm not…"

"I know," he murmured. "You're not casual. I like the way you are." Moving carefully, he nipped her ear then kissed her shoulder—and wasn't quick enough to avoid the slap that landed on his face.

He flinched and gave a surprised laugh. Her next swipe cut off the laughter.

"You've made your point," he said, ducking number three.

She dropped her arms to her sides. He could hear her hard breathing, and see the glimmer of tears on her cheeks. "You're going too fast for me," she said. "But I shouldn't have hit you." She sounded upset, but not sorry.

"I'll live," he said. "I deserved what I got."

Blue looked at the sky and felt a stillness capture them both. "Why would you deserve it? You couldn't know I'm not ready…for anything, really. Maybe one day I'll tell you why. Not now."

He moved as if he would touch her but pulled back. "Okay. I'll ask you to do that, but I'll give you some time. You need to go home and get comfortable. But I warn you, I'll be calling you again and inviting you out."

She looked at the ground. "Did you feel a raindrop?" she asked, knowing she must sound inane.

"No, but it wouldn't surprise me if it rained."

"I feel like an idiot." She arrived at her car with Roche right behind her. "You deserve better than me. I'm too much of a liability emotionally. Move on, Roche."

His heart turned and he realized the sensation was new. "Don't sell yourself short." She might not know exactly what he meant. He dealt with the kind of liabilities she talked about almost every day. It could be that they had a chance to heal each other—or create a kind of hell for themselves. Whatever the risks, Roche felt like taking them.

MEET THE
DEADLY SEVEN

Seven titles from bestselling authors and new voices that will chill and terrorize you with their tales of murder, conspiracy and suspense.

JUNE

SEPTEMBER

JULY

JUNE

JULY

AUGUST

NOVEMBER

New York Times Bestselling Author

SHARON
SALA

He killed her once...

Throat slashed and left for dead next to her murdered father,
a thirteen-year-old girl vows to hunt down the man who did
this to them—Solomon Tutuola. Now grown, bounty hunter
Cat Dupree lets nothing—or no one—stand in the way of
that deadly promise. Not even her lover, Wilson McKay.

Suspecting that Tutuola is still alive, despite witnessing
the horrific explosion that should have killed him, Cat
follows a dangerous money trail to Mexico, swearing not to
return until she's certain Tutuola is dead—even if it means
destroying her very soul....

CUT THROAT

"The perfect entertainment for those looking for a suspense
novel with emotional intensity."
—*Publishers Weekly* on *Out of the Dark*

*Available the first week of November 2007
wherever paperbacks are sold!*

MIRA® **www.MIRABooks.com**

MSS2507

Ice Storm

NEW YORK TIMES
BESTSELLING AUTHOR

Anne Stuart

The powerful head of the covert mercenary organization
The Committee, Isobel Lambert is a sleek, sophisticated
professional who comes into contact with some of the
most dangerous people in the world. But beneath Isobel's
cool exterior a ghost exists, haunting her with memories
of another life…a life that ended long ago.

But Isobel's past and present are about to collide when
Serafin, mercenary, assassin and the most dangerous
man in the world, makes a deal with the Committee.
Seventeen years ago she shot him and left him for dead,
and now he's tracked her down for revenge.…

"Stuart knows how to take chances, and this edgy thriller
shows how well they can pay off."
—*Publishers Weekly* on *Cold As Ice*

*Available the first week of November 2007
wherever paperbacks are sold!*

www.MIRABooks.com

MIRA®

MAS2500

*A thrilling suspense novel, Trapped is
every mother's nightmare and
one monster's dream come true.*

MIRA®

CHRIS JORDAN
trapped

When sixteen-year-old Kelly Hartley disappears from
her bedroom one night, the police believe that she ran off
willingly with her boyfriend, Seth. Unaware that her daughter
even had a boyfriend, her mother, Jane, soon discovers that
Seth is no boy. He is an adult—a man who met Kelly on the
Internet. Seems Jane's little girl has been hiding some
dangerous secrets.

Like mother, like daughter.

Adamant that Kelly is not a runaway, Jane hires ex-FBI agent
Randall Shane. But every step brings them closer to a cold-
blooded predator lurking in the shadows...coiled around Jane's
shameful secret...waiting to strike.

**"Riveting suspense tale.... Jordan's full-throttle style makes this
an emotionally rewarding thriller that moves like lightning."**
–Publishers Weekly

Available the first week of November 2007 wherever paperbacks are sold!

The chilling debut novel by

J.T. ELLISON

When a local girl falls prey to a sadistic serial killer, Nashville homicide lieutenant Taylor Jackson and her lover, FBI profiler Dr. John Baldwin, find themselves in a joint investigation pursuing a vicious murderer. The Southern Strangler is slaughtering his way through the Southeast, leaving a gruesome memento at each crime scene—the prior victim's severed hand.

As the killer spirals out of control, everyone involved must face a horrible truth—that the purest evil is born of private lies.

"A terrific lead character, terrific suspense, terrific twists… a completely convincing debut."
—Lee Child, *New York Times* bestselling author

Available the first week of November 2007 wherever paperbacks are sold!

STELLA
CAMERON

32425 TARGET	___ $7.99 U.S.	___ $9.50 CAN.
32353 A GRAVE MISTAKE	___ $7.99 U.S.	___ $9.50 CAN.
32278 BODY OF EVIDENCE	___ $7.99 U.S.	___ $9.50 CAN.
32219 NOW YOU SEE HIM	___ $7.50 U.S.	___ $8.99 CAN.
66734 SOME DIE TELLING	___ $5.99 U.S.	___ $6.99 CAN.

(limited quantities available)

TOTAL AMOUNT	$ _____
POSTAGE & HANDLING	$ _____
($1.00 FOR 1 BOOK, 50¢ for each additional)	
APPLICABLE TAXES*	$ _____
TOTAL PAYABLE	$ _____

(check or money order—please do not send cash)

MIRA®

www.MIRABooks.com

MSC1107BL